by Herman Cromwell Gilbert

The Uncertain Sound

Th

Also

THE NEGOTIATIONS

a novel of tomorrow

by

Herman Cromwell Gilbert

PATH PRESS, INC.

Chicago

Library of Congress Cataloging in Publication Data

Gilbert, Herman Cromwell.
    The negotiations.

    I. Title.
PS3557.I342N4   1983   813'.54   83-2186
ISBN 0-910671-00-1

Published by Path Press, Inc., 53 West Jackson Blvd., Suite
625, Chicago, Illinois 60604

Distributed by Chicago Review Press, 213 W. Institute Pl.,
Chicago, Illinois 60610

Manufactured in the United States of America

To *Brenda*, with warmest appreciation
For *Ivy*, again, with love
And in memory of *Frank London Brown*

And the Lord said, I have surely seen the affliction of my people which are in Egypt, and have heard their cry by reason of their taskmasters; for I know their sorrows.

And I am come down to deliver them out of the hand of the Egyptians, and to bring them up out of that land into a good land...unto a land flowing with milk and honey.

—Exodus 3, 7-8.

PROLOGUE ONE

It was shortly after 8:00 P.M. on Tuesday, September 1, in the Year of Our Lord 1987. The polls had just closed in the most unusual election ever held in the United States of America. Unlike in times past, white Americans had not participated in this election. Only black Americans had been eligible to vote, and they had flocked to the polling places in unprecedented numbers. Later an analysis would reveal that of those black citizens registered to vote, eighty-five percent had voted.

It was not an election of candidates to public offices. Neither was it a vote to approve bond issues for the construction of buildings, bridges, roads or other physical structures. Rather it was a referendum, through a yes or no vote, to ratify or reject the following proposition:

The Black American Council is hereby authorized to negotiate with the United States of America for the creation of a separate and independent state, within the continental limits of the United States, for American citizens of African descent.

PROLOGUE TWO

The waiting room in which the prime members of the Black American Council sat was separated from the computer room by a six-foot wide corridor. Three of the waiting room's walls were composed of portable partitions of baked grey enamel while the fourth wall, which fronted on the corridor, was made of heavy transparent glass. The Council prime members, five men and a woman, seated in light plastic chairs around a circular table of the same material and looking through the double glass of the waiting and computer room walls, were observing with intense interest the activity taking place within the computer room.

It was early afternoon on the last Thursday in September, three weeks and two days after black Americans, by a vote of fifty-two to forty-eight percent, had authorized the Council to negotiate for a separate state.

Prior to the referendum, the Council had decided that if the vote favored separation, a mechanism for selecting a chairman of the negotiating team would be developed and that this chairman would have the authority to appoint the other members of the negotiating committee, develop negotiating methodology and criteria, and generally direct discussions with all appropriate elements of the white power structure.

Following the referendum, the Council had hired a Japanese consultant firm to develop specifications and computer programs for the selection of the chief negotiator. A Japanese consultant had been selected, the Council told itself, to eliminate to the extent possible subjective influences in the design of the system which might result if either a white or black American firm were hired.

In conjunction with the consultant, the Council had developed a general profile for the chief negotiator. Then, armed with this profile, each Council prime member had drawn up a list of persons who conceivably could qualify for the job. After the names were submitted, and still operating within the criteria used to create the profile, the Council worked with the consultant to develop the basic structure of the computer system. Questionnaires were prepared and each contestant filled one out. It took approximately two weeks to write the computer programs and nearly a week of computer runs and reruns to get the programs debugged. As each change was made in a program, the reason for and result of the change had been carefully explained to the Council and received Council approval.

Now, sitting in the prefab waiting room outside the computer room of the automated data center from which the Japanese consultant firm had leased computer time, the Council prime members, through the double glass walls, were observing the final stage in the automated selection of a negotiator whose duties would be anything but automatic.

The Japanese consultant was talking earnestly to a computer operator. Nodding his head, the operator replaced a reel of tape on a tape drive, tore a piece of paper from the console typewriter and threw it in a waste basket and pressed a button to initialize a disk drive. Nodding to something the consultant said, the operator pressed another button near the console and the reel he had just placed on the tape drive moved clockwise. A fast-speed printer began to clatter, but neither the consultant nor the operator paid it any attention. Their eyes were riveted on the console typewriter. The reel of tape continued to move clockwise and the printer kept up its clattering sound. Finally the reel of tape ceased to move and the printer stopped printing. The consultant and operator, eyes still on the console typewriter, nodded to each other. The operator tore a piece of paper from the console typewriter and handed it to the consultant. In typical Japanese fashion, the consultant bowed to the operator and headed toward the computer room exit. The

Council members watched him as he left the computer room, crossed the corridor, and moved toward the door of their waiting room.

All five Council members were standing when the consultant entered. Nobody said anything as the consultant walked over to them, bowed, and laid the sheet of paper from the computer console typewriter on the table.

Printed on the paper was a single name: *Preston Levi Simmons*.

BOOK I

THE SEPARATING

Chapter 1

1:30 P.M., Thursday, September 24, 1987

PRESTON SIMMONS, wearing only a robe and sandals, was sitting in his back yard on a redwood bench, elbows resting on the matching redwood table, his chin cupped in his hands. A large multi-colored beach umbrella covered him like a canopy, its aluminum supporting pole running through a hole in the center of the table to a spearlike anchor in the ground. The yard was shielded from neighborhood sights by Simmons house on the west, his garage on the east and by eight-foot high unclipped hedges on the other sides, the hedges having long ago obliterated the cyclone fences which originally had marked the yard's north and south boundaries. The early afternoon September Chicago sun, shining brightly on the green lawn of the hemmed-in yard, appeared to isolate it and create an atmosphere of detachment. To Simmons, sitting unmoving on the bench, protected by the umbrella from the sun's ferocity, it seemed that time was standing still, a courtesy to permit him to get his fill of the calming effects of the present.

This back yard and this bench on a summer or early autumn afternoon always had had the ability to relax him, Simmons recalled now, to create in him a feeling of near euphoria. Yet, strangely, he could count the times in the nearly twenty years he had lived in the house that he had sat like this absorbing the feeling of contentment and suspension. In fact, it had not been his intention to sit out here this afternoon; rather he had planned to remain in his study in the basement, completing an

3

article for *Issues*, a national magazine. But when he had prepared himself a sandwich for lunch, he had noticed that the wastebasket in the kitchenette was filled and, in keeping with his disdain for wastebaskets containing trash, had gathered all the wastebaskets in the house and brought them outside to empty in one of the large disposal cans, converted from oil drums, which stood outside the back yard gate near the garage. The emptied wastebaskets now stood on the walkway leading to the back door, where he had placed them when the urge to sit on the bench under the umbrella had consumed him.

He knew the primary reason, of course, why he seldom sat out here alone on this bench on a balmy afternoon, deliberately seeking out the mood of the present. Basically, he did not believe that a person could successfully plan for pleasure of this type, that most often it was encountered unexpectedly. And in the years that he had lived in this house, the right combination of opportunity and receptivity simply had occurred only a few times.

The sound of a ringing telephone came through the open window of his bedroom, which was barely ten feet from where he sat. He jumped up from the bench and headed toward the side door of the house, hoping to catch the phone before it ceased to ring, at the same time reprimanding himself for having stopped outside after emptying the wastebaskets. He was expecting a number of phone calls, all of them important. Apparently the caller also considered the call to be important, for the phone was still ringing when Simmons reached the extension in the kitchenette.

The clipped, precise voice of Robert Griggs came across the wire. "Well, old man, you made it," the voice said. Griggs was executive director of the National Association for the Advancement of Colored People and chairman of the Black American Council.

"Made it? Made what?" Simmons asked, understanding of what Griggs was saying beginning to resolve in his mind, producing consternation.

'You have been selected chief negotiator. The computer

4

recommended your selection and the Council prime members confirmed it by unanimous vote."

"Dammit!"

Griggs' voice lost some of its legendary composure. "Why 'dammit!'?" he asked. "I thought you wanted the job. If not, why did you permit your name to be included?"

"Sorry, Bob," Simmons said. "I do want it. But all the time I was certain somebody else would be selected, even with the computer doing the final comparisons. The competition was heavy as hell."

"Okay," Griggs said. "But this demands a more positive attitude. You can't act in a manner to give credence to your detractors."

"What do you mean?"

"Come off it, Preston!" Griggs said. "You know as well as I do what your opponents have been saying about you for years. All intellect and no action."

"Yeah, I know. The young eager beavers who would rather act first and examine their actions later."

"I have made the announcements to the media," Griggs said. "My guess is that you will be deluged with calls for interviews as soon as they locate you. How do you plan to handle it?"

"A formal press conference," Simmons said, realizing he was speaking without hesitation, now that he had been thrust into the position where positiveness was required. Regardless of what his detractors—as Griggs called them—said, he knew that the ability to move quickly from a state of readiness was one of his assets. Even though he had not expected to be selected, he had known there was a probability that he would be; consequently, he had developed general plans. "One press conference for everybody here in Chicago this afternoon. Then nothing else until I meet with the prime members of the Council tomorrow in Washington."

"Good. What time will you reach the Council headquarters tomorrow?"

"Ten o'clock. Might as well get this show on the road early."

"Right. See you then."

5

"Wish me luck, Bob."

"I wish you luck."

Hanging up the phone, Simmons walked from the kitchenette through the dining area into the living room and sat on the couch, the circumstances and situations he and Griggs had alluded to in their phone conversation creating cameo images in his mind. Without permitting himself to concentrate on any particular detail, he attempted to fashion, for his own quick review, a lucid synopsis of events of the recent past.

The decision of the Black American Council to sponsor the Separate State Referendum had surprised a lot of people, including himself. It had been especially surprising to him because the call for the referendum came at a time when black Americans were relatively inactive, during a period of deep frustration, when no highly visible demands were being made. True, this period of inaction and frustration had followed a period which had been marked by a series of armed clashes between groups of black Americans and the police power of the country. These clashes had come to be known as "job riots" and had begun in 1983 when it became clear that the government's policy of alleviating unemployment was tied to the hope that Reaganomics would eventually work and that sufficient benefits would one day trickle down to ease the chronic joblessness in the black ghettos.

These riots, however, had ceased in 1984 following a crackdown by the government, a crackdown which had been much more ruthless than that exercised against the Black Panthers and other militant black groups more than a decade earlier. The leaders of the riots had been arbitrarily and systematically jailed and their followers dispersed and silenced. Since that time, relative quiet had existed in the black community. The black middle class had continued in its attempt to increase its political and economic power through electoral activity and normal economic endeavor, while those blacks on the lowest rung of the economic ladder appeared to sink into despair, accepting their legacy of welfare and deprivation.

However, it was during this period of apparent inaction—in

6

the winter of 1984—that the Black American Council had been created. And if prior to issuing the call for the referendum the Council had not done anything spectacular, most Americans were in agreement that the Council had done an outstanding job in helping to reduce black-on-black crime. The Council, soliciting the aid of black writers and educators, had developed hard-hitting, multi-media anti-crime materials, established local centers, and coordinated campaigns which literally were door-to-door. And the program had paid off. Unlike the situation which existed in the seventies and early eighties, when black anger seemed unable to find relief except through black murder, black Americans began to gain a measure of solace out of their mutual deprivation.

It was in this period of apparent low anger and resignation that the Council had issued its call for separation, the worst possible time, on the surface, to issue such a call. Yet, black Americans had participated in the referendum in larger percentages than they had ever before responded to an election, saying, in effect, give us something *important* to vote on, and we'll show you that we know how to vote. But even more significantly, Black America was really saying, Simmons had told himself often since the vote, that it no longer had confidence in White America. That Black America was ready to chart a course on its own, even though it had not as yet taken a good look at what lay ahead.

And now, sitting on a couch in his living room, Simmons realized that that peculiar period of inaction between confirmation of the referendum and selection of the chief negotiator had come to an end; that the white power structure must at last be confronted with the mandate of Black America; and he, the chief negotiator, must carry forward that mandate. He felt himself smiling. The time had come, as the old folks used to say, to shit or get off the pot.

As he had said to Robert Griggs a few minutes earlier, Simmons had not really expected to be selected, although he had known that there was an outside chance that he would be. True, he was not a prime member of the Council—that group

7

of black leaders which had been chosen to direct the Council's activities—yet he was familiar with the criteria written into the selection programs. And his knowledge of this criteria, plus his awareness of the scope of his own qualifications, had led him to realize that if the programs were written as objectively as the consultants had promised, his chance of being selected was better than average. Nevertheless, it was traditional, if not entirely logical, to expect that a more activist black leader with greater name recognition than himself would be selected.

Simmons got up from the couch, walked around the long, magazine-covered cocktail table to the television set and turned it on. Immediately he turned it off again. Early afternoon daytime television was not his shot.

If he had to do a profile of himself to justify his selection, how would he frame the profile? What elements would he include and which ones would be excluded? Did the curt sketches in Who's Who in the Midwest, Who's Who in America, Who's Who in Black America, Contemporary Authors and the Dictionary of International Biography capture the essence of his life sufficiently to qualify him for the task ahead? Or could the qualities which would insure success or failure in such a venture really be pinpointed by official biographers, no matter how discerning, or by computer programs, no matter how delineating? It was in those areas of the will and the spirit, he told himself, which defied premeasurement, that the determination of his fitness would be made in the heat of the battle.

But what about the profile of himself as the public would see him? he asked himself, returning to his seat on the couch. Formal education-wise, he undoubtedly would make the grade. Holder of a law degree with licenses to practice in Illinois, Washington, D.C. and New York, he also possessed a master's degree in computer technology. Although he had not majored in journalism—in fact, had never taken a journalism course—he supposed the fact that he had authored two published novels and currently wrote a twice-a-week syndicated column which ran in approximately 100 newspapers around the country, qualified him for the appellation "man of letters."

8

He was a member of a number of black organizations—and white ones, too, for that matter—ranging from middle of the road to moderately militant; yet, for the most part, he had worked in the background of these organizations and had not held a prominent leadership role in any of them.

Despite the fact that he was not very well known to the masses, Simmons realized that in the minds of middle-class American intellectuals he was something of a celebrity. His first novel, published in 1970, dealt with a school integration fight in a border state during 1950. One of the side messages of the novel was that during that period in the civil rights struggle, it was not sound tactics for black leaders to have white wives. The television publicity around the novel threw him into confrontation with a number of black entertainment, sports and political figures who had white wives, and the resultant controversy kept him somewhat in the spotlight for a year or two.

He also recalled that late in 1971 or early in 1972, when the first of what was to be a continuing string of black movies was released, he was drawn into a national dialogue around the merits of these so-called black exploitation movies. His participation in the dialogue began with the release of Sweet Sweetback's Baadasssss Song. Answering an article in Ebony, he had written:

"...It is my opinion that a work of art is revolutionary as opposed to being counter-revolutionary, progressive as opposed to being reactionary, when the positives contained in that work of art outweigh its negatives. After critical analysis, I have concluded that the positives, as related to the black liberation struggle, outweigh the negatives in 'Sweet Sweetback's Baadasssss Song'."

He had gone on to say that, in the movie, Sweetback identified with blacks struggling for survival; recognized who the enemy was; and fashioned a method for continuing the struggle. Concluding the article, he had written:

9

"...Sweetback might have come from a whorehouse—but he will not return to a whorehouse. His plight and his commitment will not permit it. In spite of himself, for his own survival, he must constantly devise schemes for collecting dues, for the enemy against whom he has raised a hand will not permit him to survive without fighting..."

With respect to the movies which followed Sweetback, he had taken the position that while some of these movies represented an unfair distortion of black life, they were no more deserving of censorship than the other distortions of American life represented by non-black movies, novels, songs, paintings, etc. In one article in a national magazine he had written:

"I have confidence in the toughness of black life. We will move past this period of bluff and bluster and enter a new era of commitment and dedication to positive endeavor. If white youths survived the Cagney and Bogart movies of the 30s, our youths will survive the Superfly's of the 70s. To believe otherwise is to believe that white youths possess qualities inherently superior to those possessed by our youths. If those who have wrapped themselves in a cloak of extreme blackness have less faith in their blackness than I, please let them step forward and repudiate me and I, too, will wear my blackness as a shroud rather than as a coat of distinction."

For the 1984 Presidential election he presented a proposal to the Democratic Party National Committee for bringing black and white voters together, attempting to bridge the breach which had first developed on a major scale in the Nixon-McGovern election of 1972 and widened in the Carter-Reagan election of 1980. Quite simply, his recommendations called for deliberately setting up black-white ethnic committees in every major city in the country where this combination represented a large segment of the population. These committees would concentrate on preparing television and radio political spot announcements emphasizing the common interests of blacks and white ethnic groups in various economic and social areas and specifying the solutions the Democratic Party candidate was proposing to enhance and solidify these interests. A typical spot announcement would have gone like this:

White Ethnic Participant:	Hello, my name is Joseph Malota, I am an Italian-American.
White Ethnic Participant:	Hello, my name is Peter Jankowsky, I am a Polish-American.
Black Participant:	Hello, my name is Robert McGee, I am a Black American.
Announcer:	Statistics prove that while Black Americans represent 10 percent of the American population, they have less than one tenth of one percent of the executive positions in major industrial and service corporations; that while Italian-Americans represent two percent of the American population, they have less than one fifth of one percent of the executive positions; and that while Polish-Americans represent three percent of the American population, they have less than one fourth of one percent of the executive positions. It must be understood that all of these corporations under question possess either or both federal and state contracts and therefore under both federal and state laws are prohibited from dis-

11

	crimination. If the Democratic Candidate for President is elected, he will strengthen the enforcement provisions of all affirmative action laws. He will guarantee that all Americans are treated equally in employment and upgrading.
All Participants:	What helps one of us, helps all of us. We are all in this together.
Announcer:	Vote Democratic.

Simmons felt himself smiling. The Democratic Party National Committee had called him to Washington, where he had spent three weeks writing scripts. Everybody appeared to be excited about the project. Yet, in the end, not a single script was used.

The sound of the telephone ringing pulled him from his reverie. Marcus Jackson, of Marcus Jackson Associates, his literary agent and man of all purposes, was on the phone.

"Where and when do you want me to set the press conference?" Jackson asked.

"At Daley Airport at five o'clock. That way I'll be able to take the six o'clock flight to Washington right after the press conference."

"Good idea," Jackson said. "You'll make all the early news shows live."

"Right. And Marc, make the plane reservation for me as well as my hotel reservation. I think I'll put up at the Washington Hotel this time."

"Okay, Preston. Anything else?"

"No. See you at the Airport in the Lake," he replied, aware that he was thinking, unaccountably, that the idea of the lake airport was probably the late Mayor Daley's number one contribution to Chicago, although he didn't get a chance to build it himself.

12

Chapter 2

2:00 P.M., Thursday, September 24, 1987

WHAT WOULD Margaret have thought about all this?

Indeed, what would his wife, tall, brown-gold and regal in his flickering first memories of her and sallow and wasted in his final haunting impression of her losing battle with cancer, have thought about the approaching probability of a separate Black State? What would the woman, who for eighteen years had been the moderator of his pleasure and pain and who nearly two years after her death was still the measure against which he evaluated so many things, have thought about her husband leading the negotiations for such a state?

The questions, and images of Margaret, consumed Simmons' mind with the fullness of near vision as he turned away from the phone conversation with Marcus Jackson and went again to sit on the living room couch. True to her complexity and changing moods, she would not have thought any *particular* thing he told himself, but a combination of many different things. She would first have been dismayed about the whole idea of a separate state—not that she respected and loved white folks, but because she had so little confidence in the ability and commitment of black folks. She loved black folks, was never ashamed to be one of them, had wanted desperately all her life to be able to surrender her desires and ambitions to the protection of a pervasive black consciousness, but she had never been

13

able to bring herself to believe that black folks were engaged in anything positive and progressive on a broad scale. She was a here-and-now, show-me type of person and, because the only evidence she considered convincing was physical, nobody could make her believe that a black identity was developing which would one day give direction to a positive black world.

But even though he knew she would be dismayed over the idea of a separate Black State, he was equally certain that she would consider him the best person to bring it off, if it could be brought off at all. He realized that although all her life she had thought he was too trusting, was guilty of the major sin of not really wanting the success he deserved, she also was convinced that he understood the motives of other people and could solve most problems that he cared about.

When he met her, she had been a fashion model—one of the best, black or white. She carried her head in a haughty manner and walked with the unhurried grace of the don't-give-a-damn, yet she was neither haughty nor uncaring. Even then, however, she desperately wanted what she considered to be the good things of life.

Looking back now over twenty years, he could not say with certainty what the single most important thing was which had drawn them to each other, caused them to get married and kept them together. Her physical attractiveness and aloof manner, without a doubt, were the primary reasons why he had approached her in the first place. And she had implied through the years—though not actually told him—that his tendency towards acquiring knowledge in a number of areas had been the main reason she had encouraged fruition of their friendship. No doubt Preston Junior, who was born in the second year of their marriage, had had a lot to do with their remaining together. There were far too many fatherless black boys roaming the streets, he had told himself during the more severe times with her, without adding their son to their numbers. And from her standpoint, there was the always looming possibility that he would turn into a genuine celebrity. Not that she was snobbish, as such, but she was a firm believer that only people

14

who had more than they needed were free to enjoy the good things of life.

He would always remember the first time he saw her. He was working for IBM at the time, teaching computer programming at the educational center on Riverside Plaza in the Loop and going to law school at night. One day, on a break from one of his classes, he stopped by an exhibition room where a commercial for a mini-computer was being filmed. Three models, two white and one black, were demonstrating the ease and utility of the computer. She had been the black model—so cool and unruffled and efficient.

He had waited until the skit was completed and approached her as she came out of the exhibition room. When she turned toward him to answer his greeting, he noticed that she carried her head tilted slightly upward, a fact which surprised him because, in her heels, she was slightly taller than his five feet nine inches and should have been looking down. When she spoke, however, her voice was pleasant.

"Hi, Brother," she said, using the vernacular of the period. "How did I do?"

"The brothers on the South Side are going to be jumping all over themselves buying computers they don't need," he said.

She laughed. "I like that. So I was good?"

"Better. What other kind of commercials do you do?"

"This is my first one. Mainly I'm a fashion model."

"Multi-talented and beautiful."

"Anything to make a buck," she had replied.

And yet, despite her pre-occupation with material things, he told himself now, she had been terribly unsentimental about them. Take this house, for instance. It was a solid brick middle-class house in a well-kept middle-class black neighborhood, accessible to the exclusivity of the white southern suburbs through which she loved to roam on looking and shopping sprees. Yet, in the late 1970s, despite soaring mortgage rates, she had wanted to sell their home and purchase a house in the suburbs or a condominium in the loop or on the near North Side.

15

"But why?" he had asked her. "There is more room here than the three of us need, and plenty of room for entertainment. Hell, we seldom use the basement, in spite of the five thousand dollars we spent fixing it up."

She had looked at him as though he were trying to be funny. "Nobody lives in just a house in the city anymore."

Then there was the eagerness with which she had discarded items when they were at the height of their utility. About two years before her death, she had gotten rid of a clothes cabinet in the basement in which he had kept his out-of-season clothing. In the argument which followed, he had become more philosophical than he usually was with her.

"Even if I didn't use the cabinet to put summer clothes in winter and winter clothes in summer," he said, "it wouldn't have done any harm to let it stay in the basement as a receptacle for old clothes which we discard. Transition is a normal process of living. It's a good idea to let a discarded garment spend a year or two passing from usefulness to uselessness. It's a respect we owe everything, even the inanimate and lifeless."

She looked hard at him, understanding of what he had said clear in her eyes. Equally clear, however, was the fact that she was rejecting his thesis.

"Bull-shit," she said.

Thinking about it now, he recalled exactly what he had felt when she had said it. He had been suddenly reminded of the wide differences between them, and, ironically, how these differences made communication between them easier. In spite of himself, he had smiled; she had laughed; and the conversation hadn't gone any further.

These differences, then, had been one of the things which had kept them together, he affirmed now. Out of the synthesis of their contradictory natures, a mutual bond had grown, if not of love, then of respect. On the night of her death, he had written:

When I think of love,
Life and the mystery of death

16

Of the agony of the bad
Times and the ecstasy of
The good
When I think of the promises
Kept and the wishes unfulfilled
Of the many things desired
And the few things received
When I think of all these things
I think of you.

He got up from the couch and walked across the living room through the dining area into the kitchenette. She seemed to pervade the house. Her presence was there in fact as well as in perception because all the furnishings had been selected and positioned by her. Neither he nor Preston Junior had scarcely moved an item since her death. Standing in the kitchenette beside the refrigerator near the wall phone, he looked across the formica-topped floor cabinets which divided the kitchenette and dining area, past the waist-high bookcases which separated the dining area from the living room to the light beige drapes which covered the living room's west wall. Limited edition lithographs of paintings by Miro, Guy Charon, Bernard Gatner, Denis Paul Noyer, Antonio Rivera, Chagall and Picasso hung in strategically selected spots on the other three walls of the living room and lined the hallway leading from the kitchenette to the bedroom, located in the eastern end of the house. A thick gold carpet of lush wool covered the living room floor, while the dining area, kitchenette and hallway were covered with tough orange and black kitchen carpet of the indoor-outdoor variety. The east bedroom and the two north bedrooms, whose doors opened off the dining and kitchen areas, were carpeted with luxuriant nylon shag rugs. Margaret had chosen the first floor furniture both for "appearance and utility", and it was moderately expensive. The first floor bathroom had been completely remodeled, and was Margaret's "pride and joy."

However, if Margaret had left her imprint on the first floor, she had gone even further in the basement. It was a full basement, which had been paneled in the early years of their marriage. In later years, the half bathroom had been enlarged to a full bathroom with oversized tub and shower, the walls and ceilings redone in African decor, with African artifacts liberally sprinkled throughout. The paintings, for the most part, were black American originals, having been purchased from museums and art fairs throughout the country.

"I can't afford the prices of white originals," Margaret had been fond of saying, "so I buy black originals. Who knows, they might end up being worth more than the white originals."

The telephone rang and Simmons picked it up before the second ring was completed. The voice coming across the wire was slow and deliberate, as though the speaker was reading from a badly written script.

"This is James P. Sneed," the voice said. "Am I speaking to Mr. Preston Simmons?"

"That you are, Jim," Simmons replied. "How are you doing?

"I was doing all right until a few minutes ago, until I heard the depressing news on television," Sneed said. "I hope what I heard isn't correct."

It would do no good to fence with Sneed, Simmons told himself. Nothing he could say would influence Sneed's opinion. "What you heard is correct, Jim," he said. "I've been selected chief negotiator for the separate state."

The silence on the line was more ominous than a threat. When he finally spoke, Sneed's words were more spaced than usual. "I really wished you hadn't taken that job, Preston. I truly thought you had better sense."

Simmons didn't say anything.

"You know I'll have to fight you, Preston."

"I know."

"You might not believe it," Sneed said, "but I always liked you, Preston."

"I believe it."

"Now I'll have to go all out to get you."

"I know."

18

"See you around, Preston."

The line went dead.

As Simmons returned the phone to its cradle, he noticed that his hand was unsteady. Things were getting off to a fast start. The opposition was moving its big guns to the front of the line. Turning away from the phone, he walked over to the cabinets which divided the kitchenette from the dining area, leaned across one of the cabinets with his folded arms resting on the formica top.

No doubt about it, Simmons told himself, Jim Sneed, *James P. Sneed*, was one of the big guns. A self-made publisher-industrialist with headquarters in Los Angeles, he was widely regarded as the richest black man in the United States. His two publications, *Black Life*, a pictorial-essay magazine, and *Roads*, a feature-fiction magazine, both had surpassed *Ebony* in total circulation. Sneed was also president of the Prudential National Bank, Los Angeles' major black bank as well as the largest black financial institution in the country, and chairman of the board of Sneed Enterprises, Inc., a conglomerate which specialized in recordings and movies. He was on the board of directors of a number of major white corporations, including General Motors.

From the very beginning, the publisher-industrialist, a man in his middle fifties, had been the most outspoken critic of the Black American Council in the black community. While he did not publicly oppose its creation, he had declined the business community prime membership, which eventually went to the head of the Urban League. He had organized a stellar group of business, entertainment and sports figures to campaign across the country against the separation referendum. Calling passage of the referendum "the most incredible act in the history of Black America," he had urged the United States government to "ignore this nonsense as though nothing has taken place."

The front door chimes terminated Simmons' reflections. He tied the belt of his robe, which had come open to expose his nakedness, walked across the living room and opened the door. Janice breezed into the room.

19

"Your neighbors are never going to improve," she said. "Still nosey as hell. That bitch 'cross the street been seeing me coming here for almost a year. But she still peeps at me from behind her drapes."

Janice's tone, as was often the case, did not match her words. She was smiling good-naturedly.

"Can you blame any woman for being jealous of you?" Simmons said. "You are the kind of female who makes other women feel useless."

"Yeh, I know," Janice said, curving her hand behind her ear and pirouetting to the center of the room in a half-curtsey. "Why don't you turn on the air conditioner? It's hot as hell in here."

"Hot in here? I hadn't noticed."

She raised her eyebrows at him. "I can see why you hadn't noticed. You don't have on any clothes, and it's almost two o'clock."

"Then why have *you* noticed," he said. "You don't have on any clothes either. Go on back to the bedroom, the window is open back there. No need to turn on the air conditioner now. I have to be leaving in a few minutes. You have heard the news?"

"Yeh," Janice said. "I suppose 'gratulations are in order."

As Simmons followed her toward the bedroom, he could feel his sex organ push against his robe. Janice always affected him like that. Sight of her, and even the sound of her voice over the phone, was enough to make him stand up with desire. It was almost incredible.

He noticed that she was wearing slip-on brown sandals, no stockings, a beige polyester skirt and a white nylon blouse. Watching her from behind, he could see where her bra strap was cutting into the flesh of her back, giving testimony to the weight of the large breasts the bra was supporting. It was obvious she wasn't wearing a girdle and his instincts told him that she was without slip or panties.

Following her into the bedroom, Simmons recalled the old saying that there were four parts to a woman's anatomy which distinguished her: legs, behind, breasts and face; that if one of

20

these parts was outstanding, the woman should be given a fair rating; two parts outstanding, a good rating; three parts outstanding, an excellent rating; and four parts outstanding, a superior rating. He supposed that was the reason why Janice rated so high in the physical department. She had beautiful legs, a gorgeous behind, luscious breasts, and a pretty face— plus a small, well-defined waistline and slender hands with long tapering fingers!

Janice entered the bedroom and sat in the rocker near the door. She reached out and touched his arm as he came into the room, looking up at him, her mouth partially open to reveal teeth which protruded ever so slightly. Her delicate round brown face was moist and her extremely light brown eyes were soft.

"Hi," she said.

"Hi, yourself," he replied.

He stood over her and she ran her hands under his robe and cupped his genitals in her hands. Her fingers were hot.

"Don't do that," he said, moving away from her and sitting on the bed. "I'm holding a press conference at the Daley Airport at five o'clock."

"So? What does that have to do with anything?"

"Hell, I mean I don't have time."

"When did it ever take you that long?"

"Well, you know...considering what's happened and all...maybe my mind isn't on it..."

She laughed. "Don't give me that. You'd fuck in the middle of an atomic attack." Then seriously: "I'm here because I had a feeling you'd need me...at least, want me."

And that was true, he told himself. He did want her, and probably needed her as well. He had always wanted her. Ever since the first time he saw her standing over him with her hand on his arm when he opened his eyes from the ordeal of having an impacted wisdom tooth extracted. Her hand on his arm had been hot that time too.

When the dentist, who was a friend of his, had walked out of the room leaving them alone he had asked: "Is this part of your job, calming the nerves of frightened male patients with your soothing touch?"

She had looked steadily at him, the light eyes approaching anger, then clearing to friendliness.

"Yes," she had said matter-of-factly.

Her demeanor had disarmed him. "Why be so honest," he said. "Why can't you pretend you have a special touch for me?"

She smiled, the light eyes becoming personal. "I touch a lot of people," she said, "but seldom do they touch back. You did."

"How's that?"

"I'm a nurse and a dental technician. My job is to assist the dentist and be attentive to patients during unusually difficult extractions. I seldom get a charge from it. This time I did. I touched you and you touched me back."

Now, ten years later, sitting on his bed in his bedroom looking at her, Simmons told himself that this had been the key to their relationship. Their ability to touch each other. And this ability to touch, or not touch, somehow represented the difference in his relationships with Janice and Margaret, with whom he had slept for so many years in this very bedroom.

In all the years he had lived with Margaret, through the good times and the bad, their personalities had never really meshed, despite the fact that they could communicate with each other. He had never been able to merge himself into her individuality so that he felt truly at home, relaxed. There was a closeness missing. And the missing thing, somehow, seemed to resolve around his inability to touch her, or permit her to touch him.

True, in the heat of passion, he could caress her and engage in all types of physical sex, but as soon as the passion subsided, he could barely touch her.

But things were just the opposite with Janice. She was the first person—woman, man or child—that not only could he touch freely at any time, but felt compelled to touch, or have her touch him. With them, there appeared to be a physical oneness transforming itself into spiritual communion. It was a thing that did not need to be spoken of, or really thought about, just permitted to exist. It was as though the inner fibers

22

of his being rejected Margaret and accepted Janice; as though the most unexplored regions of his subconscious trusted Janice and distrusted Margaret.

Yet, at the conscious level, he had felt a responsibility to Margaret that he could not bring himself to feel toward Janice. And he knew now that it was this feeling of responsibility toward Margaret that had sustained their marriage through the years of his relationship with Janice.

He got up from the bed and stood over Janice again.

"Funny," he said, "when I first met you I was married. Now I'm single and you're married."

"That's the way it goes," she said. "I couldn't wait and take the chance that you might get single. A girl needs to get married sometime."

"How is it?" he asked. "Your marriage, I mean? Better or the same?"

She shrugged. "It's a life. Like your marriage was a life. I'll never feel for him what I feel for you. Like you'll never feel for anybody else what you feel for me. It doesn't happen often. Maybe it's all sex. But if it is, then sex is the best part of it all."

He smiled down at her, feeling somewhat amazed at her ability to convey so many things with such a few words. In one sense, she was shutting him out of her marriage, as she had never tried to enter that area of his life when he was married. But in another, and almost opposite, sense, she was saying that what they had should not be contaminated by such ordinary human emotions as jealousy, distrust, and a feeling of duty. Of course, he doubted if she would verbalize her feelings in this manner, if indeed she recognized a need to do so, but he was certain these were the things she was feeling.

Yet, he was sure what was between them represented much more than sex; that the sex was a reflection of something deeper, some complex compatible communications link as yet undecipherable by the human mind. He had learned from his experiences with her that they could understand each other fully without employing ordinary methods and vehicles of communication in the usual manner. Fleetingly, he recalled the

23

times he had talked to her at length about political and philosophical things without her replying; she would only sit quietly with an enigmatic smile on her face, absorbing the tone of his voice rather than the meaning of his words.

Yet, if sex *was* merely a reflection of something deeper between them, he told himself, still smiling down at her, it projected itself as though it were a compelling force in its own right. He doubted if any two people anywhere enjoyed sex more than they.

"We've been lucky, baby," he said, kissing the top of her head. "There's no phony shit between us, and never will be."

Her hands went under his robe again, squeezing. He began to think about their sexual life together, to conjure up escapades and episodes. And as always, he began to visualize, as though in a land of fantasy, their favorite posture when engaging in the sex act.

Visionlike, he sees her naked on a rug-covered floor, on her knees and elbows, with her buttock spread to receive him. As naked as she, with his penis extended, he is mounting and entering the wet warmness of her, his stomach resting delicately along her back, his hands cuddling her breasts, and his tongue probing her ear. Her hand reaches between her legs and tenderly caresses his testicles. His penis, already rigid and enlarged, begins to swell to the point of bursting, as she pushes backward to receive his forward thrust. Cries of ecstasy are in their throats as they climax in a frenzy which explodes in the heart and echoes in the ears.

He shook his head, and the vision departed. Moving away from her, he walked over to the large Mediterranean-style dresser and stood before the center mirror. She got up from the chair and came over and stood beside him, their images becoming alive in the mirror.

"When I first met you," she said, "I was a girl of twenty. Now look at me, I'm an old woman of thirty."

He laughed. "What do you think about me. When I met you I was energetic and thirty-five. Now I've turned the corner on the road to fifty and ain't in no hurry to get there."

24

"Yeh, but you're still the finest thing I know," she said, leaning her head against his shoulder.

He began to examine their images in the mirror. Her light brown eyes seemed to reflect a mixture of contentment and expectancy and her pretty round face was relaxed. Perspiration covered her upper lip. His dark brown eyes, set deep beneath heavy eyebrows and a high forehead, looked sleepy. A slight stubble of beard marred the smooth dark brown skin of his rather square jaw lines, reminding him that he had not shaved since the day before. The high bridge of his nose and the cleft in his chin came forcefully into his awareness, reminding him that these were the two features of his face that he most appreciated, counter-balancing his displeasure at his receding hairline.

"If I'm fine on the decline," he said, "you must realize how fine you are on the upgrade. Honey, you're still five years away from that magical age."

"You mean the theory about a woman not reaching her sexual high point until she becomes thirty-five?"

"Exactly."

"If I haven't reached it," she said, "I doubt if I can live through it when I do."

He unbuttoned her blouse and pulled it off, sliding it forward over her arms.

"I thought you were in such a hurry to get to that press conference," she said.

He unfastened the hooks on her bra. He could feel his hands shaking as he slid the straps over her shoulders. Her large breasts, suddenly freed, seemed to have a life apart from her as they quivered within his double vision, in and out of the mirror. He bowed his head and nibbled tenderly at the upturned nipples, first the right and then the left.

"You said you didn't have time," she said, her whole body trembling.

He unzipped her skirt and pushed it downward where it settled in soft folds around her feet. As he had suspected, she wasn't wearing panties.

"I knew you wanted to fuck as bad as I do," she said, stepping away from the skirt, her mouth reaching for his.

With his mouth on hers, he freed himself of his robe and, in a hurry now, turned her so that she fell down across the bed. He mounted her from behind, his hands reaching for her breasts, his mouth searching out her ear. She rose to her knees and elbows.

The vision became real.

Chapter 3

5:00 P.M., Thursday, September 24, 1987

STANDING ON the podium, facing the mechanical eyes of the television cameras and the far from mechanical eyes of the approximately fifty news men and women, Preston Simmons felt like an interloper, a parader under false colors. True, he had participated in hundreds of press conferences before, had even had the distinction of appearing on the major televised national news shows, but he had always been on the other side of the camera, had always been an interviewer instead of the interviewee. Consequently, in this reverse role, he felt as though he was cheating somebody, or somebody was cheating him.

It was nearing five o'clock, and the press conference would get underway in a few minutes. Marcus Jackson had evaluated the situation correctly: the major networks considered the event to be of sufficient importance to carry it live as the kickoff to their evening news shows. He could see Marcus now down on the floor of the news hall, his full head of crinkly hair, cut in a super natural, towering above the heads of the media people, an indication of the fact that he had utilized the fame earned as a basketball superstar to launch his public relations business. Knowing Marcus, and watching the way he was moving from one news person to another, Simmons realized that he was attempting to guarantee that the press conference would come off smoothly and with some degree of continuity by prearranging the order of the questions. Marcus was big league. He had not left his excellence on the basketball court.

Simmons had arrived in the news hall about five minutes before, riding public transportation from his home to the Airport in the Lake. At 115th Street South, he had taken a Dan Ryan rapid transit train to 67th Street, where he had transferred to an Airport Special for the breathtaking, 120-mile-an-hour ride to Daley Airport by way of the recently completed Middle of the Lake Expressway. Marcus had met him as he left the train and steered him along a back corridor through a side door into the news hall, adroitly ducking the assembled reporters. Although he knew most of these reporters, none had approached him since his arrival. They were observing the sanctity of the nationally televised news conference, making no attempt to diminish it by asking questions beforehand.

And now, standing on the podium looking down and out at the media people, feeling the acids building to a slow burn in his stomach, Simmons recalled the phone conversation he had had with Preston Junior before he left home. Preston Junior had called from school shortly after Janice had left, while he was shaving preparatory to taking a shower.

After he had told the operator that he would accept the collect call, Preston Junior's excitement-filled voice came over the wire.

"Dad! You made it! This restores my belief in the objectivity of Japanese and computers."

Simmons laughed. "Some people say they are the same thing. *Japanese* and *computers*, I mean. But as you say, I made it. Maybe you can figure out just what."

Preston Junior's voice was serious when he replied. "I see what you mean. It's a mind-shattering situation. It's hard to get used to the idea of blacks seriously considering a separate state. How do you really feel about it, Dad?"

When the question came, instead of immediately searching his mind for an answer, Simmons began first to think about his relationship with Preston Junior, a relationship which permitted his son to ask him easily and smoothly to probe for a possible different answer to a question which, based on his acceptance of the assignment, should have only one answer.

28

And because he and Preston Junior had come safely through the ambivalent, uneasy, shifting stages of father-son communication to arrive at a plateau where the major current between them was sincerity, he replied:

"Son, I don't know. I honestly don't know."

There was a slight pause, then Preston Junior's voice came across the wire, firm and assured. "Well, you'll find out. As you've told me many times, truth most often is revealed in the process of living. And one thing I know about you, when you see a truth, you act on it. You don't believe in fooling yourself—and other people."

He had a difficult time fighting back the tears. "Thanks, son," he had said.

And now, thinking about that phone conversation, waiting to reveal his uncertain truths to the world, he was still feeling proud of his son. Preston Junior definitely had been fashioned from the best of Margaret and himself. Somehow her desire for material excellence had merged with his spiritual self-sufficiency to produce a son who had both the toughness of independence and the humaneness of dependence, a son who loved his mother and respected his father and had sufficient confidence in himself not to have any hangups about either emotion. In that respect, he and Margaret truly had been lucky.

Marcus Jackson detached himself from a small knot of reporters, walked to the front of the room and jumped upon the podium to stand behind Simmons. Some lights in the room were dimmed and the glare of others increased. The reporters took their seats. The conference was getting underway.

The first question came from Ron Thorn, a writer from one of the so-called quality magazines. Thorn was about thirty-five, round-shouldered, with a short beard and heavy glasses. Simmons knew him well.

"Pres...Mr. Simmons," Thorn said, "will you briefly review for us the reasons why, in your opinion, blacks decided to vote for seperation?"

"Mr. Thorn," Simmons said, "you have requested a rather tall order," hoping his voice sounded firm without quivering.

"As you know, in the past few months, a number of writers, you and me included, have addressed themselves to that question in numerous articles in many publications. However, it's my opinions you want, and I'll try to capsule them without taking up too much time..." He was satisfied with the sound of his voice.

"Agreement to hold the referendum and the vote to separate came about," he continued, "primarily because black leaders and black citizens generally have come to the conclusion that this country, as it is being run, will not give them equality. And they are further convinced that during no time in the foreseeable future will they be able to bring about changes in the way the country is being run.

"Okay? Now why is this country being run like it is? Why have we, since 1972, been cursed with a combination of high inflation and economic stagnation? Why have we permitted the decline of some industries, profits to soar in others, while unemployment mounts? Why has the government, especially in recent years, brutally suppressed demonstrations and other forms of dissent? In short, why have we permitted fascism instead of democracy to advance in this country during the past two decades?" He rested his hands on the stand in front of him, keeping his eyes fixed on Thorn's.

"The more blatent moves to reverse the gains blacks made during the sixties," he continued, "came with the election of Ronald Reagan in 1980. I say 'more blatent moves' because the climate for such a reversal was well underway before Reagan's election, or he would not have been elected. Many far-sighted people could see what was happening in 1972, when organized labor joined with the business establishment to defeat George McGovern. And why did these two powerful groups get together to defeat McGovern? Because McGovern was talking about distributing power and wealth in this country in a way it had never been distributed. He was talking about sharing the wealth through *guarantees of annual income*, and that meant central planning for the operation of the entire economy of the country. The powers-that-be not only had to defeat McGovern, they had to discredit him and his ideas for all time by making him look ridiculous. But something equally damaging happened during that election campaign. Because organized labor deserted McGovern, thereby pulling white blue-collar workers away from him, the schism between these workers and blacks was widened, setting the psychological stage for what was to follow.

"Under ordinary circumstances, the fall of Nixon would have halted the country's slide to the right, since Nixon without question was a right-winger. But the Nixon drama was so filled with psychological undertones, that most Americans didn't really view his fall as being basically political in nature. So when Gerald Ford—another right-winger, but a good-natured one—wound up as Nixon's successor, the public thought it had gotten a good deal.

"Jimmy Carter, propelled into office on a promise to make the government as decent as the American people, probably could have kindled a spirit of common purpose in the country. But although Carter was a populist in rhetoric, he was a conservative in belief. Consequently, he was doomed to preside over an administration which in four years did not find a central theme. He simply straddled too many issues without unfurling a banner around any. He destroyed his goodwill among blacks in a single stroke, when he made Andy Young the scape-goat in the PLO controversy. In short, when Carter left office blacks were no beter off than when he entered, and we were infinitely more isolated from the mainstream of American life."

Simmons paused. He felt that he was taking too long to give a satisfactory answer to Thorn's question. Although he could not detect any restlessness in the eyes staring up at him, he realized these media people were not the real audience. He wanted to appear concise and knowledgeable to the American public.

"Now back to Ronald Reagan," he said. "Reagan came into the 1980 campaign trumpeting a simple chorus. Big Government was the source of America's ills. Therefore, get government off the backs of the people and inflation would subside, unemployment would go down, and industry would revitalize. How would he accomplish these things? First, drastically reduce government spending. Second, relieve the people of the burden of government by cutting taxes. His theory: reduced government spending would slash the inflation rate while lower taxes would cause people to invest in the economy, thereby boosting employment and cutting unemployment. We, of course, are all acquainted with what happened. Because Reagan was a warmonger, he couldn't bring himself to cut military spending—but rather increased it—so all the cuts had to be made in the social programs. Also, because he believed in fewer instead of more government controls, he couldn't bring himself to establish machinery to insure investments, therefore investments did not increase and the economy became even more sluggish. By the beginning of his second year in office, Reagan had a mess on his hands—in all areas. Specifically, with respect to blacks, you know the story. Black unemployment became sky-high and black business failures reached record proportions. At first, blacks became angry, then despairing, and finally, by 1983, angry again. When the so-called job riots were put down with such force, many blacks became more and more convinced that something drastic had to be done."

"But Reagan was defeated in 1984," Thorn said, "yet the separation question wasn't raised seriously until 1985."

"Exactly," Simmons replied. "The post-civil rights, anti-black mood in the country which began under Nixon and intensified under Reagan still persists. And this feeling is primarily responsible for the failure of blacks and working-class whites to develop the kind of coalition which is necessary to end conservative political control of this country. Even though President Dorsey Talbott Davidson is a Democrat, he won because a majority of the voters in 1984 rejected a continuation of Reagan's style rather than his philosophy. There is still a deep-down feeling that supply-side economics can work, if given the chance. Although the Congress and the business

32

community don't seem quite willing to turn the country over to Reaganomics, they aren't ready to shut the door on it either. The country is afflicted with a middle-of-the-road psychology—and going to hell."

"So you're saying that it was out of the frustration and hopelessness created by the situation you just described, that the move for a separate state was born?" Thorn asked.

"Yes, and grew strong enough to register a majority vote."

"Thank you," Thorn said.

Pete McCall, a tall, sallow-faced reporter in his middle sixties from the Chicago Tribune was standing. Despite efforts of the Tribune in later years to free itself of a racist image, McCall was a hewer to the old line. Simmons had chastised him in writing on more than one occasion.

"Mr. Simmons," McCall said, his voice sarcastic, "isn't it true that the vote to separate does not represent the true feelings of black Americans on the question?"

"I don't follow you, Mr. McCall. True, it was a close vote— 52 to 48 percent. I suppose it represents the sentiment of black Americans to that degree."

"That's not what I mean," McCall said. "I'm talking about the fact that normally only about 60 percent of eligible black Americans vote. But on this question approximately 85 percent voted. Yet, the vote was only 52 to 48 percent in favor of separation. Most analysts agree that had blacks voted in the same numbers they usually vote, the referendum would have been defeated. This means that the more stable elements in the black community—as represented by Jim Sneed and his people—oppose this separation. Consequently, the vote is phony, wouldn't you say?"

Simmons felt himself trying to keep the anger out of his voice as he replied. Not that the point wasn't valid, but because of McCall's attitude. The reporter was trying hard to separate the good blacks from the bad ones.

"Mr. McCall," he said, "a clear profile of those extra voters has not been established precisely, although there is general agreement that the majority of them came from the more transient communities. Yet, because these voters don't normally vote, and did vote this time, one can assume with a degree of positiveness that they feel strongly about separation, probably more strongly than some of the more stable voters who, out of habit, address themselves to every question. Consequently, contrary to the implication of your question, some of these voters might work harder than most to make separation work. However, Mr. McCall, that is not the point. Democracies can't afford the luxury, if it can be called that, of attaching point values to votes. The philosophy of one man one vote is good enough for me."

McCall was not finished. "Mr. Simmons," he said, "while I applaud your high idealism, I must question the practical sense behind this move for separation. Do you honestly believe the majority of blacks would follow you to a new nation, even if you succeeded in getting the United States government to let you set up one?"

"If you applaud my idealism," Simmons said, "you know my answer to that question. A majority of blacks voted to separate and I assume this majority will want to become citizens of the new state. The others we will have to convince. If not by words, then by deeds. You see, Mr. McCall, I have confidence that the unique experiences of black Americans make us as qualified as any people on earth to create a society that is fair and free at the same time. And as you know, that takes some doing."

Reluctantly McCall sat down, and E. Somerset Vaughn, a columnist for the Washington Post, stood up. Vaughn was of medium height and stocky. He still wore the type of crew cut he had worn when Simmons had first seen him, nearly twenty years before. His brown hair was sprinkled with grey.

"Mr. Simmons," he said, "we have heard a lot about where blacks would like this state to be located, but nothing concrete has come from the Council. Since you have been selected to head the negotiating team, what territory are you going to push for?"

This had been one of the most discussed aspects of the separation issue, and Simmons had thought a lot about it.

Actually, he had been in the process of writing an article on the subject when he received word that his name had been thrown in the hopper for chief negotiator. Because of the possibility that he would be selected, he had not finished the article, figuring that if he were selected, it might prove disadvantageous to have too many specifics on the table. Consequently, for the same reason, he decided to dodge the question now.

"There are a number of alternatives," he said. "We will present them when the time comes."

"I understand the Council prime members favor the states of Florida, Georgia, Alabama, Mississippi and Louisiana," Vaughn said. "Any truth in that?"

"Of course, there is truth in it," Simmons said. "But the prime members are not all of the Council leadership, and some other leaders do not favor those states."

"I understand those states are favored because they are close to the black republics in the Caribbean?" Vaughn said.

"That is one of the reasons," Simmons said.

"Another angle which has received almost as much attention as the location of the separate state," Vaughn said, "is the name of the state. As you know, it is common knowledge that considerable disagreement exists among the prime members, as well as among other leaders of the Council on this question. Will you comment on this and give your preference for a name?"

Simmons had hoped this question wouldn't come up, but he had known it would. For a time, shortly after passage of the referendum, a heated debate had indeed raged among Council leaders and black citizens generally around the name of the separate state. Some groups had even held demonstrations to push their favorite names. During that period, many names had surfaced, held favor among certain segments for a few glorious days, then rapidly declined. Only a few names had survived that hectic shake-down period, and these were the ones from which the final selection would probably be made. They were: Republic of New Africa; Commonwealth of New Ethiopia; Malcolmland; Martin's Country; and Federation of

Black America. On a number of occasions, he had been requested to give his opinions on the subject, once to write a definitive article detailing the strengths and weaknesses of the most popular names. He had declined, on the grounds that debate on the name was taking attention away from the primary priorities: establishing negotiation machinery and getting the powers-that-be to negotiate. Finally, the prime members had agreed with him, and the debate had subsided, if not ceased.

"Nobody can correctly say," he replied to Vaughn, "that there is considerable disagreement among the prime members on the name of the state, because the prime members are no longer talking about it. They have taken the position that first things should be pursued first. Selected a name will come after the state has been negotiated. Probably at the constitutional convention."

"Some argue that having a name in advance could give impetus to the discussions," Vaughn said. "How do you feel about that?"

"That argument was considered when the prime members decided to postpone the name debate," Simmons replied. "I think they made a wise decision."

"And you wouldn't like to reveal your preference for a name?"

"And add fuel to the fire the prime members have extinguished? Of course not," Simmons replied.

Mary Smith of the New York Times was standing when Vaughn sat down. Ms. Smith was young and blonde with an angular face and nice figure. She was also thought of as having one of the sharpest minds in the trade. Simmons knew her on sight but had never met her.

"Mr. Simmons," she said, "I understand one of the chief negotiator's jobs is to appoint a committee to draft a constitution for the new nation. Can you tell us who these members will be?"

"You are wrong on the first count," Simmons said. "The constitution committee will be elected by the affiliated organizations of the Council, not appointed by me. You are premature on the second count. We haven't negotiated the terms of the nation yet. There is plenty of time to draft the constitution."

"But you do have some ideas of what you would like the constitution to contain?" Mrs. Smith persisted, apparently unaffected by being corrected.

"Of course," Simmons said. "There are a lot of good ideas around. We won't have much trouble drafting a constitution."

"Will you have much trouble getting the constitution ratified?"

"Probably. First we will have to come up with a method of ratification."

"Have you determined that method yet?"

"No." Simmons was getting ready to turn away from her but noticed that she was still standing, a determined look on her face. "Yes, Ms. Smith?"

"Mr. Simmons, is it true that you favor a socialist form of government for the new state?"

This was the kind of question to which Simmons didn't want to address himself this early in the negotiations. True, speculation of this type had already been in the press and some Council members had already made comments. But Simmons had no intention of letting himself be forced into a position where every aspect of the new nation would be determined by the establishment and the media before negotiations were seriously underway.

"I can't answer that question, Ms. Smith," he said. "Many people with varying views will play important roles in creating the new nation. But there is one thing of which you can be sure. The new nation will not be governed by a system of the kind of rampant capitalism that caused the vote for separation in the first place."

Gregory Worth, the black Chicago area representative of the Los Angeles Times was standing. Worth was short, medium brown, with an arthritic left arm. In addition to his newspaper work, Worth was extremely active in political affairs in the

37

Chicago area. Simmons knew him well and considered him to be a friend.

"Preston," Worth said, "we are aware that under an already worked out agreement, you have the authority to appoint your negotiating committee. Have you come up with the persons for this committee?"

"Yes." There was a murmur from the assembled media people. Without glancing at the monitors, Simmons knew that his face was a closeup on millions of television screens throughout the country. "I have decided to ask the prime members of the Black American Council to serve with me as the negotiating team," he said.

Momentarily, Worth dropped the objectivity of a newsman and became a participant by smiling his approval. "Preston," he said, "will you give us the rationale behind your thinking?"

"Glad to. As you know, the Council prime membership is composed of the leaders of the mass organizations representing the black community. Embodied in these members are the collective opinions of black Americans. Also, it was the Council which first sensed the growing sentiment for separation in the black community and arranged for the referendum. It would be an insult to the Council, and through them an insult to all black Americans, not to have Council prime members on the negotiating team."

"Preston, it's a known fact," Worth said, "that some Council prime members opposed the referendum and worked hard to get blacks to vote against separation. How are you going to overcome this?"

It was a key question, Simmons told himself. A question to which he didn't have answers, although he had thought about it a lot. It was one of those situations which just had to be faced up to when he met with the Council prime members tomorrow.

"As I see it," he said, "there is only one Council prime member who is so committed against separation that he might refuse to participate in the negotiations. I'll have a better idea about that after I meet with them."

"Do you mean this member might be kicked off the team?"

"I doubt that."

"You mean he might resign?"

"I don't know. We'll see."

Some of the media people were talking among themselves. His answer had not satisfied them. He supposed he had been less than positive. But that was the way it was. He turned to face the next questioner, who was standing. It was Vincent Crowley, a right-wing syndicated columnist of national prominence. He wondered if Crowley had come from New York City this afternoon just to be in on the initial interviewing of him. Crowley was tall, probably six feet six, and big, with flaming red hair and a close cropped beard. He was about forty years old.

"Mr. Simmons," Crowley said, his voice surprisingly soft for a man of his bulk, "it has come to my attention that at least one prime member of the Council has begun rather serious consultations with certain foreign powers. My contact tells me the purpose of these negotiations is to have these foreign powers recognize your negotiating team as a sort of government in exile, to pressure the United States government to make concessions favorable to you. What comments do you have about that, Mr. Simmons?"

So this was the reason for Mr. Crowley's presence, Simmons told himself. The C.I.A. wanted him out on a limb early.

"Your intelligence is better than mine, Mr. Crowley," he said. "I don't have any such information."

"That doesn't matter," Crowley said. "Although I'm sure my information is correct, the question I'm asking is, what is your position on your committee dealing with foreign governments?"

"The Council hasn't formulated a position on that, Mr. Crowley. However, since the subject raised by you is such a sensitive one, I think it deserves further comment from me, at this time. First, Mr. Crowley, we don't consider ourselves a government in exile, but, hopefully, a government in creation. While we wish that all people, and governments, are friendly to our cause, current plans do not call for asking foreign governments to assist us in our negotiations with the United States."

"Current plans...?"

"That's what I said."

"So you don't rule out the possibility?"

Simmons felt his stomach muscles tense. Now was as good a time and place as any to tell his first diplomatic lie. "Mr. Crowley," he said, "I don't see any possibility of our attempting to pressure the United States government in that manner."

With a shrug of disappointment and a smirk of disbelief, Crowley took his seat. Simmons pushed a nagging feeling of uneasiness to the back of his mind as Marcus Jackson leaned forward and whispered in his ear: "One more."

Moses Pennmann, the revered dean of the Christian Science Monitor, was standing. Pennmann was thin and stooped and greyhaired. He seldom attended news conferences anymore and Simmons felt a rush of gratitude that the prominent news analyst was present.

"Mr. Simmons," Pennmann began in his still firm voice, "to me this is indeed a sad occasion. I never thought I would live to see a major group of American citizens seriously considering disassociation. More as an American than as a reporter, Mr. Simmons, I ask this question: What are the chances that your committee will not attempt to negotiate a separation?"

The pain in the old man's voice was genuine and Simmons felt himself responding to it with sadness. He could detect a quiver in his voice when he said: "Mr. Pennmann, I truly respect your position and thank you for your indication of loss. However, in all honesty, I must admit that I see little chance that our committee will not attempt to negotiate. We are under mandate of a referendum."

"But surely there must be something the American people can do to make you change your minds?"

"Mr. Pennmann, as you know, at the beginning of this news conference I summarized the conditions which gave rise to the separation vote. These conditions aren't getting any better. In fact, some analysts insist they are getting worse."

"But Mr. Simmons," Pennmann said, "don't you agree that

40

some actions are occurring beneath the surface which might ameliorate these conditions?"

"Which things, specifically, Mr. Pennmann?"

"I'm talking about the recent statements of Joe Rielinski, president of the AFL-CIO, and Miss Hilda Larsen, head of the National Organization for Women."

Simmons could feel himself hesitating, as different replies to Pennmann fought for dominance in his mind. However, his voice was unhesitant and firm when he started speaking. "Mr. Pennmann," he said, "I agree that Mr. Rielinski has been successful in bringing the Teamsters back into the AFL-CIO and that he has been calling for some rather progressive steps with respect to cooling off inflation and improving the job situation. But some of the unions within the AFL-CIO don't seem to be listening to him. He has a lot of opposition, influential opposition, on the Executive Board and within the Executive Council, led primarily, as you know, by Mike Nelson of the building and construction trades. I'm afraid the majority of labor leaders are still practicing the racist, warmongering, job scarcity policies which have kept black and white workers at each others' throats. Additionally, the AFL-CIO leadership is doing little to exert any progressive influence within the Democratic Party, despite statements to the contrary as far back as 1982. And this lack of influence has been one of the primary reasons why President Davidson and the Congress have taken such centrist positions on economic matters."

"What about the things Miss Larsen has been calling for?" Pennmann asked.

Simmons smiled. "I don't know Miss Larsen very well," he said, "but I have a lot of respect for her. Basically, as I understand it, she has been urging blacks to join the women and other progressive elements to force next year's Democratic Party Convention to come up with a somewhat radical platform. I agree that this would be beneficial, if it happened. But NOW called for this same thing at the last convention, and nothing happened. Since then, blacks have gotten moving on their own. No, Mr. Pennmann, romantic-sounding programs and empty promises won't do any good now. Only concrete acts to immediately bring about revolutionary changes would cause me to recommend reconsideration." He paused. "And Mr. Pennmann, do you believe such acts will be immediately forthcoming?"

"No, I do not," the old man said.

Chapter 4

6:30 P.M., Thursday, September 24, 1987

SURROUNDED BY approximately one hundred sitting and standing passengers-to-be in the spacious waiting area assigned to the American Airlines flight on which he was booked, Preston Simmons, slumped in a corner seat near the wall, looked for the mark of death upon the passengers' faces. Not that he knew what the mark of death looked like, but often he had told himself that he would recognize it when he saw it.

He had a strong, almost overpowering fear of riding airplanes and had to deliberately prepare himself for the ordeal every time he took one. Since he realized that most serious plane accidents resulted in mass deaths, long ago he had concluded that this examination of the faces of fellow passengers was as reliable a method as any to detect approaching disaster. He somehow felt—although he rejected the notion while feeling it—that mass death could not be imminent without giving some signal of its presence. He, therefore, examined the faces of all the passengers, looking for some sameness, some irrefutable likeness, which linked the owners of those faces to a common destiny.

Yet, distrusting this instinct while still clinging to it, he realized that he did not know how he would react to a signal of impending death if he received it. What would he do now, he asked himself, if he received what he considered to be a clear signal? Would he cancel his reservations on this plane and

43

book flight on another, despite the fact that he was on the most important mission of his life? Could he chance the public finding out about his fear, his phobia? And to guard against this stigma, wouldn't he merely ignore the signal and proceed to his death to protect his image? He straightened up in his seat and sighed. Time to stop this foolishness. He would accept no signal upon which he could act. He would merely rationalize away any signal he might receive. He would take this plane, as he had taken hundreds of planes before, and would arrive safely, or go to his death, at the direction of forces uninfluenced by his detection of, or failure to detect, the mark of death upon the faces of his fellow passengers.

He stood up. A white woman of about thirty-five, blonde and chic, sitting two seats away, smiled at him, then looked away. The mark of death definitely was not on her face. A middle-aged black man, stocky and brown, was in serious conversation with a much younger white man, pointing out something in a portfolio resting on the knees of the white man.

Simmons suddenly got an almost crippling feeling of the unreality of his mission. This black man seemed so at home with this white man, their lives so enmeshed. Was Pete McCall, the Tribune reporter, correct in his assertion that the referendum vote did not represent the true feelings of black Americans, that they really had no intention of separating from white America? That they had voted for separation more out of frustration than out of any intention to positively pursue acquisition of a separate state? Possibly. But the frustration *was* there. And the distrust of whites by blacks. And the contempt of whites for blacks. And the inequality. The contempt and inequality were so graphically demonstrated every day, had always been graphically demonstrated. At no time in American history had it been more forcefully demonstrated than since 1977, when the national unemployment rate of whites fell below six percent for the first time in two years while the black unemployment rate remained at approximately 12 percent. From that point, despite the passage of the so-called full employment bill in 1978, the government and the captains

44

of private industry had not taken the steps essential to put an end to black unemployment, signalling that they were willing to condemn a large segment of the black population to eternal deprivation. And the ruthlessness with which the government had crushed the so-called job riots was history, scarred forever in the bodies and souls of millions of black Americans. No, the apparent amicability of two middle-class men, one black and the other white, could not alter the facts. Black America was demanding a change.

The intercom system sputtered through a series of jumbled words, corrected itself and, in the voice of a female employee, announced that departure time was approaching and gave boarding instructions. Simmons fell in line behind the chic blonde and followed her through the tunnel-like loading platform. At the plane's entrance, two smiling stewardesses—one slender, young and white and the other slender, young and black—read seating assignments from boarding passes and gave directions without altering the quality of their smiles. His seat was on the aisle near the center of the first-class compartment. Usually he traveled coach. Undoubtedly, Marcus Jackson had decided that this trip he should fly in style.

Simmons took a seat, leaned his head back and closed his eyes. He would leave his seat belt unfastened until he knew whether the center and window seats in his row would be occupied. Tension gripped his stomach. His hands, which he alternately rested on the arms of his seat and folded in front of him, were moist.

"Fasten your seat belt, Mr. Simmons. We are getting ready to move away from the terminal."

Simmons opened his eyes with a start. Incredibly, he must have dozed off for a few seconds. The slender black stewardess was standing over him. He looked around the cabin. Only about a dozen seats were occupied. This flight didn't have many first class takers.

The stewardess was still standing over him, smiling. Her eyes were sharp and sparkling and her features unusually thin. She was jet black. Simmons found himself wondering why he hadn't noticed the uniqueness of her blackness and beauty when he entered the plane.

"I saw your press conference," she said.

"You did? Where?"

"Caught it on TV in the hostess lounge."

"How did it go?"

"Great. You socked it to 'em."

She touched his arm, walked to the front of the cabin, where she went into the standard routine of telling the passengers where the exits were located and demonstrating the use of the oxygen supply masks. The plane was now taxiing toward the runways.

As the plane turned into its take-off runway and began accelerating its engines for the race down the strip, the stewardess breezed down the aisle and stopped by Simmons.

"You shouldn't be alone," she said.

"What do you mean?" he asked, gripping the arms of his seat, bracing himself for the take-off.

"You are going to head the negotiations for our country," she said. "You are sorta like the President of the United States. You should have bodyguards and all that." She flashed him a serious smile and went back to her take-off station.

The plane lifted from the runway, banked sharply above the sundrenched murky waters of Lake Michigan and began a steep climb into its assigned airlane. Simmons realized that his stomach was taut with more than his usual fear of flying. The stewardess' words had sent a shiver of mixed exhilaration and apprehension through him, reminding him that even he had not fully come to grips with the implications of the job for which he had been selected.

The signal sounded which turned off the no smoking light. The stewdaress moved from her station and began taking cocktail orders from the passengers. Watching her smiling in the impersonal manner designed to appear highly personal, Simmons wondered if she truly identified with the idea of the separate state with the intensity she had conveyed to him. He supposed people still took a lackadaisical attitude toward the negotiations because of the gradual, unbelievable step by un-believable step by which the negotiations had become a reality. It was a thing that few people, even the proponents, believed would ever happen.

First, there had been the question of the Black American Council seriously debating the separation proposition. The media people had laughed, but in the end the Council had debated the proposition and passed it. Then there had been the question of with how much enthusiasm the Council would campaign for the proposition. The media had sneered that middle-class influential blacks would never endorse such a proposition through their organizations and churches. Yet, most such organizations did endorse the proposition, even though the majority of middle-class blacks did not vote for it. Black activists, disillusioned by years of low electoral partici-pation in the black community, had feared that non-committed blacks would ignore the proposition. Yet, the reverse had been true. The faceless black masses had carried the day for the proposition. The passage of the separation proposition reminded Simmons of the incredible accumulation of circum-stances which had forced Nixon out of the presidency in 1974.

Often it appeared, he told himself, resting his head against the back of the seat, that history was made not through the logical step-by-step development of events, but by ironic leaps and twists, in a manner totally inconceivable beforehand. For instance, who in December of 1955, at the beginning of the Montgomery bus boycott, would have thought that fifteen years later segregation in the South would successfully have been challenged by a series of bold attacks everybody believed blacks to be incapable of mounting? Also, who in November of 1972, when Nixon was being returned to the presidency in the most devastating landslide in American history, would have believed that a mere two years later he would be forced from office, broken and humiliated, by a series of events so astound-ing that the mind was boggled and the imagination shattered? Likewise, who in the winter of 1974 would have believed that in November of 1976, the black vote would be the single most important factor in electing Jimmy Carter to the Presidency, marking the first time a Southerner (if Lyndon Johnson could be rightfully called a Westerner, as was his wont) had occupied the White House in more than a hundred and twenty-five years? Who among the blacks in that winter of 1976, with their hopes raised by Carter's promise of a more equitable life, would have been believed that his weak and vacillating performance would condition the American people to accept Ronald Reagan by 1980? Most Americans for years had used Goldwater's overwhelming 1964 defeat as a kind of assurance that Reagan could never make it to the White House. Likewise, who, even in 1980, believed that such a massive loss of faith in America would occur among blacks that by 1987, this year, serious demands for a separate state would be raised? He shook his head, smiling to himself. But wasn't it equally strange that he, a middle-class black, moderate in so many manners and attitudes, would be leading the negotiations for such a state?

The signal sounded, turning off the seat belt light. The Stewardess was standing in front of him.

"Would you like a cocktail, Mr. Simmons?"

"Yes, bring me a dry sherry...So you really go for the idea of the separate state?"

She bit down on her bottom lip and nodded her head. "It's about time we got something of our own," she said.

"How do you like this job?" he asked

She smiled. "Some days I like the hell out of it." Her voice became serious. "This job's not the problem. It's the fact that the powers that be just don't give a damn about black people. If we are lucky enough to get a break, okay. But nobody's got us in their plans any more."

The plane had stopped climbing now. Simmons unfastened his seat belt, relaxed for the first time. One down and one to go, he smiled to himself, referring to the fact that since the take-off had been accomplished without mishap, only the landing in Washington, D.C. remained as the primary obstacle to a safe trip.

But the feeling of unreality surrounding his mission would

not relent as he sat back in his seat to await his drink. The attitude of the United States government toward the separate state idea had been strangely tolerant from the beginning, and this he had spent considerable time pondering over. Of course, various government officials had addressed themselves to the question with varying degrees of speculation, but none had said anything which could be construed as an official position. From the President of the United States, that southern gentleman with the pompousness of a Sam Irvin and the cunning of a Lyndon Johnson, had come only two comments of significance. When the Council voted to hold the referendum the President had said: "The First Amendment to the Constitution gives citizens the right to express themselves on any question they desire." When the separation proposition was approved the president had commented: "Citizens have the right to petition their government for redress of any wrong, real or imagined." When a reporter had asked, "Does that mean that you will negotiate with them?", the President had replied: "Under the Constitution I must accept the petition for redress. I cannot avoid that responsibility." Basically, that had been all. Congress, of course, true to its reputation for expressing almost as many opinions as it had members, had not failed to express these views. But even there, because the leaders were divided, no genuine majority position had been reached. True, the Council had not attempted to utilize any federal, state or local government body in carrying out the referendum, but the Council had made use of lists of registered voters to determine which blacks were eligible to vote. Also, prior to the election, the Council had launched a massive registration campaign and so far as he knew, the feds had not pressured local authorities not to cooperate. Although the voting itself had taken place in black churches and other black establisments, very few governing bodies had protested when the Council called upon off-duty black policemen to help keep the peace at the polling places.

The United States government had not opposed the Council in the referendum, Simmons told himself now as he had told

49

himself many times before, for one of two reasons: it was in favor of the separate nation idea; or, so far, it didn't take seriously the efforts which had been expended in that direction. The U.S. government would be in favor of separation for one reason and one reason only: blacks were more valuable to the United States outside of it than inside. And this, would only be the case if blacks were causing the power structure more problems than it felt competent to solve. This was not to say, Simmons cautioned himself, that a separation could not be negotiated without resorting to wholesale violence or all-out civil disobedience. In any case, he told himself, if agreement of the government came at all, it would come at the *end* of negotiations, not *before* they started.

The stewardess brought his drink and stood by his seat while he sampled it.

"Good sherry," he said.

"The best for the best," she replied, her voice flirtatious with mock seriousness.

"Thanks."

"My pleasure." She moved across the aisle to the next passenger who ordered a drink.

The United States government, he told himself, wasn't engaged in vicious opposition to the separation idea simply because it didn't look upon the matter as being serious. To put it another way, the government had little respect for blacks in general and for the Council in particular. Yet, he had little doubt, he told himself, feeling the sherry warm in his stomach, that the government had to re-evaluate its assessment of the situation, now that matters had gone so far. He had always believed the government hadn't expected the separation proposition to carry at the polls. But the proposition had carried, a chief negotiator had been selected, and he was on his way to Washington to begin the big push. The people in high places had to be getting worried, and very soon they would be getting nasty. The history of the late sixties and the early eighties made it clear that *The Man* had nothing against kicking asses and taking names when he became disturbed.

He drained the last drop of wine from his glass and set it on the pull-out table in front of him. The stewardess had said he needed a bodyguard. One of the reporters at the press conference had asked if he would solicit help from foreign governments. He had little doubt that many militant groups, both black and white, were standing in the wings ready to give violent support, or violent opposition, to his cause. In the days to come, all of these things, with or without his consent, would create a confused pattern across the face of history. Hopefully he would be able to weave something of his conscience and concept into the design.

He settled back in his seat and closed his eyes, feeling the drone of the jet engines in his ears as they hurled the giant plane toward the nation's capital.

Chapter 5

10:00 A.M., Friday, September 25, 1987

"PRESTON," ROBERT Griggs said in his precise voice, "we have discussed your selection as chief negotiator in some detail, and we want you to know that we are satisfied with it. This is not to say that you were the first choice of all of us, but none of us was committed against you. We thought you should know this from the outset."

From his position at the head of the conference table, Simmons looked along its mahogany surface at the six Council prime members seated at its sides, three on his left and three on his right. He had been ponderng just where this meeting would fall on the list of important gatherings which had been held by blacks in America, concluding that only the events growing out of this and future meetings could make such a determination possible. Anyway, it was best he concentrated on what was happening now, on the things that were being said at this moment. And what Griggs had just said proved that he had been correct in selecting the negotiating team: the obvious advantages of utilizing the Council prime members in this role would not be reduced by antagonism toward himself.

"Thanks," he said. "Thank you very much."

"Even though we had given the chief negotiator the authority to select his own team," Griggs continued, "quite frankly we were worried about the role the Council prime members would

52

play. While we didn't think the chief negotiator's hands should be tied, we didn't want to be kept out of things, either." Griggs smiled. "We appreciate the simplicity, and wisdom, of your decision."

Simmons had always marveled at the peculiar deliberativeness of Griggs' speaking style. Each word had a tendency to stand apart from the other words in his sentences, not unlike the singsong rhythms of a child learning to read, yet somehow the total of his words reflected both warmth and erudition.

"Thanks again for your kindness," Simmons said, the lightness of his tone matching Griggs' demeanor.

Simmons had walked the four or five blocks from Hotel Washington to the Black American Council offices, surprised that he had not been accosted by reporters in the lobby of the hotel or in the vestibule of this building. He supposed they figured that, at this juncture, the separation story had been milked for all it was worth. And this was partially true. His picture had stared at him from every newspaper on every newsstand he had passed during his walk from the hotel to the Council building. When he got off the elevator and entered this twelfth-floor conference room, exactly one minute late for the ten A.M. meeting, the Council prime members were waiting for him. And now, with the hand-shaking and the expression of support out of the way, Simmons, sitting behind his ritualistic cup of coffee and observing the Council members behind their equally ritualistic cups of coffee, was turning over in his mind the things he knew about each of them, trying to eliminate from his thinking those things which for the moment didn't matter.

Seated to his left were Robert Griggs, Rubye Ransome and Sam Muhammed. On his right were William Green, Albert James and Benjamin P. Patten. He knew them all well and at one time or another had written a profile-type story on each of them. He considered at least three of them—Robert Griggs, Rubye Ransome and Albert James—to be his personal friends.

Robert Griggs. Staring at the side of his coffee cup, his handsome, light tan face a perfect extension of the expensive brown gaberdine suit he was wearing. In his late thirties. Had

53

served one term in the U.S. House of Representatives from New York City before resigning to become executive director of the NAACP in 1980. Council member since 1984 and president of the Council since 1985. Harvard law graduate. Executive ability and management skills his chief assets.

Rubye Ransome. Round, doll-like, honey-colored face, with straight black hair worn short. In her middle forties, but appearing to be under thirty-five, with her low-cut blouse and flashy earrings. Educated as a nurse, and married to a prominent doctor before finishing nurse's training. Began her public life as an officer in one of the better-known social-charity clubs so popular in Chicago during the sixties and seventies. Mother of two children in their early twenties. Divorced ten years after her first marriage and remarried four years later to a civil rights activist. Had been divorced from him for two years. One of the organizers of the League of Black Women in the early seventies. Instrumental in keeping black women from flocking into the white-dominated feminist organizations. Outstanding fund raiser, direct and rather earthy manner of talking. Primarily instrumental in building the League into a national organization in the late seventies. Elected to the Council when it was founded.

Sam Muhammed. Sitting nervously on the edge of his chair, fingers tapping the table, his thin, medium-brown face taut. In his middle forties. Leader of the black nationalist consortium of the Council. Original name: Samuel Johnson. Assumed the surname of Muhammed in his early twenties, but insisted on turning his first name into plain Sam. Muhammed for his ancient birthright and Sam for his modern slave experience in the United States. Has been dope addict, dope pusher and pimp and insists that because he has cleansed himself of these things, he has the purity and courage possessed by few persons. Clever quipster. Detailed knowledge of black history.

William Green. Executive director of the national Urban League. Generally represents the more right-wing black viewpoint on the Council. Approximately seventy years old, light brown-skinned with a full head of grey hair. Tall, slender and stoop-shouldered. Thirty years ago, built the Urban League of a midwestern city into national prominence. Resigned from that position in the early seventies to become executive vice-president of a black publishing firm. Called back into Urban League service in 1979 to head the national organization. Strong believer in the capitalist system. Knows more members of the white power structure than any other black in the country. Represents black business interests on the Council, the position initially refused by Jim Sneed. Voted against the separation proposition when it was being considered by the Black Council. Worked against its passage at the polls.

Albert James. Elbow on the table, chin resting in his right hand. Big, approximately 260 pounds, tall, about six feet five, black, and sixty-five years old. Communist Party member in the late forties and early fifties. Drifted away from the Party in the middle fifties because the Party opposed his position of full black autonomy within its ranks. Helped to organize most of the Negro voter's leagues of the period. In sixties and seventies worked with blacks in the construction trades and in 1976 organized a national black labor relations league. In 1982, following the murder of his son by Chicago policemen, became even more aggressive than in the past, so that by the time the Council was formed, he was among the outstanding leaders of the left of center organizations, consisting of PUSH, SCLC, CORE and his own Black Labor League. Became the representative of these groups on the Council. Has supported the separation proposition from the beginning.

Benjamin P. Patten. The Reverend Doctor Benjamin P. Patten. Eyes closed, wide-nosed, thick-lipped, dark-brown features in repose. Short, stocky, solidly-built body covered by a well-cut, dark silk suit and white shirt with clergy collar. Approximately fifty years old. Disciple of Martin Luther King Junior. Holder of a masters degree in sociology and doctorate in theology. Pastor of one of the largest black churches in New York City. President of the National Baptist Convention. Builder of a bridge between the conservative and progressive wings of the black ministry. One of the founders of the Black

American Council and the religious representative on the Council. Possessor of outstanding skills as a mediator and conciliator. When the separation proposition came before the Council, Patten had neither supported nor opposed it. Rather he had urged church bodies and individual ministers to follow their consciences. Yet, he had also urged ministers to make freedom of choice available to their congregations by opening their churches as polling places. Refused to permit his name to be submitted for chief negotiator, insisting that his primary talents lay in mediation and not in initiation.

Simmons' analysis of the Council members was interrupted by Rubye Ransome pushing her chair back from the table and standing up, smoothing her blue, floor-length knit skirt in a delicate gesture. Long skirts and low-cut, revealing blouses were a fixture with Rubye, Simmons recalled, additional evidence of her belief in the effectiveness of contrast.

"Before Preston opens this meeting up for business," she said, "I'm going to get another cup of coffee. You see, I really drink the damn stuff." She headed toward the rear of the room where a coffee percolator stood on a small table. Her movements were smooth and unhurried, so unlike the harshness of her words.

"Anybody else?" Preston asked. Griggs joined Rubye at the percolator. Bill Green stood up but did not move away from his place at the table. When Rubye and Griggs returned to their seats, Green continued to stand.

"If you'll take your seat, Bill," Simmons said, "we'll get underway."

"I have something to say," Green said, "and I might as well say it now."

"Okay, Bill," Simmons said, noticing for the first time that there was a pained expression on Green's face, broad lines cutting deep into his age-worn features.

"Before you start making plans," Green said, "I think it is only fair for me to inform you that I cannot accept appointment to the negotiating committee."

"What!" Bob Griggs and Albert James said together. Rubye,

in the process of raising her cup to her lips, set the cup on the table without taking a sip of coffee. Ben Patten sat up straight in his seat, his eyes alert. Sam Muhammed jumped up from the table and stood facing Green.

"What the hell is this!" Sam cried. "You didn't say anything about not participating yesterday when Simmons was selected!"

"This has nothing to do with Simmons," Green said.

"Just why can't you serve on the committee, Bill?" Simmons heard himself ask, noticing that beads of perspiration were standing on the old man's forehead, despite the coolness of the air-conditioned room.

"I cannot in good conscience work to bring about a situation in which I do not believe," Green said. "As you know, I do not believe in the separate state."

"But you did not believe in the separate state when we voted on the proposition," Bob Griggs said, "yet you participated in that process."

"You damn right you did!" Sam said. "If you were going to resign, you should have quit when your friend Gene Wild pulled the Congressional Black Caucus out, and saved us the humiliation of this double blow."

The other prime members were probably thinking the same thing, Simmons realized, reliving that entire painful episode in the history of the Council. United States Representative Eugene Wild from Cleveland, Ohio, chairman of the Congressional Black Caucus, had been the representative of the black elected officials on the Council when the decision was reached to hold the separation referendum. Prodded by Caucus members, as well as other black elected officials, Wild had resigned his seat on the Council, explaining that it would be improper and probably immoral for him to remain in Congress while serving as a member of a body which was urging black citizens to separate from their country.

"Sam has a point," Griggs said. "Bill, why didn't you resign at that time?"

"That was different," Green replied. "I believe in majority rule and in the supremacy of freedom of choice. When we voted

57

on the separation proposition, the question before the Council was whether the proposition should be placed before black voters for acceptance or rejection. When the Council voted to submit the question to the voters, I felt duty bound to participate in the process because the people had a right to make the final decision."

"Then, why didn't you pull out when that vote went against you?" Sam asked.

"Because I had no reason to believe that the Council would be asked to join with the chief negotiator in leading the negotiations. When Simmons announced yesterday that the Council prime members would comprise his team, I knew I couldn't serve."

"Yet, you didn't say anything until today," Albert James said.

"I figured this was the best time," Green replied. "It made sense to me to tell the Council and Simmons at the same time."

"You can't trust a goddamn Uncle Tom!" Sam said.

"*Mr. Muhammed*!" Simmons could hear his voice exploding in the room, competing with the sound of his fist crashing against the top of the table. "*You are out of order!*" He was vaguely aware that he had hurt the knuckle on the little finger of his right hand.

Sam Muhammed threw up his hands in a gesture of helpless disbelief and sat down. "Damn!" he said. "A break in our ranks before we get started. Niggers can't ever do anything right!"

William Green continued to stand, leaning forward with his hands resting on the table. His bottom lip was quivering.

"Sam, if you're worried about the image of the negotiating team," Simmons said, "I don't see how Bill's refusing to serve will adversely affect that. In fact, when you think about it, his refusing to serve might enhance the team."

"How do you figure that?" Sam asked.

Simmons looked at the other Council members. All except Dr. Patten, who was nodding his head in agreement with what Simmons had said, appeared to need convincing.

"Let's look at it this way," he said. "Everybody knows that

Bill is against the separation idea. He has spoken against it, written against it, and worked against it. It would strain credibility for him to suddenly begin negotiating for a separate state."

"Right," Benjamin Patten chimed in. "Bill's resignation represents an act of purification. Through public disassociation from him, the rest of us will appear more determined, more resolute in our will."

"I don't know about that," Rubye said. "The niggers on the streets are going to view it as a dude not being able to stand the heat. And they gonna start making bets on who the next one's gonna be."

Simmons smiled. "I'm always impressed by the unpretentiousness of your idioms, Rubye," he said. "But believe me, The Man is going to view Bill's resignation the way Ben looks at it, without the profundity of Ben's symbolism, of course."

Dr. Patten laughed. "Thank you, counselor," he said.

Sam Muhammed stood up, turned in a small circle beside his chair, and sat down again. "I can buy it," he said, "if we request Mr. Green's resignation, rather than his voluntarily submitting it to us. That way, we will be taking the lead in this purification process."

"That makes sense," Albert James said.

"It doesn't make any sense to me," Bill Green said in a low voice. "I will not permit myself to be used in that fashion."

"You will not permit yourself to be used!" Sam cried. "What the hell do you think you're doing to thirty million black Americans?"

"I'm not harming black Americans. I'm helping them. Do you really believe we could run a nation, even if this country would let us establish one? Which it won't."

"That's it!" Sam screamed, jumping up. "That's been it all along! He doesn't believe we can run a nation!"

Simmons got the feeling that the discussion was getting melodramatic, without any purpose. Apparently Rubye was feeling the same way.

"Cut out the show-timing, Sam," she said. "I thought you

knew all along that Bill Green believed we were incapable of running a nation, or *anything* important, for that matter. He's going to quit, and we can't keep him here."

"My sentiments exactly," Albert James said.

"I'm only trying to be honest with everybody," Green said, looking at Simmons.

"And believe me, Bill, we appreciate that," Dr. Patten said.

Simmons leaned back in his chair. "Okay, let's see if we can wrap this up." He looked hard at Green. "I suppose you're going to release some type of statement. What are you going to say?"

"Exactly what I've said here. I'm resigning because I don't believe in a separate nation."

"Okay. And are you resigning from the Council, or just from the negotiating team?"

"What do you mean?" Sam cut in before Green could answer. "How can he resign from one without resigning from the other?"

"Easy, Sam, as I see it," Simmons said. "I appointed him to the negotiating team. He was elected to the Council."

"Right," Robert Griggs said. "There is nothing in the Council bylaws which says that every Council member must participate in every Council endeavor. He can sit this one out and still remain a Council member. What is it going to be, Bill?"

"I'll keep my seat on the Council," Green said.

"Well, I'll be damned!" Sam said, slapping his hand against the table.

"I'll let you see my statement before it is released," Green said, talking equally to Griggs and Simmons. "I disagree with you deeply and totally, but you are still my friends, and my brothers and sister. We have been through a lot together. And we will go through a lot more—in the days ahead." It appeared to Simmons that Green had regained some of the self-assurance for which he was known.

"Thank you, Bill," he said, suddenly feeling affection for the old man. "Does anybody else want to say anything before Bill leaves us?"

60

Nobody said anything. Simmons stood up and offered his hand to Green, who took it. There were tears in the old man's eyes. All the other Council members except Sam shook his hand.

And then, with head thrown back, body as straight as his stooped shoulders and age would permit, William Green, respected leader of Black America for nearly a half century, marched away from one of the most critical undertakings in which his people had ever been involved.

Chapter 6

11:00 A.M., Friday, September 25, 1987

"WELL, THAT'S that," Preston Simmons said.

He stood up, took off his blue knit suit coat, walked across the room and hung it in the clothes closet attached to the conference room wall near the door. "If anybody has anything to do, do it now," he said as he came back to the table and took his seat. "And don't take but five minutes. We've got to get down to the business which brought us here."

"Damn right!" Sam said. He pulled a cigarette from the pocket of his shirt, lit it, took one nervous puff, and mashed the cigarette out in the ash tray in front of Rubye. She had also lit a cigarette and was leisurely smoking, head resting against the back of her chair, eyes half closed. She glanced sideways at Sam.

"You smoked that cigarette like a true Moslem, Sam," she said.

"Get off my back, Rubye!" Sam said. "You know damn well I'm not a practicing Moslem. Have never been, nor professed to be."

Rubye smiled. "Take it easy, Sam. You're uptight." Sam shrugged, got up and left the room.

"Guess I'll run down the hall to the office," Griggs said. "Be back before the deadline," he added, nodding to Simmons.

Normally, Griggs spent one day a week in the Council office and four days in his NAACP office. However, since the separation proposition became the primary consideration of the Council, Griggs had divided his time about equally between the two offices.

Benjamin Patten stood up. "Want to stretch your legs?" he asked Albert James.

"Might as well," James said. "The chairman deserves a break. Let's leave him alone with the beautiful lady."

"Go to hell, Al," Rubye said.

When they were alone, Simmons asked: "Was that crack about the Moslem and the cigarette necessary?"

Rubye leaned forward, placed her elbow on the table and rested her chin in her hand. "I guess not. I suppose I like to needle Sam. But then, deep down, I can't forget that if Sam hadn't beat out Ali Pasha as the representative of the nationalists on the Council, the followers of the late Elijah Muhammad would be working with us."

Simmons smiled. "What do you want, Sam Muhammed and Elijah Muhammad, too?" Then seriously: "Maybe things turned out for the better. In the last few years the Black Muslims have become more and more isolated. Maybe it's just as well they are not officially represented on the Council. If they didn't have Sam's not being a true believer in Allah to complain about, they'd come up with something else. Of course, believe me, I appreciate what they have done to instill in blacks a feeling of self-reliance."

Rubye shrugged. "You'll get no argument out of me. How do you think this is going?"

"Can't really say; considering we haven't really got started. But I'm not alarmed about the loss of Bill Green. That was to be expected."

"Ben Patten is right," she said. "We'll be stronger now that he's not participating. We still have too many different viewpoints on this negotiating team, if you ask me."

"Do you mean you think I made a mistake in selecting the Council prime members to work with me?"

63

"Not really that. To have done otherwise would have been worse. I suppose some days I want things to be sweet and simple."

"Getting soft, Rubye?"

"Maybe just a little bit tired."

Sam Muhammed, Ben Patten and Albert James returned to the room together, closely followed by Robert Griggs.

"My office was full of reporters," Griggs said. "I told them we would have a formal statement, in about two hours. Ted Blackwell is standing by to help with the statement." Blackwell was the executive director of the Council, Simmons recalled, truly a top-notch technician.

"That's another reason why I asked the Council to work with me," he smiled. "I don't have to look for a staff. We already have one. Did the reporters get to Bill Green?"

"I don't think so," Griggs replied. "Ted said he didn't stop by the office. The reporters probably think he's still back here."

"Good. Bill will probably wait until he gets back to League headquarters in New York before releasing his statement. That way, the media will hear it from us first." Simmons paused, then began in a more formal tone of voice. "Okay, let's get started. As I see it, we should first discuss some of the specifics of our demands. Then decide to whom we are going to address these demands. Does that sound reasonable?"

"Sounds reasonable to me," Griggs said. "Before that, however, I think we must look at the legal aspects of our demands, from a constitutional point of view. Now Section Three of Article Four of the United States Constitution says....."

Sam stood up. "Pardon me, Bob," he said to Griggs. "All that's well and good, but before we get into technicalities, we better see if we are together with respect to our mission. Simmons said a couple of things in his press conference yesterday that disturbed me. We better get those things straight first."

"Only *two* things that disturbed you, Sam?" Griggs asked. "I'm happy to know that... We're listening."

"In response to a question from columnist Vincent Crowley"—Sam turned to Simmons—"you said that current plans do not call for us to ask foreign governments to assist us in our negotiations with the United States. Now you know, and everybody here knows, that the United States will negotiate seriously with us only if its position becomes untenable. In other words, we got to put pressure where we can, and in doing this, we got to utilize every pressure source we have."

Simmons looked into Sam's eyes. They were sharp and bright and prodding.

"Sam, I remember that question well," he said. "You will remember that Crowley, who is little more than a mouthpiece for the CIA, called especial attention to my use of the phrase 'current plans.' So I finally said, and this is an exact quote, 'Mr. Crowley, I don't see any possibility of our attempting to pressure the United States government in that manner.' The question before us now is, was I jiving Crowley, or did I mean what I said. The correct answer is what I said at first. As I see it, *current plans* shouldn't call for us to ask foreign governments to assist us in our negotiations."

Sam began to speak again, but Albert James had his hand up. Simmons raised his hand to cut Sam off, nodding to James.

"What you're saying, as I see it," James said, "is that we shouldn't begin these discussions in an atmosphere of confrontation. That we should approach the negotiations as though we are trying to settle a family argument."

"Exactly," Simmons said.

"But that's naive!" Sam cried. "We black Americans are the only people in the world who believe there is good will in a bear fight. In such a fight, you better carry your shit with you; not ask your little brother to bring it to you after the fight gets started!"

"Sam, if you think that way," Simmons said, "I suppose you'd be in favor of asking the militant groups to support us with violent actions?"

Sam's eyes blinked, but he didn't hesitate in his answer. "Damn right I'm in favor of that!" he said.

"Look, Sam," Simmons said. "I can understand your frustrations. At times I feel the same way you do. In the final analysis, it might boil down to doing what you want. But we can't start off doing it. We can't get nasty first. There is still such a thing in the world as good will. And wherever this thing leads, our position has to be that we tried to negotiate in good faith."

"Amen!" Ben Patten said.

"Preston," Rubye said, placing her hand on Sam's arm to silence him, "back in Chicago, when we were running together more than a decade ago, we had a saying which dealt with a person's ability to act when his or her back was to the wall. Remember we used to ask: 'Do you have any *fuck you* money?' Okay, Preston, where is your *fuck you* money in this situation?"

Simmons felt himself smiling. He hadn't thought about that phrase in years. "Good question, Rubye," he said. "Okay, our fuck you money is precisely our hesitancy in dealing with foreign countries and resorting to violence. We'll keep the good will of the white Americans we already have, and will gain the good will of others, especially if the United States government gets nasty first. On the contrary, if we follow Sam's advice, we'd be spending our fuck you money up front, not holding it in reserve."

Robert Griggs laughed. "I'm getting more respect for computers every day. We have a chief negotiator who is both brilliant and down to earth. Sam, I recommend that you rest your case."

The other Council members laughed agreement.

"Okay," Sam said, "I won't pursue that point any longer, although I'm not convinced. But I said Simmons said a couple of things at the press conference I disagreed with. We might as well air the other one."

Griggs looked at Simmons for approval. "Might as well," Simmons said.

Sam bowed in mock graciousness. "In response to that old phony from the Christian Science Monitor..."

"Moses Pennmann," Dr. Patten cut in, "and I really don't think he's phony."

"Yes, Moses Pennmann," Sam agreed. "Well, phony or not,

66

in response to his plea that we *not* negotiate a separation, it seemed to me that Simmons gave the impression that black Americans want a separate state as a *substitute* for something more desirable. In fact he said: *'only concrete acts to immediately bring about revolutionary changes would cause me to recommend reconsideration'*. I say nothing should cause us to reconsider. We want a separate state as our first, second, third and *only* choice!"

"Sam," Simmons said, "the thrust of my statement was that there is nothing on the horizon to indicate the types of revolutionary changes which would cause us to alter our position. In fact, I pointed out to Mr. Pennmann that we are under the mandate of a referendum to negotiate."

"I know you did," Sam said, "but you did not say that under *no* circumstances will we reconsider. You did not point out to him that Black-White Unity is a farce, has always been a farce. You did not stress that we have no intention of merely exchanging white capitalist bosses for white socialist bosses, which your revolutionary changes would mean!"

When Sam finished speaking, Albert James was standing, his great height and size contrasting sharply with Sam's short, slender frame. He stared down at Sam from directly across the table.

"Sam," James said, "why do you always take things out of context to aggravate the differences of opinion on this Council? Hell, you know Preston wasn't stating that position just for himself, but for the majority of this Council, and for most of the black people in this country, for that matter."

"That's a matter of opinion," Sam said.

"Let me finish!" James interjected. "All my life I've believed in Black-White Unity, even when we called it Negro-White Unity back in the forties and fifties." He paused, then added as though the thought he was expressing had come to him for the first time. "You know something. I'm glad white people didn't agree with me thirty, twenty, or even ten years ago. I'm glad we are being forced to fight for self-determination. We'll be stronger people for it." He paused again. "Even more important, we'll be a respected people." He sat down.

Sam, still standing, asked quickly: "Does this mean that *now* you don't see any circumstance where you'd stop fighting for a separate state?"

James looked up at him. "I didn't say that," he replied. "I said that from this on out, whatever happens, white people are going to run everything past us for our input." He lowered his head, as though feeling sudden pain. "You don't have to worry about me, Sam. After what they did to my boy, I can never trust them again. You don't have to worry about me."

"I'm glad to know that," Sam said, a hint of embarrassment in his voice.

"I know something else, Sam," Dr. Patten said. "We need to be getting on with the business of mapping strategy for our negotiations. Our chairman's been trying to get us to do that all day."

Rubye clapped her hands. "This time I'll say amen for you, Dr. Patten," she said.

Simmons looked at Sam. With a shrug, the black nationalist leader sat down, apparently as unconvinced on this question as he was concerning the Council's posture in its relationship with foreign governments. Simmons was acquainted with Sam's intransigence only through reputation. His firsthand experience with it was proving to be both frustrating and stimulating.

"Bob," he said, turning to Griggs, "it seems that hours ago you were talking about the legal aspects of our demands. Will you go ahead with that?"

Griggs stood up. He had an opened book in his hands. "As a starting point," he said, "I'm going to read verbatim Section Three of Article Four of the United States Constitution, a passage we have become very familiar with in recent months." He read: "New States may be admitted by the Congress into this Union; but no new State shall be formed or erected within the Jurisdiction of any other State; nor any State be formed by the junction of two or more States, or Parts of States, without the Consent of the Legislatures of the States concerned as well as of the Congress."

"And the point you're making, Bob?" Simmons asked.

"The point I'm making is this," Griggs said. "Legally, we're going to have a hell of a time negotiating a separate state. From a strict legal standpoint, we'd have to go through the legislature of every state involved."

"Would this hold true even if we raised the old argument of the Black Belt?" Dr. Patten asked. "I mean if we only asked for the old Black Belt counties in certain southern States?"

"It's the same thing," Griggs said. "Remember, the Article I just read says no new state can be created within a state, by the combination of two or more states, or parts of states, without the consent of the legislatures of the state or states involved. It's very clear."

"I take this to mean," Albert James said, "that a constitutional amendment is required?"

"Possibly," Griggs said. "Or a very unusual ruling by the Supreme Court."

"How's that?" Dr. Patten asked. "I haven't heard that one before."

Griggs turned backward a page in the book he was holding. "Sections One and Two of Article Three of the Constitution deals with the power of the Supreme Court," he said. "Omitting those things which are not pertinent to what we are talking about, this Section reads: 'The judicial Power shall extend...to Controversies between a State and Citizens of another State...'"

"You mean," Dr. Patten began...

"Yes, that's right," Griggs said. "Black citizens of this country, because of historical deprivation, could sue the states we are concerned with to give up all their territory to us. We would bypass all lower courts and go directly to the Supreme Court for a ruling."

"But wouldn't the constitutional amendment route be more binding," Rubye asked.

"Of course it would," Griggs said, "but it might be more difficult to get. Remember, an amendment requires a two-thirds majority in both houses of Congress and ratification by three-fourths of the states."

"But neither the President, the Congress nor the states would honor such a ruling by the Supreme Court," Dr. Patten said. "Especially when Article Four is as clear as it is."

"You might be right," Griggs said.

Sam crashed his fist down on the table. "Why the hell are we wasting time!" he cried. "Why are we talking about all this crap when we already know the answer? The whole thing, as you lawyers well know, is an extralegal process. If we can convince the powers that be to give us a separate state they'll find a way to do it. Our only concern is having the power to convince them. That's why I've been pushing for us to use all the pressure..."

"Sam is right," Simmons interrupted before the nationalist leader could reopen his argument about utilizing foreign governments and militant groups. "It is an extralegal process. However, our discussing the legal ramifications is not a waste of time. Although we know that, in the final analysis, what's legal is what's politically feasible, the American people, for the most part, still believe in the consitutional process. Therefore, these legal aspects must be fully and publicly discussed."

"You are right on that score," Dr. Patten said. "We can never permit ourselves to become so cynical that we forget the power of the traditional, and the romantic. Nixon forgot it...to his downfall."

Sam waved his hand impatiently. "I'm not forgetting it. I just don't want us to act like that's all there is to it."

"Believe me," Albert James said, "we're not forgetting the way The Man is. We've been black all our lives, just like you, Sam."

"Okay," Griggs said, looking at Simmons, "how should we approach this thing? Whom should we contact to begin our negotiations?"

"I've been thinking this over for some time," Simmons said, "and the approach I'm going to recommend is probably the best, at this stage at least. First, we definitely should start dealing with the Congress, through the Judiciary Committees of the House and Senate. Whether the legislation or the amendment route is taken, the Congress must initiate the process. We also should try to sit down with the President, the Attorney General and the Secretary of State as soon as a meeting can be arranged."

"Do you think we should talk to all three at the same time?" Griggs asked.

"If possible," Simmons replied. "However, the President might want us to see those two Cabinet officers first. Just as a matter of protocol."

"Anybody else?" Rubye asked.

"Not at this stage. The Supreme Court approach should be used as a last resort. And we definitely don't want to deal with the states directly, unless we have to."

"What preliminary work do you want the staff to begin doing?" Griggs asked.

"Ted Blackwell and the Council staff," Simmons said, "should start pulling together position papers on the following: the arguments surrounding the secession of the southern states; the theories undergirding the Back to Africa movements of John Delaney and Marcus Garvey; the reasoning behind the moves to establish a black nation in the Black Belt counties of selected southern states; and the thinking which spurred the attempt to create a black nation out of the Oklahoma territory near the end of the last century. We must be as prepared as The Man when we sit down with him."

"Good deal," Griggs said. "I'll remain here in Washington all next week to work with Ted. What about you, Preston?"

"Ummm. I have a few things to take care of in Chicago over the weekend. This is Friday. I tell you what. I'll go back to Chicago this afternoon, and return to Washington Sunday evening. Okay?"

"Fine," Griggs said.

"What about the rest of us?" Rubye asked.

Griggs looked at Simmons. "It won't be necessary for you to remain in Washington," Simmons said. "If we need you during the preliminary stages, we'll call you. Of course, you will be expected to be here for all negotiation sessions."

71

"Fine," Sam said. "I have to get back to New York."

"Same here," Dr. Patten said.

"And me to Los Angeles," Albert James said.

"Okay, that's it," Simmons said. "Rubye, stick with me while Bob and I get with Blackwell. I want to talk with you before I leave."

"At your service, Sir," Rubye smiled, a twinkle in her eyes.

Chapter 7

1:00 P.M., Friday, September 25, 1987

IT WAS a glorious day. A day when the bright heat of the sun, the blue clearness of the sky, and the tender caress of the air joined in such perfect union that there was communion with the harsh concrete of the city, producing an impression, a feeling really, of summertime listlessness and the droning of bees. It was a glorious day. A day to go on forever, or never come at all.

Preston Simmons, walking in this day, his hand on the arm of Rubye Ransome, gently directing her along Pennsylvania Avenue toward 14th Street, was aware of a feeling of celebration within himself. The session with Bob Griggs and Ted Blackwell and the later meeting with the news media were done with, and he and Rubye, supported by the guise of looking for a suitable place to have lunch, were strolling not so much along a street in the nation's capitol as into the world of their memories, now made somewhat false and even more fanciful by the urgent reality of the present.

"Rubye Ransome, girl so handsome," he said in a singing voice...

"Please come home with me," she replied, also singing...

"I'll hug you, and I'll kiss you," he continued...

"And screw you 'til you pee!" she concluded.

They stopped in the middle of the sidewalk, laughing into each other's eyes.

"I'll be damn," she said, "I wouldn't have remembered that ditty in a million years."

"Shows how romantic I am."

"You call *that* romance?"

They started walking again.

"How long have we known each other?" he asked.

She looked up at him, her eyes teasingly serious. "Between us, or for the record?"

"Between us."

"Well, let me see. We met when we were in seventh grade. I think I was twelve and you were thirteen. That means we have known each other thirty-two years."

He smiled down at her, a woman nearly as old as he, yet looking not much older than the girl of their childhood.

"You're still the finest thing around," he said.

"You're not so bad yourself, with your hawk nose, dimpled chin, and just-right mouth."

"What do you mean—just-right mouth?"

"You know, a mouth with lips that are not too thin and not too thick."

"I see, not too thin like the honky's and not too thick like the nigger's."

She glanced at him, amused. "Go to hell," she said.

He placed his hand on her back, above the neckline of the low-cut blouse, steering her along the sidewalk. Although the noontime crowd had thinned somewhat, there still were a lot of people on the street, as befitting this section of Washington, D.C. Her back was cool to his touch. He recalled that her skin was always cool, contrasting sharply, in his memory of female skins, with Janice's, which was always hot. Yet, in appearance, and in the directness of their approach to things, Rubye and Janice had always reminded him of each other. Not in the extent of their concerns—for Janice had never shown any real

74

interest in broad social and political issues—but in their attitudes toward the things with which they *were* concerned.

Near the corner of 14th Place, a large restaurant spilled out of a long, low building onto the sidewalk and into the parkway between the sidewalk and the street, creating an outdoor cafe of four- and two-person tables, each table, covered with a brightly colored cloth, nestling under a large, beach-type umbrella even more distinctly patterned than the table.

"Want to eat here?" Simmons asked.

"It ain't Paris," she replied, "but I hear the food is okay."

"In fact, it's good," he said. "And the drinks are even better."

They were directed to a table in the parkway by a thin blonde waitress who showed little enthusiasm for her job, yet still managed to give an appearance of competence.

"How is your mother?" he asked, waiting for their cocktails—a sherry for him, a scotch and water for her—to arrive.

"Mother is fine. She lives with me now, you know. New York seems to agree with her."

When he had last seen her mother, some five or six years before, she had been a fidgety, birdlike woman in her early sixties, nervously losing out in the race to keep pace with the varied activities in which she involved herself. But, then, her mother had always been like that.

"I started to come to the funeral," Rubye said, "but decided against it. Margaret wouldn't have wanted me there."

He looked sharply at her, remembering that ever since he met Margaret, Rubye had been defensive about their friendship. And this defensiveness, bordering on guilt, apparently had lasted longer than Margaret's life.

"It's funny," he said, "that we've never gone to bed with each other. Yet, everybody thinks we've been fucking since high school."

"Yeh, everybody," she replied. "My husbands, your wife, our lovers and friends."

"Why?" he asked. "Not why they thought we were, but why we *weren't?*"

She raised her hand and patted her hair, tucking her bottom

lip beneath her teeth in the gesture he remembered well. "I don't know," she said. "Maybe you didn't ask me early enough, or keep after me persistently enough."

"I've asked you from time to time," he said.

"Yeh, I know. But most of the times when you asked me, I was tight with somebody else. And you know, I'm basically a one-man-at-a-time woman."

The waitress brought their cocktails and took their food order. When the waitress was gone, he said, "I've thought about this, Rubye. It must be something more than you just said. Hell, both of us have screwed people that we didn't care one-tenth as much about as we do each other."

"I know," she replied, sipping her drink. "When there is not much in a thing, you don't expect to get much out of it. With you, I'd expect a lot. And I don't believe you would give it to me."

"Why?"

She appeared flustered.

"Why?" he persisted.

"Well," she said, "to me, you always took sex too lightly. It seemed...seems to me that to you fucking is like taking a drink of water."

He felt himself smiling, but the smile was tight on his face. "Janice says I'd fuck during an atomic bomb attack," he said. "In fact, she repeated it just yesterday."

He could see anger mounting in her eyes. But there was no anger in her voice when she spoke, only a weary kind of reprimand.

"Bully for her," she said. "And bully for you. That's really wanting it. But the only eagerness you've shown me is, as I said, that of a person taking a drink of water."

"Rubye, that's not fair."

"It isn't? Why isn't it? Preston, I haven't told you this before. But even before high school, I had you staked out. And I thought you had me staked out. I thought it was understood that we'd make it. I took it for granted. Everybody else took it for granted. And I thought you took it for granted. But then, in

76

our sophomore year in high school, you began making it with Gwen."

"Gwendolyn Mosley?"

"Yes, Gwendolyn Mosley. After that everything ended."

"But we remained friends," he said, hearing the consternation in his voice.

"Yes, we remained friends. But for a long time I felt betrayed. I knew you had never wanted me and needed me like I wanted and needed you. Later, when you tried to make up, it just wasn't the same." She smiled grimly. "You know what I've told myself about you for a long time?"

"What?"

"That I'd follow you anywhere—except into the bedroom."

As the sound faded away, he examined her voice, trying to detect the whimsey in it. He stared into her eyes, looking for the laughter which must be in them. But there was neither whimsey nor laughter. Only the seriousness of an old hurt at long last revealed. She really believed that he did not need her, had not ever really wanted her with the depth which produces need, he told himself. This, then, was the answer to why she had rejected him sexually through the years. For if she gave herself to him in the absence of need, she would feel used, violated. And if she felt violated as well as betrayed, their friendship would be seriously undermined, if not destroyed. And this, he realized, she did not want to happen.

The waitress brought their food. She attacked her medium-rare steak with the relish he recalled she reserved for good food.

"Okay, love of my childhood who evidently is not going to be the love of my old age," he said, tearing into his broiled filet of sole, "tell me something about what you are doing these days. Who are you making it with."

She smiled. "Do I have to be making it with anybody?"

"Yes. You were looking so satisfied when I saw you this morning."

"Okay, now that you've caught me, I might as well admit it," she said. "I'm going with a guy here in Washington. A doctor."

"Right back where you started," he said.

She laughed. "Oh yeh. My first husband was a doctor. The father of my children. Dr. Raymond Jones."

Simmons was thinking about her first husband *and* her second husband, The Reverend Peter McGee, disciple of Dr. Martin Luther King who had introduced Benjamin Patten to the great man. However, unlike Benjamin Patten, Peter McGee never recovered from Dr. King's death and ever since had gone from enterprise to enterprise searching for something he could again hold on to. Simmons knew firsthand, and with a sense of sadness, that Rubye merely had been one of these enterprises. Yet, Peter McGee had not been much worse than Raymond Jones. Although a successful gynecologist, Ray Jones had been an insecure runner after phony values and parader of frivolous trappings. His nasty ways and wild parties had been the talk of the in-crowd during the years of their marriage. He would be surprised if the new doctor did not possess some of the same traits.

"So you'll probably be spending the weekend in Washington," he said.

"Yeh, I'll be leaving Sunday sometime. My bags are over at his pad."

"Have fun."

"Thank you."

If she wanted to think that they had failed to get together because of his lack of need for her, he would not contradict her, he told himself. It was not that he did not need her, but rather her definition of need that he could not satisfy; her requirements of need that he could not fulfill. The traits in him which attracted him to her as a companion/brother, failed to respond to her as a lover. His apparent sureness of himself, his stability, paralleled rather than complemented her own strengths. On the love scene, he told himself with a smile, she was a chick who needed to give rather than receive the favors.

He glanced at the table to his right. Two young white couples, who were whispering and looking at him, suddenly stopped talking. He smiled at them, nodding affirmatively to the question in their eyes.

"I told you so," one of the women said.

"I didn't say it wasn't," one of the men replied.

"You celebrity, you," Rubye muttered under her breath.

"You're one too," he said, as though it were a dirty word.

Rubye was occupied with her knife, trying to separate the last, reluctant piece of steak from the bone. She noticed him watching her and smiled.

"Mr. Celebrity," she said, "are you satisfied with the way this morning's meeting went?"

He shrugged. "As good as I expected. Are *you* satisfied?"

"Yeh, except for Sam."

"What about Sam? You think he's going to give us trouble?"

"What do you think! Of course, he's going to give us trouble! You don't believe for a minute that Sam's not going to use every contact he has, in the way *he* wants to use it?" She gave up on the reluctant remnant of steak.

"No, I don't. What do you suggest?"

"Put somebody on him. At least, that way, you'll know something of what he is doing."

He nodded. What she said made sense. Rubye was being her practical self. The waitress came and stood over them. He paid her, adding a sizeable tip. She removed the dishes and left.

Rubye laughed, getting up from the table. "Seeing you paying that bill without asking for help reminded me of the old days," she said.

"Yeh, I know. You were always paying bills for me and the rest of my would-be-writers friends. Especially after you latched on to Dr. Raymond Jones. Know what we used to say about you, Rubye?"

"What?"

"That you were the only good-looking chick in town who didn't mind spending her own money." He got up from the table and stood beside her.

She grabbed his arm and they walked away from the outdoor cafe, headed along Pennsylvania Avenue toward Fifteenth Street. She was her old free and easy self, now that they were again playing their accustomed roles.

79

"I noticed something else peculiar about this morning's meeting," she said, leaning her head against his shoulder.

"Yes?"

"Nobody mentioned the Congressional Black Caucus, even though we decided to make the House Judiciary Committee one of our main targets. My friend, the lady from New York City, is the second-ranking Democrat on that Committee, you know."

"I know. Is her position still the same?"

"Yeh, She really isn't for separation, but the people in her district voted big for it. She's keeping her own counsel, because she knows she has to face these voters again next year. That is, if we heven't won our separation by that time."

"I'm glad you brought that up, Rubye," he said. "As you know, the Congressional Black Caucus members are split almost down the middle on the question. In my opinion, at this stage, it's to our advantage to ignore the Caucus, and hope like hell the opposition does the same. We can't afford to have the government exploiting the split. After all, our battle is with the white power structure. We have to keep it that way."

"I agree," she said. "But do the other Council prime members see it that way?"

"I think so. Especially after the Green walkout. I'll talk to them and make sure."

They reached the corner, walked north for a half block and stopped near the side entrance to Hotel Washington.

"What time are you leaving for Chicago?" she asked.

"In about a half hour. I'm taking a three o'clock plane from National."

"Give my regards to the Windy City." She released his arm. "I'll hop a cab from here."

"Okay." He kissed her, lightly on the cheek, at the same time signalling the lead cab standing at the curb. With a half wave of her hand, she backed away from him.

As he watched her lift her long skirt to get into the cab, he was filled with the strange, ambivalent feeling he often got when separating from her. Suddenly he was struck with the notion of forcefully pulling her from the cab, taking her to his hotel room and consummating what had been thirty years in the offering.

But the notion fled, abruptly, on the warm afternoon breeze. As the cab pulled away from the curb, he realized with a start that he had not asked her the name of her latest lover.

Chapter 8

4:00 P.M., Friday, September 25, 1987

THE TALL, thin blonde attendant leaned across the white male passenger in the aisle seat, her slender hand groping for Albert James' plastic glass, which had contained his fifth bourbon and water since leaving Washington National Airport nearly three hours before. James picked up the glass and gave it to her, their hands touching lightly over the unused center seat.

"Thanks, Mr. James," the attendant said, smiling her appreciation. "May I get you something else?"

"No," he replied. "Not just yet."

The attendant widened her smile to include the passenger in the aisle seat, turned away and headed with careful steps toward the front of the plane.

As he had done a number of times since leaving Washington, the man in the aisle seat squirmed nervously and glanced at James like he wanted to open a conversation but didn't know quite what to say, or figured what he did say would be unwelcome. This time, however, he overcame his hesitancy.

"The stewardess keeps calling you Mr. James," he said. "Are you the Albert James on the Black American Council?"

The man was young and compact and dressed in an expensive sports outfit. He had a high, broad forehead, made all the more prominent by thinning brown hair. He had a serious look about himself.

"One and the same," James said.

"I saw your picture in the paper this morning," the young man said. "You don't look much like it."

"They never print the ones that look like you," James said.

The young man nodded. "I also saw that fellow, Simmons, on television yesterday. Some of the things he said were convincing."

"I hope so," James said.

The young man looked at him expectantly. When James didn't add anything, the young man shrugged, picked up a magazine, opened it, then added: "Well, good luck." He laughed nervously. "Maybe that's not the thing to say, considering what you are trying to do."

"It all depends on the point of view," James said.

"I suppose so. But it seems so unreal." The young man's tone of voice indicated that he had said all he intended to, that he wouldn't bother James any further.

It was not that he didn't like to talk to strangers, James told himself. A person in his business had to talk to everybody, white strangers included. But sometimes you got tired. Especially of white folks.

James leaned his head back against the seat cushion, listening to the drone of the powerful jet engines. He could detect a slight rising and falling as the heavy aircraft zoomed through the turbulence which must be raging outside. More than halfway home, he calculated.

God, he had been at it a long time. More than forty years. First, it had been the Westside Improvement League—the westside of Chicago, that is—organized when he was twenty-four years old. Then the Chicago League of Negro Voters, organized in 1958. He smiled, remembering something he hadn't thought about in a long time. A trip he had taken to St. Paul, Minnesota in 1960, to attempt to sell the League's latest ideas to leaders of the NAACP, which was holding its national convention there that year. The ideas were contained in a pamphlet entitled FREEDOM NOW! and subtitled *A Plan to Increase the Political Power of Negro Citizens*. He hadn't been able to sell the ideas in the pamphlet to the NAACP leaders, but a young hostess from Atlanta had almost sold *him* an idea—to leave Sarah, to whom he had been married ten years, for her. It had taken him almost five years to get rid of that young lady. But the experience had taught him something important about himself. He was too straight-forward to be a player. He hadn't strayed from the straight and narrow in all the years since.

He stretched, feeling his big body strain against the sides of the seat. He never had enough room on a plane, even on a luxury liner like this one. He let his hand fall into the empty seat, glad that it was unoccupied. Whenever he could, he got himself assigned an aisle or window seat with the center seat empty.

Simmons' first meeting with the negotiating team had gone pretty well, he told himself. Simmons seemed to have gotten a handle on the situation already. But then he would. James had known Simmons a long time and had always found him to be competent, possessing the ability to come up with logical answers quickly, plus the comprehension to back them up with historical and philosophical documentation. Yet, even though he liked Simmons, something about him worried James, had always worried him. Simmons seemed too...detached...uninvolved. He was too...non-partisan. Simmons was smart enough for the job. No doubt about that. But was he tough enough?

He hadn't opposed Simmons because the other leading candidates were too partial to individuals, he told himself. Leaning too much toward Green, Griggs, Muhammed or himself.

Then, there was that damn computer. Although they, as Council prime members, could have over-ridden the computer's selection, the damn thing was still intimidating. The kind of thing you couldn't argue with without appearing to be a fool. But still... He wasn't *unconvinced* about Simmons, but he wasn't convinced either. On that question, he supposed he was just about where he figured Simmons stood on all questions... in the middle.

The young man in the aisle seat stopped the attendant and requested a drink—a scotch on the rocks.

"What about you, Mr. James, do you want a refill?" she asked.

He shook his head. Five drinks in a single afternnon were more than enough.

"It's a damn good thing air travel is fast," the young man said, "or most business and professional people would be alcoholics."

"There could be a limit placed on the number of drinks," James said, more to prove he didn't mind making light conversation than out of conviction.

The young man laughed his nervous laugh. "I hadn't thought about that," he said.

James folded his arms, dismissed the young man from his mind, and picked up his train of thought. Being where he was, the representative of the center/left groups in the Council, wasn't due to any super-worthiness on his part, he told himself, as he had many times before. True, he had longevity. But he had never been a charismatic leader and, based on this quality, the head of either PUSH, SCLC or CORE should have his spot. But at the time the Council was established, he had been hot—still riding the crest of hard work brought on by the need to avenge the death of his son.

James tried not to think specifically about Paul these days and the way he had died that Friday night in February 1982 in a tavern on the westside of Chicago at the hands of three white policemen, out to get even for the killing of two of their fellow white officers a few days earlier. Paul, during that terrible week in Chicago, like many other black men, had been caught in a dragnet of prejudice and hatred. Only where the others had been abused and beaten, Paul had been murdered.

James pushed his mouth hard into his hand, feeling tears stinging the back of his nostrils. It had been harder on Sarah than on him. While he had turned his frustration into work, she had withdrawn from most activity. While he had embraced with new dedication the religion of black self-determination, she had given up hope. Of course, looking at her, most people couldn't tell. But he knew. And for this reason, as much as any other, he could never forget Paul's death and the way he died. He closed his eyes, summoning up again from the darkroom of his mind images of what happened on that cold February night....

The tavern stood under the L tracks at the intersection of California and Lake streets, one of the less than a dozen buildings still standing in a four-block square area. Most of the other buildings had been destroyed in the 1968 riots following the assassination of Dr. Martin Luther King, Jr., and others had since succumbed to public neglect and private assault. But because the tavern was on a corner connecting the two major streets, it stood out like a beacon in a cold desert of urban isolation.

The two young men, heading toward the tavern along California Avenue, were bent forward into the sub-zero north wind, as though it was aiding rather than impeding their progress. Both were tall and slender and created near-identical pictures, dressed as they were in waist-length leather jackets and tight-fitting dark pants tucked into heavy boots. One, however, was hatless, his thick Afro stubbornly confronting the wintry blast, while the other wore a woolen cap pulled low over his ears.

Despite the cold, the young men were in a jubilant mood, as they alternately clapped their hands together and punched each other on arms and shoulders. However, there was nothing unusual about the picture the two men made; in fact, it was rather an ordinary scene to those who frequented the tavern: Johnny Ash, young propietor of the tavern, and Paul James, his part-time helper and full-time friend, hurrying to their place of work in the early hours of nightfall.

A few yards from the door of the tavern, Johnny Ash said to Paul James, "So the papers came through today, huh?" He touched his Afro with his heavily gloved hands, as though to protect it from the wind.

"Yeh," Paul said. "I'm going to be a full-time law student. I think I'm ready now. Finally got the baseball out of my system.

I know I could have made it. But you know how it is. If you're black, you gotta be a superstar. The marginal slots have 'white only' signs on them."

"We really gonna miss you," Johnny said, half teasingly.

"Hold on!" Paul said, punching Johnny on the arm. "I'll need that gig now more than ever, to relax."

"You got it, Partner," Johnny said, opening the door of the tavern to let them enter.

Inside, the place had been given its usual Friday night sprucing up, masochistically set right so that the large, rowdy crowd could disarrange things in the hours to come. Tables, with neatly arranged chairs, were lined along the right, front and back walls. Tall stools, precisely spaced, were standing along the bar which ran the full length of the left wall. The floor had been recently swept, as evidenced by splotches of wetness and traces of sawdust on the concrete slabs.

About ten customers, all regulars, were in the place, three at the bar and the others scattered here and there at the tables. The disc jockey, Red Henry, was sitting at his stand behind the bar near the front, getting things together. It was warm and cozy inside. Johnny and Paul began shedding their outer clothing as they made their way to a table at the back where they sometimes sat when not working.

"What you fellas knowing?" Princess called from behind the bar. "I thought you guys were gonna leave everything to me tonight." Her voice was teasingly reprimanding.

"Ain't no rap, Baby," Johnny said. "Me and Paul been kickin' it most of the afternoon. His acceptance letter came this morning. He's startin' law school next week."

"Congratulations, Sugar Man," Princess said, resting her elbows on the bar and looking at Paul with smiling eyes. "That doesn't mean we're gonna lose you, does it?"

"No," Johnny replied for Paul. "He's gonna stick around."

"Swell," Princess said.

Johnny Ash didn't fool himself. Princess was one of the main reasons the tavern was a success. She had a way about herself, the ability to let people in and keep them out at the same time;

the ability to make men feel that she didn't believe she was better than they, yet didn't have to go to bed with them to prove it. She was slender and shapely and yellow, and this month was wearing her straight black hair in loose cornrows and long braids. Princess was precious to Johnny, just like Paul was precious to him, and he felt he was lucky to have two such quality friends. Princess and Paul were making it but he didn't care, even though he had to admit to himself that he wanted her too.

"I'll be with you in a few minutes, Princess," he said, just as Red Henry began to play his first number of the evening, a tantalizing piece by the Jones Girls.

"Take your time," Princess said, her voice calm beneath the sound of the music.

Outside the tavern, like a harbinger of doom, a dark blue police van pulled almost silently to the curb. The doors opened and seven white police officers got out. As though previously rehearsed, two stood beside the van, one on each side, and five crossed the street to the tavern. Sentry-like, two of the officers planted themselves on either side of the door and three went inside, where one stood near the door and two moved toward the center of the tavern, one in the direction of the bar and the other at an angle facing the right wall. The weapons of all three were unholstered and pointed downward.

The officer nearest the bar shouted to Red Henry: "Turn that motherfuckin' noise off! You can't hear yourself think in here!"

When the police officers entered, everybody in the tavern had stopped what he or she was doing, becoming virtually frozen in place. Paul and Johnny had piled their jackets, gloves and cap in the center of the table, and Paul was sitting in a chair against the wall, half-leaning across the table. Johnny was standing beside the table, his hand resting near the discarded garments.

"I'm the owner of this place," Johnny said. "What's the problem, Officers?" His voice sounded unusually distinct in the silence created by the discontinued talking and interrupted music.

Both officers moved forward, raising their revolvers. "We got a report of a disturbance in here," the same officer said. "A woman with a gun."

Johnny glanced at Princess, a question in his movement and eyes.

"There's been no trouble in here," Princess said. "Everything's been quiet."

Johnny moved away from the table, spreading his hands outward. "Officers," he replied, "why don't you put your guns away. There's no need to act like this."

The officer who had done the talking charged forward like a man obsessed and rammed the barrel of his revolver against Johnny's chin, forcing his head back. "If you breathe, nigger, I'll blow your brains out," he said.

There were gasps of anger and disbelief from the customers in the tavern. Coming as they did, from widely scattered points, the gasps sounded collective and somewhat threatening. The other officer, the one who had not spoken, looked wildly about, brandishing his revolver in an erratic arc.

As the policeman glanced away from him, Paul placed his hands on the table and stood up, moving slightly to his left as he did so. The policeman, hearing the movement, turned to face Paul, steadying his revolver in the same motion. The eyes of the two men met and held and, in that split second, both men felt a strange kinship, as though standing hand in hand together on the brink of hell.

Paul spoke as the policeman fired. But nobody could ever remember what he said, or the nature of the words he spoke— whether curse, plea or cry of pain.

Albert James opened his eyes. It always ended like this. With Paul speaking but no words coming. But he didn't need Paul's words to know what had to be done. His anger and determination had provided all the direction he needed.

Of course, he had tried to bring the policemen to justice. There had been investigations and hearings at all levels of the system—city, state and federal. But nothing had come of it.

Now, the only thing he had was his zeal and determination to help make the separate state work. Paul's revenge, and his salvation, depended on it.

A sudden change in the behavior of the plane made him more aware of his surroundings. The plane seemed to be picking up speed. Then James realized that the plane was actually losing speed, as it began its descent into the Los Angeles area. They were further along than he had thought. In a half hour, he would be at home.

He fastened his seat belt and brought his seat forward. Might as well be ready for the landing. It would be nice to see Sarah, to discuss with her how the latest milestone had been successfully reached.

He laughed sardonically. Once the separate state idea had seemed foolish to him. Yes, laughable. Until five years ago, he had been a Black/White Unity man, and before that a Negro-White Unity man. He didn't try to fool himself. He had changed because of what happened to Paul. Paul hadn't been perfect, slightly over-indulged, too much taken with things like sports and good times, but he didn't deserve to die. Especially, when he was beginning to get himself straightened out.

He sighed, feeling the sorrow coming again. He now knew that he couldn't ever again place confidence in a society which had permitted Paul to die, which had *caused* Paul to die; and then, like a stone wall before your eyes, or a wet blanket over your nostrils, blocked off any chance of your doing anything about it. It made you feel so un-belonging, so helpless.

He realized that other young black men had been killed before, in ways just as shameless as Paul. And he had been able to rationalize these deaths and still cling to his Negro-White Unity. But Paul's death had struck something deep inside him, or torn something loose. Paul's death had made him *see* the truth. Had made him understand that there was no place for black people in this white-dominated society. He was not ashamed that it had taken a personal loss to do this, didn't feel guilty, like maybe Simmons would, that Paul's death could do to him what the deaths of other young black men had been unable to do.

He didn't fool himself. The world was manipulated by individual desires, hates, joys, sorrows, even whims, and it would be that way as long as people were human. He was just glad that *something* had made him see the truth.

He smiled again. Maybe he shouldn't be so hard on Simmons. Somebody had to cool passions, take the many-sided approach to things. Everybody couldn't be like he was, simple and straight-forward, holding a single conviction, and following one star at a time. He was convinced the separate state idea was the correct path to take, and should be pursued to the end. If negotiations didn't work without violence, then they should be coupled with violence. But the negotiations should be tried first without violence, if for no other reason than this method would be less costly to black people. This was why he had ignored all approaches from the Black Liberation Army and other such groups. He didn't believe in mixing things. It only led to confusion.

A bell sounded and the seat belt light came on. As he touched the belt which was already tight around his waist, he could feel the plane banking for the descent into the airport.

He was in a hurry to get home to Sarah now, then back out into the field to his work.

He would be all right in the days immediately ahead, he told himself, aware that the last vestiges of gloom and grief were falling away from him, bringing the brisk, gruff efficiency for which he was known.

Chapter 9

4:30 P.M., Friday, September 25, 1987

PRESTON SIMMONS got off the rapid transit train at 79th Street, having tranferred from an Airport Special train at 67th Street where the Middle of the Lake Expressway junctured with the Dan Ryan Expressway. The flight from Washington had been uneventful, setting down at the Airport in the Lake at 3:55 P.M., five minutes ahead of schedule.

As he moved toward the unoccupied one of the three telephones located on the station platform, he was keenly aware that his preoccupation with the past had not diminished. Even when he had boarded the plane in Washington, his fear of flying, and participation in the usual rituals to counteract this fear, had not succeeded in pulling him out of his almost spiritual absorption with past experiences.

His walk down memory lane with Rubye earlier that afternoon was part of the reason. But the interlude with her had merely heightened his preoccupation, not caused it. For ever since yesterday, when he had received notice of his selection from Bob Griggs, he had been sifting through the past, trying to find that single incident which could serve as the fountainhead for the energy and inspiration he would require in the days ahead. Or, maybe, the reverse was true, he told himself. Maybe he was trying to return to the relative safety of the past because deep down he realized there was no fountainhead, no balm of Gilead, to inspire and protect him in the difficult job for which he had been selected.

In any case, he concluded, stepping aside at the last moment to let a rushing heavy-set black woman reach the phone ahead of him, his preoccupation with the past was the reason why he had gotten off the train at 79th Street instead of going on to 115th Street, the stop closest to his home, where he had boarded yesterday. For 79th Street had contributed more to his development than any other street on which he had lived or along which he had trod. He had been born just off this street, on Wabash Avenue, during the second year of the United States' involvement in World War II, the only child of a high-minded young school teacher and an ambitious young soldier, who later was to become a fighter pilot and die over Italy in an uneven contest with a German ace. The insurance money of the father he was never to see and the dedication of the mother who was never to remarry, had made his childhood comfortable and kept it in tune with the middle-class community of his birth, from which the last white family vanished when he was about twelve years old. By the time he finished high school, his mother had become one of the first black high school principals in the city. In the twenty-third year of his life, shortly after he received his masters in computer technology and entered the University of Chicago law school, his mother had died suddenly from a massive coronary. As far as he knew then, or ever found out, she did not have a history of heart trouble.

The young girl on the middle phone, who had been whispering seductively into the mouthpiece, hung up with an audible "See you later", and Simmons moved into the slot she vacated. The heavy-set woman was still busy on the phone she had strong-armed him out of, talking loudly about how somebody had insulted her in a store in the Loop.

When he had Marcus Jackson on the line, he brought the public relations expert abreast of the day's occurrences in quick, whispered sentences.

93

"Here's where it gets nasty, Marc," he said. "We've got to keep close check on Sam Muhammed. And you've got to arrange it."

"Where is Sam now?" Jackson asked.

"In New York City. He said he was leaving Washington for there as soon as the meeting ended."

"What are you looking for—precisely?"

"Anything, and everything. But we suspect he'll be working with the violent groups and making funny deals with some foreign governments. You ought to get on it right away. In fact, I should have called you before I left Washington."

"That urgent, eh? Okay. I take it you want him wired?"

"Damn right. Him, his office, and all his close associates."

"This means I'll have to deal with some strange people."

"Just so they keep quiet."

"These people don't know how to do anything but keep quiet. Their existence depends on it."

"Okay. I'll be at home tonight. Drop by so we can work out reporting procedure. This is the first and last time we'll talk about this assignment on the phone."

Relinquishing the phone to a slender young man, Simmons took the escalator at the east end of the platform and rode to the street level of the station. Exiting through a revolving gate, he headed east, walking slowly along 79th Street toward Martin Luther King Drive. He was wearing the same blue knit suit he had worn at the meeting earlier in the day and carrying a large attache case. Often when going to Washington or New York for an overnight stay, he didin't bother with an extra suit, merely packing an additional shirt and a change of underclothing in his attache case. Although he seldom wore a hat, in or out of Chicago, he always took one with him when leaving the city. This afternoon he was wearing a blue safari hat of lightweight velvet.

Moving slowly along the street he had called home for the first twenty-five years of his life, Simmons tried to recall just how long it had been since he had walked like this along the "main drag" of his youth. True, occasionally, he drove along

79th Street, on his way to a meeting in South Shore or some other point east. But to stroll leisurely along this street, between State and King Drive, past Fitzgerald's Funeral Home, Count's Lounge, Matilda's Beauty Parlor, Eunice's Reducing Salon, the Chatham Medical Center, and on to the Brown Girl Lounge, was an experience he had not had in many years.

After his mother's death, he had kept their home on Wabash for two years—until he got married. Following his marriage in 1967, and the publication of his first novel three years later, he had continued to come to the street, primarily for meetings with Rubye and Henry Smith at the Brown Girl, meetings which at the same time had been going on for more than a decade. But Henry had died in the spring of 1972; and later that year, Rubye had ditched Dr. Raymond Jones for good and split Chicago, taking her two children with her. When she returned two years later, shortly to become the wife of her beloved civil rights leader, Simmons had gotten out of the habit of coming to the Brown Girl, which pleased Margaret immensely. He supposed it had been fourteen years since he had been in the place.

Now, passing Fitzergald's Funeral Home, and telling himself that it was one of the few places on the street which had not changed for the worse, Simmons recalled that he had been introduced to professional writing, political action and Henry Smith at practically the same time, and at the same place. It had been the summer of 1958, the summer he was going into his Junior year in high school. A new community newspaper had opened in the area, on South Parkway near 79th, and armed with the fact that he had written for his high school paper, he had stopped by to see if he could convince the editor to permit him to write for the paper during the summer. The editor had hired him and another youth his age, who turned out to be Henry—a jet-black, good natured boy with a sharp mind and an uncluttered writing style. The editor, during that summer of 1958, was also organizing a Negro Voters League, as the initial thrust in his plan to enter a black candidate in the 1959 Democratic Party primary for a major city-wide office. He and Henry, eagerly assisting with the formation of the League, had cut classes the following spring to work precincts all over the city in the unsuccessful attempt to make political history in Chicago.

He was abreast of Count's Lounge now, or what used to be Count's Lounge. Both the lounge and the Chinese restaurant next door were vacated, the empty bar and booths looking strangely forlorn through the dirt-smeared glass windows. He couldn't recall noticing that Count's had gone out of business the last time he had driven through the area.

He crossed Indiana Avenue, walking against the light. For the first time he became aware that the traffic on 79th Street was not as heavy as he remembered it. He realized that this was due to the large number of business enterprises which had closed in recent years, both on the west and east ends of the Street. Seventy-Ninth Street was fast becoming extinct as a center for business and pleasure.

In front of Eunice's Reducing Salon now, he became sharply aware that Eunice, or her successor, miraculously was still in business. He recalled how he, Rubye and Henry had laughed when Eunice had opened the place, nearly twenty years ago. Rubye had said: "How the hell does she expect to make any money in a business like this, with all the Y's open and all?" But Eunice, apparently, had made money. The double storefront windows were still decorated with luxuriant wool drapes, only the color had changed from royal blue to screaming gold. The neon sign announcing the business, mounted high above the building, was one of the most prominent displays on 79th Street between State and King Drive.

The Brown Girl Lounge was directly across the street from Eunice's Reducing Lounge. Movement of somebody, or something, in the window caused him to assume the place was open. With a mixed feeling of reluctance and anticipation, he stepped off the sidewalk to begin the crossover. As he walked across the street, the fourteen-year gap suddenly closed, the crossing becoming just an extension, a continuation of the hundreds of other crossings he had made through the years. It was a strange, eerie feeling. He was shaking when he stopped before the door. With a sigh, he pushed the door inward and entered the lounge.

The place appeared somewhat smaller than he remembered it. Reasons for this flitted inside his head, his thoughts finally centering on the conclusion that in recent years he had grown romantic about the lounge, thereby rendering it larger than life. Reprimanding himself for useless rationalizing, he began examining the physical aspects of the place, permitting details to force themselves up from his memory.

The Brown Girl Lounge was composed of two rooms—a small room in the front and a large room in the back, separated by a partition made almost entirely of glass in which a doorless doorway was cut in the center. The small room served as the package goods section. Large, ceiling-high, self-service coolers containing beer and soft drinks stood along the right wall of the room, while along the left wall, behind a waist-high counter, were shelves and racks containing liquor, cigarettes, candy, other sundries and knick-knacks. The large room was the barroom. A huge juke box stood against the right wall, just inside the partition, while most of the remaining space along that wall and a portion of the space along the rear wall were occupied by booths. A triple deck of shelves containing bottles of alcoholic beverages ran along the left wall. About five feet from the wall, facing these shelves, was the bar itself, its red, imitation-leather arm-rest matched by approximately two dozen bar stools of the same material.

Standing in the doorless doorway which separated the two rooms, pushing from his consciousness the feeling that the lounge had decreased in size, Simmons realized the place was exactly as he recalled it; that is, except for the juke box, which was newer and larger, and the bar stools, which appeared to have been reupholstered. Even the small wash rooms, with their faded *Kings* and *Queens* signs, were as he remembered them, crammed into the corner formed by the juncture of the right and rear walls.

There were only five people in the place, including the bartender. A young woman, medium brown and big-bosomed, was sitting on a stool near the front end of the bar, while a middle-aged man, grayhaired and rawboned, was sitting near the rear end of the bar, as though they were trying to get as far from each other as possible. A young couple, in their early twenties, occupied a booth near the juke box, both sitting on the seat facing the doorway, the young man talking softly and intently to the young woman. Simmons was smiling to himself when he took a seat at the bar, precisely midway between the young woman and middle-aged man.

"What'll it be?" the bartender asked, looking at Simmons as though he were vaguely familiar.

"Sherry. Bristol if you have it, if not then the house sherry."

"Bristol, it is," the bartender said. He was tall, heavy and light-skinned, handsome in an over-indulgent sort of way. When he poured the drink, he scarcely looked at Simmons, returning quickly to his conversation with the young woman at the end of the bar. The bartender probably had made up his mind that he wasn't who he had thought he might be.

This reaction was not new to Simmons. Often he had wondered about his ability to move unnoticed in situations where people whose names were less known would be immediately recognized. True, he did not possess any outstanding physical characteristics; neither were his facial features the type which prompted immediate caricature. But it was more than that, he had concluded. It was also the will to anonymity. Often he was so pleased with his own company, so enjoyed reflecting alone, that he did not want to share himself with others. Therefore, he supposed, through mental signals which went out to those around him, he gave notice that he did not want to be recognized, in fact did not want to be bothered.

If this were the case, the signal apparently did not get through to the man sitting at the end of the bar. "Sure is a beautiful day," the man said, looking directly at Simmons. "The kind of day when a man is glad he doesn't have anything to do. Just sit and have a drink and think." The man's voice was

98

the kind that his mother used to refer to as "proper"; now, however, it was slurred with alcohol.

Simmons raised his glass. "It is indeed a day for reflection," he said. The man nodded. At least part of the signal had gotten through to him: he hadn't recognized Simmons, and he didn't attempt to continue the conversation.

Simmons half-turned on his stool and looked at the row of booths on the right wall, past the young couple to the booth near the washrooms. Henry used to sit there so many days, writing. He became a fixture in the place and nobody disturbed him. He would sit there, writing and waiting, until Simmons, Rubye and others of their set dropped in to get the conversations going. And Henry would be the life of the party. He appeared to need so little, yet was willing to give so much. But Henry was dead. What had he written when he got over the shock, and feeling of guilt, of his dying? "If death must call," he had written in the last line of a poem, "why not herald the obtuse, the uncaring, the insecure?" Henry had been none of these things, yet death had called.

The girl eased out of the booth, across the knees of the young man, and went over to the juke box. She was slender and brown and moved without apparent awareness of herself. She studied the selections for a minute, dropped some coins in the box, punched her selections, and went back to her seat.

Simmons noticed for the first time that the juke box was one of those video/audio "entertainment systems", which had become popular in the past two years, where certain selections could be seen as well as heard. Usually the video screen for such a system was located behind and above the bar in a tavern or lounge. Simmons searched for the screen and found it—high on the wall behind the bar, not too far from the "proper" middle-aged man.

When the music started, Simmons regonized the voice and face of a well-known black female singer, Willia Adams, an associate of James P. Sneed, the black arch-enemy of the separate state movement. However, despite her politics, Willia Adams had done more than any other singer to make love ballads popular again in Black America. The song she was singing had a haunting lyric with an Oriental lilt to the melody. She wailed:

> Only dreamers reach heaven
> For heaven is out of this world
> The door to paradise will open
> When dream clouds unfurl.

The woman sitting at the bar was singing along with the singer. "Great tune," the bartender said. Simmons nodded. The haunting melody continued:

> Only dreamers reach heaven
> To parade in rustic hue
> Across hills and valleys
> Where joy lights dim the blue

Simmons raised his glass to the bartender. The bartender understood the signal and refilled his glass.

"I used to come in her a lot, years ago," Simmons said. "Does Maude still own this place?"

"No," the bartender replied. "I own it now. Bought her out about five years ago. She still drops in now and then."

Simmons nodded. The woman at the bar was swinging her foot. Her legs were crossed, as attractive as her breasts. The bartender moved down the bar to stand in front of her again. The singer was riding the bridge of the song now, wailing her heart out:

> For heaven is a place of wishing
> And hoping the best comes true
> Only dreamers reach he-a-a-a-v-e-e-n
> And my dream is y-o-o-o-u!

The wailing voice and stringed instruments behind the voice rose to a crescendo, cried and died with a crash of cymbals.

"Singing bitch!" the bartender said, as the screen darkened and Willia Adams' face faded.

"You ain't no lying man!" his woman visitor replied.

It had been in that very booth where the young man and girl were sitting, in August of 1970, exactly seventeen years and one month ago, that Henry had told them he was dying. Rubye had laughed nervously, her voice begging Henry to tell them he was kidding. But it had been no joke. Henry was dying for real, from leukemia. And so it came to pass that in the thirtieth year of his life, in March of 1972, Henry Smith, brilliant, exuberant, lovable, published author of a volume of short stories and a highly acclaimed novel, fighter for black dignity and human rights, died, leaving a mother, father, two inseparable friends, and a host of other relatives and acquaintances to mourn him.

He would always remember the night of the day before Henry died, the last time he talked to him. During Henry's final stay in the hospital, he had gone to visit him almost every day, except for the three days which immediately preceded their last conversation.

"I had planned to get there today," he said. "I'll be there for sure tomorrow."

"Yeah, man," Henry had replied, "I understand."

He could tell by his voice that Henry realized that he had given up on him, had abandoned him to death. And because Henry was truly perceptive, he knew he understood that he, Preston Simmons, was shunning identification with him, was abandoning him, only because he could not help him. Yet, he would always feel guilty that he had turned his back on death when it was staring his best friend in the face.

Another song was emanating from the audio of the juke box now, a bouncy number with a slurring, soulful undercurrent. The song was being performed by a superstar quintet, Potential Unlimited, reminiscent of The Temptations in sound and style, In soft, dulcet tones the lead singer was crooning:

> Take the tang outa wine
> Won't have no wine

Take the sugar outa syrup
Won't have no syrup
Take the bitter from tea
Won't have no tea
Life would be empty
Take you from me!

A tall, stoop-shouldered young man came through the doorless doorway, glanced absently about the lounge and headed toward the washrooms in the back. He was wearing dirty dungarees and a sloppy sweat-shirt. He was medium brown, long-haired and rail-thin. The bartender nodded to him as he passed. The bartender's companion was popping her fingers to the music, spinning around on the bar-stool. An even softer lead voice had taken over for the quintet:

Take the air outa wind
Won't have no wind
Take the blue outa sky
Won't have no sky
Take the water from the sea
Won't have no sea
Life would be empty
Take you from me!

The young man came out of the back with a mop and bucket and began to mop the floor. He worked very carefully, as though he were getting a lot of pleasure out of the job. His face was very intense. The young man in the booth called to the bartender: "Two more beers, please!" The man with the mop leaned the mop against a stool, close to Simmons, and stood at the bar, almost at attention. The bartender gave him the beers to take to the young couple.

All together now, and with harsher, more strident tones, Potential Unlimited hit the bridge of the song:

I used to *walk* along by myself

Drunk with selfish pride
But since that day, you came my way
Need you by my side...

The handyman brought the beer money to the bartender, picked up the mop and bucket and carried them to the back of the lounge. As the song on the juke box ended, the handyman came out of the washroom and took a seat in one of the rear booths.

"Has anybody heard the late news?" the middle-aged man sitting at the rear of the bar suddenly asked, looking from Simmons to the bartender.

"No," the bartender said. "What's happening?"

"I hear the Council is asking the President for an audience."

Simmons felt his heart flutter. In the past few months, before and after its passage, he had discussed the separation proposition before all types of audiences. However, except for the press conference yesterday and the Council meeting today, he hadn't been placed in an advocacy position since he became so personally involved.

The woman at the bar crossed and uncrossed her legs. "I say what I've always said. I can't see my elf living with that many niggers."

"Well, I don't know," her bartender friend said. "If I could figure out a way to dispose of my business here I wouldn't mind. Hell, all of my customers are black, and we ain't gonna be so busy building that new nation 'til we stop drinking." He laughed.

"But that damn many niggers in one place!" the woman said.

"My sentiments exactly, though not in those words," the middle-aged man said.

The bartender and the two bar customers were looking at Simmons. Without saying anything to them, he turned to the young man and woman in the booth. "What about you two? What do you think?"

The young man looked up, his dark brown, thin-featured face serious. "To me, it's a new frontier," he said in a smooth

103

voice. "We need something like that."

"Right on!" the young woman sanctioned.

The woman at the bar laughed derisively. "Some frontier!" she said.

"I know there are a lot of details to work out," the bartender said. "But hell, I'm for trying anything."

"This damn thing's going to break us up yet," his friend said.

"No way, baby, No way!" the bartender told her.

The handyman stood up and walked slowly to the center of the room. He looked like he wanted to say something, but was afraid to.

"What do you think?" Simmons asked him.

The handyman gave him a surprised look.

"Go on," Simmons said.

The surprise in the man's eyes gave way to gratitude. When he started to speak his voice was hushed.

"Let me tell you something," he said. "Let me tell you how bad things are for me and a lot of people like me. When I was a kid, I knew people on welfare. But we were never on it. My old man believed in working, and he worked all his life. Now he and my mother are living off his social security. But you know something? I come out of high school in 1975. I'm almost thirty years old, and I ain't never had a job. Been looking for one for almost twelve years, but I ain't never had a job. Think about it. Me and thousands and thousands of other young men, black and white, but especially black, who want to work, but ain't never had a job. And ain't got much chance of getting one." He paused. "Shit! And you talk about not separating! Why not? Things can't get any worse."

The handyman turned, walked back to the booth, and sat down.

Simmons could feel tears stinging the back of his nostrils. He had said the same thing at the press conference yesterday. But how much more final, and frightening, reality was! It was the kind of thing which incensed the gut as well as convinced the brain. He cleared his throat.

The bartender was looking at him strangely. "Mister, you

haven't told us what you think," he said, his voice indicating that he too had been affected by the handyman's eloquence.

Simmons took off his hat and laid it on the bar, turned slowly on his stool toward the couple in the booth, then back to the bartender.

"Look at me," he said. "Do you recognize me?"

"Recognize you?" the bartender asked.

"Yes. Do you recognize me?"

The woman at the bar got it first. "Well, I'll be damned!" she said.

"What is it?" the bartender asked.

"Don't you see who it is?" Her voice was excited.

"Are you..." the bartender began.

"Yes," Simmons said, "I am Preston Simmons."

The young woman in the booth leaned forward, peering around her companion. The middle-aged man at the bar slid from his stool and moved a step closer to Simmons. The handyman, head erect now, stared straight ahead.

Everybody began to talk at the same time.

Chapter 10

7:30 P.M., Friday, September 25, 1987

HIS FRIENDS called him "Philip", "Phil" or "Jerry". No. That was not exactly right, because he didn't consider himself as having any friends, these days. So what he meant was, the people he used to know from his high school days, from that long ago another time, when he chanced to meet them on the street, called him by these names. Occasionally, even, he ran into an old woman or man, who knew his father and mother in those old good times, and the old man or woman called him "Junior"; or, peering at him with doubtful eyes, asked: "Ain't you Junior Benson?" For his name was, or at least he had been named, Philip Gerald Benson Junior.

People now, in these days without beginnings or ends, called him none of these names. The people he knew now, on street corners, in alleys, and in the taverns of The Street, called him "Benson" or plain "Ben", in the manner of the disaffiliated who eternally make things less than they are. Or—and this was more and more the case every day—they simply called him "Hey, Man".

But what his name was, or what people called him, was not really the problem. The real problem was deeper, much more personal. He didn't know what he called himself. Some days, when he was consumed more than usual in the fog of his unimportance, he did not call himself anything. Other days, when he was vaguely aware that he should have been somebody and wasn't, he called himself, not exactly called himself but sort of permitted to exist an image of himself, *The Man Who Had Never Had A Job*. But there were other times, growing fewer and fewer now, times when the joyful ambition of his childhood merged with the longings of the present, that he again became Philip Gerald Benson Junior.

Now, walking out of the Brown Girl in the dying sunlight of the late afternoon, was one of those latter times. For he had just seen, talked to, and shook hands with the great man. He was happy and sad at the same time, hopeful and despairing all at once. And in this contradictory state, he realized a truth he had not bothered to realize before: Joy and agony were cut from the same cloth. They both made you acutely aware of your existence. And because he realized this truth, he also realized its opposite: Only a numbing indifference, the kind of indifference he lived with more and more these days, blotted out existence and ushered in the fog.

And so, still Philip Gerald Benson Junior, he walked eastward away from the Brown Girl Lounge, more swiftly than usual, whistling the lively tune which had been playing on the juke box, the one about taking the air out of wind and the water from the sea and life being empty if one lover was taken from the other. Without slackening his pace, he gave a brisk raise of his hand and a curt nod of his head to greetings of "Hey, Man", coming from acquaintances whom normally he would have joined in a desultory stance at the edge of the sidewalk, indifferently affirming, "Man, ain't nothing happening".

He was still Philip Gerald Benson Junior when he entered the small grocery store on the southwest corner of 79th and Prairie and began the almost daily ritual of searching for bargains among the hardening breadstuffs, the rotting fruits and the stale lunchmeats. The proprietors of the store—a small, wizened Greek and his equally dried-up wife, who had run the place as long as he could remember—assisted him in his

107

search with their usual enthusiasm. However, his forage through such obvious trappings of poverty, regardless of his recent contact with the mighty, dampened his spirits, so that when he left the store with a bag containing five slices of bologna, four sweet rolls and two apples, he was only partially Philip Gerald Benson Junior.

From 79th street, he walked north along Prairie Avenue to 78th Street, then east along the north side of 78th Street toward King Drive. The building in which he lived was located in the middle of the block. It was a three-story brick structure, with two apartments on each floor, rising like a square fortress above the single-family houses on the block. The building had been constructed within the past decade and was bordered on both sides by empty lots, as if, through isolation, the other residents wished to show their resentment of the building's presence.

Unlocking the outside door, the man who now was considerably less than Philip Gerald Benson Junior entered the vestibule of the three-story building, made his way slowly up the stairs to the top floor and entered the rear apartment.

The apartment was not an apartment in the usual sense of the word. A dimly-lit hallway, its floor covered with cheap linoleum and its walls painted a dull grey, ran from the entrance door to the rear wall, splitting the apartment down the middle. Four of the five rooms to the left of the hallway had been remodeled into individual units to accommodate single men tenants, while the four rooms to the right of the hallway retained a semblance of apartment identity, in that they served as a living room, bedroom, bath and kitchen for the lessee of the apartment, who sublet the individual rooms. The fifth room to the left of the hallway was the bathroom for the four tenants. A pay telephone was attached to the rear wall at the end of the hallway.

"Is that you, Cousin!" inquired a booming voice from the landlord's living room.

"Yes, it's me," he replied, rather distinctly, so that the landlord could catch his voice, knowing that his having been

108

addressed as Cousin meant nothing, since the landlord called everybody by that name.

"Oh, I thought it was one of the other guys," the landlord said.

"No, it's just me," he replied.

"Okay, Cousin," the landlord said in the tone of a person who is finished with a conversation.

Standing in front of the second room on the left, fitting his key in the lock, he reminded himself that "one of the other guys", to whom the landlord had referred, was either of the homosexuals who lived in the third or fourth room. They were both tight with the landlord, who was also a homosexual, though far from an obvious type. The landlord, a man in his early fifties, often appeared to worry about his much younger friends.

He entered the room, closed the door firmly behind him, kicked off his shoes, and fell across the bed, on his back. It was a drab room, sparsely furnished. In addition to the bed, the landlord-provided items in the room were a dresser with a single-panel cracked mirror, a straight-back chair and a clothes closet, protruding from the wall like an afterthought. He had added a portable radio, a small-screen black-and-white television set and four glasses to the collection. He had occupied the room slightly more than eight years, ever since he left home shortly after his twenty-first birthday.

From the shadows of his memory of an all but forgotten book, he recalled that the protagonist, about whom he remembered little, had agonized over his room in these words: "Once my room was my sanctuary, now it is my prison. Once I used it to shut myself in from the world, now I use it to shut the world out from me." How lucky this protagonist had been to have such positive feelings about his room! Sanctuary. Prison. Anything was better than this dull extension of his eventless life. He rolled over on his side. Eventless? Hadn't he just this afternoon talked with and shook the hand of Preston Simmons, and in that talking and touching contributed somehow to the thinking which would go into the formation of a new and mighty black nation? He sighed. That was part of the trouble. The ecstasy of the moment of the meeting was gone, the agony of the realization that he could not extend that moment was also gone, leaving only what had been before: dullness. Indifferent, damning, non-productive dullness. The soul of him, The Man Who Had Never Had A Job.

The clanking, spasmodic sound of typewriter keys came through the thin partition separating his room from the one next to the bathroom. The room was occupied by a retired postal worker, a short thin man nearing seventy-five, who fancied himself as being a writer, although he had never had anything published. The man wrote day and night and talked intensely of the big deals he was on the verge of swinging. He wrote everything—novels, plays, short stories, poems and letters to the editor. He constantly lamented that if he had not stayed in the post office for forty years, he would have been one of the world's great authors. Nobody took him seriously, and he doubted if the old man took himself seriously; yet, still he wrote, pecking away against the fortress of boredom and approaching death.

The Man Who Had Never Had A Job sighed and sat up on the side of the bed, his eyes drawn to the snapshots of five young women stuck by adhesive tape along the sides of the mirror of his dresser. Four of the pictures represented the women who had passed fleetingly through his life in the past decade, now lost forever in the fog of his failure. The fifth picture, newer and less faded than the others, was the image of the one woman who still had an occasional drink with him and, less occasionally, suffered herself to be the vessel of his desire. The woman had promised to call him tonight. And she just might, he told himself, since she knew he had received his welfare check only two days before.

The door of the apartment opened and he heard the shrill voices of the landlord's two friends as they cane down the hall.

"And I said to that bitch, 'Baby, I'm not buying that drink for you, I'm buying it for your man,' " one said.

"And what did she say?" the other asked.

"The bitch was game. She said, 'I got everything my man needs.' "

"Some shit!" the second one said, apparently standing before his door in the process of opening it.

"Cousin!" the landlord called from his living room. "Is that you?"

"Yes, it's us. Both of us," the second one said.

"Come in here for a minute," the landlord said.

"Only a *minute*?" the first one asked. The sound of their laughter was cut abruptly off, as the landlord closed his door after admitting them.

The Man Who Had Never Had A Job glanced at the bag of food he had placed on the dresser. He knew he should eat something, but he didn't feel up to it. He also knew he should take a bath, for he could smell himself in the warm room. But his call might come through while he was in the bathroom. And if the call didn't come, there would be little use of taking a bath. He settled for turning on the radio and stretching out again on the bed.

These were the worst times for Philip Gerald Benson Junior. The times when he thought he might have something to do. Especially when he was here in this room in this apartment of misfits, hearing the typewriter clanking in the other room and imagining what might be going on across the hall. The waiting for a little living to enter where there was no life.

He got up from the bed and took two pieces of bologna and a roll from the bag. When he started to eat, he realized how hungry he was. Within a few minutes he had emptied the bag.

The sound of the phone in the hall was unusually loud. He waited for it to ring three times before going to answer, leaving his door open.

It was her all right, but he could tell by the caginess in her voice, when she asked him how he was, that she wasn't going to make it.

"There are some friends of my sister," she said. "They want me to go to a party with them. A kind of ritzy party," she added, thereby letting him know that he was excluded.

111

"I see," he said, apparently with more disappointment or reprimand than usual, for she came back with : "It's not my fault."

"I know, baby. It's nobody's fault."

His voice still wasn't docile enough for her. "There's no future for us," she said.

He felt fear at the bottom of his heart. "What does that mean?" he asked.

"Maybe we shouldn't see each other anymore."

"Do you have somebody else, somebody serious?"

"No. But I'm not getting any younger."

"I don't take up much of your time."

"I know. But I don't have much of that kind of time."

"Does that mean you won't be calling again? Or for me not to call you?" He couldn't keep the sadness out of his voice.

"I didn't exactly say that," she said, her resolve overcome by his sadness. "Why don't you call me up sometime and see."

"Okay."

"See you around."

He hung up the phone and went back into his room and closed the door, wishing desperately that the hurt in him would give way to the indifference he was so accustomed to feeling. But it wouldn't. He stretched out on the bed, on his back, and covered his eyes with his arm. He had known that there was a better than even chance that she would cancel their date, yet his disappointment was still like a hard blow to the stomach. Not that he cared that much for her, but everybody needed somebody who they felt had special consideration for them. As little at it was, she had been all he had.

He turned over on his stomach, balling his fist into his mouth to ckeck the sobs which were rising from his stomach and spreading through his chest. Then the tears came, springing effortlessly from a well which appeared to be bottomless. He relaxed, no longer trying to fight the tears, feeling an almost spiritual surrender in the embrace of his self-pity.

Chapter 11

10:00 A.M., Monday, September 28, 1987

THE DRAMA was being performed on four separate stages. No, that was not the case. It was being performed on four separate tiers of the same stage. No, that was not true either. The drama was being performed on the surface of the same stage, with each of the four classes of players consigned to separate and distinct positions.

Of course, none of the above was literally true, Philip Gerald Benson Junior told himself, for the drama was not being *performed* in the usual sense of the word, nor were the participants actually *players*. The situation was too real for that.

The scene was the construction site of a Safety Department district headquarters, about two blocks from the employment office at 63rd and Maryland, from which he had just come. According to the newspapers, it was the first such district headquarters building to be constructed since passage of the city ordinance, some three years before, which combined the fire and police departments of Chicago into a single Safety Department.

Since the mid 1970's, when some suburban towns surrounding Chicago had combined their fire and police departments, the City of Chicago had been under varying degrees of pressure to follow suit. In fact, during his last years in office, Mayor Richard J. Daley had made half-hearted promises to move in that direction; yet even on those occasions, he had indicated that he would never combine the two departments to such an extent that policemen and firemen would be interchangeable; but that he might consider permitting them to take management direction from a single source. Mayor Jane Byrne, who was elected to the first full term after Daley's demise, actually created a Safety Department in the second year of her administration. But this move, as many of her acts, was merely a subterfuge for another purpose. In this case, she needed a high-sounding title for the black Acting Superintendent of Police, whom she was getting ready to dismiss as head of the Police Department. The Safety Department she created had a low-level administrative function and the duties of its director were strictly ceremonial. The ordinance establishing a genuine Safety Department, along the lines Daley had discussed, was not passed until 1984—approximately nine years after Daley made his original verbal concession.

Philip Gerald Benson Junior was thinking about these things, as he stood with the fourth class of players—the spectators—carefully recording in his mind the scene before him.

Forty to fifty workers were in the process of completing the block-square building foundation, some grouped around giant concrete trucks, others pushing wheel barrows, some others leaning on shovels, and others nailing foundation boards, all caught up in that peculiar stance of inactivity which always appeared to be the main happening around a construction site, making him wonder how anything was ever accomplished. He could spot only four or five black workers in the group.

Next were the cops, forming a tight cordon around the workers, standing on the sidewalk bordering the construction site on all four sides, facing the streets with sullen eyes and ready clubs. The cops appeared to be all white, although he believed be could make out a black face or two on the side farthest from him.

114

The streets were filled with demonstrators—black demonstrators. Some were marching, some were milling about, and some were standing still. But they all were singing. Singing a song from the 60s which somehow had survived the indifference of the 70s and endured the calamities of the 80s:

> "We shall not,
> We shall not be moved
> Just like a tree, planted by the river
> We shall not be moved!"

And then there were the spectators, the group to which he belonged. The spectators, for the most part, were congregated on the sidewalk across the street from the construction site, separated from the workers by both the cops and the demonstrators. Some of the spectators, of course, were mingling with the demonstrators, singing with them, and feeling their sense of participation. The spectators, like the demonstrators, were all black.

Under normal circumstances, he would not have joined in watching the demonstration at the construction site. In fact, he had never participated in a demonstration of any kind; not even during the early 80s, before the government crackdown, when it seemed that everybody was out demonstrating for a job, whether they wanted one or not. But he supposed his meeting with the great man on Friday had changed him, in subtle ways. The wave of self-pity which had swept over him after the phone call, although it had lasted all day Saturday and most of Sunday, had not been strong enough to force him back into his state of total indifference, to check his reaching out, to break the connection, no matter how weak, he had re-established with the world around him.

So when he had awakened this morning, feeling it was the beginning of another day of nothing, a small voice in the back of his mind had whispered "not quite". He had gotten up early, took a bath, put on the best clothes he had, and caught a bus to the employment office. Not even the mechanical attention of the employment interviewer to his problem—as she made entries on the computer console typewriter and received a negative message on the display screen—had been able to re-establish the feeling of hopelessness. He even went so far as to initiate a conversation with the interviewer.

"Do you think I need to re-register?" he asked.

"Have you had any work experience, or acquired any training or additional education, since your last visit?" she asked.

"No."

"Then there is no need to re-register."

But that hadn't satisfied him. "I heard," he said "that if there is no activity on your application, no referral to a job or anything for a certain length of time, your application is taken out of the file. Any truth to that?"

The interviewer smiled, interest showing in her dark brown eyes for the first time. "That used to be the case," she said, "before computer technology advanced to the state it has. At that time we had to perform occasional manual file searches. But that's not the case anymore. Believe me, if that screen says there isn't a job for which you can qualify, there is no such job." She smiled again, but there was sadness in her eyes.

He shrugged. "No sweat," he said.

Yet, here he was, standing on the sidewalk two blocks from the employment office watching with growing interest what three days ago he would have considered a futile demonstration. It was a dull, cool morning. A light mist was falling. Sometime during the night Chicago had begun to live up to its reputation and the weather had changed from middle summer to late fall.

The singing had stopped now and the leader of the demonstration was speaking. Most of the demonstrators had forsaken the other sides of the site to form a wedge around the speaker, on the southwest corner of the lot. The leader was short and stocky and stood on a box to address the crowd.

"In 1975," he was saying, "the Assembly of Black State Executives and black members of the state legislature began to work in earnest for guarantees that blacks be given a fair share

116

of construction jobs paid for with public funds. Under the skilled leadership of Roland Burris, then the chairman of the Assembly of Black State Executives, and Congressman Harold Washington, then chairman of the Judiciary Committee of the Illinois House, these black brothers and sisters demanded that in every construction project in which public funds were involved, and where there was more than one prime contractor, at least one of these prime contractors be black. They further demanded that the prime contractors employ a fair number of black sub-contractors."

He paused to make sure that his followers were with him. After he was satisfied that they were by their applause and the usual cries of agreement, he continued:

"Brothers and sisters, more than sixteen years after creation of the first Chicago Plan to provide meaningful employment to blacks in the building trades, twelve years after the thrust of Burris and Washington, and ten years after the passage of legislation embodying many of the employment demands of the black community, we are still being bull-shitted! Look around you, brothers and sisters. This is the heart of the ghetto. A building is going up supposedly to help provide safety in the ghetto. This building is being built with your tax dollars and my tax dollars. And yet..." He paused for effect. "And yet," he cried, jabbing his finger toward the center of the lot, "these honkies have our jobs! And worse than that"—punctuating the words with the jabbing finger—"these cracker cops are wasting some more of our tax dollars keeping us from getting our jobs!"

An angry growl emitted from the demonstrators, as though from a single throat. They surged toward the workers, but the cops shifted into position, feet spread, billy clubs gripped in both hands and held across their chests. The workers, as though responding to a spoken command, stopped what little work they were doing and stood almost as still as the cops.

"Halt!" The word, sharp and whip-like, came from the leader of the cops—a young lieutenant, blond and slender. The cops inched forward, arms rigid.

The demonstrators stopped their forward surge and began milling around, grumbling. The young lieutenant walked over to their leader.

"Another move like that, and you go to jail," he said.

"Another move like what?"

"Inciting these people to riot."

Benson had moved inside the area occupied by the demonstrators, so that now he was as close to the cops as were the front ranks of the protesters. He was feeling light and funny. Maybe he had been missing something. Since he hadn't been able to find a job, didn't have anything else to do, maybe he should have been protesting all along. At least it had purpose to it.

"It is our constitutional right to protest," the leader of the demonstrators said. Despite the cool weather, the armpits of his shirt were soaked with sweat.

"It's a narrow line between genuine protest and inciting a riot," the Lieutenant said. "And I make the decision." His eyes were mean.

"I thought a judge made those types of decisions," the leader of the demonstrators said.

The Lieutenant laughed, harsh and mirthless. "Sure, the judge can make any kind of decision he wants to," he said. "After the fact. After we have busted a few heads."

"That's telling the nigger!"

The words came from a middle-aged heavy-set man with blunt features and a receding hairline, one of the workers who had broken ranks and moved almost into the line with the cops.

When the worker spoke, Benson heard his words with a feeling of resentment, not so much for what he said, but because the words broke his preoccupation with the conversation to which he had been listening, invaded a private territory he had set aside for himself. He felt his body jerk as he glanced sharply at the worker, who was separated from him only by about ten feet of space and a shifting line of cops.

The angry growl came from the demonstrators again. "Motherfucker!" somebody said. The cops inched forward.

"I advise you to tell those workers to keep quiet," the leader of the demonstrators said to the Lieutenant.

"You should have thought about that before you started shooting off *your* mouth," the Lieutenant said.

"I won't be responsible for what might happen if these workers don't stay out of it," the leader said.

"And I won't be responsible if you aren't responsible," the Lieutenant said.

Benson and the worker were looking at each other. He got the impression that the worker's eyes were larger than they should have been, larger and more liquid, bluish-grey pools of frozen water. He felt as though the eyes were drawing him into them, daring him to take the dive. Fleetingly, he wondered if his eyes were affecting the worker in some similar fashion.

"I advise you to pull your demonstrators out of the street, back up on the sidewalk," Benson heard the Lieutenant say. "If you don't, I'm going to call downtown, get more policemen and break the whole thing up."

"I got permission to demonstrate," the leader said.

"But not permission to incite a riot."

Benson and the worker were closer to each other now. Although he had been standing still, as the cops had inched forward, the worker had moved with them. Suddenly, the man screamed, "Goddamn black bastard!" and broke through the line of cops, heading in his direction.

Because he and the worker had singled each other out for special attention, Benson had somehow gotten the feeling that a closeness, not a closeness really, but a recognition, had been built up; he therefore felt surprised, and in a sense betrayed, at the venom in the curse words and the hatred on the man's face as he bolted toward him.

But the time for a decision was at hand, Benson told himself with surprising clarity. Whether to run or stand and fight. A cop reached for the worker, missed him, and started out after him, glancing at the Lieutenant for instructions.

The worker was nearly upon Benson now, the flat face contorted, the liquid eyes consuming. Suddenly he got a vision

119

of himself, broom in hand, moving numbly about the Brown Girl, lying listlessly on his bed, sick with loneliness. *The Man Who Had Never Had A Job.*

Philip Gerald Benson Junior felt something inside himself exploding against the memory of these things, against the agony and despair and the days of nothingness, against the audacity in the eyes of the onrushing white worker. A warmness, like burning liquid, spread upward and downward from his stomach, fueling his muscles and setting his limbs on fire. Then he was moving, with outspread, grappling hands.

Dreamlike, as though in slow motion, he could see the white worker floating to meet him, left shoulder upraised, right fist cocked. It would be so easy, his mind told him, so easy to evade the clumsy punch and fasten his hands around the aging neck and squeeze the contempt out of the liquid eyes.

As his hands touched the rough texture of the worker's clothing, sounds, separately distinct yet strangely blended, were in him and all around him: his cries, the worker's curses, harsh commands from the cops, shouts of mixed anger and exhortation from the other workers, demonstrators and spectators.

Then, curiously, the sounds became an explosion in the back of his head, as his hands, for some unknown reason, lost their grip on the worker's clothing and slipped downward toward the ground. In his final vision, he detected an arm of blue rising and descending rapidly, bringing the realization that the blue arm was the driving force behind a cop's billy club which had crashed against his skull. Then the explosion dulled and the realization ceased as his face caressed the damp earth from the construction site which covered the pavement like a silken screen.

Chapter 12

2:00 P.M., Wednesday, September 30, 1987

SEATED IN a small conference room in the Dirksen Senate Office Building, Preston Simmons was trying desperately to keep himself from being overwhelmed by the history which permeated the place by attempting to concentrate on the primary reason for his being there. Three others were in the room: Robert Griggs, president of the Black American Council, his light tan face tense with expectation, or nervousness; Senator Samuel Leavitt, chairman of the Senate Judiciary Committee, brown eyes alert above the prominent aquiline nose; and Representative Thomas E. Ryan, chairman of the companion committee of the House, his round face inscrutable in repose.

The furniture in the room was dominated by a large circular cocktail table near the center of the floor, surrounded by two curved leather sofas. Simmons and Griggs sat on one sofa, facing the two congressmen who occupied the other. The room was pleasantly cooled and not too brightly lighted, conspiring with the furniture arrangement to produce an atmosphere of intimacy.

It was Wednesday afternoon of the week following the Friday when Simmons had met with the prime members of the Black Council to develop initial strategy. He had returned to Washington on Sunday evening as he had promised and began working with Griggs and Ted Blackwell, executive director of the Council, attempting to set up a meeting with the joint judiciary committees. Looking about the room now, aware of the four of them sitting there like old friends getting together for an inconsequential chat, Simmons felt himself marvelling at how totally reality contrasted with appearances.

The preliminary discussions between the staffs of the congressional committees and the Council had gone badly from the beginning. Simmons and Griggs had instructed Blackwell to press for formal discussions, with the guidelines to be worked out by Blackwell and his counterparts on the committees. The committee chairman, however, through their counsels, made it clear that they didn't consider the time to be ripe for talks, formal or otherwise; that the only action they considered feasible was the holding of public hearings, and separate House and Senate hearings at that. In fact, Representative Ryan released a statement to the press questioning the authority of the Council to even *discuss* separation, to say nothing of negotiating for it.

"No recognized authority has validated the so-called referendum," he said. "This, coupled with the refusal of respectable black leaders like Bill Green and Jim Sneed to go along, leads me to believe that these Black Council members are speaking primarily for themselves."

Before Simmons and Griggs could frame a diplomatic reply, Sam Muhammed released a statement from New York City calling Ryan a racist and threatening to demonstrate the Council's strength by amassing nationwide demonstrations.

Simmons attempted to get out of the bind by chiding both Ryan and Muhammed. "Council strength has already been demonstrated," he said in a press release, "through the most time-honored American institution—the ballot box. I am sure Congressman Ryan recalls that on the day after the referendum, the Council requested that the results be validated by the federal government, and this request was refused."

Meanwhile, he, Griggs and Blackwell were utilizing all of their contacts to get a direct line to Senator Leavitt. Communication was established on Tuesday afternoon. In a five minute phone conversation Simmons convinced the Senator that the situation was getting out of hand unnecessarily. "Okay, so maybe public hearings are needed and not formal discussions," he conceded. "But not at this stage. We should sit down and clear the air before we decide on either."

Before the conversation ended, a meeting had been generally decided upon. Leavitt was left with the task of getting Ryan to attend and Simmons had the equally difficult job of convincing the other Council members, particularly Sam Muhammed, that only he and Griggs should be present at the initial meeting.

Now, twenty-four hours and many long distance phone calls later, the four of them were getting ready to take each other's measure.

"Mr. Simmons and Mr. Griggs," Ryan said, leaning forward over the cocktail table, his hands resting on his thighs slightly above his knees, "I cannot be hypocritical. I didn't want to meet with you fellows. But Sam, here, convinced me that it wouldn't do any harm to hear what you have on your minds." His voice was a hoarse rumble, each word tripping over the one which preceded it. Even though Simmons had heard the voice often, mainly on television, he was always surprised to hear a voice so distinctive coming out of a face so bland.

"Thank you for consenting to meet with us, Congressman," he said. "I am sure, though, that you must have an idea of what we have on our minds. We have been commissioned, so to speak, by the black people of this country to negotiate for a separate nation. This, as you know, requires the most painstaking dealings with the power structure of this country. Since all of us, black and white, believe in the surpremacy of laws, I know of no better place to start these negotiations than with the maker of our laws, the Congress of the United States." He paused, searching Ryan's face for a reaction to what sounded to him, in spite of himself, like a rather glib beginning. But the mild face was unrevealing. "And you gentlemen," he added, "are the gateway to the Congress in matters like this."

"How do you know?" Ryan asked. "There has never been a

123

matter like this." His voice was the same, but his face had somehow changed. It was in the eyes. They were extremely watchful.

"Would you want the questions our mission raises to be answered some place else?" Simmons asked. "It has always been my understanding that the tough ones come before the judiciary committees."

Senator Leavitt laughed. It didn't exactly sound like a laugh of intervention, but Simmons supposed that it was aimed at both himself and Ryan. "This only points up the difficulty of your mission, Mr. Simmons," the Senator said. He laughed again. "However, for want of a more legal starting place, Tom and I agree with you that probably it is better to start with us." The voice was sharp, yet softened by apparent good humor. "Since you requested the meeting, I suppose you gentlemen should tell us what you expect from us."

Griggs looked at Simmons and Simmons nodded. "The first request we make of you," Griggs said in his clipped voice, "is your recognition of the fact that we are on a genuine mission, a serious mission. Then..."

"Wait just a minute!" Ryan cut in. "Before we get started, I don't want anybody laboring under any illusions. I can't understand how Americans, people this country has been good to, can seriously expect other Americans, patriotic Americans, to be sympathetic to their denunciation of their country. I just can't see it." He was leaning back, arms folded.

"That's not fair, Congressman Ryan," Griggs said.

"Why isn't it fair? This country has been good to my people, to Sam's people, and to your people. Oh, I know, things aren't perfect, but what the hell!" He slapped his thighs, leaning forward on his hands again.

Simmons was thinking about the things he knew and had heard about Tom Ryan, trying to determine if his display of insulted patriotism was for real. Although Ryan was supposed to be a sharp lawyer and undoubtedly was one of the most astute politicians in the country, he was nevertheless a product of small town, midwest America. In fact, he represented the district which was adjacent to Gerald Ford's old district, and had been elected to his first term in the House four years before Ford ascended to the presidency. Although he and Ford were from different parties, and though he had opposed some of the former President's more conservative bread-and-butter policies during the latter's tenure in the White House, insiders insisted that on philosophic questions and in matters of the spirit, Ryan was much more conservative than Ford. In a lot of ways, he was reminiscent of one of his early mentors, Chicago Mayor Richard J. Daley: tough, corny and Irish. No question about it, Simmons concluded, Ryan was deeply aggrieved over what he considered to be a shocking lack of patriotism on their part; yet, Simmons was equally sure that the actor in Ryan, which was present in all effective politicians, would dictate that he make use of his wounded spirit in every manner available to him.

"Congressman," he said, "believe me, I have respect for your feelings. But you have to admit that this country has not been as good to blacks as it has to your people, the Irish, and the Senator's people, the Jews. We are not denouncing America. We are only trying to build something for ourselves. As an Irishman, you must truly understand this. Your glorious history proves that you are even less tolerant of intolerance than we."

Ryan laughed. It was a laugh of appreciation, not of agreement. "Blarney flows as easily from you blacks as from us Irish," he said.

"Mr. Simmons," Senator Leavitt said, "we have read and heard a lot about the separation question. We are more or less familiar with the legal arguments of both the legislation advocates and the constitutional amendment advocates. Please answer two questions for me. On which side of the fence do you fall in this argument? And what do you think should be the posture of the government at this moment?"

Simmons looked at Leavitt, examining him intently. The brown eyes were firm but quizzical, the pupils prominent with interest. The large head, appearing even larger because of the fullness of the iron-gray hair, was cocked sideways. Leavitt, one of the foremost liberals in the Congress, had a reputation as a tough but fair negotiator. And he was one of the few Jews in the Congress who was objective where Israel was concerned. He had always insisted that peace would not come to the Middle East until the interests of all parties were addressed on an equitable basis. When Carter, Begin and Sadat reached agreement at Camp David, Leavitt, then in his second term in the Senate, was among the few American leaders who pointed out that the Accord would not bring peace because too many vitally interested parties had been excluded from the process. He had said in no uncertain terms that no agreement could last which excluded the Soviet Union, failed to bring the Palestinians into the talks from the beginning, and did not cover the Golan Heights, the Gaza Strip and the West Bank as well as Sinai. And history had proven him to be correct. For despite establishment of diplomatic relations between Israel and Egypt and the return of the Sinai to Egypt, the conflict between Jews and Arabs continued until 1985, when an agreement acceptable to all nations in the area was reached. This agreement, approved at Geneva with the Soviet Union as well as the United States participating, moved Israel back to its 1948 borders, created a Palestinian state out of the relinquished Israeli territory, parts of Jordan, the Gaza Strip and the West Bank, and placed this state under the protectorship of the United Nations for ten years, when its status would be reviewed.

Leavitt, additionally, was one of the few liberals who had a genuinely pragmatic grasp of the economic situation in the country. He was a firm ally of Joe Rielinski, the new leader of the AFL-CIO, in insisting that full employment, enforced by formal government-management-labor agreements and controls, was the most dependable weapon in the battle against political unrest, economic decline and social decay currently strangling the country. For all of these reasons, Simmons wanted to answer Leavitt as honestly as possible.

"Senator Leavitt," he said, "I am one of the legislation

advocates. In my opinion, Section 3 of Article IV of the Constitution makes it clear that Congress has the authority to pass this type of legislation, without going the amendment route."

The Senator ran his long fingers through his hair. "I know that, Mr. Simmons, but that section also says that such legislation must have the consent of the legislatures of the states concerned as well as the Congress. If you are requesting that a number of states be set aside for you, as I have heard, how do you propose to get the consent of these legislatures? Wouldn't it be just as easy to go the amendment route?" The Senator's eyes were probing.

"No, Senator, it wouldn't be just as easy to go the amendment route. First, an amendment, as you know, would require a two-thirds vote in both houses of Congress, then ratification by three-fourths of the states. Passage of the legislation would require only a simple majority in both houses of Congress."

The Senator threw out his hand. "Okay. But how do you get the states you want to take over to vote themselves out of business?"

Simmons could feel his stomach muscles tensing in rebellion against the answer he knew he must give. But he had to be honest. They knew he was no fool, therefore he must have some type of rationale for his position.

"Frankly, Senator," he said, "we are depending on the United States government to provide the answer to that question. If the Congress and the President supported our demands in no uncertain terms, first by passing the law, then by working with the citizens of the states affected to make the necessary reparations, I am sure the legislatures of these states could be convinced to come around."

"In other words, you are requesting that the full power of the Federal government be utilized on your behalf," the Senator said.

"Yes, that's right," Simmons replied. "After all, we didn't get our forty acres and a mule."

Congressman Ryan stood up. When he spoke, his words were even more jumbled than usual. "Wait a minute," he said.

127

"Is this some kind of a joke? I am sure you don't expect us to be a party to this kind of scheme?"

Griggs half turned in his seat to look at Ryan. "I don't see why you call this a scheme, Congressman," he said. "Citizens have a right to petition their government for any redress they deem right and proper. And I can assure you, millions of black citizens don't think these requests are out of line."

Senator Leavitt appeared not to be listening to Ryan and Griggs. His eyes, more probing than ever, were fixed on Simmons. "I just thought of something," he said. "See what you think about this."

Ryan came back to his seat and sat down. "About what, Sam?" he asked.

"Suppose," Leavitt said, "the Black American Council suddenly launched a campaign urging blacks from the northern and western industrial cities to return to two or three southern states. And suppose the government and major corporate interests participated in this campaign, with the express purpose of making blacks the majority population in these states. Not just the majority population in these states as a whole, but in every electoral district, so that blacks would be in a position to take over these state governments. And when this happened, suppose the Congress passed the type of legislation you are talking about. Then the stage would be set to win the consent of the state legislatures required by the Constitution."

Simmons felt his mind accelerating with excitement, as the magnitude of the idea took hold. Funny he hadn't thought about it before. "And if the Congress didn't pass the legislation," he said, "these states could secede from the Union! The Civil War all over again, in reverse!"

Simmons could feel Griggs stirring on his right. He turned to him.

"Brilliant in theory," Griggs said. "But blacks aren't in a mood for that kind of long-range strategy. Something has to be done now."

Griggs was right of course, Simmons realized. And Leavitt saw it too, for the Senator was nodding his head. Yet, when he spoke, it was evident that the idea still appealed to Leavitt's intellectual curiosity, and to his personal involvement in history.

"When you think about it," Leavitt said, "that's the way modern Israel was born. Through mass migration. However, as you probably know, I agree with Joe Rielinski of the AFL-CIO and Hilda Larsen, president of the National Organization for Women. I believe blacks and whites in this country can still form an alliance to bring about meaningful improvements."

"I know," Simmons said. "But as Bob here pointed out, something must be done now."

"I can assure you," Ryan said, "what you want will not be done. Not through the House Judiciary Committee."

"How can you be sure?" Griggs asked.

"I'm sure. The majority sentiment is for action against the Black American Council. Not for giving in to your demands."

"There are a number of blacks on your committee," Griggs pointed out.

"And a few white militants, too," Ryan said. "But less than one-fourth of the entire committee would be in favor of voting out the legislation you request. And I am not among that fourth."

Griggs nodded. "What about your committee?" he asked Leavitt.

"The arithmetic is similar," the Senator replied. "Probably even less favorable than on Tom's committee."

"You're putting us in a helluva situation," Simmons said. "When our people realize that no effort is going to be made in the direction we request, we are going to have to move to some other form of action."

"Like what?" Ryan asked, his voice cagey.

"Well, we still are hopeful of talking to the President," Simmons said.

Leavitt laughed. "I wish you luck."

Ryan stood up again. "I don't wish to give you the wrong impression," he said. "Something is going to be done. We are still going to schedule the hearings."

"What approach are you going to take?" Griggs asked.

Ryan threw out his hands. "We are going to look at it from all angles. And you might as well know now, because there is really nothing you can do about it. We are going to be looking for possible conspiracy."

Simmons was looking at Leavitt when Ryan said this. The Senator's eyes narrowed for a split second, but he didn't say anything.

"Is this the way you read it, Senator?" Simmons asked.

Leavitt sighed. "No question about it. Fear is abroad in the land."

"And you are not prepared to oppose the prevailing sentiment?" Simmons asked.

Leavitt hesitated, but when he spoke Simmons could detect no indecision in his voice.

"I will not be with you in this thing, Mr. Simmons," he said. "The forces of progress should be marching together. Not in opposite directions."

Chapter 13

1:30 P.M., Friday, October 2, 1987

PRESIDENT DORSEY Talbott Davidson stood before the high Georgian windows in the Oval Office of the White House, looking out across the broad expanse of manicured lawn into Pennsylvania Avenue, where traffic moved in an erratic manner on the busy street. He wished the day was ended instead of having just passed the midpoint. It was a warm, early autumn afternoon in Washington and the President could discern the patterns of sunshine on the polished lawn. He yearned to be somewhere in a secluded spot soaking in the sun's calming rays rather than trapped in his office by an unrelenting schedule which grew more burdensome with each passing day.

He sighed, turned from the window and sat at his desk, the simple act making him aware that he was much more conscious of his large body than he had ever been before. He was tired, both physically and mentally. Yet so far as he knew, there was nothing seriously wrong with him other than the fairly well-controlled duodenal ulcer which had plagued him for a decade; and his fifty-three years definitely didn't qualify him for a wheelchair. But he supposed no man, no matter how young or strong, could bear up under the terrible pressures of the presidency if love of the office, or the power which went with it, did not sustain him like a narcotic. And that was the trouble. He no longer loved his job, no longer was stimulated by wielding its awesome power.

Leaning back in his chair, he ran the fingers of both hands through his long reddish-brown hair, smiling to himself as he recalled how his hair had been one of the symbols around which his public image had been built. His long, stylishly maintained hair, his ascetically featured yet strong face, and his large six-foot, six-inch frame were the physical attributes which his image-makers had utilized. His mental and spiritual attributes had been somewhat more contrived, not so much by his image-makers as by his pointing the direction in which he wanted his image-makers to go. By the time his unsuccessful run for the nomination in 1980 came to an end, he had pretty much replaced Carter in the minds of millions of Americans as the southern ex-governor who possessed the philosophical profundity of a Woodrow Wilson and the political shrewdness of a Lyndon Johnson. During the years between 1980 and 1984, stealing another page from the Carter book, he had skillfully maintained a fence-straddling posture by speaking out on all issues with such soul-searching depth that he avoided taking a clear-cut position on any issue of substance. The 1984 convention of the Democratic Party gave him the nomination on the fifth ballot.

The intercom on his desk buzzed. "Mr. President," his secretary said, "the Attorney General wants to know if you want to confer with him again before your two o'clock meeting?"

"Tell him no, Bernice," the President replied. "And Bernice, hold all calls prior to that meeting. I don't want my concentration disturbed."

"Mr. President, you have a meeting with the Secretary of Defense at two-thirty..."

"I know, Bernice," the President smiled, realizing that this was his secretary's way of reminding him not to give too much time to his two o'clock meeting with Preston Simmons, of which she disapproved.

But the meeting with the Secretary of Defense was also important, the President reminded himself. In recent years, the

Japanese had been moving closer to the Chinese, drawn primarily by the dramatic increase in Chinese-produced crude petroleum and the sharp upsurge in Chinese demands for Japanese manufactured goods. Two years before, the two nations had signed a mutual friendship pact, and the Chinese were pressing the Japanese to move from under the nuclear umbrella provided by the United States. He leaned across the desk, pressing his nose with his thumb and forefinger. Then there was that matter of accelerating tension between the Republic of South Africa and the black African nations. The threat to invade South Africa and oust the white minority, first proposed seriously by Amin of Uganda in the late 1970s, could no longer be looked upon as an idle threat. Nigeria, Zaire, Kenya, Zimbabwe, Angola and some other black nations had the combined strength to do it. South Africa was now in the same position as Israel in the late 1970s, or probably even in a worse position. There was going to be hell to pay in a few years, or even in a few months.

He got up from the desk, stretched his arms over his head, walked away from the desk, then returned to his seat. Funny how he had come into this office sure that he would be able to use his skills to solve most of the country's major problems, or at least alleviate them so that they would be endurable. Well, he had been in office more than two-and-a-half years, had less than a year-and-a-half to go on his first term, and things were more confused than when he entered office. The Union stood in the gravest danger of being split than at any time since the Civil War. And now, as then, the black question stood at the center of the controversy. He sighed. One thing was for sure. Today was Friday, and as soon as he possibly could he was going to get out of Washington for a weekend at the Palm Springs White House.

He lit a cigarette. It was only the third one he had smoked all day. He would possibly smoke two others before retiring for the night. He had sharply cut down on his smoking in the past few years. In a way, he supposed, his smoking was as controlled as his ulcer.

133

The black move for separation had caught him unprepared and he had spent the past year trying to ignore its various developments. Often he told himself that being from the South, possessing forebears whose heritage had been shattered, coming out of a history of rebellion, he should be able to understand that nothing is truly sacred, that no convention is above being violated. And, intellectually, he did. But deep down in his gut he couldn't bring himself to accept what was happening. He just couldn't relate such audacity to blacks—to *Negroes.*

When, last Friday evening a week ago, he had received the formal request from the Black American Council to meet with the Secretary of State, the Attorney General and himself, his first reaction was to ignore the request. In fact, he had instructed his staff not to respond. But when his congressional liaison informed him that Sam Leavitt and Tom Ryan had consented to sit down with Preston Simmons and Bob Griggs, and the media began to play up the meeting, he decided that maybe he had better establish direct contact in some form or other. He couldn't have that fool Ryan and that radical Leavitt setting the government position without his being in on it. At first, he had thought that the best approach would be for the Attorney General and the Secretary of State to meet with the black negotiating team without him. But he realized that the Attorney General, because of his crackdown on the job rioters three years before, was considered by blacks to be a hardliner; and the Secretary of State, although he understood the legal questions well enough, didn't have a sound grasp of domestic issues. Then, in one of those flashes of sudden decision which dotted his career, he had concluded that a heart-to-heart talk with Simmons was the answer. Just the two of them. Might as well show him the bottom line, at the beginning. He'd be damned if he was going to be intimidated by a bunch of niggers.

The intercom buzzed. "Mr. Simmons is here, Mr. President," his secretary said.

"Show him right in, Bernice."

The President had never met Preston Simmons face to face, although he had seen him on a number of television shows,

134

including the one which had been broadcast live from Chicago following his selection as chief negotiator. Additionally, the President was an occasional reader of Simmons' newspaper column and his lengthier pieces in national magazines. The President had come very close to meeting Simmons in the fall of 1984, when the Democratic National Committee accepted Simmons' proposals for bringing black and white workers together in support of his, Davidson's, candidacy. These proposals, however, had never been put into effect for the simple reason that he, the candidate, had turned thumbs down on them. The chairman of the National Committee had wanted him to explain to Simmons why his material was not being used, after having been accepted, but he hadn't seen any sense in tying himself, the candidate, directly to the refusal to use the material. So the meeting with Simmons had not taken place.

The President was thinking about these things as he watched Simmons enter the Oval Office. Rising from his seat to greet his visitor, the President noticed that the black man appeared to possess an air of quietness and that the smile on his face seemed forced. The brown eyes above the hawk nose were watchful, if not exactly wary. The President quickly concluded that, on the whole, Simmons was somewhat detached, if not by nature, then by carefully developed design. A hard one to read.

As he and Simmons sat down, the President found himself wondering just what would have happened if he had followed Simmons' plan of establishing black-white ethnic committees in every industrial center in the country as a means of dramatizing the common interest of black and white workers, and having major campaign strategy flow from these committees. If he had used such a thrust and actually got elected, undoubtedly his domestic programs would have been slanted far differently than they had in the past two years. But he had been afraid to take a chance. The conservative coalition developed by Nixon, maintained by Ford, not destroyed by Carter, and extended by Reagan had been too strong.

"Mr. Simmons," he said, "I've seen you on television attempting to explain the reasons for the extraordinary

135

demands you and your people are making. Do you think you can explain the reasons for these demands to me in down-to-earth language?" He hoped his tone sounded as blunt to Simmons as it did to himself.

Simmons smiled. It was a slow, easy smile without any hint that he had been intimidated, as he rubbed the cleft in his chin with his thumb and forefinger. His eyes were steady.

"Mr. President, I'll do my best," he said. "In a nutshell, the majority of black people have lost faith in this country."

"But that's what I can't understand," the President said. "Lost faith? Precisely at a time when there are breakthroughs in all areas. Look at yourself. You are one of the best-known syndicated columnists in this country!"

The President could feel the brown eyes turn deliberately upon him, reprimanding. "Individual breakthroughs are not the point, Mr. President. It's the obvious disrespect people in power show for black folks. For instance, when massive unemployment hit white workers in the middle 1970s the government was very innovative in finding ways to combat it. But when white unemployment was cut to an acceptable level in the late 1970s everything became business as usual, despite the fact that black unemployment was nearly twenty percent. Reagan wouldn't have been able to sell the American people on the rape of social programs if they hadn't considered these programs as benefitting primarily blacks. And a reactionary, anti-people spirit wouldn't continue to permeate our society, and give direction to our government, if the majority of whites didn't believe that a reversal would benefit blacks more than anybody else. It seems as though all elements of white society are in a conspiracy to restrain blacks."

The President had been unprepared for the directness of Simmons' statement. He had expected him to be somewhat intimidated by the office and the occupant, despite his obvious coolness.

"Granted, some of what you say is true, Mr. Simmons," the President said. "But there are other avenues of protest open to you. Citizens have a right to petition their government for redress of grievances, but the right of petition doesn't extend to destruction of the Union." He hoped his voice carried the full authority of his office.

Simmons smiled his slow, easy smile again. "Mr. President," he said, "blacks no longer trust other forms of protest. And, Mr. President, I have a confession to make. Two years ago, I thought the majority of blacks were resigned to their fate, disinclined to protest at all. I had come to this conclusion because in the past decade we had made such ineffective use of the more obvious forms of protest, such as the ballot box. But it seems that we were merely waiting for somebody to raise the big question."

The President felt his chest knot up as the sour taste of acid rose to his mouth. Although he wasn't ready to go so far as to question Simmons' sincerity, the black man's articulateness, bordering on glibness, offended the President's sense of proportion.

"A war was fought to preserve the Union," he said harshly. "Do you believe Mr. Lincoln loved his country any more than I?"

Simmons did not smile, but his voice was pleasant enough when he replied. "I don't doubt your love for your country, Mr. President. But surely you don't equate the South's fight to preserve slavery with the struggle of black citizens to win equality?"

"While we might differ in our opinions as to the degree of rightness of the two causes," the President replied slowly, "that really is beside the point. Mr. Lincoln was willing to abide the evil of slavery to preserve the Union, and I am willing to abide the lesser evil of inequality to preserve it. That is as clear as I can make it, Mr. Simmons."

Simmons nodded. It seemed to the President that his visitor had anticipated his toughness and was trying to decide whether it would do any good to continue the conversation. Finally the easy smile returned and Simmons spoke.

"Mr. President," he said, "you know and I know that there are millions of white people in this country who would be only too happy to get rid of us. Why not permit us to create a new nation?"

The President held up his hand. "Mr. Simmons you know there is more to it than that. First, all the blacks wouldn't go. Second, the new nation wouldn't be able to sustain itself, at least not at first. Third, we'd always have to worry about the loyalty of the blacks who remained within the United States. And fourth—and this is the most important—the new black nation would always represent a potential enemy on our border. Maybe I should say an actual enemy."

"How do you figure that, Mr. President? I mean the enemy nation allegation?"

The President felt himself smiling a tight cold smile. "Don't be naive, Mr. Simmons. The so-called Third World nations are constantly baying at the heels of the United States. And your nation would immediately become a part of the Third World."

Simmons shook his head. "Guarantees in those areas could be established in the separation agreement," he said. "But Mr. President, you never did comment on the fact that millions of white Americans support our desire to separate."

The President stood up from his desk. "Yes, I did," he said. "When the other objections I have raised are made clear to the American people, they will no longer support your separation demands. Both the nigger-hating racists *and* the bleeding-heart liberals can understand the danger of having a welfare state, which is also an enemy state, on our borders."

Watching Simmons, the President could tell that his remarks had struck a sore spot, producing anger. However, Simmons held himself in check. His voice was calm but somewhat sarcastic when he spoke.

"They'd rather have a welfare enemy nation within?" he asked.

"If it came to that, yes," the President replied.

Simmons got up from his chair. Standing face to face with him, the President noticed that he was shorter than he had assumed. "Mr. President," Simmons asked, "since you feel the way you do, why did you insist on seeing me alone? Why not say what you've said to the prime members of the Black American Council, so there wouldn't be any doubt where you stand?"

The President sat down and waved Simmons to his seat. "Mr. Simmons," he said, "officially, you are not a part of the Black American Council, and have played only a small role in cooking up this separation scheme. I'm certain the hearings Tom Ryan and Sam Leavitt are planning will bring out a lot of things which will surprise you. I don't see why you should go down the drain with a lot of malcontents, like Sam Muhammed. I want you to denounce this thing, and work directly with me to bring the matter to an equitable conclusion."

"An equitable conclusion, Mr. President? What do you mean by that?"

The President smiled. "When I was running for the nomination for this office, as you will recall, everybody said I had a better chance than the other aspirants of finishing up the business started by Roosevelt and continued by Truman, Kennedy and Johnson. Things like national health, quality education, equal employment opportunities. They said I could restore the coalition created by Roosevelt." He smiled again. "But things kept getting in the way. In the past two years, it's been hell just keeping the ship of state afloat."

"But Mr. President," Simmons said, "it seems to me you haven't tried to restore Roosevelt's coalition. From all appearances, you have found Nixon's coalition more to your liking."

The President frowned. It was just like a smart bastard like Simmons to mention a thing like that, to indelicately rub a sore spot. But the people *had* said he would continue the tradition of the great Democratic presidents of the last half-century. They even called him by his initials. DTD for Dorsey Talbott Davidson. Right up there with FDR, HST, JFK and LBJ. Funny how these sobriquets had escaped Dwight Eisenhower, Richard Nixon, Gerald Ford, Jimmy Carter and Ronld Reagan, as though they were unworthy of such ready identification. But that wasn't exactly fair. Eisenhower, Ford and Carter had been called by names even more personal and intimate than their initials: Ike, Jerry, and Jimmy. And when you thought about it, Nixon had had his sobriquet also. The people had called him Tricky Dick. And now Simmons was comparing him to Nixon.

"It's easy for you to downgrade my performance, Mr. Simmons," the President said, spreading his hands. "But I couldn't take a chance on being more progressive. The time wasn't ripe."

"Is the time ripe now?"

"I have a feeling it might be. With Meany and Kirkland gone from the labor movement and Rielinski in the top spot, who can tell. The convention comes up next year. Maybe we can get a fresh start in the next term."

"Are you telling me you are willing to come out for the things Rielinski is talking about, such as *guaranteed* full employment, nationalization of certain basic industries and utilities, and strong government-management-labor committees to give direction to the overall economy?"

"I'm not prepared to go that far. After all, the free enterprise system has been the lifeblood of this country."

"You'd have to be prepared to go that far, Mr. President. It's the only way we'd be able to convince black and white workers, black and white Americans, that they have a common interest. It would take that kind of public pledge from you, Mr. President, for me to even *discuss* with the Council the possibility of *postponing*, not withdrawing, the separation demands. And that pledge would have to be made *now*."

The President suddenly felt as tired as he had felt before Simmons entered his office. He had reached another one of the thousands of impasses which had contributed to his lack of effectiveness. The kind of deadlock which made him acutely aware of his inability to reason with, to even understand, far too many Americans. And it made him angry. "It might take a while to prove it, Mr. Simmons," he said coldly, "but as of this moment I consider you an enemy of this nation."

Without looking at Simmons, he pushed the intercom switch on his desk. "Bernice, is the Secretary of Defense waiting?" he asked.

140

"Yes, Mr. President."

"Send him in, Bernice. Mr. Simmons is leaving."

Then the President's anger fled. He was smiling to himself, almost gleefully, as Simmons headed toward the door. He was certain his latest remarks had struck that spot in Simmons which is not immune from fear, even in the strongest men.

"Good day, Mr. Simmons!" he called to his departing visitor.

As the black leader reached out his hand for the door knob, the President noticed that his touch was unsteady, almost like a blind man feeling his way.

141

Chapter 14

9:00 A.M., Saturday, October 3, 1987

THEY WERE all there, the members of the negotiating team, in the same conference room where he had first called them together one week plus one day ago, four men and a woman waiting eagerly to begin their analysis of events since that time. It was nine o'clock on Saturday morning, and looking at the negotiating team members sitting along the table—Rubye Ransome and Sam Muhammed on one side and Robert Griggs, Albert James and Benjamin Patten on the other— Preston Simmons was imbued with a sense of well-being, which he had not felt since his meeting with the President yesterday.

Maybe the feeling, he told himself, was nothing more than the relief one got from the sharing of misery; sort of like baring one's soul in a confessional box, or crying in one's beer. Or maybe—and he hoped this was the case—it was the feeling of assurance which comes from calling upon the collective strength, and wisdom, of one's associates to find a solution to a problem one could not find alone.

All the members of the team, except Sam, had been in Washington since Wednesday morning, where they had come

142

anticipating a meeting with the judiciary committees of the House and Senate. Sam, of course, had also made the trip to Washington; but when it had been decided that only Simmons and Bob Griggs were to meet with the two chairmen, he had returned to New York City, threatening all kinds of dire consequences. And when the President had insisted that his initial participation in the negotiations be limited to a private audience with Simmons, it had taken three intense long-distance telephone conversations with Sam to keep him from crying "sell-out" to a world eager to pounce on any morsel of information.

The other members of the team had not exactly jumped with joy at being left out of the meetings; but none of the others had assigned any conspiratorial role to him in the exclusion. Rather they had philosophically concluded that he and Griggs, where the committees were concerned, and he, in the President's case, could at least get a picture of the government's mood. And to the best of his ability, through individual phone calls and meetings, he had transmitted to them what he gleaned this mood to be.

Now, sitting in the conference room, with copies of the country's major newspapers spread before them, they were ready to begin their collective analysis of this mood and determine their immediate course of action.

The Saturday morning newspapers were highlighting two themes: the plan of the Senate and House Judiciary Committees to hold joint hearings, and the President's apparent support of this approach. This also had been the accent of the Friday evening television news shows. Neither Tom Ryan, Sam Leavitt nor the President had released any of the details of their conversations with him and Griggs. But the direction they intended these hearings to take were clear in the general statements they did release, especially those of Ryan and the President.

"First, we shall inquire into the validity of the mandate," Ryan had said. "Determine if the referendum was conducted in a proper manner. Second, we shall seek to determine from

143

those groups which originally supported the referendum whether they still support the separation idea. Third, we shall examine the legitimacy of those individuals comprising the so-called negotiating team. And fourth, quite frankly we shall seek to determine if there are any un-American elements, domestic and/or foreign, playing significant roles in this separation move."

When asked if he had evidence of significant activity by un-American elements, Ryan had smiled cryptically and replied:

"As I said, that's one of the reasons for the hearings. But it's not our purpose to waste the taxpayer's money."

The President had been very pious in his pronouncement. "There is a possibility that we are facing the greatest threat to the preservation of the Union since the Civil War. We are as determined as was Lincoln to preserve it, and at much less the cost."

When asked if blacks weren't justified in their demands, considering the discrimination they had faced for more than three centuries in this country, the President had replied: "You don't burn down your house to effect minor repairs. I say to you what I said to Mr. Simmons. If Mr. Lincoln was willing to abide the evil of slavery to preserve the Union, definitely I am willing to abide the lesser evil of inequality for a minority of our citizens to preserve it."

Senator Leavitt had taken a similar but broader approach, and in a softer tone. "I look upon the separation request as a petition for redress of wrongs. But regardless how grievous the wrongs against black citizens might be, the petition is too extreme. I and millions of other white Americans stand ready to join with our black friends in support of a more reasonable petition."

When asked to be more specific, the Senator had replied: "Not everything is on the table yet. This will be a long drawn-out process."

Then there were other statements in the newspapers, ranging from support of a number of well-known black leaders and a

144

few progressive white leaders who looked upon the United States as an incurably racist society, to support of two admittedly white supremacy spokesmen who declared in a joint statement that the country would only strengthen itself by getting rid of the "inferior minority which for centuries has been dragging the majority down to its level". Sandwiched in between these extremes were new statements by Joe Rielinski and Hilda Larsen, urging the Black American Council to disavow the separation goals and join with them in the formal formation of a black-white progressive alliance. All in all, on this Saturday morning, the newspapers of America had played the separation issue as the number one news item.

"Preston," Albert James said, breaking into Simmons' reverie, "just how did the President say you were an enemy of the nation? Was he just saying it to make a point, or did you get the feeling that this is going to be their major line of attack?" He wiped his round face with a handkerchief, his chair squeaking from the movement of his large body.

Simmons would always remember the President's words, the coldness in his eyes when he said them, and the sickening feeling in his own stomach as he instinctively recognized the sincerity of the threat.

"The President meant it, Al," he said. "And that's the approach they're going to use in their attack. Of course, being smart politicians, they're going to build up to it. We have to prepare for that type of approach. His statement to the media bears that out."

"Damn right!" Sam Muhammed said. "Throw the book at the leaders and scare the rest of the niggers off!"

"So I can look forward to a thorough airing of my Communist Party background," James sighed. "Got to go through that bull all over again."

"You didn't expect anything different did you?" Sam asked.

"I don't suppose I did," James said.

Simmons was thinking about the report he had received late last night from Marcus Jackson in Chicago, giving him updated information on his surveilance of Sam Muhammed.

145

During the past week, Sam had met publicly with a number of Third World diplomats and American black nationalists, generally considered to be a part of his broad constituency. However, he had met secretly, on three separate occasions, with a black-white team known to those-in-the-know as political mercenaries. This, in itself, didn't mean anything, since it was common knowledge that Sam occasionally used force to keep dissidents within his organization in line. But it also meant that Sam was not about to curtail his activities because he expected a speedup in government spying.

"Preston," Dr. Patten said, "I was somewhat intrigued by that proposition raised by Senator Leavitt, the one dealing with the voluntary migration of blacks to one or two southern states for the express purpose of taking over those states. Was the Senator serious or merely intellectualizing, as is his habit at times?"

"Both. But he wasn't recommending it to us—at least not at this time. Is that the way you read it, Bob?"

Griggs nodded. "But, Preston, I got the idea the Senator would be advancing this as a serious proposal, if he wasn't supporting Rielinski's position."

"To hell with the Senator and Rielinski," Rubye said. "How does the idea sound to us? Does it make any sense?" She flicked her right hand in a delicate gesture. As usual, her movement contrasted sharply with the tone of her voice.

"Rubye, how can you say to hell with the Senator, when it is his idea?" Dr. Patten asked.

Rubye shrugged. "Okay, to hell with him, other than it was his idea." Everybody laughed.

"The idea makes a lot of sense," Simmons said, answering Rubye's question. "Only I keep getting the feeling that the idea has come too late."

"What do you mean?" Dr. Patten asked.

"Well, let's put it this way. If somebody had got the idea to use this approach back in 1975 or 76, when blacks first started reverse migration to the South, it would have been a novel innovation, whether the final intention was to govern a few

146

states or build a nation. But now, blacks are all set to build a nation. That approach would amount to gradualism at this stage."

"You're damn right!" Sam said. "Nobody has time for that kind of bullshit now!"

Simmons held up his hand. "I'm beginning to feel uncomfortable, Sam," he said.

"Why is that?" Sam asked.

"That's twice you've agreed with me today."

After the laughter had subsided, Dr. Patten said: "I'm not quite finished with that approach. It has possibilities for the future, as well as for the past. Suppose, for instance, we fail in our current endeavor to secure a separate state. And suppose Rielinski's plan of building a black-white alliance to bring equity to this country also fails. In that case, we'd be right back where we are today, only worse off. I suggest, therefore, that the Black American Council develop this plan as an alternate, in case of defeat."

"I can't buy that," Sam said.

"Why?" Simmons asked.

"It's negative thinking. We can't permit ourselves to think of failing."

"That's where you are wrong, Sam," Simmons said. "It's more negative not to have an optional plan. If we fail, your children and mine must be left with a legacy of hope, not of despair. Bob, I suggest that you have Ted Blackwell put his fertile mind to work on this plan, have him explore it in all its ramifications, and come up with an approach for the future."

Griggs saluted. "Gotcha," he said.

Dr. Patten placed his elbow on the table and cupped his chin in his hand. "Let's take a look at the Rielinski proposal again," he said. "Preston, what aspects of it is Senator Leavitt in accord with, and does the President endorse anything of what Rielinski is saying?"

"I don't know about Rielinski," Griggs said. "His economic approach appears sound enough, but his social thinking, in my opinion, is scrambled. As you know, the NAACP has locked

147

horns with him over school bussing and his unwillingness to relent on employment seniority guidelines."

"But his answers to your objections make a lot of sense," Dr. Patten said. "He might be right when he contends that guaranteed full employment would solve many of the social questions, as well as the economic ones."

"What's all this got to do with us?" Sam Muhammed asked. "Hell, Rielinski's plan as much pie in the sky as Leavitt's."

"I don't know about that, Sam," Dr. Patten said. "What we need to do is —"

"Just a cotton-pickin' minute!" Rubye said, slapping the table top with her right palm. When all eyes were on her, she turned from Sam to Dr. Patten. "May I have you gentlemen's permission to try to break this thing down to the nitty gritty?"

She took out a cigarette and lit it. Behind a thin screen of smoke, she said very slowly: "Before the referendum was put before them, our people had been failing to make their wishes known by staying away from the polls and by showing a lack of interest generally. This separation question has been the only thing that's made black folks get up off their asses and express themselves, one way or the other, in a long time. So far, nobody has shown me anything that we can substitute for the hope the separation issue has brought black folks. Okay, so maybe Rielinski is sincere. Maybe my friend, Hilda, is also sincere. But they haven't come up with how the thing they're pushing can be done. And that's the name of the game—doing it! Okay, maybe we haven't come up with how to do our thing, either. But there is one difference. This thing is our thing. And I ain't for trading my thing in on somebody else's thing until they show me their thing is a damn sight better than my thing."

Sam Muhammed clapped his hands, shaking his body in an imitation Holy Ghost seizure. "That's telling it, Sister!" he shouted.

Rubye gave him a mock bow by bending her body forward across the table.

Simmons looked at Griggs, James and Dr. Patten. "Are you gentlemen in agreement?" he asked.

148

"Well, let's look at it like this," Albert James said, smiling at Rubye. "We were for doing our thing when we selected a chief negotiator; we were for doing it last week; and as the good sister says, ain't nothing come up since then to make us change our minds."

Griggs nodded and Dr. Patten said, "Amen!"

Simmons stretched out in his chair, locking his hands behind his head. "Okay," he said. "Now the next question is: precisely, where do we go from here?"

"We take the offensive," Sam said. "They're getting ready to start these damn hearings, and we must demonstrate our strength ahead of the hearings."

Albert James nodded. "I agree," he said.

"Demonstrate our strength how?" Simmons asked.

"On all fronts," Sam said. "Get the nations who are friendly to our cause to come out for us. Get the United Nations General Assembly to issue a resolution in support of us. And demonstrate like hell on the home front!"

Bob Griggs leaned forward across the table. "I'd steer clear of involvement with the United Nations or foreign governments at this stage," he said.

"Why?" Sam cried turning sharply in his seat in a gesture of disgust. "Isn't it clear that the white folks are getting ready to throw the book at us? We better bring our shit up front!"

Albert James wiped his face with his handkerchief. "I'm tempted to agree with Sam," he said, "but something about the timing worries me. During these hearings, they're going to hit us with charges of all kinds of foreign involvement. Their primary goals will be to scare black Americans into withdrawing their support, and making white Americans brand us as traitors. It seems to me, since this is the case, we better hold off on the foreign governments until we can gauge the impact of the hearings. Also, I don't know about the United Nations, at this stage."

"Hell, that's not logical thinking," Sam began, but Simmons held up his hand, nodding to Dr. Patten, who also had started to speak.

"I agree with Al James," Dr. Patten said. "However, I do believe we should begin laying the groundwork for utilizing the United Nations—not for issuing a resolution, but for defending our civil liberties."

"Explain that, Doctor," Simmons said.

"Well, let's look at it like this," Dr. Patten said. "During these hearings they'll be trying to establish evidence to prove that our exercise of the constitutional rights of protest and petition are in fact acts of conspiracy and treason. And they will attempt to indict us on these charges. We should begin now to assure that, at the proper time, certain forces in the UN charge the United States with violating our civil liberties. Out of this process, then—which would really be a defensive action on our part—would come the other forms of UN and international support, mentioned by Sam."

When Dr. Patten finished speaking, Simmons could see agreement on the faces of Rubye, Bob Griggs and Albert James and something akin to consternation on the face of Sam Muhammed. For his part, he was marvelling, as he had marvelled before, at Dr. Patten's ability to synthesize fragments of viewpoints into a consistent, workable theory.

"A very good analysis of the situation, Dr. Patten," he said. "Bob," he added, turning to Griggs, "I suggest you and Dr. Patten begin working with Ted Blackwell to get this UN thing going immediately."

"Something like yesterday," Rubye said.

Sam hunched his shoulders in disagreement, but said nothing.

"Okay," Simmons said. "That leaves the action on the home front. What are we talking about here?"

"The usual types of things," Albert James said. "Expressions of support from all the organizations making up the Council, except the Urban League, which we won't get. Mass meetings. Prayer meetings. Demonstrations before Federal buildings, etc."

Rubye and Griggs nodded.

"Anything to add, Dr. Patten?"

"There are a number of groups which agree with us that don't have Council membership," Dr. Patten said. "They should be asked to participate. Also, it's time to ask the black members of Congress who are on our side to stand up. Our front must be as united as possible—to offset the defectors, if for no other reason."

"I'd rather not deal with the Congressional Black Caucus members," Simmons said. "Although it is true a number of them agree with us, remember the Caucus pulled out of the Council over this issue. Public support on their part would only cause the Caucus chairman to denounce us, and that might more than offset the support of a few members. In other words, keep the Caucus out of it and hope its members remain silent."

Dr. Patten spread his hands. "I'll buy that for the time being," he said.

Simmons nodded. "Have we forgotten anything, Sam?"

Sam hunched his shoulders again.

"Okay," Simmons said. "Bob, I suppose Albert James should take the lead on this one, with upfront assistance from Rubye and Sam."

"When do we start?" Rubye asked.

"To borrow your phrase," Simmons replied, "something like yesterday."

Chapter 15

8:30 A.M., Sunday, October 4, 1987

HILDA LARSEN woke abruptly, the caption for the editorial she had been mulling over the night before suddenly clear in her mind, as though it were already set in bold type on the editorial page. This was often the case with her, she recalled. Sleep really did knit up the raveled sleeve of care. But it was more than that. She had a capacity for being able to awake suddenly from a deep sleep with her mind completely unblurred, as though she had not been asleep at all. None of that business of waking up in a strange apartment and thinking she was at home, or finding herself in bed with a man and not knowing who he was. And what was even more unusual, the drinking of alcohol or the smoking of pot prior to going to sleep made no difference. She always awoke with a clear head.

Of course, on this Sunday morning, she smiled to herself, there was nothing about her circumstances to test the validity of her pet phenomenon. She was in her own large round bed and the man lying beside her definitely was not a stranger.

She uncurled her fingers from around the rigid, gristle-like object she was holding in her hand. It was David's penis, now erect, hours after she had given up coaxing it. She smiled. Why not give the devil his due. The penis had performed satisfactorily three or four times last night. It shouldn't be blamed for her extreme horniness, nor for the fact that she hadn't seen its owner for more than a month.

She turned over on her side, her movement fanning the sheet covering David and her, unleashing the dank smell of stale come. The smell revived memories of the night before and she felt a relaxation deep in her vagina as warm moisture began to generate.

She was the only bitch she knew, she reprimanded herself, who got her kicks by wallowing in her own dirt. She'd better write that caption down before she forgot it. She rolled off the bed, walked across the wide expanse of white shag rug to the curved, multi-mirrored dresser, took a seat on a dresser stool and picked up a pad of paper and pencil that she always kept there. WE BELIEVE YOU'RE EQUAL, MR. SIMMONS, she printed in large block letters. Sticking the pencil in her mouth, she squinted at the letters, nodded her approval, then began writing rapidly.

"Mr. Simmons," she wrote, "in one of your early novels you developed the thesis that democracy could not move forward in this country until black Americans (then called Negroes) won equality on the economic, political and social fronts. You further stated that for blacks to win this equality, two psychological phenomena had to take place: blacks had to believe they were equal and white folks had to believe they (blacks) were equal. In our opinion, Mr. Simmons, you were extremely prophetic in that novel. The civil rights victories of the sixties, the employment protests and the separation demands of the eighties all have contributed to the building of the knowledge of equality within blacks. You might not believe this, Mr. Simmons, but these same things have also gone a long way toward forcing white folks to accept you as equals. Mr. Simmons, your point has been made. Now is the time to join us in building the democracy of which you wrote so eloquently in that novel. *Mr. Simmons, we believe you are equal...*"

"You should be over here fucking instead of over there writing," David's mildly cynical voice came from the bed.

"You had your chance, buddy," she replied, "now it's Mr. Simmons' turn."

"Oh, it's like that, uh?"

"It's like that."

David rolled over to the curve of the bed nearest her, the sheet wrapping around his lower body to reveal his broad shoulders and muscular arms. He brushed his long black hair away from his high forehead, his thin sensitive face serious. "You and your causes," he said.

"You should appreciate my causes," she said coquettishly, "they get me ready for you. Didn't last night prove it?"

David laughed. "That's one way of looking at it, all right. But there is also another way of looking at it."

"How's that?"

"Trying to satisfy the accumulated desires of a big healthy girl like you at one session is hell. I'd like to be around so I can take care of business, a little at a time."

It always came to those two things, she told herself. A reprimand for her socio-political activities. And a proposal of marriage. One she was compelled to do, and the other she was equally compelled not to do. But he was right about one thing—she was a big healthy girl!

Yes, he was right about her being mission-oriented, Hilda repeated to herself. And sex-oriented. But she used sex to bring objectivity to her other endeavors—not the other way around, as was the case with so many women she knew.

Looking back now, it seemed to her that she had been a political activist as long as she could remember. With hundreds of other sixteen-year-olds from the Minneapolis/St. Paul area, she had traveled with Eugene McCarthy to New Hampshire in the spring of 1968 to test voter attitudes toward Lyndon Johnson's Viet Nam policy in that state's bellwether presidential primary. Four years later, as a senior in college and editor of her college newspaper, she had joined the staff of Senator McGovern in what she referred to as the "first serious attempt at changing the American system since the early days of the New Deal."

Shortly after graduating from college in August of 1972 (she had had to attend during the summer to make up for the time lost in the McGovern primary campaign), she had joined the

154

staff of Ms. Magazine as a junior editor. Within five years she was editor and approximately ten years from the date she started on the magazine, she was elected president of the National Organization for Women. This, of course, meant that during her first ten years on the magazine, she definitely had engaged in more activities thàn selecting, editing and writing articles. During this period, she became an activist in the women's liberation movement, somewhat of an activist in the civil rights movement, and made numerous friends in what she often referred to as the "parallel movements".

Now, in the fifth year of her presidency of NOW and the thirty-fifth year of her life, she had another mission—turning the black separation movement into a joint black-white thrust against American fascism.

Her reverie was interrupted by David's hands on her breasts, cupping them. Momentarily, she felt resentment surge up in her. Struggling to curb the resentment, she turned around on the stool and looked up into his blue eyes, which appeared deep-set because of the dark circles around them. This was one of the things she hated most about herself, she thought. The tendency to bore too easily, expecially in personal matters. And through the years she had paid a heavy price for it—in short-lived love affairs. Unhappy love affairs for the most part, especially for the men involved.

She stood up from the stool and wrapped her arms around his waist, drawing him to her. Her face was level with his and she kissed him on the mouth, tenderly nibbling his bottom lip. His penis pushed against the inside of her thigh. She stepped back, unfolding her arms from around his body.

"I can't see why it can't be like this," he said huskily.

"Don't punish yourself," she said. "Let well enough alone."

He turned from her and sat on one of the stools. "Hell, Hilda, you act like we are the most incompatible persons in the world—like I am a male chauvinist or racist or something. In a way, I'm part of the crusade also. I was one of the first white entertainers to be invited to Black Expo, when Jesse Jackson opened it to whites in 1974."

"I know, David. If it could be anybody, it would be you."
She put her hand on his shoulder. "Believe me."

He ran his hand through his hair. "I was hoping you'd go
with me to Las Vegas. I open there tomorrow night."

"I know. But I can't."

"What's your itinerary next week?"

She reached for her robe which was lying on the dresser, but
changed her mind, realizing he might look upon the gesture as
shutting him out. "Later on today I plan to call Rubye Ransome. She might be here in New York, or she might be in
Washington."

"In other words, you might go to Washington."

"I might."

"I see."

She didn't like his tone. "Hell, David, you know how I feel
about this thing. You heard the news last night, and read the
papers." She waved at the papers scattered about the room.
"The President and the chairmen of the judiciary committees
are rushing into these hearings. And Simmons and his people
are calling for mass demonstrations. You know what that
means? The type of confrontations nobody will be able to
stop!"

"When have you ducked confrontations before?"

She threw up her hands in a gesture of disgust. "Don't be
funny, David! If people like me continue to sit on our asses,
we'll never be able to turn this thing around." She hated the
harshness of her tone.

"I just don't want you to leave me," he said.

She smiled, feeling suddenly tender toward him. She went
over and ruffled his hair, pulling his head against her stomach.

"Let's take a shower," she said. "Then let's fuck enough to
last both of us until the next time."

Chapter 16

11:30 A.M., Sunday, October 4, 1987

THE UNNATURALLY blue water of the swimming pool sparkled under the bright midday California sun, eluding the shade of the huge umbrellas which formed a crescent around the north edge of the pool, causing the shadows to fall away from the water and reach toward the patio of the house. The now unoccupied, blatantly upholstered benches, chairs and lounges, which were scattered along the pool's concrete embankment, somehow seemed to emphasize the sun's brightness and the water's blueness, creating an impression of opulent neglect.

James P. Sneed was conscious of these things as he sat with his two guests, a man and a woman, on the patio, looking at the pool through the back door, which was really an opening in the floor-to-ceiling sliding glass wall. The patio was located in the east wing of his sprawling Culver City residence, a place which joined with his New Jersey country estate, his San Francisco apartment, and his Virgin Island villa to create the famous quartet of abodes Sneed alternated in calling home. Except for him and his two guests, the Culver City place was vacant at the moment. Reginia, his wife, had left for San Francisco on Friday, taking her maid with her. Other than for entertainment and maintenance purposes, Sneed didn't like servants. They made him feel useless. When he and Reginia were not eating in restaurants, they prepared their own meals. He made no attempt to disguise his reason for owning four homes. They were symbols of his success, a testimonial to the viability of the American private enterprise system.

James P. Sneed often told himself—and this he did with genuine sincerity—that nobody, black or white, believed more devoutly in the American way of life than he did. In public speeches he had a habit of building up America by, in a sense, downgrading himself. "If I can do it," he said, "anybody can. Look at me, I'm just an ordinary Negro, medium brown, medium height, with a minimal education, and not really too smart. Yet, I publish books and magazines, produce records and movies, run a large bank, and serve on the board of directors of a number of major corporations. I'm what America is all about, and America is what I am about. I defend America because America defends me."

Now, sitting on the patio of his half-million dollar Culver City home, Sneed told himself that his two guests were also about the business of America—or at least they should be. In a lot of ways, the country had been good to them as it had to him.

"Jim," the male guest said, "I'm sure you wouldn't get us out here this early without offering us a drink. Even you wouldn't be that inhospitable."

Sneed realized that he possessed the fault of many strong-willed persons in that he had a habit of attributing his likes and dislikes to those around him. However, he was seldom resentful when reminded that such was not always the case. Consequently, he waved his hand in the direction of a small bar which stood in a far corner of the patio. "You know where everything is, Macey," he said in his disjointed tone of voice. "However, you've implied the reason for my oversight. It is early."

"Not too early for me," Macey Roberts replied. "Nor for Willia either, if my memory isn't failing."

"You always did assume things you shouldn't, Macey," the woman guest said in a soft voice. "I'm just fine."

"Suit yourself, Sweetie," Macey said. "A little gin and tonic is good for the disposition, even before noon."

As Macey went over to the bar and fixed himself a drink, Sneed found himself reflecting on the relationship between

158

Macey Roberts and Willia Adams. They were former husband and wife, highly publicized darlings of the black jet set, who had come to a parting of the ways some two years before. But their separation had not ended their friendship, nor their love affair. They were present at most of the Hollywood events that counted, either together or with other partners. It was generally assumed that they truly had their game together.

But it was not their collness in personal matters which impressed Sneed, but rather the influence they exerted in business and politics, an influence based primarily on their success in their individual careers. Macey was head of a firm which represented athletes in major league sports, a business he entered when his career as a premier running back was cut short by a knee injury just as he was on the threshold of replacing Jim Brown, O.J. Simpson and Walter Payton in the record books. Following the injury, he had attended law school where he had developed a close association with Lester Cohen, a brilliant white student. It was out of this association that the firm had been created, with well-defined areas of concentration for each partner. Macey's primary role was to sign up athletes, leaving the job of selling their services to the sports operators to Cohen. And this technique had paid off. Within five years, they had outstripped the competition. Roberts & Cohen Associates was now the first choice of most athletes desiring to have their professonal careers launched and maintained on a sound footing.

Willia Adams' successful career, Sneed told himself, stemmed primarily from two factors: the multiplicity of her talents and her ability to manipulate men without generating revengeful tendencies in them. She was an actress and singer of the first order. But beyond that, everybody—directors, producers, financial angels—seemed eager to do something for her, to let her have her way. To this, he could give personal testimony. She had used him, but for some reason he didn't resent it. Part of the reason for his acceptance of her misuse was because she had come through for him with five gold albums and four box office smashes in the past five years.

There had been a time—shortly after her marriage to Macey had gone sour—that he had thought she loved him. Yet, she had refused to let him into her mind, to surrender her independence, her individuality, to him. Later, he had learned that at the time he had thought he was closest to her, she had been having similar affairs with at least two other guys. When he had confronted her with his knowledge, she had smiled demurely and said: "But Jim, did I ever tell you anything differently?" And he had had to admit that she hadn't. He supposed she had that indefinable quality which made every man conclude that if circumstances were just right, she would reserve herself exclusively for him. Once a friend of his, talking about a woman with similar traits, had made a statement which came very close to summing up Willia Adams. "She looks like a lady and acts like a lady; therefore, she can get away with being a whore."

The sound and movement of Willia standing up cut into his reflection. "If Macey is going to drink and if you, Jim, are going to muse, I suppose I have to find something to do," she said.

"Take your pick," Macey said. "Drink with me or muse with Jim."

"I think I'll drink with you. Pour me a glass of white wine."

"Come and get it," Macey said.

Sneed watched her as she headed across the patio in that careful way she had of walking, as though she was not quite sure where she was going. However, on second glance—and this was an impression he often had of her—she seemed to be gliding like a proud bird, serene and secure.

Reaching the bar, she accepted the drink from Macey with a slight curtsy, spreading her skirt with her left hand. "Thank you, Sir," she said.

"My pleasure, Madame," Macey replied.

Watching them standing there, side by side, Sneed found himself being affected by their magnetism. Macey was tall and slender appearing, probably the same weight as when he was breaking records on the gridiron. His face, unusually thin and delicate for a football player, was remindful of Harry Belefonte

160

of twenty years ago. Willia was not pretty, in the sense that movie stars are supposed to be pretty. Her features were too heavy for that. But her eyes, large and expressive, animated her face and enlivened the normal immobility of her features with a compelling vitality. She was one of those women who appeared to change coloring with her surroundings: with brown-skinned women she appeared brown, with yellow women she appeared to be yellow, and when she was around white women she seemed to be damn near white.

"Okay, Jim," Macey said. "Now we are ready to hear why you called us out here."

Sneed could feel his mind shifting into gear, as he cast aside his indulgences of the past few minutes. When duty called, nothing should be permitted to stand in the way.

"Have you read the papers this morning?" he asked.

Macey nodded his head in the affirmative. "I haven't," Willia said.

"But you have heard the latest news on television?"

"I suppose so—what are you getting at?" she asked.

"I'm talking about the plans of the Black American Council to hold nationwide demonstrations."

"Oh, that," Macey said.

"Yes, that."

"What about it?" Willia asked.

"We can't let those demonstrations go unchallenged."

Macey held up his hand. "Jim, I don't want any part of it. I've made up my mind to sit this thing out. At your insistence, I got deeply involved before the vote was taken. But now that the vote has been taken, I'd feel like a fool opposing the Council."

"Jim, I have to agree with Macey," Willia said. "Opposing the Council now, would make me feel kinda like a—traitor."

This wasn't going to be as easy as he had expected, Sneed told himself. He needed them to help get the opposition moving again. Nobody was doing what they should. Even Wild of the Congressional Black Caucus, who had resigned from the Council rather than be a part of the separation vote, and Bill Green of the Urban League, who had quit the Council after the

161

vote was taken, weren't doing a damn thing to help him now. They were keeping quiet out of some silly sense of loyalty to black causes, even though they didn't believe in the separation scheme.

"Come over here and sit down," he said, "and let's talk about this thing seriously. Just because Simmons and Griggs are making fools of themselves, is no reason why we should fall into the same trap."

When Macey and Willia were again in their seats, Sneed continued. "First, Macey, let's take a look at your situation. Sports have been good to blacks, and your business is based on the fact that sports continue to be good to blacks. Now we don't always like to admit it, but blacks don't patronize sports as paying customers like whites do. Now what kind of salaries do you suppose black athletes would be making, and consequently what kind of commissions would you be drawing down, if sports had to depend on blacks for support?"

"I don't see how that enters into the equation," Macey replied slowly. "If blacks succeeded in negotiating a separate state, black athletes would still be needed in the United States. And they would be paid good salaries. Look at the salaries West Indian blacks are drawing down."

Sneed laughed. "I thought you'd bring that up. But you aren't thinking it through to a logical conclusion. Now, I ask you this. Have any of these West Indian governments, other than Cuba, ever had a serious conflict with the United States? And the Cuban athletes on American teams are enemies of the Communist government, not friends of it. Now, can't you see what would happen, if by some stretch of the imagination the Council does succeed? Of course, you can. The American sports fraternity, with the support of the American people, would ban all blacks from participating in American sports. We'd be right back where we were forty years ago."

"Forty years ago?" Willia asked.

"Forty years ago was 1947," Macey said. "The year Jackie Robinson broke the color bar in baseball."

"Oh," Willia said.

162

Sneed was watching Macey intently. He could tell that his latest arguments had affected the athlete, but he still was showing little inclination to campaign further against the separate state idea. "Don't you think I'm right, Macey?" he asked.

Macey leaned forward in his chair, rubbing his hand along the front of his face. "Everything you say is probably true," he said. "But there is another side to it. I guess I'm getting fed up with the idea that white folks and black folks expect black folks to *accept* the fact of our second-class status. Take Lester's and my business, for instance. The idea was mine, and there was a young black lawyer I wanted to come in with me. But I took the idea to a white man. Why? Because I knew he could deal with the owners better than I could."

Sneed could feel something in himself hardening against the argument. This was the kind of thinking which caused so many Negroes to fail in their endeavors. Putting pride before common sense.

"Look," he said. "Forget about that and think positive. The fact is, you have succeeded. This is America, man. A land of many races and national groups. It's a thing of give and take. The Irish know it, and the Jews know it above all. What's wrong with taking advantage of the odds?"

Macey sighed. "I know," he said. "But sometime you have to wonder."

"Wonder all you want to. But business is business. Don't think the Irish and Jews don't wonder. But you don't see them trying to break away from the country."

"Okay," Macey said. "You're probably right, but while I'm wondering, I'll get something else off my chest. Remember, about fifteen or twenty years ago, when those two black athletes were barred from further competition for giving the black power salute in Latin America?"

"Yes. What about it?"

"Okay, here is what I mean. Less than ten years after these athletes were barred for giving the salute, all American athletes—*white* as well as black—had adopted the black power salute as a victory symbol. And here is something else. Remember how white coaches and athletes used to pat their companions on their asses to encourage them? Then the black hand slap came along. Now everybody uses the black hand slap instead of the white ass pat."

"So?"

"Okay, I know this might sound far out, but I resent it. White folks always steal things that are uniquely black from black folks and claim them as their own. Now they don't steal these things because they want them, *but to keep us from having them*. You see, when they claim something that we invent, the militance leaves that thing, causing it to become sterile. In other words, by stealing black expressions, white people steal not only our possessions, but our identity."

Sneed had never heard Macey talk like this before. But as always, he told himself, when people got out of their depths, they came to conclusions which missed the mark and only confused things. "Look, Macey," he said, "instead of resenting what white people steal from us, you should be proud. Hell, if they didn't steal our talk, our walk, and our songs, what would they steal? The important thing is, the black images they steal are absorbed and become part of the whole. A part of America. Hell, I hate to keep repeating it, but that's what this country is all about!"

Before Macey could reply, Willia, moving impatiently in her chair, said: "My case is different."

The quick, uncharacteristic movement forced her skirt upward, exposing knees and thighs which Sneed considered to be among the most attractive he had ever seen. Looking steadily at him, she half raised from her chair and pulled her skirt down, repeating: "My case is different."

She was a lady, all right, he told himself. Always kept things well hidden until the time for action arrived; then she was one of the boldest women he had ever known. In spite of himself, he couldn't keep from thinking about a story he had heard about her.

When she and Macey were on the verge of breaking up, the

story went, Macey, realizing she wouldn't be his wife much longer, decided to ascertain for sure if her sex appetite extended into an area he had long suspected it did. So he invited her to join him and a girl friend in an adult game for three. Without showing anger or resentment, she had said: "I tell you what, Macey. Why don't you bring one of those young football studs home with you. I bet you I'm better at fucking two men than you are at fucking two women." Sneed had no reason to believe the story wasn't true, since Macey had told it to him one night in her presence. He, however, had had no inclination to determine if the telling of the story was also an invitation to help Willia prove her boast.

"Jim," Willia continued now, "you keep talking about business is business, and I agree with you. That's why my case is different from Macey's. It's not good business for me to continue my involvement in this separation thing."

"I don't see how you figure that."

"Well, although white people buy loads of my records, black people buy more. Young black people. And according to statistics—those carried in your own magazines—more young black people voted for separation than voted against it."

Her logic was as marred as Macey's, he told himself. That's what happened when one permitted singers and football players to participate in the mapping of social and political strategy. But he needed their influence.

"Look, Willia," he said, "you and Macey are talking like this is a campaign to determine whether Cola Cola is more popular then Pepsi. This is a campaign to keep the country, the *United States of America*, from breaking up. Now the only way to keep us from getting hurt, to keep our *business* from getting messed up, is to stop this thing before it goes any further. It's better for us to stop it than for the white people to have to stop it."

"What do you mean?" Macey asked.

"It's obvious what I mean. If we help stop it, the white people will still be reasonable. If they have to stop it by themselves, they're going to kick *all niggers* in the ass!"

"Are you sure about that?" Willia asked.

"As sure as I am of anything in the world. But there is something else, even more important, to consider."

"What's that?" Macey asked.

"A matter of personal integrity. Look, I'm not asking you to do anything you don't believe in. Do either of you believe in this separate state? Despite any grievances you might have, do either of you believe in it?"

"Of course not," Willia said. "I think we proved that when we worked with you before."

"Okay, then. It's even *more* important that you work with me now."

Macey stood up. It was a movement of sudden decision. "What do you want us to do?" he said.

Sneed could feel himself relaxing inside. He had won again, as he had known all along he would. "Like I told you," he said, "the Black American Council is planning nationwide demonstrations next week to show there is still mass support for separation. We have to launch counter-demonstrations of blacks in these same cities."

"Do we have time?" Macey asked.

"We have time. The pre-election organizations are still in place."

"Precisely where do we come in?" Willia asked.

"The same as before. You two will head the Los Angeles contingent. I'll be in touch later this evening, after I've made a few more calls."

"Okay," Macey said, "we'll do it. But there is one condition."
"What is it?"

"No violence. I can't bear the idea of blacks fighting blacks."

Sneed looked from Macey to Willia. They both stared back at him.

"All right," he said. "No violence."

Fifteen minutes after his guests had gone, James P. Sneed called a number.

"Tell the Attorney General," he said, "that things are going according to plans. The New York, Chicago, Los Angeles, and

New Orleans contingents are in place. The others will be by nightfall."

He listened intently to the voice on the other end of the line, then spoke again.

"I agree with the Attorney General," he said. "It definitely might be necessary to bust a few heads, if for no other reason than to get across the message that these people are courting violence. In any case, it is time to start bringing this thing to a close. By any means necessary."

Chapter 17

8:00 P.M., Sunday, October 4, 1987

PRESTON SIMMONS relished the solitude of a hotel room. In all the trips he had made back and forth across the country during the past seventeen years—as a novelist publicizing his books, as a newsman gathering material for stories and as a lecturer responding to speaking requests—the function he appreciated most was the act of retiring alone to his hotel room for an interlude of reflection and sleep. This did not mean that he did not enjoy the more associative activities of the travel circuit; there had been times when the clash of ideas between him and an interviewer, the sudden awareness of an unusual communicative bond between a reader and himself, or just the mere moving among a responsive audience, had been highly stimulating; nevertheless, for the most part, the highpoint of these trips had come when, a particular segment completed, he retired to his room to commune with himself, to prove again that he was his own best company.

Now, sitting in the living room of his two-room suite in Hotel Washington, Simmons realized that this ability to find pleasure in being alone was being affected by present events. It was approximately eight o'clock on Sunday evening, the day following his latest meeting with the negotiating team. He was sitting on the couch, dressed in robe and pajamas, with his feet, encased in soft corduroy houseslippers, resting on the cocktail table. He was sipping sherry on the rocks.

The feeling of comfort that he had once found in his anonymity—even the not-quite-so-certain anonymity of a near-celebrity—was completely shattered now, replaced by the apprehension of living in a display cage. And because he no longer had privacy of person, he had this odd notion that the privacy of his mind was also being violated.

He sighed. That, of course, was illogical. He had to get over this crazy feeling of being mentally exposed just because he was in the spotlight. Other people functioned, and functioned quite effectively, within the glare of continuous public scrutiny. It was just so new to him.

He replenished his glass with sherry and ice from the bottle and bucket on the cocktail table. Sipping the drink, he closed his eyes, permitting his mind to flit about the surface of events affecting him and his associates. Last night Albert James had left for the west coast, Dr. Patten for the south, and Sam Muhammed for New York City, to direct the demonstrations. Some of these demonstrations had gotten underway today, Sunday, while others were scheduled to start on Monday. Rubye was going to Chicago tonight or early tomorrow to give direction to the midwest activities. He and Bob Griggs were remaining here in Washington for a day or two, then they would leap-frog across the country, checking out the effectiveness of the demonstrations.

But the feeling of being hemmed in would not relent. He supposed it was due in part to the fact that he had been assigned police protection; that for the first time in his life, he was being guarded.

He had first become aware of it tonight when he returned to the hotel from the southwest side of the city, where he had lectured that afternoon in a middle-class integrated church and had dinner at the home of the minister. Marcus Jackson, who had flown in from Chicago the night before, had spent the day with him, as he had often done in the past. Upon their return to the hotel, Marcus had left him at the magazine counter in the hotel lobby, hurrying to his room to pack for a flight to Los Angeles. When he and Marcus had entered the hotel, he had noticed that there were more policemen in the lobby than he had ever seen there. He had gotten a fleeting notion that they were there because of him but didn't know for sure until he got out of the elevator on his floor and noticed a cop in the corridor, sitting as unobtrusively as possible in the alcove where the vending machines were located. Immediately, he had called Marcus' room, hoping to catch him before he left the hotel.

"Yes, we have set up minimum security," Marcus had admitted. "Guards at the main entrances of the hotels where you will be staying and a guard on your floor. When you travel, somebody will always be with you."

"Guards?" he had asked. "These are policemen—at least the one stationed on this floor."

"That's right. For the most part, they will be black volunteer policemen, off duty. When this can't be done, we'll make other arrangements."

"Do you think I'm in danger?"

Marcus had hesitated. "If you mean, have I heard anything?—the answer is no. But your guess about the *possibility* of danger is as good as mine. It makes good sense to take precautions. Don't you think so?"

Reluctantly, he had admitted that he did.

But even more disturbing than the presence of the policemen was the report Marcus had given him that morning on the Saturday night activities of Sam Muhammed. The information on Sam Muhammed had been received by Marcus in two separate reports—one before he left Chicago and the other after he reached Washington. After Sam had arrived in New York from Washington on Saturday afternoon, he had had a clandestine meeting with a suspected member of the Black Liberation Army, the most violent of the para-military groups existing in the country, black or white. But more alarming than

170

the meeting with the BLA was the discovery by Marcus' investigators that Sam was under a twenty-four-hour surveillance by FBI and CIA agents.

"So that means the government knows about his meeting with the BLA?" he had asked.

"Yes. And it seems to my people that Sam isn't going to any real trouble to keep them from knowing."

"Are you saying that Sam knows he is being shadowed?"

"He probably does."

"In other words, you're saying Sam's deliberately letting the CIA and FBI know he's meeting with the BLA?"

"Probably."

"Marcus, are the rest of us under constant surveillance by the FBI or CIA?" he had asked.

Marcus shook his head. "I don't think so. You are probably under periodic surveillance, but not constant surveillance. You see, the CIA and FBI know the rest of you are out-front protesters, not underground revolutionaries. So they are probably keeping just a tight enough check so they would find out within a reasonable length of time if you changed your style."

"But Marcus, in your opinion, why would Sam want the CIA to know he's dickering with the BLA? Is he hoping they'll crack down on him so all hell can break loose?"

Marcus had thought a long time before replying. Then he had only said: "Your guess is as good as mine."

He noticed that the litre bottle of sherry was nearly half empty. He had been drinking more than he thought. He glanced at his watch, lying on the end table. It was slightly past nine o'clock. What should he do? he asked himself. Go to bed or look at television? He smiled at the irony of his still possessing the luxury of two such simple choices. Maybe he should do both.

The telephone on the desk across the room rang shrilly. He walked over and picked it up.

"Mr. Simmons," a male voice said, "Mrs. Ransome—Mrs. Rubye Ransome—is down here to see you. Do you want to talk to her, or may she come up?"

"Tell her to come up," he said.

He went back to the couch and sat down. He was surprised that Rubye was paying him a visit, especially without calling first. When he had talked to her that morning, she had told him that she would be spending the day and evening with her new friend, the doctor; that she wanted to spend as much time with him as she could before taking off for Chicago tonight, or early Monday morning. In fact, if it hadn't been for the intensity of her new relationship, he was certain Rubye would have gone to Chicago the day before, in order to make use of Sunday activities in mobilizing for the demonstrations. Then why was she wasting her precious time to visit him? Maybe she had fallen out with her new friend and was coming over for him to console her. Maybe... What the hell, he thought, why beat his brains out. She was on her way up and in a minute he would know the reason for her uncharacteristic visit.

He was standing in the doorway of his suite, looking down the corridor, when Rubye got off the elevator. She was wearing a two-piece denim pants suit with a scarf around her head, and for a second he thought she was alone. Then he saw, rather than heard, her say something to the tall white woman who followed her out of the elevator and realized she had company. Then he recognized the woman. It was Hilda Larsen, president of the National Organization for Women and editor of Ms. Magazine. He stood holding the door as the two women came down the corridor toward him, the Larsen woman towering over Rubye's short slight figure. Hilda Larsen walked with slow, half-bouncing confident strides, and appeared to be taking only single steps to Rubye's two or three. She was wearing a tan suit, with short skirt, and her blonde hair appeared to be pulled back from her forehead.

Rubye was smiling when she came up to the door. Hilda Larsen had her arm locked in Rubye's.

"Preston, I brought you some company," Rubye said.

"Hello, Mr. Simmons," Hilda Larsen said. "I hope you don't mind." Her voice was calm, with a musical undertone.

He stood back from the door. "Come in," he said. "I hope

you ladies will excuse the way I'm dressed—but I didn't know you were coming."

"I take the blame for that," Hilda Larsen said, as they came into the suite and Simmons closed the door. "I told Rubye not to call—not to give you a chance to refuse to see me."

"I told her you wouldn't do that," Rubye said. "That you are always eager to see a woman—especially a strange one." There was a devilish gleam in Rubye's brown eyes.

"Take a seat, ladies," he said. "In those chairs, or on the couch next to me."

Rubye took a seat on the couch. Hilda Larsen pulled the chair from under the table on which the phone sat and positioned it so that it faced the couch. Simmons noticed that he had been correct about her hair. It was pulled back from her head and held in a clip at the base of her neck, its ends falling down her back over the lightweight suit jacket. Taking a seat in the chair, she crossed her legs slowly, as though to make sure that in crossing them, attention would be drawn to the act itself. She had nice legs.

"Would you ladies like a drink?" he asked. "I don't have anything but sherry, but I can order."

Rubye picked up Simmons' glass and took a sip, frowning. "I don't like this sherry," she said. "Too sweet. Anyway, I have to be going. I just brought Hilda by."

"I hope you don't mind, Mr. Simmons," Hilda Larsen said. "I told Rubye I had met you a few times."

"I remember twice," he said. "One time we were interviewers on a televised news show, and the other time we were fellow panelists at a NAACP workshop."

"That's right," she said.

"Were there any other?" he asked. "I mean...you said we had met a few times?"

She smiled. "I don't suppose you call two a few, do you?" she asked.

"Sure you do," Rubye said. "If you want to." The amused tone was still in her voice.

"Why do you have to go?" Simmons asked Rubye.

"You know what I have to do," Rubye said. "I have to be in Chicago tomorrow morning for a nine o'clock session."

"That's almost twelve hours from now," he said.

"I know," Rubye said. "But in that twelve hours is included travel time and goodbye time."

He noticed that Hilda Larsen was smiling. "I see you have been brought up to date on Rubye's new thing," he said.

"And what a thing," Rubye said, standing up.

"You didn't tell me if you drink sherry?" he said to Hilda Larsen.

She leaned forward and read the label on the bottle. "Yes, I drink sherry," she said. "In fact, I prefer it."

Rubye laughed, moving toward the door. "Well, at least, you have that much in common," she said. "I hope you-all don't kick too much shit out of each other."

"If we do, we have a referee outside," he said.

Rubye stopped near the door, "I know," she said seriously. "So they think things are getting rough?"

"They just don't want to take any chances."

Rubye nodded, her hand on the door. "Well, Hilda," she said, "I delivered you to him. But as I told you, we gotta play this string out."

"I understand," Hilda Larsen said. "But I wanted to plead my case face to face. Thanks, Rubye. See you around."

Rubye looked at Simmons. The amusement in her eyes was gone, replaced by a look of questioning uncertainty. He knew she was feeling what he was feeling. He didn't know exactly how to deal with Hilda Larsen. Then Rubye smiled at Hilda, grinned at him and went out the door.

In the deep silence following Rubye's departure, he took a glass from the cocktail table, stripped off the plastic covering, fixed a drink for Hilda and handed it to her. She took a sip, smiled her approval, set the glass on the cocktail table and stood up.

"May I pull off my jacket?" she asked, taking it off before he replied and hanging it over the back of her chair. Then she sat down again, crossing her legs in the same methodical manner.

She was wearing a brown blouse with a collarless neck and long sleeves. The blouse was plain, totally without adornments, but her large breasts, straining against the soft cloth, made the blouse appear somehow decorative. He noticed that unlike a lot of women with large breasts, hers did not swell out from the neckline but moved in an almost straight line outward considerably below that point, creating the atmosphere of a cavity at the top of her chest. In spite of himself, the words "mysterious well" came into his consciousness, bringing with them a nagging desire to peep down the neckline of her blouse and examine for himself the secret place where her chest and breasts made juncture.

He was overreacting to her, he told himself, recalling that white women always created in him an uneasiness that he couldn't quite fathom. They always made him either too bold or too shy, or brought forth an indifference that he suspected was false. He realized, of course, that different women, black or white, evoked in him individual responses; but, somehow, with white women there seemed to be a sharper edge to his response: a more acute awareness of their presence.

"I'm a great admirer of your work, Mr. Simmons," she said, "especially your novels." The words sounded unrelated to the situation in which he found himself, so that he had to concentrate to grasp their meaning. He was sure he was too long in replying.

"Thanks," he said. "You are not a bad writer yourself."

She took a sip of her drink without taking her eyes off him. "I used one of your novels as a point of reference for an editorial I wrote this morning," she said.

"Which one?"

"*The Pregnant Issue*, the one where you developed the thesis that black men, especially black leaders, shouldn't have white wives." Her eyes were twinkling.

"Oh."

"But that's not the reference I'm using in my editorial. I'm dealing with the theory where you said that democracy cannot advance in this country until black Americans win equality;

175

and that since blacks are the key to democracy, they are the most important people in America."

"I see," he said. "And what did you conclude, in the editorial?"

She reached in her purse for a cigarette and held it in her hand. "I said I agree with you," she said.

He picked up a book of matches from the table, stood up, lit her cigarette and took his seat again. "There is one major fallacy in that book," he said. "I assumed that the majority of white people in this country wanted democracy to advance. That assumption was a mistake."

"Do you think the majority of blacks in this country want democracy to advance?" she asked.

"Yes, I do."

"Why do you believe we are so different?" Her eyes were serious, probing. He took a sip from his glass, framing his reply carefully.

"Because most white people," he said, "have been convinced that they don't really need any more democracy. That they have enough already."

She nodded, shifting her eyes slightly. "I suppose this was the point you were making in your second novel, *The Campaign*, where the white liberals refused to support the black candidate for Mayor, even though he was one of them—I mean a liberal like them—and was the best-qualified for the job."

"Exactly. That's what I meant in the novel, and that's what I meant at the televised press conference Thursday before last, the day I was selected chief negotiator."

She pulled her chair closer to the cocktail table and flipped the ashes from her cigarette into an ashtray.

"Why don't you sit over here on the couch," he said. "It's better than going through all the gymnastics."

"I like to look at you when I talk to you," she said.

"We can still look at each other," he said. "There is such a thing as turning sideways on a couch."

She laughed, got up and walked around the cocktail table

and sat on the couch. She placed her arm on the back of the couch, crossed her left leg over her right in that slow controlled fashion and looked hard at him. "Like this?" she asked.

"Yes, like that," he replied, turning so that he was facing her. "Now, where were we?" he asked.

"We were talking about the failure of white liberals, and white progressives for that matter, to demonstrate an interest in working with black people as equals," she said. "But things are changing."

"I can't see these changes," he replied. "Maybe your eyes are better than mine. What is your evidence?"

She rested her chin on the arm she had stretched across the back of the couch. "One evidence of the change is me," she said, "and the people I represent. I realize the mistakes which were made in the women's liberation movement vis-a-vis black people in the 1970s. We feel guilty that in far too many cases employment gains for white women were made at the expense of black men, and we want to try to correct this. Then there is the labor movement under Joe Rielinski. He's a firm believer that only *guaranteed* full employment can begin to solve the problem. And he wants to stop talking, and start *fighting*, now!"

Her eyes were bright with excitement. He reached out his hand and touched hers, then pulled it back.

"Miss Larsen...Hilda," he said. "Look at it like this. Black people have waited for white people to extend a hand for a long time. Finally, we have gotten the nerve to take a bold step on our own. It might not be the right step, but it is our step. You can't ask us not to take it without offering something concrete."

She moved toward him, touching him on the knee with her hand. "Preston, I can see your point," she said, "but please look at mine. I believe we're closer to getting the type of coalition we've all dreamed about than ever before, than we'll ever be again if we let this chance slip away. I can't prove it, but I can feel it—the majority of white people are ready to join us. Join you, me, Joe Rielinski, and all our people. Only we'll have to give the word. And we'll have to give it together!"

She was aflame with conviction, of that he had no doubt. She was breathing rapidly, her beautiful breasts heaving. He had to say something to force her from the peak she had ascended.

"I can't do it, Hilda," he said. "As I said before, it is our step—and we must take it."

"But, Preston, we might never get another chance!"

"Maybe so. But I still can't do it. I can't do it—not even for a beautiful white lady." That should do it, he told himself. Should bring her back to reality.

For a moment she seemed stunned, then color rushed to her face. But she was tough, and bold. She picked up her glass and drained it. Her voice was sarcastic, yet a little bit apologetic, when she said: "Never in my life have I tried to use my sex, or my race, to give me an advantage in matters like this."

He looked into her eyes. The flame of dedication was no longer present; yet, if anger was there, he could not detect it. She seemed to realize that she had been pushing too hard, and did not resent the method he had employed to tell her to ease up. But he had hurt her, and for that he was sorry. He hoped his voice was light and airy when he replied.

"You might not have tried to use your sex to gain an advantage," he said, "but there would have been plenty around to *force advantages on you*, if you had decided to become head of General Motors instead of the National Organization for Women."

The look of caginess fled, and she laughed. "Preston, you are full of an unsmelly kind of shit. But anyway, thanks for not believing that we women liberationists are a bunch of homosexuals."

Now it was his turn to laugh. The tension was gone, yet he realized they were fencing with each other behind the protective facades they had built up through the years and not responding from the core of their beings. But he had little

178

doubt that she would play the game through to any conclusion he desired. This he could tell by the seductive way she was leaning back, pointing her breasts at him, daring him with veiled eyes.

But was she daring him, or inviting him? While the trait probably was not as overt in her as in others he had known, he suspected that she was afflicted with the universal curse of liberal and progressive American white women: the desire to do something *protective* for some black male. But protection always marched hand-in-hand with control. And he wanted no part of either.

Yet, at the same time, he realized he was probably too harsh in his judgment of her. She probably was merely reaching out to him, woman to man. Indeed, the mysterious well above her breasts was still enticing, and he was as eager as before for exploring. But the time for that was past, at least for the moment. They both deserved much more than that. He had got a glimpse into the depth of her soul and fleetingly had experienced the communion of spirit which was possible between them. And this he would not debase.

"Friends?" he asked, reaching for her hand to shake, not to caress.

The veil lifted from her eyes, and he could tell that she understood.

She thrust her hand forward. "Friends," she said in a firm voice.

Chapter 18

6:00 A.M., Tuesday, October 6, 1987

"ONE, TWO, three, four! One, two, three, four! One, two, three, four!" With hands on hips, feet close together, Joe Rielinski bent forward, straightened up, bent backward, straightened up, then repeated the movements over and over again, careful not to break the cadence set by his muted voice. "One, two, three, four! One, two, three, four! One, two, three, four!"

It was six o'clock on a Tuesday morning. Dressed only in boxer shorts, he was in the basement of his home in Washington, D.C., completing his morning exercises. The exercise room was in the back of the paneled and comfortably furnished basement and contained most of the paraphernalia for physical fitness. Although occasionally he used this equipment, his daily exercise consisted mainly of the calisthenics he had learned while training as a marine for service in Viet Nam. He especially liked the bending exercise he was finishing up with now, using it to determine the condition his body was in. If he could bend forward until his torso was parallel to the floor without feeling a painful pull on the muscles of his legs and bend backward at a forty-five degree angle without feeling a tear at his stomach, then he considered his body to be in the proper condition.

He picked up the tempo now, both in the speed of his count

180

and the extremity of his bends—"One, two, three, four! One, two, three, four! One, two, three, four! One, two, three, four!"—finishing up with a flourish.

Stepping out of his shorts, he went into the bathroom, which was adjacent to the exercise room, to take a shower. He was sweating, but not profusely, and he felt relaxed. He smiled to himself. This was the only way to begin a day. Make sure the body was in shape and you didn't have to worry about the mind being ready for action.

Finished with his shower, and enjoying the sensation of a terry cloth robe wrapped around his tingling body, he walked the length of the basement to the stairs which led up to the master bedroom. As he moved through the basement, he admired the richness of the pecan wall paneling, the boldness of the red and black leather couches and chairs, and the well-stocked mirrored bar which his friends and associates so appreciated. Entering the bedroom, he could hear his wife, Rosa, moving about in the adjoining kitchen. Within a few minutes she would stick her head in the door and tell him breakfast was ready.

He moved over to the king-sized bed, the head of which nestled against the far wall of the room, and picked up Rosa's pillow and placed it on top of his. Without removing his robe, he stretched out on the bed, his head resting on the stacked pillows, and pushed the button which activated the television mechanism recessed in the opposite wall of the bedroom. As the mammoth screen infused with light, he flipped the switch which tuned in the *Today* show. The announcer, as he knew would be the case, was just beginning the first news highlights of the day.

"Monday's activities," the announcer was saying, "marking the second day of the demonstrations called by the Black American Council to show support for its demands for a separate state, were carbon copies of Sunday's protests in that the demonstrations were varied, depending on the sections of the country, but everywhere massive. In Atlanta, the protesters marched from City Hall into outlying neighborhoods, while in

St. Louis, they marched from the black ghettos into the main business district. In Los Angeles, the demonstrations were confined primarily to the Watts area, while in Chicago federal buildings marked the focal point of activities. Everywhere there was a tenseness, creating an impression that violent confrontation between the demonstrators and law enforcement personnel cannot long be prevented. Preston Simmons, speaking for the BAC from Washington, D.C., has vowed that the demonstrations will continue until appropriate national officials agree to meaningful negotiations. Meanwhile, Representative Thomas Ryan, chairman of the House Judiciary Committee, stated that plans are continuing to begin hearings on the BAC demands as soon as possible. Senator Samuel Leavitt, of the Senate Judiciary Committee, and President Davidson have not enlarged on their statements of last Friday, when the President stated that there is a possibility that the country is facing the greatest threat to the preservation of the Union since the Civil War and Senator Leavitt said, in effect, that the actions of the BAC are too extreme to represent a mere petition for the redress of wrongs. In any case, the people of this country, as well as the peoples of the world, are watching and waiting...."

Joe Rielinski sighed and pushed the button to turn off the television mechanism. The feeling of near euphoria which had engulfed him at the completion of his exercises was subsided now and he was aware, as he had been aware often in the past month, of a vague sense of personal failure. After all, he was the president of the AFL-CIO, had been elected as a reform candidate on a platform which promised to bring economic and racial stability to the country, and in his position he definitely was one of the major wielders of power in the nation. But not only had he been unable to bring stability to the country, all of his efforts had not been sufficient even to help maintain the status quo. But neither had the other power brokers been able to do anything—the President, the Congress, the barons of industry. And in a sense, he had been able to do more than the others, especially in his specific area of responsibility. He *had* been able to bring more unity to organized labor than had existed since the early sixties, when the automobile workers had pulled out of the AFL-CIO.

Immediately upon his election to the AFL-CIO presidency in 1983, he recalled now, he had launched a highly visible campaign to bring about labor unity. Straightening out the few remaining problems resulting from the automobile workers's re-entry into the AFL-CIO had been relatively easy because Lane Kirkland and Douglas Frazier had done a good job putting the pieces back together when the split was healed in 1981. Next he had tackled the United Mine Workers Union and the National Association of Education and within a year the job was completed. The re-entry had been formalized in a special convention in August of 1984. But the teamsters had been another matter, the major problem being the influence of organized crime in the union. Yet, by July of 1986 the deed had been done, without the necessity of another special convention.

However, in his attempts to create racial harmony he had failed as dismally as other national leaders. He had been unable to keep the Black American Council from holding the separation referendum, and had been equally as ineffective in his attempts to dissuade them from moving to consummate the outcome of that referendum.

He drew his knees up and locked his hands behind his head, staring at the ceiling. The question kept coming up, inside his own mind and from others, of just why he felt it was so essential to keep blacks from establishing a separate nation, to keep them a part of the United States. Many of his associates and friends kept telling him that whites in this country would be better off without blacks, that with the absence of blacks white workers could go about the business of establishing genuine democracy, free from the divisive influences of racial differences. But he knew this would not be the case. First, if blacks did establish a separate nation, probably one-fourth of the blacks in the country would not migrate to it, but would remain within the borders of the United States as citizens. And this situation, rather than decreasing the race problem, would intensify it. Second, white Americans tended toward complacency in the absence of stimulating influences. Throughout American history black demands had moved American whites to action. And now that blacks had momentum going for what was probably their second biggest demand, it made sense for white workers to latch on to this momentum for their own interest. But most importantly, he did not want a separate black movement to shatter the vision he had of America as one land composed of peoples from all lands. If America could be made to work, then the destiny of mankind as a single viable species was closer to assurance.

He turned over on his side, enveloping his jaw in his hand. Maybe, as some black leaders said, he had been guilty of putting too much stock in the value of economic security; that, in so doing, he had played down the importance of social equality, thereby alienating himself from some of these black leaders who had given their lives to a civil rights movement oriented basically toward winning social equality. And, to an extent, this was true. In the early stages of his drive toward the top in the labor movement, he *had* concentrated on the so-called bread-and-butter issues. This had been necessary to win the support of the white ethnics. But, really, there was nothing inherently contradictory in the approaches. He believed now, more than ever, that social equality and cultural fulfillment grew out of economic security for all, and not the other way around.

Then there was another influence, insidious yet helpful at the same time. It had been clear since 1977, the first year of the Carter administration, that the white middle class, which held the balance of voting power in the country, wanted the majority of benefits. And middle class white America was convinced that the few social and economic gains blacks had made—not so few from the white viewpoint, of course—were at the expense of middle-class whites. The tax revolts of the late 1970s, such as the California Proposition 13, were merely expressions of this sentiment. Consequently, from the beginning a major thrust of his labor leadership had been to convince the white middle class that the benefits and power they were seeking had to come from those who had it—the corporate structure of the country. And the best way to fight for this power was to join forces with those who needed power the most—the millions of blacks and other disadvantaged minorities.

This was also the message he had been attempting to bring to black leadership during the past few years. The trouble was, black leaders had not been listening to him because they were convinced middle-class white America was not listening to him; that they, the blacks, were being asked to de-emphasize their social demands while middle-class white America, including millions of union members, was solidifying its psychological and economic alliance with the power elite of the nation.

But he *knew* things were changing, *had* changed. Sentiment within the labor movement *had* taken a sharp turn to the left in the last few years. It couldn't be otherwise, considering the concessions Reagan and the supply-siders had forced upon organized labor in the past six years. And in his more than two years in office, Davidson had taken few steps in utilizing the government to change the climate created by Reagan. This was the key reason the separatist movement was so strong among blacks. They had lost faith in their government. The burden, therefore, was on him and organized labor, and other groups of like persuasion. Labor was ready to assume the lead. He would prove it at the AFL-CIO convention coming up in San Francisco in a couple of weeks. Prove it by the passage of specific resolutions which the majority of so-called experts were swearing couldn't be passed.

But first, he told himself, and the sooner the better, he was going to sit down with Preston Simmons and have a knockdown, drag-out conversation about the whole thing. Simmons understood where he was coming from; the job was to convince him that he had a chance of getting where he was going. The news announcer had said that Simmons was in Washington. He would attempt to locate him as soon as he reached his office.

He got up from the bed, letting the robe drop from his body, and stood naked before the mirrored wall. He liked his body, had always liked it, as far back as he could remember. And he had good reason to, he told himself now. His neck was muscular, his shoulders broad, his chest wide and rounded in the right places, his arms long and sinewy. His upper torso tapered into a slender waist and narrow hips. He wasn't quite as tall as he wished—only five feet ten—but this was because his thighs and legs had not attained the near-perfection of the rest of his body. His thighs were a little too heavy and his legs were a little too short. He shrugged his shoulders. What the hell. A person couldn't have everything. Knotting his forehead so that his brows came together above his deep-set grey eyes, he frowned at himself, then deliberately turned the frown into a smile. His face was almost as good as his body. Maybe a little too round, but his lips had a sensuality to their fullness and his nose was high-bridged and tapering. Broadening his smile into a grin, he glanced down at his genitals. He was well hung, as the boys in the plant used to say, recalling that in his youth in Southeast Chicago he had been tagged with the nickname "Nigger-Cock Rielinski". Later, when he had learned more about black idiom, he realized that the nickname should have been "Nigger-Dick Joe".

But seriously, he told himself, still staring into his eyes, he had come much further in life than he had imagined he would. The reality of his present far exceeded the dreams of his past. In the days after high school, in the middle sixties prior to going into the Marine Corps, he actually had wanted to be a policeman. In fact, he had taken and passed the police exam and was waiting to be called when he was drafted. At the time, he was working in an East Chicago steel mill where his father, Leonard Rielinski, was a union steward. And despite the fact that increasing numbers of Americans were growing sick of the war in Viet Nam, for him there was no possibility of attempting to beat the draft. His father, who was both affectionately and mockingly known as "America First" Rielinski—after a Chicago-area politician of that nickname who made a habit of running for every available office on both major party tickets—had imbued the son with his brand of patriotism, and there was no doubt that Joe would end up wearing a uniform.

But he had returned from the war, he recalled now, as opposed to the conflict as any draft resister. He had seen too much in Viet Nam: too many heartless and useless killings, too much squandering of public funds and neglect of public property, and a cynical destruction of the spirit of young men and women.

He returned to the bed and sat down, then stretched out on his stomach, folding his arm under his face. One element of his father's philosophy had been retained, he reminded himself now. Upon returning to the plant, he became an active member of the union. But where his father had really, deep down, been pro-company, he became rigidly pro-worker. It was during this period that he first began to forge his concepts about economic security and full employment being the starting point for all social and cultural progress in the United States. But he had kept most of these ideas to himself and fought strictly on the bread-and-butter issues. In 1973, at twenty-eight years of age, he was elected president of his local union. Later that year, despite his heavy schedule, he enrolled in a union leadership program at the University of Chicago. From that time and all during the years he served as district director, until he launched his fight in 1977 to take over the steelworker's union, he was an almost continuous student at the University, broadening his horizon with courses in politics, philosophy, economics, statistics, accounting and history. And as his insight deepened, his belief solidified that economic security was the starting point for advancing American democracy.

Immediately prior to launching his fight for control of the steelworkers' union, he recalled now, he had begun developing an alliance with the heads of the teachers' and public workers' unions, aiding them in their struggles to win meaningful collective bargaining agreements from stubborn local, state and federal governmental entities. These leaders, the most intellectual and among the most cunning in organized labor, were his staunchest allies when he made his big push for the top job in the AFL-CIO.

He rolled over on his back, locking his hands behind his head. If the public sector unions were among his strongest supporters, it was equally clear from which unions his strongest opposition was coming: the building trades and the teamsters, a new alliance led by his old nemesis, Michael S. Nelson. Looking back over the past decade, Rielinski realized that he and Nelson had been waging a battle to the death for control over organized labor since he won the presidency of the steelworkers' union. And this was as it should be, for Nelson was the undisputed leader of the unregenerate, old-line, right-wing forces in the labor movement. As president of the carpenters' union and head of the building trades council, he looked upon himself as the rightful heir to George Meany.

Rielinski smiled bitterly to himself, a picture of Nelson clear in his mind: long gray hair waving in the breeze, thin arms outstretched, bony chin thrust forward. A writer once had labeled Nelson the "Neanderthal Man of Organized Labor", and the name had stuck; yet few questioned the sharpness of his mind or the acid in his tongue. He often ranted, and not always in private circles, about "Niggers and Polacks getting together to the detriment of more deserving white folks." Rielinski sighed. Nelson was a problem, all right. He might as well face it. There was no way he could get his program passed in San Francisco without breaking Nelson's stranglehold on the building trades' or teamsters' delegations.

"Well, aren't you a beauty," Rosa's voice said from the doorway.

Rielinski spread his arms and legs. "Look what you can get for nothing," he said.

Rosa smiled at him, brown eyes sparkling in her mobile Italian face. She had an apron tied around her waist, over her thin night-gown, and one of her large breasts had won the uneven battle with a delicate shoulder strap. Looking at the reddish-brown nipple of her exposed breast, Rielinski felt his penis stiffen and begin a slow elevation. After fifteen years of marriage, he bet he could still set a record in getting an erection for his wife. It was a damn shame, he smiled to himself.

Rosa glanced at his rising penis, moved swiftly to the bed and made a playful grab for it. Instinctively, he closed his legs, but seized her arm and pulled her down on top of him, appreciating the lush softness of her body. She struggled against him, pulling out of his arms.

"No, no," she said. "Breakfast is ready."

He slapped her ass. "Don't I have a choice of food?"

She laughed, tapped his chin lightly, and got up from the bed. "The food in the kitchen will get cold," she said, "but this has a built-in burner. So first things first, huh?" She gave him a coquettish grin and marched out of the bedroom.

Still lying on the bed, Rielinski shook his head from side to side, smiling. He was glad their relationship had come through the fire and passion of the early years, through the misunderstandings of the middle years, to the freedom and ease of the present. They had been married in 1972, the year before he became president of his local union—Joe Rielinski, the dogged, determined Polish veteran to Rosa Maita, the fiery, beautiful Italian school teacher. From the beginning, they both had wanted children, tried desperately for children, but to no avail. When the doctor had concluded that she was barren, he couldn't accept it. Of course he didn't tell her that he couldn't accept it, but somehow she had known. And his knowledge that she knew lay like a wedge between them, stifling communication. Gradually they drifted apart.

He began to stay at the union hall later than usual and to spend unnecessary hours in the library. His few spare hours, which should have have been spent with her, he began spending with the boys, and then with the girls. He watched her withdrawing into herself, but he was unable to say the word or provide the touch which would halt the inward movement. So he had watched miserably as she, who had always enjoyed the world outside her eyes, began to live exclusively in a world within her mind.

He got up from the bed and put on his robe and stood

looking again in the mirrored wall. He supposed he would always remember the episode which removed the wedge between them and started them on the road to recovery. During the depth of her depression, when he was coming home less and less, she had gotten in the habit of keeping the dinette table set for two at all times—all day long, whether at mealtimes or not—a plaintive cry to him from the locked regions of her soul. And, somehow, he had summoned sufficient perception and courage to heed the cry.

One afternoon, when he knew she was at the store, he had come home about two o'clock, sat down at the table, folded his napkin across his knees, and waited for her. When she came into the house, she stopped in the kitchenette door, looking at him. It was a look of mixed bewilderment and surprise. He stared back at her, hoping that his eyes revealed sincerity, tenderness, and a prayer for forgiveness.

"Rosa," he said, "I came home because I am so hungry. I haven't had a proper meal in a long, long time."

He was watching her eyes as he spoke. He knew his actions could cause her to go either way: bring her back to the open world she loved or lock her forever within the closet of herself. Then, like shadows fading before sunlight escaping from behind a cloud, the surprise and bewilderment moved from her eyes and joy entered: a sparkling joy, emblazoned with tears. She dropped the bags she was carrying, ran over and threw her arms around his neck. "Joe, you came back to me!" she cried. "Joe, you came back to me!"

And so he had.

Now, smiling bitter-sweet at the memory, he turned away from the mirror and headed out of the bedroom toward the kitchen. Rosa met him at the door.

"I told you the food was getting cold," she said, half perturbed. "What have you been doing in here?"

He placed an arm across her shoulder.

"Thinking how much I love you," he said.

190

Chapter 19

10:00 A.M., Tuesday, October 6, 1987

PRESTON SIMMONS had never been a person to observe birthdays and holidays with much enthusiasm nor underline dates on calenders with undue relish. To him events made their mark on history more by the enduring nature of their contributions than by the beginnings or endings of specific occurrences. For this reason, he was surprised that on this Tuesday morning, sitting in the living room of his suite in Hotel Washington getting ready to go to the airport for an eleven o'clock flight to Los Angeles, he was preoccupied with the fact that it had been exactly two days short of two weeks since he had received the call to serve as chief negotiator for a separate black state. But he supposed in this case he could excuse himself for his date-keeping tendencies for, by any measuring stick, the past two weeks had been the most important of his life.

He leaned back on the couch, locked his hands behind his head, and placed his feet on the cocktail table. He felt nervous. The reports on the demonstrations—coming from Dr. Patten in Atlanta, Albert James in Los Angeles, and Rubye in Chicago—gave cause for serious concern, for each had stated that there was a tenseness in the air, an indication of impending violence. But even more alarming were the reports that large numbers of blacks were among the counter-demonstrators. Apparently Jim Sneed's call, publicly issued on Sunday evening, was having a definite effect. He had not received a report from Muhammed in New York City, but he had heard from

Marcus Jackson, who had been dispatched to that city more to keep an eye on Muhammed than to direct demonstrations. Jackson's report was similar to the others; however, he also stated that Muhammed didn't appear to be taking a personal interest in the demonstrations, but was leaving these activities to his lieutenants. This action, or lack of it, was in character with Muhammed, Simmons realized, since Muhammed had indicated at last Saturday's meeting that he didn't consider demonstrations to be the most important project for the Council to engage in at this time.

Simmons picked up a glass from the cocktail table, got up from the couch and moved toward the refrigerator with the intention of getting a drink of sherry; however, upon reaching the refrigerator, he poured a glass of water instead. He couldn't permit himself to get in the habit of drinking alcohol this early in the day, he told himself. There were too many things to do, and to think about. He went back to the couch and sat down.

The other project they had agreed upon at last Saturday's Council meeting was moving ahead satisfactorily. On Monday, Bob Griggs and Ted Blackwell had contacted representatives of selected UN member nations and launched the plan to have the U.S. government charged with violating the civil liberties of Council members should they be hit with charges of conspiracy or treason against the United States. Nigeria, Sweden, Brazil, Mexico and China had agreed to carry the ball on this one. Simmons smiled. That was covering the whole front: North America, South America, Europe, Asia and Africa. Considering the breadth of support, no wonder Muhammed wanted to ask for resolutions from foreign countries. He sighed. But the support was more symbolic than real. The lack of UN effectiveness during the past twenty years was tragic testimony to the fact that the United States and her friends still carried the big stick in world affairs.

The phone rang. Bob Griggs was on the line.

"Thought you were on your way to Atlanta, Bob?"

"I am. Getting ready to leave now. But I'm glad I caught you before you left for Los Angeles."

"Why?"

"Joe Rielinski just called the Council office looking for you. Says he must see you right away. Today. Immediately."

"You told him I was heading for Los Angeles?"

"Yes. But he insists on seeing you."

"Did he say specifically what he wants?"

"No. But you *know* what he wants."

Simmons sighed. "Yes, I know. What do you think, Bob?"

There was a pause on the other end of the line. "Well, you gotta do it one day soon. Now is as good a time as ever."

"You're probably right. I've had a meeting with Hilda Larsen of the National Orgainzation for Women. And she wants another one, tomorrow, in Los Angeles. So I might as well see Rielinski today. I'll take a later plane out. Where does he want this meeting to take place?"

"Anywhere you select. I'm to call him back and tell him the time and place."

"Okay, Bob. Tell him here, in my hotel suite. An hour from now."

"Got you. See you, Preston. And good luck."

"Thanks, Bob."

Simmons had been in the same room with Rielinski a number of times. In fact, on one occasion shortly after Rielinski had been elected president of his East Chicago local union, he had spent three of four hours alone with him, interviewing him for a profile which later was published in *Issues* magazine. And each time he saw Rielinski, he had no reason to change the impression he had formed during that interview, some fourteen years ago. When interviewing a person, he had a tendency to search for a single word which in his mind best summed up the interviewee. *Strength* was the word he had selected for Rielinski. Strength of character. Strength of purpose. And strength of intellect.

Now, sitting in his hotel suite facing Rielinski across a cocktail table on which sat two glasses of water, examining the man's strong face and observing his rippling neck muscles

193

through his open shirt collar, he realized that Rielinski had changed very little through the years. He had grown bolder, somewhat more confident, both changes seeming to add to his strength of purpose. If his years of dealing in the intricacies of union politics had forced him to deal in shit, probably subtracting from his strength of character, he had been smart enough to keep his image clean.

Rielinski, sitting in the chair where Hilda Larsen had sat on Sunday night, cupped his chin in his hand and leaned forward. "I see things are heating up," he said. "Everybody is expecting trouble. I'm talking about the policemen in the lobby and the one outside your door."

"I didn't order them," Simmons said.

Rielinski smiled, his grey eyes sparkling. "But you didn't dismiss them either," he said.

There was another thing different about Rielinski, Simmons thought. He seemed to be less intense than he remembered him, projecting a genuine sense of humor. He returned the labor leader's smile. "No, I didn't release them," he said.

Rielinski leaned back in his chair. "Okay, let's get down to brass tacks. Trouble is coming to this country. Now, I don't mind trouble, but I hate to see good effort wasted. This country belongs to all of us, to you as much as me. It needs straightening out, true. And that's job enough for all of us. Preston, I'm here to officially ask you and your people to join forces with me and my people to get the job done."

Rielinski had spoken in his famous whip-like style, as though he were on a platform, yet at the same time his words communicated a certain intimacy, a person-to-person appeal. Simmons was affected by the man's directness.

"Joe, I appreciate your getting to the point," he said. "So I'll get to the point. As things stand now, I don't see any chance of our getting together, if you are talking about the Black American Council backing off from our attempts to negotiate a separate nation."

"Aren't there any conditions under which you'd reconsider?" Rielinski asked.

194

"Yes, there are some conditions," Simmons said. "The ones I stated at my televised press conference Thursday before last. But frankly, Joe, I don't believe you are prepared to deliver those conditions. White Americans aren't ready to live equitably with black Americans. And I doubt if they ever will be."

Rielinski leaned forward again. His voice was quiet when he spoke. "What do you want, Preston—guarantees? There are no guarantees in this life." Suddenly, he smiled. "But anyway, Preston, how do you know whether I can meet your conditions? Ask me some questions? I just might have more going for me than you think."

Simmons got up from the couch, went over to the refrigerator, took out a half-filled bottle of sherry and set it on the cocktail table. "More than an hour ago I told myself it was too early to drink," he said. "It isn't now. All I have is sherry. Do you want that, or should I order you something?"

Rielinski laughed. "Man, you know I'm married to an Italian woman. Just try offering me anything else but wine."

Simmons smiled, again reminding himself of Rielinski's improved sense of humor. He took their glasses from the table, poured out the water and poured in the wine. There was nothing in the world he liked better than a good conversation, especially a one-on-one confrontation with a person whom he considered to be his intellectual equal.

"Okay, Joe," he said, taking a sip of wine, "you are always talking about economic security and full employment, about the healing powers of these things, how they can cure our social, cultural and, to a certain degree, our moral problems. Why do you think we have failed to accomplish full employment, especially since a Democrat was in the White House before Reagan and one is there now?"

Rielinski gave Simmons a quizzical look, as though he were somewhat surprised at Simmons' summary of his pet theme. Then the look left his eyes as he prepared himself to accept Simmons' challenge, more than to grasp the opportunity to talk things out.

"I've never been able to understand the failure of blacks and progressives at the Democratic Party Convention of 1976," he said, "the year Carter was first nominated. Oh, I know Carter came into the Convention riding an anti-big government wave, yet, at the same time, the Democratic Party platform called for implementing full employment, as embodied in the Humphrey-Hawkins bill. Yet blacks and progressives didn't raise the proper questions about how this concept was to be implemented."

"What blacks and what progressives failed to raise the proper questions?" Simmons asked. "And what were the proper questions?"

Rielinski took a sip of wine for the first time. "Answering your questions in reverse order," he said, "raising the proper questions would have meant introducing a new theme into the convention, and into the campaign which followed. It would have meant pointing out that full employment really meant, at least, coming up with new sources for additional jobs, other than through stimulating the private sector and expanding public service employment."

"What new theme should they have introduced?"

"Well, for a starter," Rielinski replied, "the progressives and blacks should have called for using the regulatory agencies to expand employment in the public utility areas—in the light, gas and telephone industries, by turning profit dollars into jobs. Because these industries are in fact protected monopolies, a good case could have been made for this proposal. American working people have always resented the way these companies deal with the public, especially since the people can't switch to another source of supply when service is unsatisfactory. This move, at that time, could have prepared the people for the demands we must now make—nationalization of the utilities, railroads, airlines and the oil industries."

"Now tell me who were the blacks and progressives who should have called for these things?" Simmons asked.

"Well, people like George Meany, Senator Harris and Jesse Jackson should have led the call. And they should have been backed up by people like you and me."

196

"But we weren't at the convention," Simmons said.

"I know we weren't," Rielinski replied, "but we had influence, even at that time. You were busy writing a novel, and I was busy scheming to get control of the steelworkers' union." He smiled.

Simmons felt himself smiling in return. "You're right, of course," he replied, "about the questions which should have been raised. But you know why those theories weren't advanced. The Republicans were saying that to use public service jobs to boost employment was just another way of perpetuating big government. And the Democrats avoided the subject to keep from getting trapped in a contradiction of their own making, in view of the fact that their standard bearer was anti-government. So the Democrats tried to outdo the Republicans in pretending that full-employment could be brought about by stimulating the private sector. And despite the passage of a watered-down Humphrey-Hawkins bill, they are still talking that crap, while generation after generation of black children are being stifled by a welfare society."

Rielinski took another sip of wine and looked hard at Simmons. "Be fair, Preston," he said. "You are talking like you've forgotten the Reagan years and their effect on the minds, and pocketbooks, of workers. Remember the concessions workers in the auto and steel industries have been forced to make? Only a few workers now believe that private enterprise, left to its own devices, can keep the economy going and expanding. I honestly believe that the overwhelming majority of the American people are ready to accept nationalization of the basic industries."

"Do you *really* think they're ready to go *that far*, Joe?"

"If not that far, they're at least ready to accept control of those industries by government-management-labor committees. The point is, Americans are finally beginning to realize that the forces shaping and directing the economy of our country, and the economies of the world, are too complex to be permitted to operate by themselves, without constant, expert monitoring and control. This month's AFL-CIO convention is going to be more than a convention. It is going to bring together a majority of the liberal and progressive forces of this country to develop plans for a new day. These plans are being worked out right now. The supply-siders have had their day, and failed. Now it's our turn."

"Which groups are joining you?" Simmons asked.

"All of the major church groups, the major women's organizations, and the intellectual societies. The black groups are the only ones that are missing. We need you."

Simmons refilled their glasses, avoiding answering the question implicit in Rielinski's last statement. "A number of leading blacks have serious problems with you," he said. "They complain that your preoccupation with the economic question has caused you to deemphasize important social questions. They further charge that you have taken the wrong position on questions like affirmative action and school busing solely to endear yourself to ethnic whites and advance yourself in the labor movement."

"What do you think?" Rielinski asked quietly.

"I've always believed you to be sincere. Additionally, I've agreed with most of your positions. As you know, I've long stated, and written, that some way had to be found to bring black and white workers together. But I must admit that your approach always seemed to place the burden of the first move on blacks. And that attitude among white progressives and liberals, as much as anything else, has caused blacks to despair with this country."

Rielinski nodded his head. "I know. But whites have been so polarized on the race question since the late sixties that I figured emphasis had to be placed on the one thing of *major* common interest to both blacks and whites. And if I appeared to lean toward whites, it was deliberate." He smiled. "After all, they are in the majority." The smile faded. "But thanks to you, things are turning around now."

"How is that?"

"It's like the late fifties and early sixties," Rielinski replied. "When Martin Luther King and his followers proved that they were ready to sacrifice their lives to end legal discrimination, well-meaning whites joined in the struggle. They are ready to join with you now—to advance democracy in this country."

Simmons got up from the couch and walked across the room, turned and came back to the couch and sat down. He felt charged up, like he always felt when explosive ideas were picking away at his brain. It always boiled down to what *blacks had to do* in order for whites to respect them enough to believe blacks deserved equality. In the fifties, black leaders believed whites would respond affirmatively if blacks believed they, the blacks, deserved equality. In the sixties, it was felt that if blacks pushed boldly for power, whites would be willing to share the wealth of the land. Now, Rielinski was telling him that because blacks were carrying their quest for self-determination to the point of demanding a separate nation, whites were willing, at last, to deal with them as equals. It was something to think about.

"Okay, Joe," he said, "so you think you have the leaders of most of the liberal and progressive white groups lined up with you to turn this country around. *But how do you know?*

"Attitudes have changed," Rielinski replied. "They have been changing for a number of years. Maybe you can't see it, but I can. I've been observing these changes from close up."

"I'm waiting to be convinced," Simmons said. "So expound, man, expound. Give me some history."

Rielinski took a long drink from his glass. His eyes were sparkling from the intensity of his thinking. "I began to notice a change in the late seventies," he said, "when jobs began to disappear from the basic industries, especially in steel, because of foreign intervention and technological advances. When jobs continued to disappear from steel, auto, textile and other industries throughout the early eighties, and the captains of industry, because of their multi-national relationships, did little to stop the trend, labor leaders, at my prodding as you will recall, began to urge workers to save their unions and them-selves by attempting to bring these problems to the bargaining table."

"But you didn't have any success in these endeavors," Simmons pointed out.

"I know we didn't," Rielinski replied. "That's why the workers are ready to follow me in my new approach. Turn these industries over to the government, so the whole country can sink or swim together."

Simmons stood up from the couch again. "It doesn't seem to me that white workers have learned all you say they have," he said. "If they had, they wouldn't have opposed affirmative action programs so strenuously during the past few years."

Rielinski held up his hand. "I agree that white workers have opposed affirmative action programs. In a job-scarce economy, where nobody had essential protection, white workers believed they had to fight anything which threatened their seniority and other hard-won advantages. But when blacks fought back, and also showed no sign of relenting, something had to give. A compromise had to be reached. I believe that compromise has been reached—a compromise which should have been the main program in the first place."

"And that is?"

"The majority of white workers now understand that the only way both black and white workers can acquire the benefits they deserve is through an enlarged base of resources, guaranteed by the government."

Simmons sat down again. He looked hard into Rielinski's eyes. "Do you really believe the majority of white workers have learned these lessons?"

Rielinski stared back at him. "Indeed I do," he said.

"And you believe you'll be able to get your program past the delegates in San Francisco?"

"I'm confident I will."

Simmons pulled his eyes away from Rielinski, picked up his glass and took a drink. Rielinski didn't appear to be faking his confidence, and he probably wasn't. Throughout his career Rielinski had made a habit of coming up with bold answers to hard questions. Take, for instance, the disability/retirement consolidation plan he had been instrumental in getting introduced into the 99th Congress in 1985. Known as the Comprehensive Disability and Retirement Act (CDRA), it was a proposal to create an entirely new disability/retirement program out of existing systems: social security, railroad retirement, federal civil service retirement, various state, county and city retirement plans, and the major private industry pension plans. Practically everybody had scoffed at the legislation when it was first introduced—by Senator Sam Leavitt—but now it was given an even chance of passage. He was sure that this was one of the programs Rielinski intended to push at the up-coming AFL-CIO convention.

"Joe, I have to take my hat off to you for the way you have stuck with that consolidated disability/retirement program," Simmons said. "That program, if passed, will not only kill a lot of sacred cows but will close the till to many sticky fingers, especially in the labor movement."

Rielinski smiled. "I know. But the whole idea is so logical. First, all workers, public and private, should work under the same type of disability/retirement plan. It cuts down on resentment. Second, the method of payment and the rate of payment should be as nearly the same as possible. This is key. For example, a lot of hell is being raised about the increases in social security taxes. Yet, most federal and some state workers pay a much higher rate into their plans and you don't hear the same hue and cry, because these plans are looked upon as being much superior to social security. I'm also convinced that it is much more desirable to have workers contribute to the fund than to have employers, public or private, pay the whole freight, even though the workers have given up other benefits for such agreements. To have contributed gives a retired worker a sense of accomplishment. Oh yes, a single plan, transferable from job to job, public or private, is the way to go."

"And controlled by the government or a public corporation," Simmons said.

"Right," Rielinski agreed. "Sound investments and an end to all these money scandals."

"Good work, if you can get it, Joe," Simmons said. "But you have a long way to go, on that and many of your other programs. What about Mike Nelson and his group and John Radicci and the teamsters? It is my understanding that these two groups hold the balance of power. Mike is against most of your economic programs and the teamsters haven't agreed to your disability/retirement program. A narrow victory won't do you much good—especially when you're trying to change a country. You've got to win big in San Francisco, and I don't believe you can."

Rielinski sat back in his chair. "Mike is a problem, I admit," he said. "But I'll find a way to overcome him."

"That's not good enough, Joe," Simmons said. "Before the Black Council would even *discuss* your proposition, they'd have to have some guarantees. Now how are you going to handle Mike Nelson?"

Rielinski smiled, tightly. "If you walk through a bed of snakes time and time again and don't die from snakebite, it proves you know something about snakes," he said.

Simmons laughed. This guy really had developed a sense of humor. "Very good," he said. "But it proves no such thing. It might merely indicate that what you thought were poisonous snakes were the harmless garden variety."

Rielinski's eyes were serious, yet there was a glint of amusement in them when he replied. "You know something about the members of the AFL-CIO Executive Board and Executive Council. How would you classify them?"

"You know how to stay out of the way of dangerous snakes, all right," Simmons replied. And they laughed together.

Simultaneously, Simmons and Rielinski stopped laughing, looking sheepishly at each other. "I know," Simmons said. "This matter is too vital for laughter. But what do you want me to say?"

"I want you to say yes."

"I know. But you know I can't. Not now."

"That sounds like you believe you might be able to, some day soon."

Simmons shook his head. "I didn't say that. I said before the Black Council would even *discuss* your proposal, you'd have to give us some guarantees. This is the beginning of the second week in October. And you'll be having your convention during the last week of this month. Let's talk after the convention is over."

Rielinski stood up. "Is that the best you can do?" he asked.

"That's the best I can do."

"Things are moving fast. They might get out of hand before that time."

"I know."

"Why don't you call off the demonstrations? Sort of coast until after the convention?"

Simmons shook his head. "I can't do that."

"You're taking a big chance, you know."

"I know. But it's a chance I have to take," Simmons replied.

Chapter 20

10:00 A.M., Sunday, October 11, 1987

LONG AGO, *in a past so distant it seems like a dream, when you were absorbing the precise theories of computer logic and convincing yourself that the strict disciplines of the physical sciences were not the domain of the white world alone, you developed a disdain for the occult, harbored contempt for the mystic, and closed your ears to the voices of the spirit calling to you from the land of your fathers. But you were blessed, as few are blessed, and soon learned—or at least permitted yourself to feel you had learned—that the atoms of the body, the molecules of the mind and the elements of the spirit are parts of the same world, and that the mysteries of one will not be unraveled until the door shutting out knowledge of the others is finally unlocked. And it is for this reason you feel in the secret recesses of your being that nothing is ever lost, that each thought, each act somehow influences everything that occurs in the universe.*

So, now, Sunday again, calmed by the quiet hours of morning, sitting in the living room of your suite in Hotel Washington, a room which is more a place of refuge than of abode, you tell yourself that although in one sense you have lived two lives during the past week, in another sense it has been only one life, probably more inextricably intertwined by the apparent contradictions. One life has been concerned with directing the nationwide demonstrations to make the powers that be more susceptible to the demands for a separate state, while the other has been aimed at forging a relationship with a woman who is both familiar and strange, new and old, in the eternal battle between man and woman. And because you have been occupied with both at the same time, you realize that both lives have suffered, yet have been immeasurably enriched by the influences of the one on the other. Nevertheless, during the hectic week just passed, neither life has progressed to your satisfaction. But you accpet this, for your experience has taught you that nothing is ever as definite as wishing expects nor as fulfilling as hoping demands.

But your acceptance carries with it a feeling of guilt because the balance, the tidy evenness by which you govern your existence, has not been maintained; for in this hour of calm you are reflecting more on what has happened between you and Hilda Larsen, the woman, than on what has occurred in the struggle for your people.

It is Tuesday night in Los Angeles, following a session with Albert James to assess the results of a street demonstration which has extended from a long afternoon into a tiring evening. Dinner completed, you are sitting in a quiet restaurant talking to her, having permitted analyses of specific incidents to transform themselves into a discussion of things in general.

"It might not be a good idea to value things too highly," you say; "for when you do, it is too painful to give them up."

"Is that your formula for living," she asks—"don't get into things for fear you will have to give them up? It seems like a plastic way to live, or rather, to not live."

"I know," you reply, smiling. "But believe me, it's better to have never loved than to have loved and lost."

She shakes her head. "There is another way. You don't have to let them take the things you want away from you. You don't have to give them up."

"That calls for clarification," you say.

"You are talking about going on living after your loss," she

205

says. *"There is another way, you know. You don't have to go on living. You can die fighting to keep the things you want."*

You laugh. *"It always comes back to the basic question,"you say. "Whether living at any price is preferable to dying."*

Then, after a few more cocktails and slightly more intimate talk, the conversation returned to the same general theme.

"Only fools apply revolutionary tactics to evolutionary situations,"you say.

She smiles sweetly. *"Probably true. But on the other hand, cowards are the ones who keep revolutionary situations from coming into existence by constantly engaging in evolutionary tactics. Am I correct in assuming that you are not a coward?"*

The next night, in San Francisco, you are feeling poetic. The demonstrations have gone well. At her urging, a number of women's groups have joined the demonstrations, not to support your demands but to voice their support of your right to make them. You are in a taxicab, returning to your respective hotels from a session with a newspaper editor, and in your poetic mood you are strangely reflective, putting into words something you have not thought about in a long time.

"I believe,"you say, "we exist simultaneously at different levels of consciousness. And each level of consciousness has its own continuity."

Her leg brushed against your leg, momentarily breaking your trend of thought. *"How's that?"she asks.*

"How's what?"

"What proof do you have for what you have just said."

"The best proof in the world,"you reply. "From my own experience. For example, often when I get a fever from a cold or some other bacteria or virus, I go back and connect with thoughts I had and experiences I went through the last time I had a fever. Things I don't think about at all when I don't have a fever. It is also the same with dreams. In dreams I often complete philosophical analyses I have started in other dreams, continue experiences I have begun nights or months before."

She leans against you. *"Ummm,"she says, "I understand*

206

*what you mean. The same things happen to me. But tell me,
Preston, have you ever gotten the impression that you were on
the verge of a major breakthrough in communication, that if
you could just get past a certain barrier, you could experience
things that few persons have experienced before?"*

"In what way?"

*"That you are about to free yourself from self-entrapment,
almost have the ability to move vertically from the present into
the past or future, and horizontally into the minds of other
people."*

*"Yes," you reply, aware of the eagerness in your voice. "My
most vivid impression of having lived before relates to a recur-
ring dream. In this dream I am a slave trying to escape from a
plantation by way of the Mississippi River. For some unknown
reason, I am tied to the propeller of a boat and I am stifling
from the murky waters swirling about me. That's where all the
dream sequences end. I suppose in an earlier life I drowned
trying to escape."*

She touches your leg, ever so lightly.

"You poor dear," she says in a soft voice.

*In St. Louis, on Thursday, the demonstrations do not go
well at all. The march from the black neighborhoods to the
federal building is impeded by mobs of angry whites. Hundreds
of blacks join the whites and violence erupts on a massive scale.
Scores are injured. In the forefront of the march, you miraculously escape with only a few scratches. After the legal
maneuvers of charges and countercharges are out of the way,
you decide to have dinner in your hotel room. Since she has a
room in the same hotel, after genteel bickering, the decision is
reached that she will have dinner with you. But the soft moods
of the other nights have flown before the violence, and when
the time for the inevitable self-revealing conversation arrives,
you are filled with a strange harshness.*

*"A person who looks upon the possession of power as an end
in itself," you say, "is much more difficult to deal with than a
person who aspires to power for a specific purpose. If you can*

207

somehow accommodate the latter's viewpoint, convince him that you support his philosophy, then you can work with him and be relatively free from his suspicions. However, on the other hand, the only way you can safely coexist with a person who yearns for power for itself, is to inhabit that person's skin."

"Yes, but is that an advantage?" she asks. "I mean, if you are dealing with a person whose ideas are repugnant to you?"

"Of course not. Not if you really want to advance a certain point of view. However, although the guy who wants power for a specific reason might be more dangerous to your cause, you at least know where he stands. But the other guy will cut your throat for no rhyme or reason."

Again, a little later, you say: "To believe that the creation was as it is described in the Bible is to do a disservice to the wonder and majesty of the universe."

"Why do you say that?"

"The creation as described in the Bible is extremely simplistic. Beautiful. But simplistic. The story in the Bible doesn't begin to approach the grand scope of the physical universe, to say nothing of the wonder of the human creation."

"Maybe that's the reason why the story is so simple," she says. "Because words and ideas could not be found to depict the complexity and grandeur of the subject matter."

You smile at her. You can tell she has gotten your point. "Exactly," you say. "We don't understand these things. And until we do, we should say we don't. Not go around creating images for a knowledge we don't possess. All else is hypocrisy on the grandest scale."

She looks at you, her eyes consuming. "What you say might sound logical," she says, "but it stops short of truth, and you know it. To follow what you say to its logical conclusion would also say that since the mystery of the human existence is so complex and so frightening, the most compatible person is one who can keep us from looking into ourselves; that the most rewarding experiences are those which keep us distracted, prevent us from probing into the core of our being."

You smile at her. "I suppose you have me there, because if

208

what I said was true," you reply, "by implication things like making love, having children, building governments, etc., are only make-believe artifacts with which man has surrounded himself to keep from looking into the hell, or heaven, of himself; because he cannot look too deeply into himself and still live, or at least, remain sane. Such logic would doom humans to a life of inaction."

She holds up her hand in a manner which indicates that she is ignoring what you just said, although both of you know she isn't. You realize she has grasped a thought which she must state before it eludes her. "As an indication that a person doesn't know where the core of his/her being is located," she says, "consider just what part of you you are talking to when you speak to yourself. Are you talking to your face, eyes, forehead? Or to your brain, or heart? Or some other inner repository of yourself? Or are you talking to all of these things at the same time?" Her eyes are sparkling.

Now, it is your turn to hold up your hand. "You talk too much," you say. "This is neither the time nor the place for me to answer that."

When you arrive in Chicago on Friday afternoon, Rubye has everything under control. She has scheduled a rally for one o'clock at the Dirksen building on South Dearborn in the Loop and a solidarity parade through the black neighborhoods for Saturday morning. Things, however, are not going well at all in New York City. According to newscasts and confirmed by a phone call to Marcus Jackson from O'Hare Airport, police are battling your demonstrators in that city. Jackson swears the police are acting like they have orders to go on the attack.

When you, with Hilda at your side, arrive at the Dirksen Building shortly after three o'clock the rally is winding down. The moderate-sized crowd is surprisingly good-natured and you are wondering how the reaction can be so different in New York and Chicago on the same day. Rubye is standing on the sidewalk surrounded by a knot of dignitaries when you join her. After the dignitaries have dispersed and you, Rubye and

Hilda are alone, Rubye says teasingly, but somewhat sharply: "The last I saw you two you were together in a hotel room. Have you been together ever since?"

You are surprised at the depth of Hilda's blush. "Don't be silly," she says. "I'm not really with Preston. I'm observing the demonstrations for my organization."

Rubye chuckles. "And the best way to observe them is up front with the head man, ain't that right, now?"

Hilda glances at you, but you deliberately avert your eyes, so she replies: "Right. I always heard that the front seats were the best seats."

Rubye gives Hilda a sideways glance. "Are you making any headway in your campaign?" she asks.

"What campaign?" Hilda asks.

"Have you forgotten so soon? The campaign to get us to forget about the separate nation and join you?"

Before Hilda can answer, you enter the conversation. "Hilda hasn't been proselyting since her initial efforts failed Sunday night. All week she has been the courteous guest."

"And you have been the gracious host," Hilda says.

Rubye looks intently at the two of you, then she laughs. "A person would think I'm jealous," she says. "And how could I be? After all, I was the one who brought you to his hotel room. Right?"

"Right," Hilda replies.

And you take them by their arms, Rubye on your right and Hilda on your left, and guide them to the waiting car for the trip to your hotels.

In the early hours after nightfall, the three of you, in the company of two bodyguards, tour the city, you and Rubye pointing out to Hilda sights of general interest and places you revered in a time long past. You even take her across 79th Street and show her the Brown Girl Lounge, but you do not enter.

And when the night grows relaxing with October coolness, you pick up junk food—hamburgers, ribs and shrimps—and, *giggling like teenagers, go to your home. And there amid the memories of Margaret, the three of you eat and talk and drink under the aura of a soothing companionship, bask in a soothing relationship, almost eerie because of its intensity and intimacy. And in the atmosphere of this relationship, you recount to them a dream you have never before revealed to a living soul.*

"In this dream, shortly before Margaret's death," you say, "I had a vision of Margaret and Preston Junior at a funeral, supposedly my own. Margaret is leaning on Preston Junior's arm. The only trouble is, Margaret looks much younger than she was at the time and Preston Junior much older—so that they appear to be about the same age."

"How do you figure that?" Rubye asks.

"I have thought and thought about it," you say. "I have finally come to the conclusion that in Margaret's mind, something important in our relationship died long ago—long before her physical death and, of course, long before mine."

When you finish speaking you are observing them closely. Rubye laughs, hysterically, and covers her face with her hand. Hilda is looking straight ahead, almost as though transfixed, but her eyes are glistening with tears.

"I'm so sorry," she says. "So sorry for her, and for you."

So now, in the sweet solitude of Sunday morning, savoring the memory of the wanderings of the spirit and the cleverness of the tongue which the new relationship has brought forth, you realize that the harsh things of the past week—the feet-numbing marches, the throat-parching shouts, the head-cracking attacks—are somewhat reduced in your remembering, like muddy water made almost clear by the sieves of a filter. And this, you know, despite philosophizing to the contrary, is not as it should be.

Suddenly, you are filled with a consuming sadness which tingles the nostrils and blurs the eyes, for you realize that surrender to reality-altering reflection is a luxury you no longer can afford; that though tendency toward such reflection will follow you all the days of your life, you must bar your mind

211

against its beguiling entrapment, like a curtain shutting out a glimpse into an enchanted land. So placing your head in your hands and closing your eyes tight against intruding visions, you feel a shudder go through your body; then the shudder passes, like a person shaking off a chill which has run its course.

And when you open your eyes, the world is real again.

Chapter 21

1:30 P.M., Sunday, October 11, 1987

GENERAL BRADFORD Weyland, retired, sat in his big chair behind his massive desk and surveyed his large office, which extended approximately fifty feet in front and more than twenty feet on each side of him. The office was vulgar in its opulence, he told himself, as he had done many times before. Yet, even as he reminded himself of the ostentatiousness of his surroundings, he could feel a glint of satisfaction in his eyes, for this was the kind of vulgarity he took pride in—the kind of comfort he believed he deserved after nearly forty years of service to his country and more than fifty years of conscientious dedication to the American way of life.

Everything about the office was indeed of the highest quality, he reminded himself, suppressing his pride of ownership and appraising the office with the cool objectivity of which any military man worth his salt should be capable. A deep-pile wool rug of luxuriant gold stretched from the wall behind his desk to the doorway which opened into his secretary's office, the continuity of the carpet broken only by a bubbling fountain in the front right corner, around which an artistic arrangement of purple cyclamen, blue hyacinths, red gloxinias and pink begonias grew in dense glory. Large ferns were positioned strategically along the walls of the office and potted plants—

some of which he could not call by name—hung from the ceiling, positioned in such a manner that they did not interfere with the recessed lights which could be dimmed or brightened by switches under the eave of his desk. The walls of the office were composed of imported heavy oak slabs, deliberately polished to a dull finish. Other switches or buttons under the eave of his desk could open panels in the wall to reveal a huge television screen, a safe, bookcases and a doorway to living quarters. The doorway to the living quarters—composed of a sitting room, bath and bedroom—opened from the rear wall of the office, behind his desk.

The only other furnishings in the office were three large leather chairs, facing the desk, unwaveringly arranged four feet apart and ten feet from the desk—close enough so that conversation could be heard without effort, yet far enough away to preclude unwanted intimacy. He didn't believe in couches or conference tables in private offices, especially in his. When the rare occasion existed for him to talk to more than three persons at a time, he used a conference room; and when intimacy was required, he used his living quarters. Proper order had to be maintained at any cost.

General Weyland leaned back in his chair, enjoying its protective hugeness and relishing the quietness which surrounded him. It was early Sunday afternoon. He suspected he was the only person on the floor on which his office was located, and probably was one of only a dozen or so people in the entire building, located on North Michigan Avenue in Chicago. In any case, he knew he was the only employee of Services International on the job today. And that was the way he wanted it. He could reflect alone, in the inspiring atmosphere of his office, without interference from his secretary, subordinate officers, clients and other well-meaning persons of that ilk. Of course, all of these people had to be dealt with, and with as much courtesy as was essential to the success of his mission, but that was no reason for him to play down the fact that the most important ideas had been hatched in his own brain and carried through because of his iron will.

214

He was the executive vice-president of Services International, and as such he realized he was one of the most powerful men in America. Yet, few among the masses of Americans had ever heard his name, not many persons in high places were aware of his existence, and even fewer were acquainted with the nature of his business. He smiled wryly. That was okay with him. *He* knew what Services International was about.

Leaning forward across his desk, he removed the pen from a monogrammed pen-and-ink set and began scratching on a pad. Objectively, he supposed, Services International was one of those select few organizations which were in the business of mixing the cement to hold the military-industrial complex together, on an international scale. Although he didn't close his ears to the language of his detractors—in fact, he often used their terminology when thinking about some of his projects—he was more than satisfied with his job; proud of the fact that his military experience had prepared him to serve as a liaison between the military and major manufacturers of military equipment. He also considered it an honor to be among those privileged few who were called upon to represent the United States government in its dealings with foreign military establishments. And in these roles he had served the American people well, regardless of what the enemies of America, both foreign and domestic, had to say about it. What did it matter if a few corners were cut in arranging for contracts? Only incompetents let impediments like competitive bidding, cost overruns and affirmative action stand in the way of maintaining an adequate defense for the free world. And what person in his right mind gave a damn about the occasional ouster or assassination of a head of state of some half-ass country which was plotting against the security of the United States? The pleasure had been all his every time he had been asked to participate in such a venture.

Pushing back his chair from the desk, General Weyland got up and headed across the room toward the fountain, his feet tingling to the springy sensation caused by the thick padding beneath the soft carpet. He was a small man, slender and only five feet seven, and he was aware that he carried his body ramrod straight. His awareness of size, however, was gone from his mind by the time he reached the fountain, where he stood staring down at the gurgling water, feeling a closeness with the orderly array of flowers around the indoors pond. A few of the blue hyacinths appeared to be withering, he noticed. On Monday, tomorrow, he would call the outfit which serviced his flowers and give them hell.

He returned to his desk, took a batch of papers from the center drawer, and began to go through them, making an occasional note. They were routine papers, dealing with employee budget matters, and before long he found his interest wavering.

Although he liked his job, he told himself, it was time for him to be moving up to the number one spot in Services International. It was time for the President, Admiral Clyde McCullough, retired, to retire in fact. The old man didn't have it anymore. He was getting too cautious. In last week's meeting with the Attorney General, he had recommended a go-slow policy toward the leaders of the Black American Council. Imagine! They were insurrectionists, and should be treated as such. But then, McCullough had always had a soft spot for niggers, both domestic and foreign. His recommendations a decade ago had contributed to the United States supporting the silly idea of black majority rule throughout South Africa. Clyde McCullough and that nigger, Andy Young. Now Rhodesia and Southwest Africa were united under a black government and South Africa itself was divided into two countries, one black and one white. And the blacks were occupying the majority of the choice land.

He sighed. Oh, well, one can't have everything. But he would like to move up to the presidency of Services International where, by virtue of the position, he would head up the Washington office, and be closer to the center of things. Not that there was anything wrong with this Chicago office, located as it was on North Michigan Avenue, in one of the city's best and newest buildings. But, hell, he had been headquartered in

Chicago too long. It was time to move on. And he had a feeling that Nancy was ready to move on, also.

General Weyland could never think about his wife, Nancy, without admitting to himself that she was one of the few persons he had known well whom he could not understand. She seemed genuinely aloof from and unaffected by the insecurities common to so many women. He and Nancy no longer slept together. In fact, they had not engaged in sex with any degree of passion for nearly a decade. But she didn't appear to have any hangups about it. He now suspected that she had never really enjoyed sex, only put up with it for his benefit. Yet, he had to admit that he had enjoyed his life with her, had really gotten genuine pleasure out of the way she had adapted to the inconveniences and uncertainties of being stationed all over the world; and, in later years, the skill with which she had handled their more exalted station in life, rubbing shoulders with the economically powerful and socially prominent as though she were to the manor born. One thing he could say about Nancy: she had class. Yes, he liked Chicago, liked their large house— an estate, really—on Longwood Drive on the Southwest side of the city. The house was set so far back from the woodlined street that to passersby it appeared to be unoccupied.

The telephone on his desk rang. He glanced sharply at the instrument before picking it up, thereby registering his disapproval of the intrusion upon his privacy. Cheryll was on the line.

"You said you were going to call me last night," she said, her voice pouting. "You promised to take me to Wisconsin to the Americana Club for the weekend."

"Something important came up," he replied, "and I couldn't get away."

"But you could have called," she said. "I sat around all night waiting for you to call."

"You should have known better than that. I've never told you to sit around waiting for me."

"I know you haven't, but I wanted to be with you," she said, her voice still pouting.

217

"Why?"

"You know..."

"Why?"

"I love you, but you don't believe it."

She didn't love him, of course, he told himself now, but neither did she look upon him as an old fool from whom she should wrench every advantage. She respected him, liked him, and feared him just a little: the right combination of feelings for a twenty-five-year-old mistress to have for her sixty-year-old keeper. She lived in one of those lakeside condominiums, about five blocks from his office, and he had been paying her mortgage for nearly two years. He liked her because, for the most part, she knew how to play the game. The only hitch was, she reminded him of his own twenty-six-year-old daughter. Everytime he went to bed with her he had a slight feeling of guilt. Nothing compelling, but guilt nevertheless.

"You don't love me," he told her now, "and stop pretending you do. Do you still want to go to Wisconsin?"

She hesitated. "No," she finally said. "We'd be too rushed." Then her voice softened. "Why don't you come by here? I want to do things to you."

That was one of the best things about Cheryll. She knew her role, and how to play it. And she really enjoyed the role she played. She was smart without being ambitious, accepted nice things as though she really appreciated them—and was one of the cleanest women he had ever known. Naturally clean. Even after strenuous sex, there was nothing of the cunt smell about her. And she didn't hold back where sex was concerned. It was almost incredible. He had to admit he was lucky where the two women in his life were concerned.

"Didn't you hear me?" she breathed into the phone.

"Yes, I heard you," he said. "I was just thinking."

"Thinking about what? Afraid you can't get one up." Her voice was teasing.

"It hasn't happened to me yet," he said. "Especially with you." He was thinking about the subtle tricks she employed to arouse him. When she Frenched him, she had a habit of not

218

approaching his penis directly, or head-on, so to speak, but from the side, as though she were too bashful to perform the act.

"I'll tell you what," he said. "I'll work here for another hour or so. I'll be hungry by that time." He glanced at his watch. "So why don't you come by here—about three o'clock—and we'll catch an early dinner. Okay?"

"Can I get in the building?"

"Yes, there's a guard on duty in the lobby. I'll call him and tell him to let you up when you arrive. When you get to our floor, ring the bell to our outer offices and I'll let you in. Okay?"

"Suits me, Love. See you at three."

He pushed the horizontal phone bar to disconnect Cheryll, released the bar, dialed the lobby service station, and told the guard to let her up when she arrived. He shuffled the budget papers into a neat stack and returned them to the desk drawer. Then he pushed the button which controlled the panel covering the safe. When the safe was exposed, he went over, opened it by manipulating the combination lock, and took out a manila folder. Returning to his desk, he opened the folder, spreading a number of sheets of paper in front of him. The papers contained notes, in his handwriting. He studied the notes for a few minutes, then took a blank sheet of paper from the folder and began writing. As he wrote, he smiled to himself. He was developing a case against Admiral Clyde McCullough detailing his inconsistencies over the past few years. When his documentation was completed, the information checked and re-checked, pressures brought to bear in the appropriate places, he would leak the report to the right people, making sure that its authorship could not be traced to him. He was hopeful that the New Year would see him in McCullough's job.

He wrote for thirty minutes, pausing only to chuckle to himself. He was so absorbed in his writing that he didn't see the three men until they were inside his office. Then it was too late for him to push the button which would have locked the door to his office and lowered an iron shield in front of it.

When he noticed the men, they were moving toward him, not

knotted-up together, but widespread, stalking silently across the thick carpet. They were tall, black and young, almost carbon copies of each other, dressed in casual suits of green denim. Then he realized that their sizes, color and suits were not the primary reason he had gotten the impression that they were carbon copies of each other. It was their headgear. Each man's face was covered by a dark handkerchief, drawn tightly across the nose and mouth, leaving only the eyes uncovered; and on each man's head rested a green fez with gold braid and black letters. The large letters, embossed across the fezzes, were BLA. *Black Liberation Army*!

General Weyland had always looked upon himself as possessing more than his share of physical courage. And he had demonstrated his courage on numerous occasions, as a combat Lieutenant in Korea and as a regiment commander in Viet Nam. But in all of these situations he had had time to prepare himself to meet the coming danger. But this was different. He had gotten out of tune with the necessity to personally face danger. Besides, the odds were too uneven. The men moving toward him were younger, larger, probably as professional as he, and three to his one! For the first time in his life, he knew real terror.

"What the hell is this?" he cried.

The men did not say anything. They were nearing the desk now and he noticed that the one in the middle had a gun in his hand, a military automatic. The man with the gun moved up to the desk, while his two companions circled the desk, one at each end.

General Weyland could feel the terror leaving him, to be replaced by a burning anger, as much at himself as at the men. There was a gun in a bottom drawer of his desk, but he knew he couldn't reach it. His instincts told him that talk wouldn't do any good. His only chance was to act quickly, to go after the man who was holding the gun.

"Goddamn niggers!" he cried, and threw himself across the desk, reaching for the man's throat. But he didn't make it. One of the other men grabbed him from the rear, pinning his arms to his sides. Then he could feel a coarse piece of cloth in his mouth, held there by a strong hand, stifling his cries. He was aware of being lifted from his feet and then he could feel a solid structure beneath his back, and he realized that he was stretched out on his desk. Momentarily, his primary emotion was disgust over the near certainty that the equipment on his desk and the papers on which he had been working—the secret papers—were now scattered untidily across the desk and on the floor.

Heavy hands were fumbling at his clothing, unbuckling his belt and unbuttoning his trousers. Then his trousers were pulled down to his ankles, his shorts ripped open, and he could feel rough fingers on his penis and testicles, fondling them.

Then, suddenly, his existence was a world of pain. Searing, grating, lacerating pain, bringing tears to his eyes, and sweat to his armpits. Pain made all the more unbearable because the cloth in his mouth prevented him from crying out. Then nausea came, followed by a shimmering wave of blackness.

But before darkness descended and consciousness fled, he could feel himself thinking in a strangely detached and sardonic manner: My God, the BLA is cutting the nuts out of the military-industrial complex.

Chapter 22

8:30 A.M., Monday, October 12, 1987

As is the case with most major news stories, information about the attack upon General Weyland was released to the public in stages, and a clear picture of what had happened did not come into focus until more than twelve hours after the occurrence. Sitting in his room in the Hotel Washington on early Monday morning, from where he had followed periodic television reports of the incident since late Sunday afternoon, Preston Simmons realized that the general's prominence was not the only reason why the attack upon him had been one of the lead stories in Sunday afternoon's news; it was also because the Black Liberation Army—or persons posing as members of that group—had been the perpetrators of the attack.

The first spotty reports had merely stated that a white businessman in Chicago had been brutally attacked by what was believed to be "members of the Black Liberation Army." Later, the nature of the attack had been amplified by calling it a "mutilation", without saying how the victim had been mutilated. All reports, however, had indicated that the victim was in critical condition, but was expected to survive. Then somewhat later—after the victim had been identified as a retired general who had something to do with military contracts—the newscasters had begun speculating on the "truly ominous nature" of the attack, bringing into their stories for the first time quotes from statements the Black Liberation Army had made in the past against the "war machine." Finally, as though by prior agreement, the opinion-makers from all the major television networks had hit upon a code name for the attack—referring to it as a "symbolic castration of the military-industrial complex." It was only after the news reports had settled into this mold, that the information which offered definite proof of the Black Liberation Army's involvement had been revealed. According to this information, the group had left a copy of the symbol by which it was well-known at the scene of the crime: big, black gold-bordered BLA letters, affixed to a rectangular green background. And this symbol had been tied by a string around the neck of the victim!

Now, sitting in his hotel room in his pajamas, more rested than he had thought possible when finally he had gone to sleep about four o'clock, Simmons was preparing himself for the ordeal he knew he had to face within the hour. As soon as the news broke, he had called Bob Griggs and together they had decided not to issue a statement until this morning. Simmons realized there were thousands—probably millions—of Americans, both black and white, who believed there was a connection between the Black American Council and the Black Liberation Army. In fact, he knew, many of these people looked upon the BLA as the military arm of the BAC and would consider the attack upon Weyland and the nationwide demonstrations to be companion tactics in a coordinated strategy. The United States government, of course, knew better, but he was certain that both the President and Representative Ryan would be pushing this coordinated strategy theory for all it was worth, employing hints at this stage instead of direct charges.

Ryan, in fact, was already moving in that direction. Appearing on the *Today* show this morning, he had stated: "While we have no proof that the BAC is involved in this dastardly deed, neither do we have any proof that it is not. These are times of revolution. And in times like these, the country must be prepared for the worst." As yet, the President hadn't issued a statement, but Attorney General Richard Lawrence, making it clear that he was speaking for the President, had said on another network: "For security reasons, we must withhold detailed information concerning the relationship between the BAC and BLA. However, it would be foolish for Americans to assume that there is no contact between these two groups." And the trouble was, Simmons told himself now, there was a grain of truth in what the Attorney General had said. There was *some* contact. During the past two weeks, according to Marcus Jackson and his agents, Sam Muhammed had been consulting boldly with representatives of the BLA.

Simmons got up from the couch, walked toward the bathroom, but returned to the couch and sat down again. He wouldn't dress for the trip to the Council office, and his ordeal with the news media, until he heard from Rubye. Last night he had called her at her Chicago hotel and told her not to comment to the press but to find out all she would about the attack on Weyland. She had promised to get back to him this morning. He didn't know what additional information she would get, but as enterprising as Rubye was, she would probably come up with something. He felt suddenly hungry, but decided not to call for room service. He would have something brought up to the Council office after he had faced the press.

The phone rang, the bell-like peals sounding unusually loud in the room. He picked up the phone. Rubye was on the other end.

"The shit has hit the fan," she said after their brief greetings.

"You can say that again. Have you heard anything new?"

"Well, I don't know what's new," she replied, "to you, that is. But I'll tell you what I know, and you can tell me what's new." Suddenly, she asked: "Is your phone tapped?"

He laughed. "I don't know. But I bet you can't tell me anything they don't know. I just want to know it too. So shoot."

She sighed. "Okay. First, the woman who discovered Weyland—Cheryll Hopkins—wasn't one of his aides, like the news say. She was his mistress."

He started to ask how she knew, but decided against it. If his phone, or hers, were tapped, he didn't want her to give away her sources.

"Second," she said, "they have no real proof that the guys who hit him were members of the BLA. They haven't been able to come up with a make from Weyland's description."

"But they do know it was three black guys?"

"Right. And it is true that they left the BLA's calling card."

"Okay. Did anybody see them enter or leave the building?"

"No. But they did find out the way it was done. They came in through the employee parking lot in the rear of the building, through a door which opens into the air conditioning service room. The door was unlocked."

"Is it usually unlocked?"

"No. Speculation has it, they went out the same way."

"Anything else?"

She hesitated, making humming sounds. Finally, she said: "One more thing which might be important. When the police arrived, Weyland was lying on top of his desk, and a lot of papers were scattered about on the floor near the desk. Those papers might be important."

"Why do you say that?"

She paused. "They just might be important."

"Okay," he said. "Is that all?"

"That just about covers it. What are my instructions for the rest of the day? Are the demonstrations off?"

"I don't know yet. I'll let you know later, after I talk to the press and consult with Bob Griggs. Okay?"

"Okay," she replied, but she did not hang up the phone, the silence from her end suggesting that she had something else to say.

"Yes?" he asked.

She was silent for a few seconds more, then asked: "By the way, Preston, where is your lady friend these days?" She sounded as though she wanted him to believe that she had just thought of the question.

"What lady friend?"

"You know I'm talking about Hilda." Her tone was direct, in

her usual manner. So he had not been wrong in Chicago last Friday, he told himself. She was concerned about his relationship with Hilda Larsen.

"I suppose she's in New York," he said, "taking care of her business and, I hope, letting ours alone. When we left Chicago Saturday evening, she didn't come by way of Washington, but went straight to New York. Okay?"

"Okay," she replied. This time she hung up the phone.

Fifteen minutes later, dressed in the most conservative suit he could find in his traveling bags and surrounded by six bodyguards, Preston Simmons stepped out of the Pennsylvania Avenue side of the hotel into a throng of screaming, pushing news media representatives. As four of his bodyguards tightened their cordon about him, literally encircling him with clasped hands, the other two cleared a path through the crowd with their shoulders, arms and elbows. He looked intently into the faces of the newspersons, detecting in the eyes of some a hostility he had never before seen. He and his protectors were headed for the large limousine parked at the curb, which was to take him to Council headquarters. He wouldn't be making the trip on foot this morning, as he had on other occasions during the past two weeks.

"Mr. Simmons! Mr. Simmons!" voices were shouting, as microphones were thrust into his face across the protesting arms of the two advance bodyguards. "Just a few questions, Mr. Simmons!"

He glanced at the car at the curb, then looked again at the surging newspersons, their sound recorders and cameras ready. He had intended to withhold comments until he conferred again with Bob Griggs at the Council Office, then issue a written statement. But he had gone too long already without making a statement, and continued hesitancy would be construed as his having something to hide. Besides, some of these newspersons had been waiting for hours to interview him, and it was only right that he told them something. He knew how it was, having been in their place so often over such a long period of time.

226

"Hold it, fellows," he said to his bodyguards, but loud enough for the reporters to hear. "This is as good a place as any to hold a press conference."

"Hurray!" a television reporter whom Simmons knew slightly said, as the other newspersons stopped pushing and formed a circle around him and his bodyguards. A few others made noises of approval.

"Ladies and gentlemen," Simmons said, "I'm going to make a short statement, then take a few questions, but only a few. They are waiting for me over at the Council headquarters. I'm sure you can understand that." He paused, then continued: "First, I wish to say that I deplore that attack upon General Weyland, as I deplore all violence, including that which interrupted our demonstrations during the past week. Second, I wish to say that neither the Black American Council, nor any of its representatives, had anything to do with the attack upon General Weyland. And third, it is my profound hope, and the hope of the Council, that the persons responsible for this deed be quickly apprehended."

"Mr. Simmons," a woman with a tape recorder asked, "are you convinced that the Black Liberation Army is responsible for the attack?"

"I don't know," Simmons replied. "It is my understanding that the attackers have not been tied directly to the BLA. I just can't say."

"But, according to the police," the woman said, "one of the BLA's logos was found around General Weyland's neck?"

"That is also my understanding," Simmons replied, "but that in itself doesn't prove anything. A BLA logo is not that hard to come by."

"Mr. Simmons," a tall, white male reporter called from the edge of the crowd, "does the Black Liberation Army have any connections whatsoever with the Black American Council?"

"None."

"But I have reports that some of your people have been seen talking to agents of the BLA," the man said.

"Well, I have no way of disproving the validity of your

reports," Simmons said. "But even if they are true, it doesn't prove anything. People supporting us talk to everybody. But you can be certain the BAC does not work with, nor approve any BLA programs where violence is involved."

E. Somerset Vaughn, the Washington Post columnist, had his hand up. Simmons had not seen him since the Chicago press conference. "Yes, Mr. Vaughn?" he said.

"Mr. Simmons," Vaughn said, "will this attack on General Weyland cause you to alter your present tactics? I mean, will your nationwide demonstrations continue?"

"The demonstrations of the past week, Mr. Vaughn," Simmons said, "were called to show that the majority of black Americans still support our attempts to negotiate for a separate nation. In this respect, I believe, the demonstrations of the past week proved successful."

"Does that mean, then," Vaughn asked, "that the demonstrations will not be continued?"

"I didn't say that," Simmons replied. When Vaughn started to speak again, he held up his hand. "We haven't decided yet whether the demonstrations will continue another week, two weeks or what. That is one of the things we will be deciding today. But in any case, it is not definite that what happened to General Weyland will be a contributing factor."

"But it could?" Vaughn asked.

"Yes, it could," Simmons replied.

Frank Marshall, a black reporter for the Washington Post was waving his hand.

"Yes, Frank?" Simmons said.

"Preston," Marshall said, "I suppose you've heard what the Attorney General and Representative Ryan said this morning?"

Simmons nodded.

"Do you think it is really their intent to attempt to tie the BAC to this thing?"

That was the key question. Simmons knew it, and he could tell the other newspersons present knew it. He could feel an air of expectancy as they waited for his answer.

"Yes, I think that is their intention," he said slowly.

"Do you think they'll succeed?" Marshall asked.

Simmons shook his head. "No, Frank, they won't," he said. "Not unless they do it with lies," he added quietly, and began walking toward his limousine.

Hands went up all around him, as reporters called his name, urgently seeking his attention. But he kept moving, his bodyguards gently pushing the crowd out of the way. At the door of the car he stopped, and looked carefully at the reporters.

"An additional statement will be ready in about an hour," he said. "It's been nice talking to you."

When Simmons arrived at Council headquarters, Bob Griggs, immaculately dressed in a grey silk suit, met him at the doorway to his private office and gestured him inside. There was a tautness about the Council president's thin mouth, making him appear less handsome.

Ted Blackwell, his moon face unreadable behind mod, horn-rimmed glasses, was seated at the small conference table in the corner of the office, sipping something from a large mug.

Griggs waved at the table. "Preston, there are coffee and rolls. If you want something else, we'll send out for it."

Simmons shook his head. "Coffee and rolls are fine, Bob," he said, crossed the room and took a seat at the table across from Blackwell. Griggs glanced at his desk, went over and picked up some papers, then joined Blackwell and Simmons at the table.

"Here is a statement Ted worked up," Griggs said. "It looks okay to me."

Simmons nodded, pouring himself a mug of coffee from the electric coffeepot in the center of the table. "I'll read it later," he said, taking a sip of coffee. Ted Blackwell was one of those staff executives who had the uncanny ability of being able to write for almost anyone. Simmons knew he would have few, if any, changes to suggest.

"Albert James, Dr. Patten and Marcus Jackson have called within the past half hour," Blackwell said. "They all want to know about the demonstrations."

Simmons laughed without mirth. "The news media just finished badgering me with the same question," he said.

"What did you tell them?" Griggs asked.

"I told them we would decide in this meeting." He turned to Blackwell. "Have you heard from Sam Muhammed?"

"No," Blackwell said, shaking his head. "From my schedule, Sam is supposed to be in Philadelphia today. Marcus was in Philadelphia when he called. Said he hasn't seen Sam. In fact, he lost track of him in New York Sunday morning."

"Where were Dr. Patten and Albert James when they called?"

"Dr. Patten was in Atlanta, arriving there from New Orleans yesterday. And Albert James was in Denver. He arrived there from the West Coast Saturday. I take Rubye is still in Chicago."

Simmons nodded. "I talked to her about a half-hour ago. So that accounts for all the top-line coordinators, except Sam."

"Right," Blackwell said.

Griggs' secretary stuck her head in the door which connected her office to Griggs'. "There is an important news flash on television," she said. "I'm sure you gentlemen want to hear this." She walked over to Griggs' desk and pushed a button which activated the television mechanism on the wall near the table where they sat.

"...To repeat," the announcer was saying, "the Black Liberation Army struck twice today, apparently speeding up its war against the American establishment. We have just received word from New Orleans that a statue of the Virgin Mary in one of the largest churches in that city was defiled late last night or early this morning. The defilement was of a simulated sexual nature. Meanwhile, less than thirty minutes ago, in New York City, an explosion ripped the head off the Statue of Liberty. Reports indicate that two workers probably have been killed. And in both of these instances, the Black Liberation Army has claimed credit for the acts. In New Orleans, a note to this affect was fastened to the door of the church, while in New York, a telegram was sent to the New York Times. Today's atrocities, following yesterday's mutilation of General Bradford Weyland, must lead inescapably to the conclusion that the Black Liberation Army has declared war on America's cherished institutions. We will interrupt our regular programming to bring you information as it is received...."

Chapter 23

10:00 A.M., Monday, October 12, 1987

"I'LL BE damned!" Ted Blackwell said, placing his elbows on the table and leaning forward, resting his chin in his hands.

Bob Griggs shook his head from side to side, a look of consternation on his face. "Tough luck," he said.

Simmons could feel a hollowness in his chest, just below his heart, and he got a sensation of the room, everything, spinning out of control. He placed his hands over his ears, attempting to steady himself, to force himself to grapple with the latest news.

A commercial had replaced the announcer on the screen now and he closed his eyes to shut out the vision. His heart fluttered across the hollowness in his chest, then gradually resumed its normal beat. He removed his hands from his ears and leaned back in his chair. Slowly, his mind, like unsure feet searching for firm ground in a muddy path, began to seek out essential aspects of the shocking news, to determine just how the events of the past twenty-four hours would appear to the American people, after the occurrences had been filtered through the image-making machinery of the news media. He smiled to himself. He had found the firm ground. His mind was sharp and analytical again.

The American people would look upon the BLA as having, in the language of the most common vernacular, cut the nuts out of the military-industrial complex, fucked orthodox religion, and splattered the brains of America's vaunted freedoms.

It was a sonofabitch!

"It's a damn shame people seldom get a chance to control the direction of the things they set in motion," Ted Blackwell said.

Simmons glanced sharply at him. Blackwell had taken off his glasses and was rubbing his huge brown eyes. Simmons got a faint shock as he reminded himself that this was the first time he had seen Blackwell without the glasses. He realized that Blackwell was suffering from the same feeling of helpless frustration he had felt a few seconds before.

"I suppose we have been too romantic about this thing," Simmons said. "History is not going to single us out for special dispensation. There never has been a revolution without violence, and I don't suppose there ever will be."

"What's worrying me," Bob Griggs said, his clipped voice firm in the room, "the violence is not coming from us, nor from our main opponents. I can't understand why the BLA is putting us on the spot. In the final analysis, they ought to be on our side."

"Maybe they think they are," Ted Blackwell said, putting his glasses on again. "Maybe they think we aren't moving fast enough."

Blackwell probably had a point, Simmons told himself. Without a doubt, Sam Muhammed agreed with that view; at least up to a point. However, it was equally probable that the BLA was being manipulated by the government. The Black Panther Party thrust of the late sixties and the jobs movement of the early eighties definitely had been maneuvered in this manner in order to turn the mainstream of American public opinion against black demands. He voiced his thoughts to Griggs and Blackwell.

"And there is a third possibility," Griggs said.

"What is that?" Blackwell asked.

"It would be to the advantage of Rielinski's group to make our position untenable," Griggs replied. "After all, they've stated they want us on their side, and I believe they do."

"I'll agree with you about one thing," Simmons said. "They do want us on their side. But I doubt if the social democrats and socialists controlling Rielinski's group would initiate violence. In that way, they are like us."

"Black social democrats and white social democrats, moving in opposite directions," Blackwell mused.

"But there are elements in Rielinski's group that he might not be controlling," Griggs said. "Some people think he moved too fast in bringing the teamsters back into the fold."

There was an element of truth in what Griggs was saying, Simmons had to admit. But Rielinski was smart, and tough, and he knew how to keep his thing in hand. He would concentrate on the other two probabilities.

"Blackwell," he said, "have Marcus Jackson fly in this afternoon for a conference. We'll instruct him to broaden and intensify his surveillances. In the meantime, we have to make a decision on the demonstrations."

"Right," Griggs said. He got up, went over to his desk and turned off the television. Opening the door to his secretary's office, he said: "Eunice, keep the television on in your office. Notify us of any developments." He closed the door, came back to the table and sat down. "Okay, Preston," he asked, "where do we go from here?"

Simmons leaned back in his chair, locked his hands behind his head, trying to marshal his thoughts. "I'll think this out while I talk," he said. "When I arrived at this office this morning, before we received word of the other attacks, I was inclined to recommend that the demonstrations continue as is. My thinking was that if we didn't discontinue them last week when violence struck us, we shouldn't call them off just because of an attack on one of our opponents. However, these latest developments have put things in a different light. It is now clear that somebody is out to turn the public opinion against us in the most vicious way. Therefore, to continue mass public demonstrations would only be subjecting our people to calculated harm."

"But we have to do something," Blackwell said. "You said yourself that violence goes hand-in-hand with revolution."

"I know. But, first, let's examine the reason why we called

234

the demonstrations. We called them to demonstrate to the government that the majority of blacks were still on our side. Okay, we proved that last week. But I doubt demonstrations this week would prove the same thing."

"Why do you say that?" Griggs asked.

"Well," he replied, "let's look again at the vote for separation. It was fifty-two percent for and forty-eight percent against. We've known all along that in that forty-eight percent are some of the most influential blacks in this country. Except for Jim Sneed, they haven't been too vocal against us up to this time. But they haven't been converted. And if the government in the next few days succeeds in tying us to the BLA, in any way, these blacks will come out against us in mass. We can't afford to have that happen."

"In other words, you believe we should hold off on the mass demonstrations until we see which way the wind in blowing?" Griggs said.

"Right."

"Then what are we going to do to take the place of the demonstrations?" Blackwell asked.

"Hold forums within the black neighborhoods."

"Who'll participate in these forums?" Griggs asked.

"Everybody in the communities. Those black who are for us, and those blacks who are against us. Remember, Rielinski's convention begins next week. He's been appealing to black leaders to join him. We don't know how successful he's been. We need to find out. Therefore, the forums will be a vehicle to recalculate our strength: to determine how many blacks are with us, how many like Rielinski's brand of demands, and how many aren't willing to take either radical approach."

"You think Rielinski's approach is truly radical?" Blackwell asked.

"I do, if he can marshall as much white support as he thinks he can."

Griggs was looking at him, intently. Finally, he asked: "Do you think the time has come to re-examine Rielinski's proposal?"

Simmons shook his head. "No, not the way you are asking. If

we even *considered* to stop pressing our demands now, Rie- linski would never be able to sell his conglomeration of workers, professionals and intelluctuals a program in which we could participate. The firmer we are, the more he will press. It doesn't help the establishment to be caught in a squeeze play. But we need to know our strength. The forums will help provide that knowledge."

Blackwell was smiling. "Preston," he said, "you sound like you are glad we have Rielinski as a rival."

"No, not exactly," Simmons said. "But anything that weak- ens the real enemy can't be all that bad."

"Okay," Griggs said suddenly, "I'll buy your idea of the forums." He turned to Blackwell. "Ted, call Dr. Patten, Albert James and Rubye and tell them about the decision. Tell them to remain where they are, and get the forumes going in the same areas where they organized demonstrations last week. Okay, Preston?"

"Right," Simmons replied. "But Bob, since Marcus will be coming in to get new instructions, somebody will have to cover the New York area. Do we have anybody?"

"Yes, plenty of capable people in the area. But I would rather have somebody from this office directing things."

Blackwell held up his hand. "I haven't been in the field in a long time," he said. "How about me?"

Griggs looked at Preston. "Do you think we can get along without him around the office?"

Simmons shook his head. "We can't, but we'll have to. I don't believe in keeping anybody from becoming a front-line soldier."

"Amen, Brother," Blackwell said.

Chapter 24

1:30 P.M., Monday, October 12, 1987

SIMMONS AND Griggs returned from lunch to find the FBI waiting for them. Two agents, one black and the other white, were sitting in the vestibule outside Griggs' secretary's office, on opposite ends of the soft leather couch. When Simmons and Griggs, accompanied by two bodyguards, entered the vestibule from the corridor, the agents stood up immediately, quickly displaying their credentials as though they had been holding them in their hands.

As Simmons examined the credentials, he realized he was not displeased that the agents were there. Their presence at least indicated that the government had decided to make a move of some kind.

Shortly before he and Griggs had gone to lunch, Ted Blackwell had left the office to pack for his trip to New York City, still elated over going into the field. Earlier they had called Rubye, Albert James, Dr. Patten and a few other key persons to get the forums started. Then they had updated the statement Blackwell had drafted to include references to the two latest BLA attacks, released it to the media, and settled back to await further developments. So far as he could discern, there had been none. The latest news announcements had not materially enlarged on the information given in the first news flashes, except that it definitely had been established that two workers in the Statue of Liberty had been killed.

"It is imperative that we talk to you, Mr. Simmons," the black agent said in a soft, smooth voice, looking directly at him. "And you, Mr. Griggs," he added, nodding in Griggs' direction. Then glancing at the bodyguards, he added: "In private."

The black agent was tall and thick-bodied, with a big natural and a heavy mustache. His eyes looked sleepy in his cinnamon-colored face. He was wearing a tan, casual cotton suit and a patterned, dark-brown shirt, open at the collar. The white agent was about an inch shorter than his black companion, heavy-set with a round red face. He was dressed in a blue knit suit and a white turtle-neck sweater. The FBI's mod look, Simmons mused.

"Is there somewhere we can go?" the white agent asked. His twangy voice and gray eyes were alert.

Simmons never had quite accepted the validity of black American law enforcement officers, even though in the seventies he had participated in the battles to outlaw discriminatory police examinations and for the equitable hiring and upgrading of minority and women police personnel. He had done these things because he realized that, overall, black communities received better service from black law enforcement personnel and, generally, black citizens were harrassed less by black police officers than by white ones. But he just couldn't feel comfortable with the idea of a black person being willing, in some cases eager, to put his life on the line to enforce the laws of a society which discriminated against him and his people in so many ways. He knew he would feel differently about law enforcement in a society which black people controlled, or in a society where black people enjoyed equality.

But if he had this feeling about black ordinary law enforcement personnel, he told himself now, the feeling was magnified many times where the elite of the profession was concerned.

The sight of a black FBI agent made him angry and the mere thought that black CIA agents existed made him furious. These agents did not have the excuse of needed service to the black community to justify their existence. They existed for one reason only: to undermine political self-determination in the black community. The havoc they had wreaked on the Black Panther Party and other militant black organizations of the sixties and seventies was glaring testimony to this fact.

"What do you want to talk to us about?" he asked, looking hard at the black agent, trying to make contact with the sleepy eyes.

The agent shifted his gaze to the bodyguards. "Our business is with you and Mr. Griggs," he said.

Griggs stepped forward, so that he was standing beside Simmons. "We don't have any quarrel with that," he said, "but you haven't answered Mr. Simmons' question. He inquired as to the nature of your business."

The black agent glanced at the white one, confirming for Simmons what he had suspected: the white agent was in charge—if not by rank, then at least in the mind of the black agent.

Turning deliberately away from the black agent, Simmons said to the white one: "Mr. Griggs and I want to know what you want to talk to us about."

The white agent stared at him, the alert eyes probing. "We should rather state our business only to you and Mr. Griggs," he said.

"Oh, is it that important?" he asked.

"Yes, it is that important," the agent replied, a smirk in his voice.

At one level of thinking, Simmons told himself, there was no good reason why he shouldn't dismiss his bodyguards and escort the FBI agents into Griggs' office or the conference room and find out what was on their minds. After all, FBI agents were always calling on people at all levels of society. Yet, at another level of thinking, there was absolutely no reason for him and Griggs to deal with the FBI agents. In the past two weeks he had consulted with the President of the United States, he and Griggs had held conferences with the chairman of the Senate and House Judiciary committees, and he had talked by phone with the Attorney General. Also during this time, Ted Blackwell and other Council staff members had engaged in numerous conversations with lesser government functionaries, all of whom held higher positions than these two FBI agents. Therefore, to talk officially with these agents—especially for *Griggs* and *him* to engage in such a conversation with them— would, in effect, constitute lowering the level of their negotiations with the federal government.

Feeling his body tingle with sudden decision, and placing his hand firmly on Griggs' shoulder to ward off contradiction from that quarter, Simmons said to the white agent: "Well, I'll tell you this. If what you have to say to me and Mr. Griggs is too important for our associates to hear, it is too important for you to be saying it. Your bosses should be saying it to us."

The head of the black agent jerked like it had been pulled by an invisible string. He opened his mouth to say something, but the white agent held up his hand.

"Which bosses?" the white agent asked.

"Your big bosses," Simmons replied. "The Attorney General and the Director of the Federal Bureau of Investigation."

The white agent continued to stare at him. Finally he asked: "How do you expect me to get such a message to the Director?"

Simmons smiled. "You don't have to worry about that. Just tell the man who sent you, and let him do the worrying."

The white agent glanced at the black agent, but the black agent appeared to be sulking. Suddenly, the white agent smiled. "You got a point there, Mr. Simmons," he said. "We'll do just that."

"Right," Simmons said, "you do just that."

One hour later, Simmons and Griggs were sitting in a small room in the Justice Department, not far from the Attorney General's office. Upon their arrival at the Department they had been directed to this room because it was reported that the

240

Attorney General was holding a meeting in his office and, according to an aide, didn't want to inconvenience them by having them wait in the more public area reserved for that purpose. Now, sitting in the small room with its neat conference table, comfortable leather chairs, and muted fluorescent lighting, Simmons was appreciative of the courtesy, although he knew somebody would attempt to exact the price later. Attorney General Richard Lawrence was not a man from whom a person could expect small favors.

But one had to admit that the Attorney General *was* a man of quick decisions, Simmons told himself. This conclusion was supported not only by the man's reputation, but by the speed with which he had disposed of his and Griggs' disagreement with the FBI. The agents had been gone from their office no more than twenty minutes when the Attorney General's office called. The Assistant Attorney General who placed the call had asked only one question: Could he and Griggs meet with the Attorney General, in the latter's office, in forty-five minutes? Taking a cue from the man's conciseness, he had been equally concise. He simply had replied that they would be there.

Simmons crossed his legs, the movement causing him to push his chair slightly back from the table. Glancing at his watch, he said to Griggs, who was sitting across from him: "The forty-minutes are up, with five minutes to spare. The illustrious chief attorney for the United States should be summoning us to his office shortly."

Griggs laughed. "It's about time," he replied. "Either that, or run the risk of tarnishing his reputation for punctuality." Then seriously: "So you really think the FBI chief is pissed off with us for not being nice to his agents? That this is the reason why Lawrence is meeting with us by himself?"

"I'm sure of it. Director Hutchins is an old line bureaucrat who is in the habit of sticking up for his men. He also is as right-wing as they come, and is not about to be caught dealing with two subversives on an equal basis."

"But Lawrence sees the whole thing differently, huh?"

"He might not see things differently, but his role is to act

241

differently. They want to find out what we know, see how we are standing up under pressure. And somebody has to do the job."

Griggs nodded. "You are right about one thing. They want to talk to us, all right. Otherwise they would have put us in cold storage after we snubbed their agents."

Suddenly, the door to the room pushed inward, and a man entered. He came into the room so swiftly that he was standing by the table looking down at them before Simmons recognized him. It was Richard Lawrence, the Attorney General. Simmons realized that another reason he had not instantly recognized the Attorney General was because he had not expected him to come to the room in person, but to summon them to his office through an aide, probably the same one who had directed them to the room in the first place. However, the reason why Lawrence was here soon became evident. He intended to talk to them in this room, because, as he and Griggs began scrambling to their feet, the Attorney General, with a curt wave of his hand, gestured them to remain seated.

Richard Lawrence was a big man, tall and heavy-boned, so thick through the center of his body that his shoulders appeared somewhat narrow. His large head was almost round and covered with bushy red hair, trimmed to a semi-crew cut. Although his face was wide and flat, his nose was incongruously high-bridged and so thin at the tip that his nostrils appeared to be located in the sides of his nose rather than at the end.

Lawrence, Simmons recalled, usually had a happy-go-lucky, expansive air about himself, a sort of Northern Good Ol' Boy attitude. And today was no exception. He was dressed in brown slacks and a short-sleeved tan shirt, open at the throat, giving an impression of being ready for action. Even the smell of the man was distinctive. The cologne he was wearing hovered around them like a separate presence, pungent and persistent.

Pulling the chair back from the head of the table, the Attorney General sat down, draping his right leg over the arm in

242

almost the same motion. This was to be an extremely informal meeting, his demeanor was saying; so informal, Simmons told himself, that Lawrence hadn't bothered to shake their hands.

"Glad you gentlemen could make it," Lawrence said in a sharp, rapid voice, folding his arms across his chest, looking from Simmons to Griggs, his intense blue eyes shooting bullets. "Glad you could make it."

"Always ready to oblige, Mr. Attorney General," Simmons said, leaning back in his chair. He was wondering if Lawrence would mention that they had refused to talk with the FBI agents, and decided that he wouldn't. He was not the kind of guy who wasted his time covering old ground, especially if he had come out second-best in the previous encounter.

"Mr. Simmons, I was relieved to hear what you told the news media this morning," Lawrence said with a chuckle. "Very relieved."

"I am always glad when anybody is relieved," Simmons said. "But what specifically did I say this morning to cause you relief?"

Lawrence glanced sharply at Simmons as though he believed he was being mocked. "You disavowed knowledge of, and participation in, the recent acts of the Black Liberation Army," he replied. "The recent acts of the Black Liberation Army."

Simmons looked at Griggs. Griggs had his hand over his mouth and the glint in his eyes told him the hand was hiding a smile on his lips. What the hell was Griggs smiling about? Then he remembered. Griggs was smiling at a quirk in Lawrenece's speaking manner, which was well-known and talked about in the Washington inner circle. The Attorney General had a habit of making a statement, then summarizing the statement in an additional sentence. Often this habit gave a ludicrous twist to his statements, rather than the emphasis he intended. But Lawrence's speaking manner wasn't what was important. The things he was saying were.

"Does this mean, Mr. Attorney General," Simmons asked, "that you no longer believe the things *you* told the media this morning? As I recall, you said that it would be foolish for

243

Americans to assume that there is no connection between us and the BLA."

Lawrence shook his head, vigorously, his bushy hair moving so out of place that he had to push it back into place with his hand. "I'm not saying that, Mr. Simmons," he said. "I meant that I'm relieved that you have *publicly* disavowed knowledge of the acts of the Black Liberation Army." He paused, shifting his eyes from Simmons to Griggs. When he started speaking again, he was smiling—a deliberately plastic smile. "Therefore, when we prove otherwise," he said, "most Americans will look upon you as liars as well as traitors. Liars as well as traitors."

The words came out so casually that for a second Simmons was certain he had not heard the Attorney General correctly. Then he looked hard into the man's eyes; rather, felt himself being drawn into the bottomless blue sea of his eyes, and knew that Lawrence had said what it sounded like he said. From the periphery of his vision, he noticed that Griggs had placed his hands on the table and half-lifted himself from his chair. Suspended in that comic pose, Griggs said angrily:

"Mr. Lawrence, we didn't come here to be insulted!"

Lawrence was sitting straight in his chair, his arms folded across his chest. There was a satisfied smirk on his face.

"Believe me, Mr. Griggs," he said, "I am not trying to insult you. I am only doing my duty as the chief law enforcement officer of this nation. And this duty compels me to tell you that you are viewed by this nation in the terms I have stated. Definitely in the terms I have stated."

Griggs sat back down in his chair, a look of wonder on his face, as though he could not quite believe that the Attorney General existed. "But hell, man, what kind of proof do you have? As the chief law enforcement officer, you must know there is no proof of your allegations!"

The smirk on Lawrence's face became even more self-satisfied. "Proof?" he asked, looking more at Simmons than at Griggs. "You gentlemen know, must know, that truth is defined more by how it is *perceived* to exist than by how it *actually* exists. However, in this instance, one doesn't have to

244

depend upon philosophical concepts to make a case. There is a preponderance of circumstantial evidence to support my allegations, Mr. Griggs. A preponderance of circumstantial evidence."

"What circumstantial evidence?" Griggs asked.

Lawrence unfolded his arms, made a pointer out of his index and center finger, and slapping his fingers down on the edge of the table, began to intone what he considered to be circumstantial evidence. "First," he said, "Mr. Griggs, you, Ted Blackwell, and other members of your staff have been busy working with various nations, trying to make a case against the United States..."

"That has nothing to do with the Black Liberation Army," Griggs cut in. "Besides, you know we are only trying to protect ourselves against unwarranted charges..."

"It doesn't matter," Lawrence interrupted. "We have evidence of more direct involvement with the BLA." He paused. "Second," he said, slapping his fingers against the table again, "BLA members were observed playing prominent parts in last week's demonstrations, and attending some of your meetings."

"You know meetings and demonstrations can't be screened," Simmons said. "And you know we don't have the facilities to determine who are members of the BLA and who are not. And we are not expected to."

Lawrence laughed. "What you are saying might be true, Mr. Simmons," he said. "Under ordinary circumstances. But you have decided to start a revolution. And that means everything goes. Everything goes."

"What you have listed so far is very weak circumstantial evidence, to say the least," Griggs said.

"Maybe so, by itself," Lawrence replied. "But when it is added to our other evidence, a pretty good case can be made."

"What other evidence?" Griggs asked.

"Third," Lawrence said, striking his fingers agaisnt the side of the table—"and this is what I had in mind a minute ago—a member of the Black American Council has been observed during the past few weeks consorting with known officials of

245

the Black Liberation Army. I'm talking about Sam Muhammed." He paused, smiling his plastic smile. "And you can't deny this, because your people have been seen observing the same thing. Observing the same thing!"

When Simmons had given Marcus Jackson the assignment of keeping Sam Muhammed under surveillance, he had not for a moment believed that the actions of Jackson and his representatives would go unobserved by government agents. He simply had wanted to be kept as informed as possible of Sam's activities. Therefore, it would be foolish to condemn his decision now, he told himself. Given the same set of circumstances, he would come to the same conclusion again. It was the only logical option open to him.

"Mr. Attorney General," he said, "our surveillance of Sam Muhammed is not evidence of our complicity with the BLA, but evidence to the contrary."

"Then you admit Sam Muhammed is an agent of the BLA?" Lawrence asked gleefully.

"Of course, we don't admit any such thing!" Griggs said. "It's no secret, especially to you, that Sam Muhammed has been calling for more militance in our attempts to negotiate a separate state. We didn't want to be the only ones who didn't know what he was up to. Sure we've observed him talking to known BLA officials. But what does that prove? Nothing, so far as I know."

"Do you know where Sam Muhammed is now?" Lawrence asked.

Griggs glanced at Simmons. "No, we don't," he replied.

"Then, so far as you know, Muhammed might be with the BLA at this very moment?" Lawrence said.

Griggs looked steadily at Lawrence. "So far as we know, he could be in China," he said. "But I doubt if he is with the BLA. We haven't heard from him since early yesterday."

Lawrence nodded, and got up from the table. He seemed suddenly to have made up his mind about something. "Okay," he said, "I might as well tell you now as for you to find out later. The Department is going to release a statement officially tying

246

Sam Muhammed to the BLA and charging him with complicity in their acts. We are also going to issue an order for his arrest."

"On the slight circumstantial evidence in your possesion?" Griggs asked.

Lawrence held up his hand. "I'm not finished," he said. "We further are going to state in our official release that all prime members of the Black American Council, including its chief negotiator, are being kept under close observation. Under close observation."

What the Attorney General planned to do didn't surprise Simmons. In fact, anything less would have been surprising. The reason Lawrence had sent them to this room was now also clearly evident: he had no intention of giving them the respect of meeting them in his office.

"Let's get this straight," Simmons said, looking up at the Attorney General. "You are going to take a series of weak assumptions and try to turn them into facts, in the minds of the American people. In effect, you are going to tell the American people that: first, the BLA is definitely responsible for the atrocities of the past two days; second, Sam Muhammed is in complicity with the BLA; and third, the Black American Council is supporting Sam Muhammed in his complicity. Right?"

The Attorney General smiled down at him. "Right, Mr. Simmons. That's exactly what I am going to tell them. I'm going to place the burdens of defense and denial on you. Defense of the BLA. And denial of your own guilt." He laughed.

"I don't suppose there is any need to ask just why you are doing this?" Griggs asked.

Lawrence laughed again. "I don't mind telling you, Mr. Griggs. In fact, Mr. Simmons has been told before, by the President of the United States. Friday before last, I believe. On that occasion the President told Mr. Simmons that he considered him to be an enemy of this nation. Today, I extend the same courtesy to you, Mr. Griggs."

247

Then laughing silently, as at a private joke, the Attorney General turned away from the table and walked out of the room, the smell of his distinctive cologne lingering in the air like the memory of a bad dream.

As Simmons watched him go, he felt suddenly tired, as though he were trapped under a heavy blanket in a close place. He glanced at Griggs. The forced smile on his companion's face was a poor cover for the shocked expression in his eyes.

"Bob, let's get the hell out of here," he said lightly, "before the bastard comes back and throws us in jail."

Chapter 25

8:00 P.M., Tuesday, October 13, 1987

SITTING IN the pulpit of Mount Moriah Baptist Church in the heart of Manhattan, Ted Blackwell was trying to determine just how he felt about being where he was. There were a number of ironies involved in his being here in this pulpit, he told himself, sitting up here like a dignitary looking out into the dimly-lit sanctuary at three hundred or so upturned faces, getting ready to conduct a forum on black opinions.

First, he hadn't planned on seeking a field assignment, hadn't even thought about it, until that precise moment yesterday afternoon in Council headquarters when he had uncharacteristically made the request of Griggs and Simmons. Second, he was surprised that they had acceded to his request as easily as they had; no, more than that, had acted as though they were honored to have him assume the assignment. This was something new to him, for he looked upon himself as being essentially a staff person by nature, and he believed others viewed him in the same light. Consequently, he seldom sought out roles where he was expected to take the lead in implementing projects or programs.

Now that he was playing such an unfamiliar, uncharacteristic role, he asked himself, glancing out of the corners of his eyes at the two people who sat with him in the pulpit, how was he reacting to the situation, responding to the challenge, so to speak? With the duplicity of a good staff person, of course, he told himself with a wry smile: for as near as he could determine, his present mood consisted of an equal mixture of tension and detachment.

The people in the pulpit with him were the pastor of the church and the president of the New York City chapter of the NAACP, both staunch supporters of the BAC. They were among the first persons he had called yesterday afternoon when he had begun arranging for the forums in the New York City area.

The reason for his tenseness couldn't be attributed entirely to the fact that he was to conduct the meeting, he told himself. For in his role as head staffer for the BAC, he often conducted meetings. But almost without exception they were meetings of other staff persons, where plans were kicked around and formulated for others to act on. In short, he was used to conducting meetings of persons like himself, whose attitudes and responses could be anticipated and controlled. Not like the multi-faceted crowd which was gathered beyond the pulpit's footlights in Mount Moriah's sanctuary.

The reason for his feeling of detachment was another matter, of course. It was part and parcel of his nature. He had a reputation for being able to adapt to any viewpoint, and that was essentially true. He was aware that he could present strong arguments for many sides of an issue, and could do so without prejudice. Possibly his extreme objectivity was due to his not possessing any definite viewpoints of his own. He felt himself smiling. He was being too unkind to himself, for in some things he really did have preferences. But not strong emotional preferences. Basically, he was an arranger and presenter of ideas. Ideas which, for the most part, had been forged by others in the furnace of their conflicting emotions.

He raised his eyes and looked out across the assembly hall. Most of those present were seated, but some were milling about in the corridors or standing in small groups around aisle seats, their collective voices creating an echo-like drone. No newcomers seemed to be arriving through the double entrance doors. He glanced at his watch. It was nearly eight o'clock.

Picking up the cue, Bernie Kigh, the NAACP president, who was seated on his right, leaned toward him. "Think we should get started?" he asked. He was a thin, light-brown man with a taut face, sharp eyes restless under heavy brows. His hair was short, straight and iron-grey.

The pastor, Dr. Maceo McGrowder also leaned inward, so that their three heads were almost touching. "It's about that time," he said. In appearance, he was almost the opposite of the NAACP president: a much younger man, roundfaced and dark brown, with a bushy Afro.

"Might as well," Blackwell said. "How are we going to do it? I mean who's going to talk first?"

Bernie Kigh laughed. "I'm here for moral support. I might talk if the going gets rough. But basically this is your and the reverend's show."

Dr. McGrowder nodded. "Since this is a forum to solicit opinions, I don't see much need for Bernie and me to do much talking, because our opinions are already known to Council headquarters. Ted, I'll introduce you, and you can take it from there."

"Okay, Reverend," he said. "Give them the ground rules, and I'll take over." His stomach was tight, but he had a feeling it would loosen up as soon as he started talking. He flipped on his tape recorder, which was sitting beside him on the pulpit floor, as Dr. McGrowder walked over to the podium and rapped for silence.

It turned out that the crowd was in a highly receptive mood. Strict attention was given to Dr. McGrowder as he outlined the procedure. Those persons wishing to speak would so indicate by raising their hands and waiting for recognition before going to one of the four microphones located strategically about the floor. Three minutes would be the maximum time allowed for any person to express an opinion. Each speaker would state his/her name and organizational affiliation, if any. No person would be allowed to speak a second time until everybody contending for a microphone had been given a chance. Dr. McGrowder would be the timekeeper and Ted Blackwell would select the speakers. In case a serious dispute arose over a ruling by Blackwell, Bernie Kigh would arbitrate the situation. However, before the give-and-take got underway, Ted Blackwell, their illustrious visitor from Washington, D.C., who just happened to be the executive director of the Black American Council, would put the reason for their being here in proper perspective.

It also turned out, Ted Blackwell told himself as he started to speak, that he was in good form. His words, precise and to the point, came out without being forced, almost as though they were creatures of their own creation. Quickly he recounted the essence of what had taken place in the recent meetings with government officials, including the President and the Congress, revealed the rationale behind the demonstrations of the past week, and deplored the violence of the last three days.

Concluding his introductory remarks, he stated: "We now stand at what must be considered a new threshold. Although it was nearly two months ago that black Americans marched to the polls and declared their allegiance to the idea of a separate state, that allegiance must be declared again and again if the idea is to survive. On this night, at this moment, in many parts of the country, men and women not unlike yourselves are meeting to reaffirm this allegiance. But this allegiance cannot be affirmed by the mindless spouting of slogans. The Black American Council, in whose hands you have placed your trust, needs your honest opinions to guide it during these dark days. *We want to know what you really think*! So please, as we make available the microphones to your words, do not hesitate to open your minds and pour out your hearts as well."

And they did not fail to heed his invitation, if the stating of different points of view meant anything. Since he was taping the session, he didn't attempt to keep an accurate count of the number of speakers who supported separate statehood as compared to those who opposed it. That he could do later. What intrigued him was the unique, individualistic reasoning

252

behind the positions expressed by a number of speakers. Although some appeared to be quoting canned phrases, for the most part what was said had the ring of sincerity.

One young woman, tall, medium-brown and pretty, who gave the name of Vivian Malone and said she was a model by profession, struck a highly emotional chord in the audience with her defense of a separate nation.

"I know that in the past ten or fifteen years or so, it has become fashionable to say that money is the name of the game. During that time, more and more of our women have taken to ripping off whitey any way they could. I'm talking about using sex to get what we want. Some of us believe that because the white man is willing to pay, he looks upon us as equal. But that is not the case. The white man doesn't believe his own woman is his equal, so you can just guess what he thinks about us. Even when he marries us, he's just doing it for a kick, to show how liberal he is. He doesn't actually feel it..."

She paused for the applause to subside, then continued: "I'll tell you something else. Our men have suffered so much from the white man, from this system, until some black women are turning to white men out of the need to survive. Others of us are going along with the game because we can't do any better—sort of grinning and bearing it. But none of this is a healthy situation. We need our own country so that we, black men and women, can get back together and save ourselves from destruction."

The response was deafening.

An elderly man named Moses Turner, a retired postal worker, made probably the most appealing pitch for joining forces with Joe Rielinski's group.

"Dreams die hard," he said. "All my life I have dreamed one dream, that I would like to see the day when the things that Martin Luther King talked about would come to pass—when white men and black men, white women and black women, would work together as equals to make this country a paradise on earth. I had this dream when I was a young man, and now I'm an old man, but I still have it. I read in the papers today that

Joe Rielinski is getting ready to team up with the Urban League and the Congressional Black Caucus to put pressure on the rich and the mighty of this country to make them understand that their riches belong to the people. That's been the trouble all along. We have let the rich divide us, one from the other, black from white. For the most part, it's been the white folks' fault. Now it seems they are willing to take the lead in correcting it. We should be willing to extend a helping hand."

Then there was the young man who insisted that a separate black nation could come into existence only through violent struggle. He said his name was Abdul Sharieff and that he was presently unemployed. He was tall and brown and bearded.

"The time has come for us to get rid of our adolescent approach to reality," he said. "Nobody has ever won a revolution without fighting and dying for it. Birth and death and blood are inseparable. And the killing must begin with those of us who sell out to the enemy!"

The crowd responded loudly, and with mixed feelings.

"I was a teenager in Chicago in late 1976 when Mayor Daley died," Sharrieff continued. "I watched as Wilson Frost and those other black aldermen sold out to the white political machine. I was sick to my stomach. Since then, I've been sick every day of my life, because every day some of our people in high places sell out. In any other battle for freedom, anywhere else in the world, these sellouts would be the first to be ripped off. Look at what happened in Kenya during the Mau Mau uprising. We are going to have to start doing the same thing. Hell, I don't see how we won what little we did during the civil rights struggle of the sixties without doing it. We sure didn't win the job rights fight of the seventies without doing it. And we sure won't win this self-determination fight of the eighties without doing it!"

The applause was thunderous.

Adherents of the Back-to-Africa Movement were also present. Their spokesman was articulate, if not convincing, a middle-aged man with close-cropped hair and a smooth brown face. He was a self-employed tailor, named Jerome White.

254

"Throughout the world," he said, "black people revere the name of Marcus Garvey. And they revere him with justification, for he was the first to raise the banner of Mother Africa calling her children home. But Garvey was ahead of his time. He launched the Back-to-Africa Movement at a time when Mother Africa was herself enslaved, when her children would have had no place to go had they responded to Garvey's call. But today, things are different. Powerful, independent nations, black nations, are flourishing in Africa. The time is indeed here when we can afford to go home. It is immoral for us to contest the white man for land he stole from the Indians. Instead, let us send a message to our brothers and sisters in Mother Africa, letting them know that we are ready to *return to our heritage!*"

And so it went, on and on. Blackwell found himself searching for a common thread in the opinions being expressed. And he found it. The common thread was dissatisfaction. Dissatisfaction with things as they were. Dissatisfaction which had broken out of the borders of apathy and frustration and spilled over into a mood of rebellion. It was no longer a matter of getting a separate nation or nothing, of going back to Africa or accepting conditions unchanged in the United States; the options were broader now. Something was going to give. A people on the move had everything to gain and nothing to lose. He found himself glancing at his tape recorder, whirring silently on the floor beneath his chair. Maybe this time he, the purveyor of other men's ideas, would have a few ideas of his own to carry back to Simmons and Griggs.

Finally, there came a time when the intervals between concluded and beginning speeches lengthened, when speakers began to stammer and listeners began to murmur among themselves. The three men in the pulpit looked at each other in silent agreement. The session had run its course. Blackwell took his seat and Dr. McGrowder moved to the podium to begin the dismissal ceremony.

Exodus from the church was rapid. By the time Blackwell packed his tape recorder and faced his hosts to say goodbye, only a few persons were left in the sanctuary. These were

255

standing around in small knots, talking for the most part in animated gestures.

"Things went very well, don't you think?" Bernie Kigh asked, shaking hands with Blackwell.

"Very well, indeed," he replied, extracting his hand from Kigh's grasp and extending it to Dr. McGrowder. "If the sessions the others are holding are going like this, the information should prove helpful." He patted the tape recorder under his arm.

Dr. McGrowder touched his Afro. "Ted," he asked, "how do Preston and Bob really feel about things as they stand right now? Do they believe the government is going all-out to break us? How are they responding to Rielinski's campaign?"

Blackwell could feel himself withdrawing from the questions. Not only didn't he know how Preston and Griggs felt, he didn't know how *he* felt. Especially about Rielinski. But he did have a definite opinion about the government.

"I think the government is going to keep up the pressure, Dr. McGrowder," he said. "About the other, we'll have to wait and see. That's part of the reason for these meetings."

"Ted, do you want us to drop you off at your hotel?" Bernie Kigh asked.

Blackwell looked out into the assembly hall. Abdul Sharieff and Jerome White were talking with a few other people near the door. "No, thanks," he said, offering Kigh and Dr. McGrowder his hand again. "I think I'll hear a little more about the Back-to-Africa Movement. That guy made some interesting points."

But by the time he reached the rear of the assembly hall, Jerome White had gone. Abdul Sharieff saw him coming and waited and they walked out of the church together.

The moment he stepped onto the sidewalk, Blackwell felt himself shudder. The air was moist with threatening rain, and it was downright cold. After all, this was the middle of October, he told himself.

"I'd like to talk to you, Mr. Blackwell," Sharieff said. "There's a restaurant around the corner we can go to."

Blackwell shrugged, vaguely wondering if Sharieff was an active militant, a philosophical one, or just a loudmouth. "Okay," he said. "I could use a cup of coffee."

They started walking down the sidewalk, away from the church. Suddenly Sharieff stopped, bumping against Blackwell. Blackwell looked up. Two white men wearing dark topcoats were approaching them from across the street. They were coming from the direction of a dull-colored sedan which was parked at the curb, its doors open, and apparently occupied by two or three persons.

"Watch it!" Sharieff said, seizing Blackwell by the arm.

The white men were still coming toward them, walking about six feet apart, hands in their pockets. Dimly, Blackwell could hear voices behind them, coming from the church exit. One of the voices sounded like Dr. McGrowder's.

Blackwell's grip on his arm was like a vise. The white men stopped about ten feet from them, still in the street.

"Abdul Sharieff," one of them said, extending his left hand, "we have a warrant for your arrest."

Sharieff stared at the men, his grip on Blackwell's arm loosening, but only somewhat.

Then suddenly, like a person responding to a quick decision, Sharieff started running down the sidewalk, pulling Blackwell after him.

Blackwell tried to snatch his arm free of Sharieff's grasp, almost succeeded, but the hand held on to his topcoat sleeve, still dragging him.

"Halt!" one of the white men cried. "Halt, or we'll shoot!"

The whole thing was crazy, Blackwell told himself, trying to twist out of his topcoat; but the coat was buttoned, and he was still being dragged along in that awful, awkward gait. His tape recorder fell from beneath his free arm.

"Halt!" He heard the voice again, and almost immediately heard the sound of gunfire. But before the sounds reached his ears, he had already felt the pain; the pain like probing fingers of fire at his legs, buttocks, back and skull.

Dreamily, with a peculiar kind of relief, he realized that his

257

coat sleeve was free of Sharieff's grasp. But now, both of his arms were on the sidewalk and his fingers were scratching feebly at the hard surface.

In that moment he knew he was dying; knew it with a calm detachment he had often hoped he would be capable of in a time of supreme crisis. With a sigh, he let his head sink to the sidewalk between his hands. His only regret was that he would not be able to analyze with Simmons and Griggs the speeches on his tape recorder.

Chapter 26

IT WAS strange, Preston Simmons reflected, how death threw a spotlight on a person, emphasizing and revealing things about that person which few of his acquaintances had taken the time to think about or determine prior to his death.

This was especially true where Ted Blackwell was concerned, Simmons told himself now, sitting with Bob Griggs in the latter's office around the same table at which he, Griggs and Ted Blackwell had sat only two days before, mapping strategy for the black opinion forums. He had known for some time that Ted lived with his mother, sister and brother-in-law somewhere in Washington, but before late last night—when McGrowder had called notifying them of Ted's death—he had not met a single member of Ted's family; had not, in fact, wondered about what they were like; had not concerned himself with whether they were involved in the movement. Of course, he probably could be excused for his lack of knowledge, not having been associated closely with Ted, but he could not be excused for his lack of *interest*. And yet, Bob Griggs apparently didn't know much more about Ted's family than he did, judging by the unfamiliarity exhibited at last night's meeting. He supposed it all boiled down to the fact that Ted just hadn't been the kind of guy in which people exhibited a lot of personal interest on a day-to-day basis. He hadn't seemed to need it, nor want it. Yet, nobody had played down his value. He just had been taken for granted, both as a person and a provider of expert service.

Yet neither Ted's mother nor his sister appeared to elicit the same kind of indifferent response from people. His mother, a short, thin, dark woman, had an inner vitality which reached out to you in a highly personal way, as though she were desirous of conveying a private message. The sister, a slender woman in her middle thirties, was very attractive from both a personality and physical standpoint. She possessed a sexually confident manner which could not be hidden even under the emotionally-charged circumstances of the meeting. The brother-in-law had not been at home.

Bob Griggs picked up his cup of coffee and sipped it. "Why Ted?" he asked. "Godddammit, I feel like a bystander was killed. Ted was so emotionally detached." His smooth tan face was pinched with grief and his usually clear eyes were clouded with sadness.

Simmons shook his head. "Don't do that to Ted's memory, Bob," he said. "Ted was as committed as any of us, even though he might not have known it. A man's mind is the best part of him, and Ted was committed with his mind."

Griggs tapped his fingers along the curve of his cup. "I suppose you're right. He was with me so long. Ten years as my administrative aide when I was executive director of the NAACP, and all of the three years here. But dammit, I keep getting a feeling that we never treated him like he really belonged!"

Simmons shook his head again. "Now you're doing to yourself what you just did to Ted. People are different, Bob. You know that. And there's nothing we can do about it. You and Ted complemented each other in a very wonderful way. Otherwise, you wouldn't have stayed together so long."

"I know," Griggs replied. "I suppose I'm just thinking aloud.

A person gets in that habit talking to you."

Simmons smiled. It was true. He and Griggs had come to the stage in their relationship where the no-man's-land between their talking and thinking was gradually being eliminated.

"I keep thinking about how Ted could get so much out of people without pressuring them," Griggs said. "How considerate he was of people, those for whom he worked and those who worked for him." His voice became suddenly elated. "I suppose that's as good a yardstick as any to determine a person's worth—how near they come to treating subordinates and superiors alike."

Simmons nodded, feeling emotion surge within him. "Yeh," he said. "That was Ted, all right. The living democrat. But you know something, he got it from his mother. She's some lady."

"Yet, he never talked about her," Griggs said.

"I know. Preoccupation with personal things was an imposition to Ted—an imposition on the general welfare."

Griggs laughed. It was a laugh of release. "Ted would get a kick out of that statement," he said. "He sure as hell would." He paused. "You know something, Preston? It's going to be difficult to honor his mother's request that his funeral not be a public protest."

"I know," Simmons replied. "But we'll do the best we can."

And indeed it was going to be difficult, he told himself. For at this moment, telegrams and letters of protest were pouring into Washington from all over the country. Some of these protests were being directed at the White House and Capitol Hill, demanding that the persons responsible for the death of Ted Blackwell be punished; others were coming into Black American Council headquarters, many calling for nationwide demonstrations, and an almost equal number offering support for any endeavor the Council deemed essential. He and Griggs had been in the office since eight o'clock this morning and as of now, two hours later, more than five hundred telegrams had been received. Contacts at the White House said that telegrams were coming in at the rate of more than a thousand per hour; and although it was impossible to determine precisely the

261

number of protests being received on Capitol Hill, their contacts in the offices of a number of Senators and Representatives indicated a heavy influx of telegrams.

"Do you think Ted's killing represents a deliberate attempt, on the part of the government, to establish in the minds of the American people the idea that there is no essential difference between the Black Liberation Army and the Black American Council?" Griggs asked.

Simmons stood up from the table, raised his arms above his head, stretched, locked his hands behind his neck, then sat down again. The government had released its official statement on Ted Blackwell and Abdul Sharieff shortly after McGrowder had phoned them. The government's statement had been terse and to the point. Abdul Sharieff, the statement said, had been killed by two FBI agents while trying to escape apprehension for participation in the destruction of the Statue of Liberty, which had also resulted in the deaths of two workers. Ted Blackwell had been killed while attempting to aid Sharieff in his escape. Later on, about six o'clock this morning, the Department of Justice had amended the report by adding that it definitely had been established that Sharieff was a member of the Black Liberation Army and that new evidence was available linking him to the attack upon General Weyland.

"I don't believe Ted was killed because they believed he was helping Sharieff to escape," Simmons said. "I believe he was killed even more deliberately—simply because he was with Sharieff when he attempted to run away from apprehension. Anybody with Sharieff at that moment would have been killed—man, woman or child, preacher, washwoman, or student. And, probably, white, black, red, yellow or what have you. The fact that Ted was who he was has made it convenient for the government. This plus the fact that nobody has come up with a satisfactory answer why Ted was walking away from the church with Sharieff."

"But McGrowder and Kigh said Ted wanted to talk to Jerome White of the Back-to-Africa Movement, not Sharieff," Griggs said.

262

"Exactly. But he didn't talk to White. He was leaving the church with Sharieff."

"We know that," Griggs said. "But White said he didn't talk to Ted simply because he left with friends before Ted came down from the pulpit."

"Bob, I know that. But I'm talking from the government's viewpoint, or from the viewpoint the government wants to make public. Its role is to build a surreptitious connection between Ted and Sharieff, and consequently, between us and the Black Liberation Army. And this is not too difficult, especially since Sam Muhammed has not been heard from. So to complete my answer to your question, while Ted wasn't killed because he was an official of the BAC, the fact that he was is being used for all it's worth to tie the BAC to the BLA. No doubt about it."

Griggs sighed. "Well, there's nothing surprising about that. You know what the Attorney General told us Monday afternoon. And in the meantime, the search for Sam Muhammed goes on. By the government and by us."

"And every minute that he remains hidden, more and more people become convinced that the BLA is the military arm of the Black American Council."

"You just said it."

"This connection in the minds of the people also serves another purpose, from the government's point of view," Simmons said.

"What's that?"

"It keeps down speculation about the Black Liberation Army itself. About whether it's truly a valid black revolutionary organization, or just another creation of the government's intelligence system. Sharieff can't provide any answers. He's dead. That is, if Sharieff knew anything to tell anybody."

"Preston, what do *you* think?" Griggs asked.

"Oh, I think there's a genuine BLA, only completely infiltrated and almost totally manipulated by the intelligence system. Marcus Jackson feels the same."

"Ditto here," Griggs said. "But most of the known leaders of the BLA have been arrested during the past two days. Do you think they're the ones who blew the whistle on Sharieff?"

"Probably. If Sharieff actually participated in anything. It is noteworthy though that the arrested BLA leaders swear they had nothing to do with Sunday's and Monday's happenings, even though one said he wished he had participated in the castration of General Weyland."

Griggs laughed sardonically. "One doesn't have to be a member of the BLA to wish that," he said.

Simmons refilled his and Griggs' cups from the electric coffeepot on the table. "What do you think, Bob?" he asked. "Should we call the others in from the field, cancel the forums, or let them continue until Ted's funeral Friday?"

Simmons and Griggs sipped coffee simultaneously. Finally, Griggs said: "I've been wrestling with the same question. It seems to me that we have two questions here."

"How do you mean?"

"Well, I don't think it's a good idea to continue with the forums," he replied, the usual crispness coming back into his voice. "Blacks throughout the country are so inflamed over Ted, we couldn't get objective answers. And on the other hand, we don't want to give the impression that our steadfastness needs to be affirmed by a continuing grassroots discussion of policy. In short, both sides of the coin dictate against continuing the forums."

Not a bad analysis, Simmons told himself. Yet, didn't Griggs' second reason for discontinuing the forums suggest that they shouldn't have been called in the first place? Probably not, because when the decision was made two days ago, the public most likely didn't perceive of the Black American Council as being on the defensive, while it was almost certain that such was the public's perception today. He was positive this was the subtle difference which had led Griggs to his conclusion.

"Okay," he said, "I'm with you in calling off the forums. Now what about your answer to the other question? Do we call Rubye and the gang in from the field?"

Griggs shook his head. "Of course not," he said. "They

264

should stay out there and keep those telegrams rolling in. And a few local demonstrations might not hurt. It's still true that the best defense is a good offense."

Simmons laughed, feeling good inside. It was strange how often, despite all the philosophizing and theorizing, the best strategy was rooted in the obvious. He supposed that was also the reason why direct, uncomplicated men like Griggs made the best leaders.

"Okay, Bob," he said, "that takes care of the field. Now what about you and me? How do we join in the attack from the headquarters front?"

Before Griggs could answer, the door to his office opened and Eunice, his secretary, stepped inside. "A special report is on television," she said, pushing the button on the wall to activate the television mechanism.

"...To repeat," the announcer's voice was saying, "the FBI reported just seconds ago that Sam Muhammed, the Black American Council executive sought for the past few days on charges of complicity with the BLA, has been fatally wounded while resisting arrest in Philadelphia, bringing to two the high-ranking BAC members who have been slain within the past twelve hours. Ted Blackwell was killed last night in New York City under similar circumstances. To repeat, Sam Muhammed has been slain in Philadelphia while resisting arrest. This station will keep you informed as details come in...."

Chapter 27

3:00 P.M., Wednesday October 14, 1987

IT WAS the middle of the afternoon before Simmons and Griggs again addressed the question of how to launch an offensive from Council headquarters, and by then the question was more urgently in need of an answer than when Simmons had first asked it. For now, the deaths of two Council officials instead of one, with all their corollary ramifications, had to be fitted into the equation.

Simmons and Griggs had spent almost every minute of the past few hours on telephones—seeking information, answering questions, and issuing instructions. Most of the information had been sought from Council contacts in the Philadelphia area and from government officials in Washington, while the answers and instructions had culminated from interchanges between them and Council representatives throughout the country. The news media had been avoided, with the patent excuse that a full statement would be forthcoming later in the afternoon. At the same time, they had kept the television going, determined to keep abreast of media slants and fluctuations in public opinion.

Now, back in Griggs' office, with remnants of half-eaten sandwiches before them—having issued instructions to let only the most urgent telephone calls through—Simmons was reviewing in his mind the occurrences of the past few hours and the decisions they had reached relative to these occurrences.

According to reports, Sam Muhammed had been arrested

by Philadelphia city police, and not by the FBI. These reports stated emphatically that he had been shot by members of that city's police department in a "daring escape attempt" while being transferred from police headquarters to the FBI field office. To bolster this argument, pictures of Muhammed lying in the street had been flashed on television screens around the country. However, as was the case in the shooting of Ted Blackwell, names of the officers involved had not been released.

Since, as was generally known, Sam Muhammed had no living relatives, the Black American Council, through its Philadelphia office, laid immediate claim to his body. The general idea, as conceived by Jim Griggs, was to bring Muhammed to Washington where a joint funeral would be held for him and Ted Blackwell on Friday. However, opposition to this idea was raised immediately from two fronts. First, the leaders of the nationalist groups which Muhammed represented on the Council insisted that he be buried in New York City, the area of his greatest strength. Second, Ted Blackwell's mother reminded Simmons that he had promised to keep Ted's funeral as private as possible. After a minimum of low-key bickering, it was decided to hold Ted's funeral in Washington as planned and Sam's in New York City, both at eleven o'clock on Friday morning. Griggs would be the official representative of the Council at Ted's funeral and Simmons would perform the same function at Sam's. Other Council members and staff personnel were free to attend the funeral of their choice. Marcus Jackson was given the assignment of accompanying Sam's body from Philadelphia to New York City.

Bob Griggs cleared the table of sandwich wrappings and threw them in a waste basket. He moved slowly, as though very tired.

"Sam Muhammed might not have been any prize," he said, "but he didn't deserve to go like that." He had expressed this sentiment in almost the same words a number of times in the past few hours.

"You can say that again," Simmons said, aware that his

response to Bob's statement was also basically the same as on the other occasions. Ever since he had known Sam Muhammed he had attempted to determine just how he felt about him. Although he had always admired Sam's vitality, the tenacity with which he pursued his goals, Sam's tendency to deliberately offend people had always worried him. But one thing you had to give Sam, he told himself now. Probably more than any other person, he was responsible for the Council deciding to hold the referendum on separation.

"There is something very strange about Sam being killed so soon after Ted, and in almost the same manner," he said. "It is almost as though Sam had to be killed."

"Are you saying that Sam knew something which he couldn't be permitted to tell?" Griggs asked.

"It seems that way. Sam was killed soon after he was arrested, before he got a chance to talk to a lawyer or anybody."

Griggs pursed his mouth and made a sucking sound with his tongue. "If that is the case, Sam must have found out something before he went underground."

Simmons nodded. "That's probably true. He must have been on to something; otherwise, there would have been no reason to go underground."

"On to something, or *up* to something," Griggs said. "You could never tell about Sam."

Simmons nodded again. "Well, in any case, we'll keep digging. We have to make sure that Marcus keeps somebody busy trying to find out Sam's whereabouts since Sunday. Okay?"

"It's okay with me," Griggs replied. "But I have a feeling we'll never know." Suddenly, he spoke again, with the spontaneity of a new idea. "If, as we think, Sam was killed before he could tell something he knew—I can't see why the feds brought the Philly cops into the picture. That's unnecessarily complicating things."

"They brought the Philadelphia police into it for the reason you made the statement," Simmons said.

"How's that?" Griggs asked. "Oh, I get you. Most people's

268

first reaction to the apparent complication will be the same as mine. And with some of them, the first reaction will become the final conclusion."

"Right. Any little old doubt helps. Especially where political assassinations are concerned."

"Okay," Griggs said, resting his folded arms on the table and leaning forward, "now what about our statement. The one we've been promising the media all day?"

Simmons locked his hands behind his head and stared at the ceiling. "Try this on for size," he said, speaking slowly. "I believe we should go all-out in our attack. We should accuse the government of engaging in systematic extermination of the leadership of the Black American Council. We should say what we've just said—that the Philadelphia police were used in the slaying of Sam to divert attention from the FBI. We should hit hard on the manner in which Sharieff was killed, charge excessive force by pointing out that, in the opinion of witnesses, Sharieff could have been stopped without killing him and especially without killing *an innocent bystander*. Unless, of course, the aim was to kill the bystander also. The last will tie in with the first—the intention of the government to eliminate all BAC leaders."

Griggs whistled. "That's hitting hard, all right. Do you believe what you've just said?"

Simmons pulled his eyes from the ceiling and met Griggs' probing stare. "Yes and no," he said. "I have no doubt they would like to eliminate us. But I don't believe they have a plan for it. Not yet, anyway."

"Do you believe that saying they have such a plan will delay its formation?"

"Probably. But the reason I'm suggesting that we say it is to keep us in the fight in the minds of the public. As you said this morning, the best defense is still a good offense."

Griggs laughed. "Condemned by my own words. Okay, I'll buy your approach."

Simmons noticed that Griggs was looking at him in a peculiar manner, and he realized they were thinking about the same thing: the time had come to ask Ted Blackwell to draft a statement from the agreement they had just reached. He could feel a tightness in his chest and a fullness in his throat, and he knew he couldn't trust his voice.

"Young Vernon White will draft the statement," Griggs said, his voice husky. "According to Ted, he is almost as good as he was."

"Okay, give it to him then," Simmons said.

The phone rang. Griggs walked over to his desk, picked up the phone and stood listening for a few seconds. He pushed the hold button and turned to Simmons.

"This is Gene Wild on the phone. He wants a conference with us as soon as possible."

So Gene Wild, chairman of the Congressional Black Caucus, wanted to talk, Simmons thought to himself. He hadn't talked to Wild since shortly before accepting the job as chief negotiator for the Council. To Griggs, he said: "Is it your understanding that Wild is coming out for the Rielinski plan next week?"

"Yes, that's what our sources say. Next week at the AFL—CIO convention."

"What do you think?" Simmons asked. "Does Wild want to tell us himself, or try to convert us?"

"Both. Also Bill Green wants to sit in on any conversation we have," Griggs replied.

Good old Bill Green, Simmons thought, He would never forget the agony in the old man's eyes the day he severed ties with the negotiating team.

"If it's okay with you, it's all right with me," he said to Griggs.

Griggs nodded affirmatively.

"Okay, then," Simmons said, "tell them we'll talk to them Friday evening, after the funerals. I'll fly back from New York Friday afternoon. Is seven o'clock all right? In my hotel suite?"

Griggs nodded, pushed the button removing the telephone from hold, and imparted the information to Wild.

He seemed very tired as he walked back to the table.

Chapter 28

3:00 P.M., Friday, October 16, 1987

SIMMONS RETURNED to Washington from Sam Muhammed's funeral in New York at approximately two-thirty on Friday afternoon. He went directly to his hotel suite, determined to relax undisturbed for a few hours before the scheduled meeting with Wild and Green. The past two days had been so hectic that he felt drained and rootless, as though he were losing his sense of purpose. Events appeared to be occurring without his having anything to do with the direction they were taking.

Sam's funeral had seemed almost like a staged affair. And in a way, it had been. The mayor of the city, anticipating violence, had left few things to chance. Upon hearing of Sam's death, he had worked out a deal with the governor to have the national guard patrol the streets, beginning on Wednesday evening. By the time Sam's body arrived in Harlem, the city was sealed up tight. Therefore, the huge crowd which attended Sam's funeral was under rigid control, even though it spilled over into a two-block area surrounding the mosque where the funeral was held.

Arriving at the mosque in the company of four bodyguards of his own and escorted by a three-car police contingent, Simmons felt insulated and unreal, enslaved and patronized at

271

the same time. The government definitely was out to prevent his charges of "systematic extermination" of BAC leadership from coming true, at least on this Friday in New York City.

The funeral services were composed of an equal mixture of Muslim and Christian rituals, respecting until the last Sam Muhammed's claim of equal identification with both groups. The ceremony was simple and impressive, consisting of songs, chants, poetry readings, prayers, and two eloquent sermons, one by a Black Muslim and the other by Dr. McGrowder. Sitting in the front row usually reserved for members of the family, Simmons almost lost his feeling of isolation during Dr. McGrowder's sermon. Calling the grave the "final democratic abode" of man, Dr. McGrowder stated that death gave "an irrefutable lie" to human distinctions. He said that Sam Muhammed, through his "quickness to choose up sides" was impatient with mankind's tendency to "disavow change and progress," thereby guaranteeing that "each of us will forever remain alien to the other." The service had closed with a series of Muslim prayers followed by a Negro spiritual, sung by the choir from Dr. McGrowder's church. Earlier, Simmons had refused an invitation to speak, and he was glad he had.

Rubye sat next to him at the funeral, resplendent in a long black two-piece tunic with a white lace veil, representing, like the service itself, a gesture toward the two cultures which Muhammed espoused. Her face, beneath the checkered openings of the lace veil, was without makeup, smooth and serene, causing him to assert, once again, that she definitely had found the Fountain of Youth. She held his hand periodically during the services, helping to push back for a while the feeling of unreality and rekindling the currents of communion which always flowed between them.

"I saw your girl friend as I came in," she said at one point.

"My girl friend?"

"Hilda."

"Oh, is she here? But she would be, wouldn't she?"

"You got that right."

And Hilda was there, of course. He spotted her as he came

272

out of the mosque, waved, but kept going. He had to get back to Washington. Rubye said goodbye to him before he entered his limousine. She was going to fly straight from New York to Chicago, and had made her own arrangements for getting to the airport.

Now, in his hotel suite, Simmons was putting on his pajamas when the phone rang. Bob Griggs was on the line.

"I'm getting ready to take a nap," Simmons said. "Things still set for this evening?"

"Yes. Seven o'clock," Griggs replied.

"How was Ted's funeral?" Simmons asked.

"Surprisingly subdued."

"I suppose you could say the same about Sam's," Simmons said. "Okay, see you sometime before seven?"

"Right."

When Green and Wild arrived at exactly ten minutes after seven, Griggs and Simmons were waiting for them in an atmosphere of expansive hospitality—like close friends who see each other often rolling out the carpet for equally close friends who are making their first trip to the city after an extended absence. Simmons had awakened at six, showered, dressed in slacks and sport shirt, and called room service for refreshments and sandwiches. Room service had responded more quickly than usual so that by the time Griggs arrived, at seven o'clock, he had eaten two sandwiches and was drinking his second glass of sherry. The plane he had taken from New York had been too late for lunch and too early for dinner. Griggs poured himself a scotch and water and joined in the wait for Green and Wild.

Standing to receive his guests as Griggs opened the door to admit them, Simmons was surprised that he hadn't noticed the general resemblance between Bill Green and Gene Wild before, with Wild being a younger and smaller version of the Urban League director. They both were light-brown skinned with thin faces and full heads of bushy hair. Only Green's hair was gray while Wild's was dark brown. Green was tall, slender and stoop-shouldered, and Wild was merely slender and stoop-shouldered, some six inches shorter than Green. However, in their movements and manner of speaking, they were not alike at all. Green moved slowly and talked slowly, while Wild moved swiftly and talked in animated gestures. He supposed this was the primary reason he hadn't noticed the physical resemblance before.

Pulling off his topcoat and handing it to Griggs, Wild said to Simmons: "Man, they have you locked in here like Fort Knox! How do you stand it?"

Simmons helped Green pull off his topcoat, took Wild's coat from Griggs and went over to the closet and hung them up. When he returned to his seat on the couch, all three of his guests were seated—Griggs on the couch and Wild and Green in chairs facing the couch, on the other side of the cocktail table. Simmons noticed that all three of his guests were dressed in modish three-piece suits.

"Over-protection is the first real indication that you have arrived," he replied to Wild's statement, his tone light. "But, then, you know that, Gene."

He had always liked the chairman of the Congressional Black Caucus and had interviewed him a number of times for articles in national publications. Now he was thinking especially about the article he had written when Wild, as chairman of the Caucus, had resigned from the Black American Council following the decision to hold the separation referendum, thereby ending Caucus membership on the Council. Even though the Congressional Black Caucus had a rotating chairmanship, it seemed that Wild's turn came up more often than anybody's else's. This was because he was the real leader of the Caucus, regardless of who was chairman, Simmons told himself.

"Fellows, fix yourselves drinks," he said, motioning to the filled cocktail table, "and have a snack, if you are hungry."

When they were holding drinks—Green a scotch and water and Wild a bourbon on the rocks—Green said to Griggs: "Bob, how are things going?" Concern was in his voice.

Griggs shrugged, but his face was untroubled when he replied. "Fine, Bill. When you get a tiger by the tail, you hold on."

Green nodded. Wild set his glass on the table and, spreading his slender hands in an outward arc, said: "Okay, let's get down to cases. We're here for a unity meeting." His sharp brown eyes switched from Simmons to Griggs, then back again.

"I'm employed by the Council," Simmons said, "and Bob is only one member of the Council. You know we can't make a decision without the Council. And I doubt if even the Council has a moral right to go against the referendum." He paused. "Now, this is not saying that Bob and I personally have any reason to want to change our positions. I'm just putting everything on the table, up front. Okay?"

Wild brought his hands together. "Okay," he agreed. "But we can talk?"

"I understand you've talked to Rielinski?" Green asked, looking at Simmons.

"Yes. I talked to Joe just before I took that swing across the country last week, whipping up the demonstrations."

"Before the shit hit the fan," Wild said with a chuckle.

"Yes, you might say that," Simmons said.

"And you might also say something else," Green said slowly. "You might say that the demonstrations were one of the principal reasons why...things have started getting out of hand."

Simmons felt himself smiling. Green couldn't bring himself to use Wild's phrase. He supposed his observation about their resemblance definitely was limited to the physical, all right.

"Yes, Bill," he said, "I suppose you could say that our decision to hold the demonstrations convinced the government that we weren't fooling. And they have responded to our peaceful demonstrations with violence. Yes, you could say that."

Wild picked up his glass, sipped, and set it down again. "Look, fellows," he said, "let's stop kidding ourselves. The government isn't going to let blacks set up a separate nation. I'm not saying the entire decision would be left to them, if blacks were united in their desire for a separate country. But we aren't, and they know it. In one respect you fellows have been right in the last few days—they'll eliminate the entire leadership of the Council before they'll let you succeed."

Simmons emptied his sherry glass, feeling the liquid warm his insides. "It hasn't come to that yet," he said, "regardless of what we've been saying."

"Yes, but why go down a dead-end street?" Wild asked. "This time there is an alternative."

"Yeh, I know," Simmons laughed. "Rielinski told me all about it."

Wild spread his hands. "Come off it, Preston," he said. "Rielinski doesn't deserve that tone of voice, and you know it. In fact, you helped develop some of his ideas over the years."

"I know," Simmons said. "But it's so hard to trust white folks. And Rielinski doesn't have the proper guarantees built in yet."

"That's why we need you," Wild said. "The militance of this separatist movement is required to keep the more conservative elements in Rielinski's group in line. Everything is a constant fight. You'd have that on your hands, even if you got your separate nation."

"Hey, Gene, back up a little," Griggs said, speaking up for the first time. "There are a few philosophical questions which need to be settled. Especially for an old integrationist like me."

"Shoot," Wild said.

"I want to ask Bill a question," Griggs said. "Bill, you have always been an integrationist—so, okay, I gave up my claim to the tag when I supported the separate nation—but you haven't. Then, how can you be joining up with Rielinski, who definitely is no integrationist?"

"A good question, Bob," Green said carefully, looking hard at Griggs. "Well, I'll tell you, it's like this. Rielinski has changed the elements of the equation, by making it in the interest of the white working class to work with us. In the past, Americans, including blacks, loved to refer to this country as a melting pot. The truth is, it has never been that. The essence of ethnic pluralism has been present from the beginning. A mosaic, not a melting pot. And that is a good thing. People want to preserve their cultures. At least at this time in history. But we can't let the special interests, the rich and powerful, continue to take advantage of this desire. This is the reason why we have to stop concentrating on the things which divide us—like integration—and start concentrating on those things in which we have a primary common interest—like redistributing the wealth of this country."

Griggs ran his thumb and forefinger along his mustache. "What you are talking about, Bill, are respect and equality. If white folks didn't respect us enough to integrate with us, how do you figure they'll respect us enough to give us our fair share when the wealth is being redistributed?"

"I'll tell you why," Wild said, before Green could reply. "They'll join with us to fight for redistribution of the wealth because they can't win it without us. And if they can win it on a pluralistic rather than an integrated basis, so much the better, especially from their viewpoint."

"Are you saying, Gene," Simmons asked, "that the 1954 Supreme Court position that separate can never be equal is dead?"

"Of course I'm saying it, Preston," Wild said, "and you know it as well as I do. Just because separate was not equal before 1954 is no reason to assume that it can't be equal in 1988. Then we didn't have the power to enforce equity. Now we do." Wild looked straight at Griggs. "I don't see why a little separatism alarms you, Bob. You're pushing for a separate nation."

Griggs laughed. "Good and funny! Remember, Gene, I put in my disclaimer before I asked Bill the question I did. But don't think I don't have an answer. And the answer is this: it's a hell of a lot different being separate in your own, than separate in somebody else's."

"Amen!" Simmons said, and poured himself another drink.

Wild hooked his thumbs underneath his vest and leaned back in his chair. "It's strange how often what's really worrying people comes out in jest," he said. "The idea is to make ethnic and racial pluralism work in a country which belongs to all of us. The reason why ethnic neighborhoods have been more acceptable to whites in the past than they have to us is because white ethnic groups have had control over the political and economic aspects of their communities, while we have not. We've merely occupied the land. As you know, the Rielinski proposal calls for a Marshall Plan for black communities. The same kind that Jesse Jackson called for in the seventies. Additionally, the proposal calls for improved loans, bonding, insurances, etc., for black business to participate more fully in the general business community like, for instance, the Loop in Chicago. Some of these ideas come from those first presented in the Minority Enterprise Act of 1976, as introduced by Baltimore Congressman Parren J. Mitchell."

"I know you always looked upon me as being the right-wing member on the Council," Green said, looking at Griggs. "And I admit I was, for a long time. But I'm no fool, and I've observed for years how big business has resisted every logical proposal to expand the base for creating jobs in this country. And the job base must be expanded, in the so-called private productive sector. The extent to which job shortages are eliminated, we can de-emphasize programs like affirmative action. And when emphasis on these programs are played down, racial and ethnic tensions resulting from them will also decrease, making it possible to increase pressure on the Man."

Griggs laughed. "Well, I'll be damned!" he said. "Bill, I never thought I'd live to see the day when you endorsed a government take-over of public utilities and certain major industries as a means of guaranteeing full employment."

"As of this day," Green said, "consider yourself as having lived so long."

"Let me say something else," Wild said, locking his fingers together and speaking rapidly. "The basis of the Rielinski plan is giving people what they want, as long as what they want doesn't limit anybody else's options. First, it calls for creating white, black and integrated neighborhoods in major cities, and letting people have choices. But the sizes of these neighborhoods will be controlled by the numbers of people expressing

278

choices. None of that business of a few whites having all the land and blacks being jammed together in high-rises. What did Jesse Jackson call it way back in 1970? Placing a quarter on a dime. The plan also calls for deliberately creating neighborhood and district-wide schools, and permitting parents to send their children to either. To encourage integration, the per capita outlay for the integrated schools will be higher, but the outlay for all schools will be sufficient."

"I can go for that idea," Green cut in, more talkative as a militant than Simmons had remembered him to be as a conservative. "If white folks don't want to integrate, let them stay separate. This might be a form of blackmail, but so be it. Seriously, though, it gives recognition to the fact that freedom of choice is the most cherished freedom we have. Only this time we're going to guarantee that black folks will not be victimized by the freedom of choice of white folks."

Wild stood up and asked where the bathroom was located. Simmons decided to do some deliberate thinking while he was gone, to determine just where the conversation was going. Wild and Green, like Rielinski nearly two weeks before, were putting up a strong argument for their position. Since World War I, however, socialist theorists and strategists had dreamed of putting together the type of coalition they were talking about. The New Deal, Fair Deal, New Frontier and Great Society of the Roosevelt, Truman, Kennedy and Johnson eras had been similar in composition, yet these coalitions had fallen far short of what Rielinski had in mind, in that they had not been class-oriented. In fact, American radical movements had always pulled back from genuine classism, succumbing to big business propaganda that class ideology was the natural enemy of democracy. It was this fear in the American people which had defeated McGovern in 1972 and caused Carter to try so hard to appease big business in 1977. He wondered if Rielinski's base, a decade later, was as broad as he thought it to be. He voiced his doubts to Wild when he returned from the bathroom.

"I believe the support is there in depth," Wild said. "The

279

traditional labor union members are behind Rielinski, having been made more radical in the past ten years by a decline in jobs due to foreign inroads in the basic industries they represent and, of course, the Reagan thrust. Public workers are solid in their support, primarily because government at all levels and public institutions have made the mistake of being in rigid opposition to collective bargaining agreements during the past decade. The Spanish-speaking population loves Rielinski. And most of the blacks who aren't following you are following him. Revolution is in the air, Preston, and you can't afford to be branded as the organization which refused to help advance democracy in this country."

Wild's eyes were sparkling when he finished speaking and Simmons had no doubt that the Congressional Black Caucus leader genuinely believed what he said.

"So you think the country will get a look at what Rielinski really has next week?" he asked.

"No doubt about it," Wild said. "Everybody's coming to the convention to testify."

Simmons looked at Griggs, and Griggs nodded.

"Okay," Simmons said. "I'll tell you the same thing I told Rielinski. Let's talk after the convention. Look at what you have, and what we have. Then we'll decide on whether to put your proposition to the Council."

Wild looked at him for a long time without speaking, eyes unblinking. Suddenly he thrust his arm across the table, reaching for a handshake.

"That sounds all right to me," he said.

Chapter 29

10:00 P.M., Friday, October 16, 1987

TIME HAD reversed itself. He was back on a job he had held twenty years ago, shortly before his first novel was published, when he had worked for a year as the assistant manager of a state centralized computer installation in Springfield, Illinois. And even though he had experienced some hectic times on the job—daily having to prove to the high-minded white systems analysts and software specialists that he was worthy of being their boss—the situation he was experiencing now made those times seem like childish antics at a Sunday School picnic. Everywhere confusion reigned. Workers, some of whom he recognized as through a dim fog, danced in the aisles. Pop and beer cans were strewn about the floors. The manager's office was just down the corridor, yet the workers did not seem to notice. They were dancing, drinking, having a good time. Some of the fellows were kissing girls, leaning them precariously against the wall of the computer room. He was walking among them, pulling at coat and shirt sleeves, yet no one seemed to notice him. He tried to shout above the noise, but he could barely hear his own voice. What if the boss came out of his office and saw this disrespect for rules, observed his inability to get the workers to stop dancing, singing and kissing? He would be in a pickle. Because, after all, he was the assistant boss and should have enough influence to get things done. He felt as though he were stifling. His arms were stiff and he could barely move his hands. He pleaded and pleaded and his voice got lower and lower.

Suddenly there was a loud pealing sound. The sound grew louder and louder until it seemed to be coming from everywhere, drowning out the noise the workers were making.

He opened his eyes. The telephone was ringing. He had been dreaming.

Turning over in bed, freeing his arms and shoulders from the covers, he picked up the phone.

"A Miss Hilda Larsen is down here," the voice of the desk clerk said. "She wants to come up. In fact, she is already on her way up."

"Okay," he said and placed the phone in its cradle.

The peculiar tenseness was beginning to rise in him. He didn't try to fool himself. It was more than the normal anticipation of being alone with a woman, even one who was still new and unexplored. This feeling was made up of the strange uniqueness he had come to associate with Hilda. Inviting and fearful at the same time.

He rolled off the bed, picked up his robe from the bedside table, and went into the sitting room, putting on the robe as he walked. He glanced at his wristwatch. Ten o'clock. Wild, Green and Griggs had been gone more than an hour.

He was sitting on the couch when she rapped softly on the door, so softly that it sounded more like a scratch than a knock. He opened the door and she walked past him without looking at him. When he turned from the door, she was standing by the couch, walking the fingers of her left hand along the couch's arm. She was wearing a long trench coat, and her hair was pulled back from her head and held by a clip at the base of her neck, the same way she had worn it the night she and Rubye came to his room. She was holding a large canvas purse in her right hand.

"Have a seat," he said, sitting on the couch. Without a word, she sat down beside him. She seemed nervous, and he wondered if he gave her the same contradictory feeling she gave him.

"I see you had a session with Green and Wild," she finally said.

He was surprised to hear her mention the meeting. Memory of it was completely out of tune with what he was feeling.

"How did you know?" he asked.

"Most of the world knows about the meeting by now," she said.

He shrugged. It was so difficult to keep remembering that, at this moment in history at least, he was one of the world's most newsworthy persons.

"You didn't come up here to talk about them," he said. "Or did you?"

She humped her shoulders. "No, I didn't," she said.

He bent slightly forward, turning his head so that he could look into her eyes. She obliged him by turning her head to meet his gaze, at the same time raising her left hand to play with her right ear lobe. The pupils of her eyes were prominent and alert.

"To what, then, do I owe the pleasure of this visit?" he asked.

Her eyes did not blink, but continued to stare, as though she were trying to see inside him. "Are you sure it's a pleasure?" she asked.

He turned his head from her and leaned back on the couch. Things were getting difficult. She was reprimanding him, as though she were there by invitation and was being treated in an inhospitable manner. Women always found a way to make everything a man's fault, he told himself.

"Pleasure? Pain? Is there really a difference?" he asked.

She didn't reply. Standing up from the couch, she nodded in the direction of the bathroom. "May I?" she asked.

He nodded in the affirmative. She picked up her purse from the couch and, moving in long yet strangely seductive strides, went into the bathroom, the poignant, exhilarating scent of her lingering around him like a fog.

The last time she was in this room, he reminded himself, he had believed he could have seduced her but had refrained because to have done so would have been doing both of them a disservice. And last week, when she followed him across the country from demonstration to demonstration, he had ended the week with a feeling that a bond more spiritual than physical was developing between them. And he had thought this was happening in her mind as well as his.

Cut out the bull shit! he reprimanded himself brutally, twisting around on the couch. Sure, he had thought these things but they had represented only a portion of his cogitative process as he had struggled in vain to formulate a conclusive opinion of her. And probably the main reason for this failure, he told himself now, was because the deliberation itself had been so stimulating! But this was not the time nor place for even that kind of deliberation. She was here and he was here. The only thing to do now was to remain cool and adjust to the unpredictability of her presence.

He glanced across the room. His eyes stopped at the small table in the corner on which were located the remnants of the refreshments acquired for the meeting. Dammit, he'd forgotten to offer her a drink. Sherry was her favorite, and there was plenty of that left.

As he stood up to go over to the table to fix the drinks, she came out of the bathroom. He stood staring at her, the drinks forgotten. She was wearing a long blue gown which came almost to the floor, the bottom gingerly caressing her bare feet. The top of the gown was cut low, exposing the swell of her large breasts where they began their outward and downward curve. Her blonde hair was hanging loose, covering the sides of her face, neck and shoulders like a silken screen. Her lips were moist and parted slightly in a half smile, revealing the edges of her teeth and tip of her tongue.

She came toward him, reaching out her hand.

His thoughts were fleeting and mixed, jumping over each other for supremacy. So that had been the reason for the large bag: to carry the gown. Anticipation of what she planned to do was the reason she had been so nervous. She was bold, of that he was sure, but even the boldest of people occasionally shrink

284

from the effects of their anticipated actions. Talk about the unpredictability of her presence! Could he remain cool as he had vowed he would? Hell, no!

He walked around the cocktail table, took her outreached hand, which was strangely cool to his touch, and pulled her to him. She yielded so completely that her body felt boneless, her large breasts suppliant against his chest, like the feel of quality foam rubber. He looked into her eyes. They were a sparkling pool of green.

"Two of the basic elements requires for lovemaking are present here now with us," she murmured, taking a long time to finish the sentence, so that it sounded disjointed and out of place.

"And they are?" he asked, feeling his penis hardening, as his thighs pressed against hers.

"Need and desire," she whispered. "You need me and I want you."

She was right, of course. About the need and desire. But he doubted if all of the need was on his part and all of the desire on hers. Both were present in both of them. Maybe not in equal parts. But both were present.

He kissed her, the knowledge that it was the first time screaming loud in his mind. Her lips felt so thin, yet so soft. He got a peculiar sensation that her mouth was smaller than it should have been; that he was kissing the mouth of a child. He could feel his penis coming to full erection. He kissed her harder and harder, consuming her lips.

Then she was moving away from him, leading him toward the bedroom.

With a sense of wonder, his hand in hers, he found himself following her.

Then, suddenly, with bounding eagerness, he caught up with her and took the lead in the race to the bedroom, desire swelling and swelling within him, overpowering his inquisitiveness and blotting out his trepidation.

Chapter 30

8:00 A.M., Saturday, October 17, 1987

As HAD been the case of late, Preston Simmons observed, the newspaper headlines were not kind on this Saturday morning following his strenuous sexual session with Hilda Larsen. He was alone in his hotel suite, sitting on the couch with papers strewn around him, keenly aware of how comforting it was to be by himself. Not that Hilda hadn't been good company, he mused, but she was a luxury he could afford only in small doses—both physically and psychologically. Additionally, he was convinced that their being together the night before had not basically altered their relationship. When she had left about one o'clock this morning, dressing quickly without fanfare as though on the spur of the moment, he sensed that there had developed between them a silent agreement of non-commitment: a subtle understanding that a more binding decision was being postponed until a time more suitable to both of them.

BLACK LEADER BLASTS BAC/AS TERRORISTS OFFER AID, one newspaper headline screamed. The black leader, of course, was Jim Sneed, calling for "detention of Council leaders, especially in view of the fact that terrorist groups are openly in support of the BAC." The terrorists groups referred to in the article, and by Sneed, were the Black

Liberation Army and the Fighters for Freedom, a white group that had been active in the job riots, and which only surfaced periodically. According to the news story, the executive boards of the two groups had met the night before and offered to aid the BAC "in any manner mutually agreed upon." In offering the aid, however, the BLA had again stressed that they were not responsible for the castration of General Weyland and the other "highly publicized atrocities" of the past week.

LABOR CHIEFTAIN/HITS UNITY BID was the main headline in another newspaper. Mike Nelson was the labor chieftain and the unity bid he was hitting was Joe Rielinski's continued attempts to get the Black American Council to join forces with him, the latest trigger being the meeting among Wild, Green, Griggs and himself. "I have warned repeatedly," Nelson was quoted as saying, "that Joe Rielinski has nothing less than a Communist takeover of this country in mind. And who are his allies? The most violent-prone left-wingers in this country, including the known traitors heading the Black American Council. Don't be fooled by their attempt to play coy. They are with Joe Rielinski and Rielinski is with them. The American people, especially American workers, will not be mislead."

Poor Joe, Simmons said to himself. He had his Nelson and they had their Sneed. Maybe they did deserve each other.

He glanced at his wristwatch. A little after eight o'clock. At nine he was due in the office for a meeting with Griggs and Vernon White to map media strategy for the weekend. He sure as hell missed Ted Blackwell. Vernon was good, but there was no substitute for experience.

There was a light knock on the door. He wasn't expecting anybody. "Who is it?" he asked, noting that his voice was cagey.

"A letter for you, Mr. Simmons," the voice of one of his bodyguards said.

"Okay, Jack," he replied, and went over and slid the chain off the door. The bodyguard handed him the letter through the opening. "It's been inspected," he said.

287

"Thanks, Jack," he said, closed the door, and went back to the couch and sat down.

The envelope was legal-sized and brown. It had been opened, undoubtedly because of the inspection by the bodyguards. Folded inside were ten or twelve sheets of white bond typing paper. He opened the folded sheets of paper, studying the first page. The page was covered with neat firm handwriting, vaguely familiar. The salutation said: "Dear Preston, Joe and Moses." He pulled the last sheet from beneath the others, searching for a signature. When he found the signature, his heart fluttered, leaving a peculiar hollowness below his breastbone. The signature was that of Sam Muhammed!

Dear Preston, Joe and Moses:

When you receive this letter, I will be dead. I can state this with certainty, for if I am not dead, you will not receive this letter. I will not tell you how I know this, for to do so will expose those persons who have been instrumental in getting this letter to you. And this I will not do. You will have to take my word for it that if my death is not common knowledge when you receive this letter, I am dead nevertheless. For you see, in a few hours I shall tell the government intelligence group (call it the FBI for want of a better name, because they are the same) for whom I have worked for ten years that I will work for them no longer, that I refuse to carry out their latest bizarre assignment. Further, I shall tell them that I am going to make a public statement exposing our relationship and giving details about the things I have done for them through the years. When I tell them this, they cannot let me live. I don't know how they will dispose of me. But they cannot let me live.

As you can tell by the date, I am writing this letter on Wednesday. It is very early Wednesday morning. By noon today, two copies of the letter will have been made and all three copies given to the proper people with instructions that if I do not personally pick them up by Friday mid-

288

night, they must be delivered to three people: Preston Simmons, Joe Rielinski, and Moses Pennmann. These people must be located wherever they are and this letter delivered to them. They are honorable men. I trust them to use it wisely.

As I said in the beginning of this letter, I have been working for the FBI about ten years. Those of you who are familiar with the biography of Sam Muhammed will recall that in 1977 I was leading a somewhat obscure group of black nationalists in New York City known as the New Movement. My group was little different from a number of other black nationalist groups trying to fill the void left by the jailing of Rap Brown, the flight of Huey Newton, the defection of Eldridge Cleaver and the conversion of Stokely Carmichal to Pan Africanism. Well, I did have two things going for me. The first was my name. As you know, I had been an orphan with the name of Sam Johnson, but I had changed the Johnson to Muhammed and kept the Sam intact: Muhammed for my ancient birthright, and Sam for my modern slave experience in America. This was probably the first time the concept of who black Americans really are was handled with psychological correctness. Second, I had wrapped the mantle of Malcolm X around myself. I had been a dope addict and a pimp, and had kicked both habits. Of course, I hadn't really kicked the dope habit, but everybody seemed to think I had. Everybody, that is, but the government intelligence agencies.

Anyway, in April of 1977 the FBI came to me with a proposition. If I would cooperate with them, they'd help make me the leader of the black nationalist groups in the country. How would they do it? Simply by putting extra pressure on my rivals and providing me with operating and expansion funds. Of course, there was the little matter of giving me money to buy all the dope I needed, or providing me with the dope outright. But honestly, it wasn't the dope which sold me on the idea. It was the operating and expansion money and the pressure on the other groups. I desperately wanted to be top dog in the black nationalist movement because I believed in it. In accepting the proposition, I considered myself something of a double agent. I told myself that one day I would find a way to out-smart the FBI, and in the meantime, I wouldn't let them make me do anything that was too far from my principles, something that couldn't be corrected when I got the chance.

For a long time, the FBI didn't give me any specific assignment. And with the money coming in and the other groups being harassed, it wasn't long before I was the recognized national leader of the black nationalists. This taught me one lesson. The primary reason for the failure of black organizations is money. Let me tell you something that is very funny indeed. I became so enthused with my organizing work, that I actually kicked the dope habit. Kicked it cold! I was slick though. I didn't let the FBI know that I kicked it, and to this day they aren't aware of it.

The first actual assignment I received from the FBI was in 1983, at the beginning of the so-called job riots. They gave me instructions to have my people storm employment offices all over the country and to not pass up an opportunity to tangle with the police. Hell, this was an assignment I liked. This kind of action was needed anyway. Well, it would have been the correct tactics if the masses of black and poor people had been ready for action. However, in the end, our boldness turned public opinion against the jobless and the poor, and the movement for full employment was destroyed.

The FBI definitely didn't like the idea of the Black American Council being created in 1984. But they realized there was nothing I could do to stop it, considering it was such a logical extension of nationalist philosophy. For a while, they dickered with the idea of my coming out against it by saying that it would be a step backward for my group to join forces with less militant groups. But I pointed out to them that this idea wouldn't wash—that it would be better to let the Council be created and I become a prime member of the governing body. I also pointed out that I doubted if they could stop it without attacking groups they didn't want to attack. In the end they bought my argument that my being on the Council was the better move.

The next thing the FBI ordered me to do was definitely in line with what I wanted to do. They thought that if the Council could be influenced to call for a referendum of separation, and the voting actually took place, the referendum would be so badly beaten that the Council would lose face with all black Americans and then the government could move in and destroy it. First, of course, we had to get the Council to vote for the referendum, before the question could be put to the people. And for a while it was close. You will recall that during the debate, Gene Wild urged that instead of calling for a separation referendum, the Council should push for a self-determination posture to be exercised in a manner and at a time to be determined by the Council. Griggs and Green supported this position, while Patten and James supported me. Rubye Ransome broke the tie when she came out in favor of my position.

The FBI was very happy. They were so sure the referendum was going to be defeated by an overwhelming margin they didn't try to interfere with the election. They didn't even attempt to get me to go slow in working for the referendum. But I had a feeling that it was going to carry. I was aware of the high level of frustration in the minds of millions of blacks and the tendency toward the spectacular in the minds of millions of others. I was certain if blacks could be convinced that this was something big, those who hadn't been voting on less important issues would come out and vote. And I was further convinced that those who had never voted would come out and vote for the referendum. Well, as you know, I was right and the FBI was wrong.

Immediately after the vote, the FBI began attempting to discredit the Council by tying it to foreign powers unfriendly to the United States and to domestic violent groups, both black and white. The FBI's position, of course, was designed to make a crackdown on Council leaders in particular and blacks in general more acceptable to the American public. The only trouble was, the violent groups didn't cooperate by committing violent deeds. Given time, of course, these groups would have come up with something. But the government didn't have time. The Council had to be discredited before the white American public started thinking the Council had the moral right to negotiate for a separate nation.

So the FBI had to manufacture some violence. They got a break when Jim Sneed and his people agreed to physical attacks upon Council demonstrators, proving that many blacks are violently opposed to the separate nation, but this wasn't really the kind of violence the FBI needed most. The Council had to be tied to something which would strike a raw nerve of resentment in the American people.

What am I about to say now I can't prove—because I wasn't in on the planning. But I have heard from a good source that the FBI and CIA made a deal to have phony BLA members castrate General Weyland. He was selected because he was getting out of hand. I don't know in exactly what way he was getting out of hand, but this source swears that he was. Sharieff was killed last night simply because the FBI had to show that something was being done about Weyland's castration. Blackwell, innocent little Blackwell, was killed for no reason other than he was with Sharieff. Of course, his being the executive director of the Council didn't hurt. If necessary, the fact that Blackwell was with Sharieff could be used to prove that the Council and the BLA had secrets to talk over.

Now I come to what was to have been my role in the scheme. A role I will never play. Early Sunday morning I came with the FBI to Philadelphia, where I was to make my big play. I was to stay out of sight until they gave the word. Then I was to call a press conference and tell the world that the BAC and the BLA are working together, have jointly been responsible for the castration of Wey-land, the defiling of the church statue in New Orleans, and blowing the head off the Statue of Liberty. Philadelphia was chosen for maximun effect—the cradle of American democracy, etc. I was to play this angle big. Defending liberty in the cradle of democracy. I was to make it clear the reason why nobody had seen me since Sunday was because I had been running for my life because the BLA had somehow got wind of what I was going to do.

They told me last night after Sharieff and Blackwell were killed that I was to call the press conference today. I acted like I was glad the time had come, so I could get a little time to myself to write this letter and get it to the proper people.

Now I know the first question which comes to mind is that since they aren't keeping such a close watch on me—in fact trust me—why don't I just go to the news media and tell my story. I've thought about that for a long time, and the more I think about it the more I know it wouldn't work. Nobody would believe me. Everybody would believe that my story was just a Council trick to make the FBI look bad. The only way my story will be believed is for me not to be around to tell it. The voice from the grave, so to speak. Oh, I know there is a slight possibility the FBI will not kill me. Will let me go and take a chance on the public not believing my story, or that I might not say anything for fear the public will not believe it. Of course, if one of these two things happen you will not be reading this letter—at least not under circumstances you are now reading it.

Now I would like to say something especially to the

*leaders of the Black American Council. I believe the time
has come for you to join up with the group headed by
Rielinski. Don't get me wrong, I still prefer a separate
black nation, but it is impossible to achieve one under
present conditions. It is much easier for the establishment
to kill blacks alone than to kill both blacks and whites.
The militant, progressive and liberal forces in this country
just might be at the stage in history where the establishment can be defeated. At least it's worth a damn good try.*

*Now, I suppose, the time has come to ask forgiveness. I
won't do it. I played the game the best way I knew how.
Anyway, it doesn't matter how each individual hand is
played, but who's the big winner at the end of the game.*

I hope I die bravely.

Sam Muhammed

Simmons finished reading the letter, rapidly shuffled the
sheets until he came to the first page, read a few paragraphs,
then shuffled the sheets again, reading and nodding his head.
He was almost estatic, a tremendous feeling of elation flowing
through him as though he had won a million-dollar-lottery. He
felt like thumping his chest with his fists, dancing in the middle
of the floor, and shouting at the top of his voice. Then, slowly,
one of the habits he liked most about himself took control of
his actions, dimming his elation. Carefully he laid the letter on
the couch beside him and began a point-by-point analysis of
the situation.

First, he told himself, he should do a preliminary check into
the validity of the letter by determining how it had been delivered. Next, he should attempt to determine, to his own satisfaction at least, if Sam Muhammed had written the letter. Then—
if the other steps proved positive—he should contact Joe
Rielinski and Moses Pennmann and see if a joint course of
action could be worked out.

Picking up the phone, he dialed the suite occupied by his
bodyguards. Jack, the guard who had delivered the letter,

answered. "Jack," Simmons asked, "who gave you that letter you brought me a few minutes ago?"

"The letter was sent up from the hotel front desk," Jack replied. "A bellhop brought it. Anything wrong?"

"No. Thanks, Jack." Simmons then dialed the registration desk. "This is Mr. Simmons," he said. "A letter for me was delivered to my bodyguards about half an hour ago. Can you tell me how this letter was delivered to the hotel?"

"Hold on, Mr. Simmons." In a few seconds the man was back on the line. "The letter was given to the registration clerk by a woman—a black woman," he said.

"Do you have a description of the woman?"

The line went blank for approximately fifteen seconds. "No, Mr. Simmons," the man said, "nobody got a description of her. The clerk thinks she was young. We sent the letter to the suite of your aides instead of directly to you for security reasons."

"I understand that," Simmons said.

He picked up the letter again and studied it. It looked like Muhammed's handwriting, all right, but it was dangerous to depend on memory. There were numerous samples of Muhammed's writing in Council headquarters. He'd check it out immediately. Anyway, it was time Griggs was brought into the case.

Less than an hour later, Simmons and Griggs had satisfied themselves that Sam Muhammed had indeed written the letter. They had compared it with a number of hand-written reports and commentary Muhamnmed had left with the office through the years, materials written primarily when he had been at headquarters attending meetings.

"It's interesting that he included Pennmann," Griggs said. "However, if Pennmann is sold on the validity of the letter, millions of Americans will be convinced automatically."

"You can say that again," Simmons replied. "The dean of the Christian Science Monitor staff is probably the most respected journalist in America."

"Sam Muhammed was truly a surprising man," Griggs said. "I wonder if he did die bravely?"

"I have a feeling he did," Simmons said. "Well, let me call Rielinski."

When he called the labor leader's Washington home, Mrs. Rielinski, speaking in her quick Italian voice, told him that Rielinski had already left for San Francisco to attend the AFL-CIO convention.

"He has a number of meetings scheduled for today and tomorrow before the convention opens on Monday," she said. "You can catch him at the Hilton in San Francisco."

"Mrs. Rielinski, this is important," Simmons said. "Did your husband receive a hand-delivered letter this morning?"

There was surprise in her voice, but she answered without hesitation. "Yes, he did," she said.

"Mrs. Rielinski, I received a similar letter. I'm sure your husband would like to know the contents of that letter as soon as possible. I could call him and read mine to him, but I believe it would be better if you did it. Will you call him and read the letter to him, Mrs. Rielinski?"

"I don't like to open his mail, especially business mail," she said.

"You don't have to open it unless he tells you to," Simmons said. "Just call him and tell him what I've told you, and I'm sure he'll ask you to read the letter to him. Okay?"

"All right, Mr. Simmons," she replied.

When he hung up the phone, Moses Pennmann was waiting on another line. "Did you get your copy of a letter purported to be from Sam Muhammed?" the newsman asked in his direct way.

"I sure did. And it seems like the real thing."

"I wish I could be as certain," Pennmann said.

"Well, you can satisfy yourself the same way Griggs and I have done," Simmons said. "We have numerous samples of Sam's handwriting here in the office. You can come by or have somebody pick up a few samples."

"I'll come by," Pennmann said. "And I'll have a handwriting expert with me."

"Fine."

"Simmons?" Pennmann asked.

"Yes?"

"If it turns out that Sam Muhammed did write this letter, what do you plan to do?"

"Well, I thought we could work out some joint action. I mean joint action with respect to making the letter public. Rielinski's copy was mailed to his home. His wife is calling him in San Francisco and reading it to him. I'm sure I'll hear from him in a few minutes, or I'll call him."

Pennmann was silent for a few seconds, then he said: "If Muhammed's letter does turn out to be the real thing, you realize it'll help Rielinski's cause more than it will yours?"

"Maybe. But it'll help us turn those violence charges around. And in one sense, that's the most important thing."

"That we agree on," Pennmann said. "Preston, if I satisfy myself that Muhammed wrote this letter—that it is not a crank letter—as a newsman I'll have to make it public. But I'll have to make it public on my own. You and Rielinski, of course, will be central characters in my news release. You just might want to call separate press conferences. In any case, the letter will be made public. And that is what we all want, it seems to me."

"Right. See you in a few minutes. Rielinski and I will have talked by then."

"Good enough for me," Pennmann replied.

Chapter 31

4:00 P.M., Saturday, October 17, 1987

SAM MUHAMMED's letter soon became a national sensation. By three o'clock on Saturday afternoon, the day the letter was received, Moses Pennmann, with the aid of three handwriting experts, had satisfied himself that the letter had been written by Muhammed. Shortly thereafter, he released the letter to the media.

"At approximately 8:00 A.M. today," his release statement said, "the attached letter was delivered to my home here in Washington, D.C. I, along with three handwriting experts, have compared the writing in this letter with that in other documents known to have been written by the person whose signature appears at the bottom of the last page. We are fully satisfied that the letter was written by the late Sam Muhammed. In releasing this letter, I do not vouch for the truthfulness of the statements contained therein. This determination will have to be made by persons better equipped than I to conduct a definitive investigation. It is my understanding that Messrs. Preston Simmons and Joseph Rielinski, who also received copies of the letter, will issue their own statements concerning the matter..."

The media, of course, didn't wait for Simmons and Rielinski to call press conferences. It came calling on them.

"Although Mr. Muhammed's letter was addressed to me

298

personally," Simmons said, reading from a prepared script outside Council headquarters, "I am speaking for the entire Black American Council, by whom I am employed. While we are insulted by the fact that Mr. Muhammed for years utilized his seat on the Council to carry out the insidious assignments of government intelligence agencies, we are prepared to permit forgiveness to become the prevailing sentiment in our memory of him; for by this final act of repentance, he has gone a long way toward redeeming himself in the eyes of his black brothers and sisters who struggle for the right of self-determination..."

The questions came fast and furiously.

"You are convinced that Sam Muhammed actually wrote the letter?"

"Yes. We employed the same handwriting experts as Mr. Pennmann. There is no doubt that Sam Muhammed wrote the letter. In addition to the handwriting, the manner of expression is typically Muhammed."

"You say forgiveness of him is the prevailing sentiment within the Black American Council. Does this mean that you are going to follow his advice and join Rielinski?"

"No. The Council has not addressed itself to that matter. The Council has promised to take up that question after the AFL-CIO convention next week."

"Granting that Sam Muhammed wrote the letter, do you believe the things he says in it are true?"

"Yes. As you know, we've been implying some of the same things in our statements all week."

"In view of Sam Muhammed's charges, how do you think the majority of Americans will now view their government?"

"I do not, and will not, presume to speak for the majority of the American people."

"Whose position has been helped more by Muhammed's revelations—yours or Rielinski's?"

"I don't know. Only time will tell."

Rielinski met the media in the lobby of the Hilton hotel in San Francisco.

"It is deplorable," he said, "that the government of the

United States, in the name of defending liberty, has resorted to the murder of its citizens and the mutilation of its most cherished symbols. When the government attempts to hide its misdeeds by blaming others for its crimes, are any of us safe from persecution? Subversion by government is tyranny."

He was questioned at length.

"Mr. Rielinski, will the Muhammed affair help your ideas to gain wider acceptability among the American people?"

"I believe my ideas already have wide acceptability. However, if you mean will this regretable affair cause *more* Americans to examine our positions favorably, the answer is yes."

"Mr. Rielinski, you accused the government of subverting its own ideals. Don't some of the programs you are pushing amount to subversion?"

"Everything we are for, we are for out front and above board. That cannot be considered subversion by any stretch of the imagination. Now if you are talking about the radical nature of some of our proposals, that's another matter. It's time for the American system to be infused with new ideas. In fact, the Founding Fathers looked upon such periodic infusions as essential to the preservation of a vibrant democracy. Thomas Jefferson said that whenever any form of government becomes destructive to the ends of democracy, it is the right of the people to alter or to abolish it. Serious alterations are now in order, if democracy in this country is to survive."

"Mr. Rielinski, do you believe this country is on the verge of a violent revolution?"

"No. This country is getting ready to enter the first stages of a *peaceful* revolution. Our institutions are malleable enough to accept change, yet strong enough to survive change."

"Do you believe you and the Black American Council will get together?"

"I believe so."

"But you aren't definite?"

"No. But I believe so."

By the time the Sunday papers hit the streets, the media had

300

fashioned a mold for the Muhammed affair. Using phrases like "posthumous revelations" and "voice from beyond the grave", print journalists declared that a "Watergate-like atmosphere" existed in Washington and hinted that President Davidson might be forced to "negotiate with the Black American Council" in order to "restore credibility" to his government.

The government's statement, when finally released late Saturday night by Attorney General Richard Lawrence, was half-hearted and unconvincing. "A thorough investigation into this affair is underway," the statement said. "There are more questions raised than answers provided by the letter which is being attributed to Mr. Muhammed. The government remains steadfast in its position that Mr. Muhammed was engaged in acts of civil disorder and espionage bordering on treason and was killed while trying to escape from lawful arrest. If Mr. Muhammed did in fact write the letter, there is nothing in his background which should cause the American people to believe these charges against the government. Results of the government's continuing investigation will be released as they are obtained and processed."

Sam Muhammed was having a day like he had never had before.

Chapter 32

9:30 A.M., Sunday, October 18, 1987

SAN FRANCISCO was one of Joe Rielinski's favorite cities. He loved the pleasant days, the cool nights, the rolling hills and the international, yet intimate flavor of the night-club entertainment. Although San Francisco was one of the leading convention sites in the country, he was among those who felt that the city was too naturally appealing to be forced to compete with the usual tourist hype for a visitor's attention. Whenever he came to the Bay City, he managed to schedule his time so that he had a few hours for strolling alone along the quaint streets, reflecting in an atmosphere which, for him, was so conducive to meditation.

This Sunday morning—the day before the beginning of the AFL-CIO convention—was the time he had originally set aside for such private use. But the receipt of Sam Muhammed's letter yesterday had forced him to reschedule urgent meetings to the extent that today must be devoted exclusively to work. He fervently hoped that when the convention came to an end on Friday, his successes would be such that he would still be in a frame of mind to enjoy what the city had to offer.

Dressed in slacks and short-sleeved shirt, he was sitting in the living room of his 40th floor Hilton Hotel suite, waiting for his first meeting to get underway. If this meeting went as he hoped, he could breeze through the remainder of the day, for this was the meeting which would dictate strategy for, or determine the necessity of, the other meetings scheduled to follow. The key meeting was with a single person: John Radicci, the tough, young president of the teamsters union. Just the two of them, in a heart-to-heart talk.

Originally, the sit-down with Radicci had been scheduled for last Tuesday in Washington, D.C. But on Monday, Radicci had phoned to request a postponement, suggesting that their get-together be rescheduled for yesterday in San Francisco.

"Don't you think that's cutting it kinda close, John?" he had asked. "We need to have things settled before the convention gets underway."

"Damn, Joe," Radicci had replied in his sharp voice, "that's two whole days before you bring the gavel down. Hell, you and I can make, or break, a world in less time than that."

Radicci, of course, had been stalling. Realizing, as he did, that the teamsters held, or came close to holding, the balance of power in the struggle between Nelson and him, Radicci wasn't about to commit himself until the last minute, especially when the issues to be brought before the convention held such significance. He didn't really blame Radicci for playing the wait-and-see game. He probably would have done the same if their roles had been reversed.

"Okay," he said, "see you in my hotel suite at ten o'clock on Saturday morning."

But the Muhammed letter had changed the day from Saturday to Sunday. Now, waiting for Radicci to arrive, he was confident the delays had strengthened his hand. He had been in the news—directly and indirectly—since last Monday's conversation with Radicci, and the media's treatment of him had been most favorable during that period. Of course, he couldn't guarantee that Radicci's conclusions would be the same as his, but one thing he did know about Radicci: he responded to good public relations, being, to such a large extent, a creation of it himself.

Rielinski glanced around the room. It was spacious and

furnished with a tasteful arrangement and selection of couches, chairs, tables, lamps and live plants. He was sitting near the center of the room in a large leather chair, the twin of which stood across from him on the opposite side of a circular glass table. Copies of three or four newspapers were stacked in the center of the table. He had exercised, showered and completed his reading nearly an hour before. The San Francisco skyline, somewhat diminished by his view from the 40th floor, again caught his attention through the half-drawn draperies, fleetingly reminding him that if things had gone according to plans, at this moment he would be many blocks away entering the second phase of his morning stroll.

The three raps on the door were bold and sharp. Moving over to the door, Rielinski looked through the peep-hole at the top of a full head of brown hair, then glanced downward until he discerned the firm, square features of the face beneath the hair. He opened the door and John Radicci walked into the room.

Rielinski had read somewhere that there were two types of short men: those who were always conscious of their lack of height and those who were mainly conscious of it when they were around women. He had also read that short men were more inclined toward personality extremes than were taller members of the species; that they were either extremely agressive or extremely retiring. He didn't know to what extent these things were true; but he did know that every time he encountered Radicci, the stereotype of the pushy short man somehow forced itself to the forefront of his mind. He supposed it was the way Radicci walked. He walked so straight, took such deliberately forceful steps, that he appeared to be leaning slightly backward. Yet, in his dealings with Radicci, he had not found him to be obnoxious. Forceful, yes, but definitely not obnoxious.

"Glad to see you, John," he said, extending his hand.

Radicci's brown eyes were watchful but warm, as he clasped Rielinski's right hand in both of his.

"It's like coming home, when I drop by to see you," he said.

"Joe, you know that."

"I'm glad to hear you say it, John," Rielinski replied, motioning Radicci to the twin of the chair he had been occupying.

Radicci, also dressed in slacks and short-sleeved shirt, walked across the room in his ramrod straight fashion. "How's Rosa?" he asked as he sat down.

"Fine. And how's Maria?"

"All cylinders working," Radicci replied. "There's no woman like an Italian woman. You know that, Joe."

Radicci never missed an opportunity to remind him that he was married to a woman of his nationality. At times it was embarrassing, but he didn't resent it. Radicci seemed so sincere. "How well do I know it, John," he said. "How well do I know it."

Rielinski sat down and leaned across the table, facing Radicci. "It's really good to see you, John," he said.

Radicci smiled, nodding his head. "We've neglected each other, Joe," he said. "The fire of friendship must be stoked to stay alive."

Rielinski had always marveled at the ease with which Radicci came up with apt metaphors. "The fire of friendship must be stoked to stay alive." Not fanned or stirred, but stoked. How long had it been since he heard that word? And Radicci didn't come from the steel mills either! He was feeling deep affection for Radicci when he asked: "How have things been *really* going, John?"

Radicci rested his arm on the table and made drumming sounds with his fingers on the surface. "Things are fine, Joe. Not perfect, but fine. I'm keeping busy to stay ahead of the game. As busy as a peg-leg man in an ass-kicking contest."

Rielinski touched Radicci's hand. "I know," he said.

Radicci's rise to power in the teamsters had paralleled his own rise in the AFL-CIO. A product of Jimmy Hoffa's old local union, Radicci, ironically, had rode into leadership on an anti-crime campaign. But Radicci was nevertheless a true Italian ethnic, in the most vocal sense of the word: fiery, tough and proud. He supposed it was Radicci's ethnicity, more than any other factor, which had made it possible for him to curtail the influence of organized crime in the teamsters. But Radicci didn't pretend that the mobsters had been completely driven from his union, only the more overt evidence of their presence. Yet, Radicci ran the teamsters, to the extent that his was the single most dominant voice. He had been among the first to support Rielinski's recommendation that the giant trucking union come back into the AFL-CIO, and together they had had the power to bring it off. Rielinski had no doubt that Radicci could swing the overwhelming majority of teamsters delegates behind his program at this convention—if he so desired.

"John," Rielinski said, "a short while ago you said that we've been neglecting each other. It hasn't been me, John. You know that. My people have talked to your people. I've talked to you. But you haven't responded. Why, John?"

Radicci looked at Rielinski, his eyes guarded. Then, suddenly, the veil lifted and the brown eyes became candid. "Joe," he said, "there's no point in my trying to fool you. I've been playing a waiting game. Frankly, at first, I didn't think you had a chance to pull your program off. In the union, and definitely not in the country."

"And now you think I can?"

"Now I think you have a fighting chance."

Rielinski felt himself smiling. "Hell, I thought your hesitancy was because you didn't agree with my programs," he said.

Radicci threw out his hand. "I don't agree with all of them. I'm no Commie, nothing like that, but I'm not a fool like Mike Nelson, either. One thing I do know—the wealth in this country needs to be redistributed. It's strange, but you intellectuals always seem to forget the history of the teamsters. Our union was started by the Socialist Workers Party."

"I know, John. But that's not the reason why you've changed your mind, about my now having a fighting chance."

Radicci laughed. "It could be that I like the way you've been

306

handling yourself. More like a Dago than a Polack."

It was Rielinski's turn to laugh. "I appreciate your letting me into the club, John. But there are a few things I need to know."

"Shoot."

"You have no real quarrel with my economic proposals?"

"I can live with them."

"What about my wanting the blacks to come in—on an equal basis?"

"I don't have as much confidence in blacks as you have—but I can live with them."

"John?"

"I said I can live with them."

"So that means you are with me then?"

"Maybe." The veil had covered the eyes again.

"John," Rielinski said, "you say you can live with my economic and racial policies, even though you aren't as enthused with either as I am. Okay, I can buy that. You say Nelson is a fool. You *know* I buy that. Yet, you still say *maybe*. What's the problem?"

Radicci stood up, arched his back, walked over to the window and stood looking out across the city. Rielinski watched him but did not move. Finally, Radicci came back to his chair and sat down. Placing both hands on the table, he leaned toward Rielinski. When he spoke, his voice was low and conspiratorial.

"Joe," he said, "you know I've been having problems with the mob. You haven't said anything about it, but I know you know. I've thought about asking you to help, but I doubt if you could have done anything, especially now that you're trying to get this other thing going. Now I know how we can help each other."

Rielinski had had confidential conversations with Radicci before, but never like this. Always Radicci had appeared to be holding something back—even when they had mapped out the strategy for the merger. But not this time. His soul was out there in plain view. "Buddy, I'm all ears," he said.

"In the two years I've headed this union," Radicci said, "I've

307

been trying to compromise with the mob. But what you've always heard is true. It doesn't work. There is nothing to compromise where one side has no principles. And the mob doesn't have principles."

"I buy that. What do you have in mind?"

"I know you know that the establishment and the mob have always worked hand in hand. Oh, they pretend to be natural enemies, but in reality they sustain each other. Look at the deal worked out between Roosevelt and the mob during World War II and the arrangement between Nixon and Hoffa..."

"You'll get no argument from me."

Radicci looked hard at Rielinski, his eyes unblinking. "I'll help you change the establishment if you'll help me destroy the mob," he said.

So this was what Radicci had been holding out for, Rielinski told himself. He wanted the mob destroyed, but he didn't believe the mob could be destroyed until the system was changed. And now he believed Rielinski had a fighting chance of changing the system.

"John, you realize I'm getting the better of this deal," Rielinski said. "By your own analysis, the system—the establishment—will have to be changed first."

"I don't see it exactly that way," Radicci said. "I hate the inequities as much as you do."

"I get your point."

"Still," Radicci said, "there's a commitment you must make up front."

"Like what?"

"You must give me something to help me sell my delegation on the idea of supporting your program."

"You can't do it as president of your union?"

"Maybe. But we can't afford to take any chances. This thing must be put across in a big way—if it is to mean anything. There is no bandwagon if half the people are on the sidelines."

This was precisely what Preston and Simmons had said, Rielinski recalled. He had to win big to be effective. "Okay," he said, "what do you want?"

Radicci leaned across the table. "The best way to make the delegates in my union—especially those who are under mob influence—go for a thing is to convince them they're taking something from somebody else. Your program calls for nationalizing the utilities and increasing government control in certain other major industries. This could also mean enlarging union participation in those areas. Right?"

"Right."

"This could also mean that jurisdictional questions would have to be settled among competing unions. Right?"

"It could come to that."

"Okay, here's what I have in mind. I'd like to plant the word that I have your assurances that when these questions arise, they'll be settled in favor of the teamsters."

Most such disputes, Rielinski realized, would probably arise between the teamsters and the pulic workers and the teamsters and the automobile and oil workers. The heads of these unions were among his strongest supporters. Maybe he could swing it without making too many waves. "I'll talk to the proper people—David Eastman of the public workers and a few others," Rielinski said. "They'll understand."

Radicci shook his head. "This is just between you and me, Joe," he said. "You can't talk to anybody. To *nobody*."

"But you do expect me..."

"It can be done, Joe. David Eastman and the others are just as committed to your programs as you are. In fact, the programs are as much theirs as yours. Tell them this is the price that bastard John Radicci is asking for not supporting Mike Nelson. That'll bring them in line." He paused. "And you won't be lying, Joe. That is the price."

"Rielinski looked deep into Radicci's eyes. The eyes were open and frank, and they were no longer pleading. Radicci knew he had made a good case. Rielinski felt the peculiar, inverted affection returning. Damn Dago, he thought.

"Okay, John," he said, extending his hand. "You're making me as dishonest as you, but you've bought yourself a deal."

309

Chapter 33

Monday, October 19 through Friday, October 23, 1987

THE AFL-CIO convention got underway on Monday with all of the media attention and fanfare usually reserved for conventions of the two major political parties. By the middle of the week it had become clear that if Joe Rielinski was not the *inherent* recipient of the benefits accruing from the Muhammed revelations, the fact that his convention coincided with receipt of the letter made it appear that he was.

On Wednesday, with machine-like precision, overpowering heated opposition from Mike Nelson and the old guard, Rielinski's forces pushed through the convention resolution after resolution relating to his economic and social programs. Included in the economic package were proposals calling for federal legislation guaranteeing full employment and the reduction of the work-week to thirty hours; to nationalize the telephone, light and gas industries; to regulate the oil, coal, automobile and steel industries in such a manner that employment, profits, expansion and contraction in these industries would be under strict government direction; and to establish a "Marshall Plan" for urban renewal, with special emphasis on the development and expansion of black and other minority businesses. Leading social proposals called for federal legislation for the creation of a comprehensive health program; the institution of a federally-directed educational system; the reorganization of federal departments to guarantee direct delivery of social services without interference from competing layers of federal, state and local bureaucracies; and, of course, the consolidation of disability/retirement programs as called for in the Comprehensive Disability and Retirement Act.

And to make sure passage of the resolutions would not be looked upon as merely a labor movement pipe-dream with little or no support from the rest of the population, Rielinski, on Thursday, paraded an impressive contingent of dignitaries before the convention to swear "allegiance" to his program. Among these testifying were Hilda Larsen from the women's movement; Gene Wild and Bill Green from the black community; the chairman of the National Council of Churches; the head of the National Organization of Hispanics; the presidents of three major universities; representatives of medical and legal groups; and spokespersons for various civic, fraternal and social organizations.

Writing for the Christian Science Monitor on Friday from San Francisco, where he had gone early in the week, Moses Pennmann stated: "On Wednesday and Thursday of this week, in the cosmopolitan city of San Francisco, the first new major American political party in more than a century was born. It is unclear yet whether those responsible for this birth look upon themselves as having created a political party, or by what name it will be known. A number of names come to mind: Progressive, Labor, Liberal, or even Radical. But, on second thought, none of these names might be appropriate. This new giant of a baby just might be the Peoples Party...."

While Rielinski was assuming a new dimension in the collective mind of the nation from San Francisco, Simmons and Griggs remained in Washington, D.C., watching and waiting. The other Council leaders were assigned to those major cities which had been the centers of their organizational strength prior to the formation of the Black American Council, with instructions to determine and report on the effects the AFL-CIO convention was having on the far-flung affiliates comprising the Council.

311

On Tuesday, Rubye Ransome reported from Chicago that the leadership of a major black women's sorority was weakening and it was doubtful if that organization could be kept in the fold. Further, she reported, there were serious rumblings within her base organization, The League of Black Women, which had launched her nationwide career.

On Wednesday, Dr. Benjamin Patten, reporting from Atlanta, stated that the executive board of the Southern Christian Association, meeting in special session, had decided to reopen the question of separation in a meeting to be held the following Monday in New Orleans. A number of the more prominent ministers were ready to defect to Rielinski's position.

On Thursday evening, following the mass confessional in San Francisco, Albert James reported from Los Angeles that a number of his long-time cohorts, who like himself had gotten their start in the labor movement, were becoming convinced that their old organizations at last were ready to fight for the welfare of working people. The breach in the Council's left-wing was beginning.

The breach in the center forces, represented by Griggs himself, also began on Thursday. The Newark, New Jersey and the St. Paul-Minneapolis, Minnesota branches of the NAACP wired him that they were pulling out of the Council if it persisted on pushing the separation issue.

And on Friday morning, Rielinski was given probably the biggest boost of the week. United States Senator Samuel Leavitt, Chairman of the Senate Judiciary Committee, appeared at the convention and offered his support.

"I have watched the morality of our government deteriorate for the past twenty years," he said. "I witnessed the downfall of Johnson, the destruction of Nixon, the vacillation of Carter, and the insanity of Reagan. Now we come to the tyranny of Davidson. I am sick, I am tired, and I am ashamed. If you can use my help, I am at your service."

The first major defection from the government of President Dorsey Talbot Davidson had come to pass.

312

Chapter 34

8:30 A.M., Saturday, October 24, 1987

IT SEEMED to Preston Simmons that he was walking down memory lane, although he had taken this same walk just a month ago. He was covering the half-block from 115th Street to his home, moving slowly along the sidewalk in the early hours of Saturday morning, watching the sun break through the haziness of the eastern horizon in its journey toward the apex of a clear sky. It would be mild today, he told himself, in the high sixties or low seventies, registering glorious testimony to the unique presence of Indian Summer.

The sidewalk along which he walked was covered with brown leaves from the huge maple trees which formed a canopy over the parkway, the branches of one tenderly touching the branches of the next in a continuing, sentinel-like line to the end of the block. The leaves still remaining on the trees were a study in the limitless variations in colors, representing every imaginable shade in nature's green-gold-brown spectrum.

Although—in ritualistic pilgrimages to the corner for newspapers—he had walked along this block every Saturday and Sunday morning in the twenty years he had occupied his home, it was the early morning forays this time of year that he had enjoyed, and remembered, most. And it was his memory of these times, as much as anything else, which had brought him here on this Saturday morning following Rielinski's San Francisco triumph to determine his future course in surroundings he knew so well and loved so much.

He had left Washington the night before, accompanied by

313

Marcus Jackson and two bodyguards. A suite had been reserved for them at the Palmer House, where they had spent the night. Early this morning, while the bodyguards were still asleep, he had persuaded Marcus to permit him to take a trip to his home alone, promising to call as soon as he arrived. Marcus and the bodyguards would join him later in the morning.

"I feel the need to be in my home by myself for awhile," he had explained.

"Dress casually, act indifferent, and grab a cab around the corner on Wabash," Marcus had replied. "Nobody'll expect Preston Simmons to be traveling so light and by himself. But when you get home, that's another matter."

"I know, but give me a couple of hours."

"You got it."

The cab had let him out at the corner. His luck had held. The driver had not recognized him.

His luck was still holding during the walk from the corner to his house. Nobody was astir on the street, which was not unusual for early Saturday morning. So far as he could tell he had not been observed, even by Clem Williams, his third-door neighbor, whose all-hours, outdoors-dickering had made him an object of whimsical commentary throughout the neighborhood.

His lawn was covered with a heavy accumulation of leaves, giving it the appearance of a plot of plowed earth in a field of greenness, as the lawns adjacent to his had been raked clean of fallen leaves. Mrs. Brimson, his housekeeper since the death of Margaret, was taking her job literally by confining her attention to the inside of the house. He would have to inform her that she had the authority to hire somebody to rake the lawn.

It was strange, he told himself as he entered the house, how the living room always looked differently than he expected when he returned from extended trips. Sometimes it seemed smaller than he remembered it, other times larger, but somehow always different. He flopped on the couch and stared at the wall in front of him. The limited-edition lithograph of Miro's Golden Isle, which Margaret had selected with so much care, was still in place, the sun-bronzed trees casting their reflections in the red-tinted water. He glanced across the row of book cases into the dining area. Letters and other mail were positioned carefully on the table in neat rows, separated, he was certain, as to types. He would have to take a look at the mail before he returned to Washington. At least, he would have to write checks for his bills.

This was one of the reasons he had given Griggs for his spur-of-the-moment flight to Chicago. But Griggs had not been fooled. Neither had felt like putting into words what they both knew faced them.

"When will you be back?" Griggs had asked.

"Sunday. No later than Sunday night."

"Okay."

"We'll talk Monday."

"Okay."

He got up and turned on the television set, but he turned it off before a picture came on the screen. Suddenly, he got an eerie feeling. He had done the same thing the day he received word that he had been selected chief negotiator. It was uncanny, his being so vividly reminded of a nervous gesture he had made on that particular day.

Getting up from the couch, he walked through the dining area and kitchenette into the bedroom. He smiled to himself in the dresser mirror, appraising with a sense of unfamiliarity the image of the man in the flop hat, circular-neck sweater, zippered jacket and casual slacks. He sure had taken Marcus's advice to dress casually. It would be ridiculous, if the whole affair wasn't so deadly serious.

The tragicomedy of the situation reminded him of Rubye, and the call she had made to him last night while he was packing. Informing him that she had returned to Washington from Chicago late that afternoon, she also had told him that "everything" was over between her and her latest friend. The fast breakup had set something of a record, even for her.

"I don't know what's wrong with me, Preston," she had said. "Maybe I want too much. I wonder why I keep trying?" She had seemed sincerely upset, and he felt concern for her creeping into his attitude.

"You're a romantic at heart," he had replied.

"You're probably right," she had responded with a nervous laugh. Then pausing for a few seconds, she had asked: "How are you making out with your latest love?"

"What latest love?"

"You know who I'm talking about. Hilda."

"If Hilda and I are in love, I don't know anything about it."

He could hear her breathing on the line. When she spoke, her tone was harsh. "You're fucking her, aren't you?"

He hadn't been exactly surprised at her question, but he had been somewhat taken aback by the anger in her voice. His answer had been careful and deliberate.

"Rubye," he had said, "I have a feeling that you and I have more important things to think about than who is fucking whom. Wouldn't you agree?"

Surprisingly, her answer had been immediate, without a trace of sarcasm. "I'm sorry, Preston," she had said.

Sounds of the front door bell, chiming impatiently, broke into his thoughts. He had been wrong, he told himself. Somebody had observed his coming home, after all. He doubted if it were Mrs. Brimson, because she would use her key. Besides, she had told him that when he was away, she seldom stopped by before one o'clock, until after the mail had been delivered.

He hurried through the house to the living room. Once he entered the room, he was careful to stay out of its center so that he could not be observed by anybody looking through the glass opening in the front door. He walked over to the window, pulled back the floor-length drapes and peeped out. Janice was turning away from the door.

He hurried to the door and opened it. "Where are you going?" he asked.

Janice halted her descent from the porch with an exaggerated movement, turned and came back up the steps, smiling.

"Have you forgotten how to open your own door, Your Royal Highness?" she asked.

316

"Come in and shut up."

She was dressed in a green jump suit, brown, short-collared blouse, and extremely high-heeled boots. She stopped just inside the door as he closed it, then reached up and took his hat off his head, her light-brown eyes twinkling.

"Didn't your mother teach you not to wear your hat in the house?" she asked.

Her effervescent manner was already getting to him, loosening him up, and he remembered with a feeling of unbelief that it had been a month since he had seen her. He touched the side of her face.

She laid his hat on the television set and walked over to the couch and sat down. "I heard on the news that you were coming to Chicago," she said, "so I took a chance that you might come here. You don't call anybody anymore."

Her tone was light but he could detect a note of reprimand. She had a right to be peeved, he told himself. But the truth was, he appreciated her more when he was with her than he missed her when she was away from him. He sat down in the chair by the window, so that he was facing her.

"Are you here by yourself?" she asked, looking around the room. "I heard that you had bodyguards and everything."

"I ditched them for a few hours," he said. "Who needs bodyguards when you're around."

She frowned. "Don't jive me, Preston."

That was one of the things he kept forgetting about her, he told himself. She could read his moods better than he could. In the ten years he had known her, there had never been a time when she hadn't known when he wanted her, needed her, or didn't want to be bothered. They always had had a feeling for each other bordering on the unnatural, and that feeling had been sustained as much by the honesty which had existed between them as by their physical and sexual affinity.

"I'm sorry, baby," he said. "I wanted to be here by myself for a few hours. But I can't say that you didn't figure in the equation. Because when I commune with the best part of me, I am also communing with you."

317

She nodded. "I know what you mean," she said. "But I don't think that's true anymore."

"What are you talking about?"

She put her finger in her mouth and looked away from him, feeling for words. "People change, Preston," she said. "They change all the time, and they don't always know when they are changing. They just wake up one day—changed."

"Yes, but what has that to do with what we're talking about? I don't feel changed."

She moved uncomfortably on the couch, trying to find the words she wanted. "Let's put it this way, Preston," she said. "People deal with each other, on a personal level, for two reasons. The other person is either good *for* them, or good *to* them. Now what I mean by a person being good for you is that the person can do something material for you—like supporting you or fighting your battles or being willing to give you whatever he has. When a person is good to you, you get pleasure out of that person, you just want to be around him, touch him, make love to him. You get what I mean?"

"Of course I get what you mean. You put it very well."

She smiled wanly. "Okay. Ever since I've known you, Preston, you've never been good for me, but you've been good to me. When I first met you you were married, but I didn't care. Later on, I got married, then your wife died. But that didn't change anything. You were still good *to* me."

"And I'm no longer good to you?" he asked.

"No."

"Why?"

"Because I'm no longer good to you. And if I'm not good to you, you can't be good to me," she replied. "It takes two to tango."

"But you don't know that," he said, "about your not being good to me?" He got up from his chair, walked across the room and stood over her. "If there is a change in my feelings about you, I don't recognize it."

She stood up, the high heels she was wearing permitting her eyes to be almost level with his. "Our worlds are too different,

318

Preston," she said. "You'll always be in the spotlight from here on out. I'm not going to kid myself, Preston. I don't fit in your world. Okay, we still feel a lot of what we have always felt. But we won't feel it for long under these circumstances. Let's quit, while we still have something nice to remember." Her eyes were pleading.

Simmons could feel compassion rising in him. He raised his hands to her face and cupped her chin, tenderly moving his fingers along her cheeks. He had made love to her for so long and enjoyed it so much that it was difficult to imagine that she was asking him not to ever hold her again, to forever refrain from touching the one person toward whom the act was always one of reaching out and never holding back. But he knew the question was as difficult for her to ask as it was for him to answer. And if she was woman enough to ask, he had to be man enough to try to provide her with the anwer she sought.

Kissing her softly on the nose, he asked: "Is that what you want, baby?"

"Yes, that's what I want."

"Are you sure?"

"Yes, I'm sure." Her voice was firm, but her eyes were still pleading, begging him to permit her to sever the bond between them.

"You got it baby," he replied.

She stepped back from him, smiling, the beseeching look in her eyes turning to one of mixed adoration and concern, as though she were bidding him farewell just before his departure on an uncertain and dangerous journey—a journey which she was awed at his taking, yet realized she didn't have the courage to take with him.

"See you, Preston," she said, turned and headed for the door.

As he watched her go, he was very close to crying.

Back in the bedroom, stretched straight across the bed on his back, forearm covering his eyes, Preston Simmons told himself that the time had come to make the decision he had been postponing for nearly a week. He had to decide, and decide this day, whether he should any longer press for a separate nation or join Rielinski and his allies in their push to advance democracy for everybody in a single nation.

It was ironic, he thought, how often major issues turned on single individuals making lonely decisions, on individual persons looking into individual souls and determining if they could live with the decisions that had to be made.

Okay, that being the case, he told himself, his first duty was to forthrightly ask himself a few questions and see if he could answer them equally forthrightly.

First, did he agree with the programs Rielinski was proposing? Of course he did, the answer came quickly, because he had proposed most of the same ideas himself through the years. Second, did Rielinski have a chance of getting these programs placed into operation? He might, the answer came more slowly, if he could secure the support of the vast majority of the American people. But the support had to be overwhelming, or the forces of greed would not permit the movement to get off the ground.

The next question was neither clear nor forthright, but subversive fragments creeping like an inquisition into his mind, mocking him to reveal what he now, this moment, thought about the separate nation idea. His response was the same as it had been during the past week: a refusal to answer, a plea for more time from the pit of the soul. This time, however, the outlines of an answer began to frame itself, ever so slowly. If we had not been so imbued with the idea of a separate nation, he told himself haltingly, so committed, so *personally* wrapped up in it as our *thing*, then we would have been able to see that the conservative hold on the people was being broken, and we probably would not have taken the final step toward separation. The past six months might not have happened.

And because he had let that idea into his consciousness, another idea which he had been suppressing for the past week, an idea based on words from Sam Muhammed's letter, forced itself into the forefront of his mind. "They (the FBI) thought that if the Council could be influenced to call for a referendum of separation," Muhammed had written, "and the voting actually took place, the referendum would be so badly beaten that the Council would lose face with all black Americans and then the government could move in and destroy it." These were the words, Simmons told himself now, that he, Griggs, Rubye and the others had chosen to ignore in their discussions of the past week. Rather, they had tried to mend their spirits by dwelling on how the favorable vote for separation had tricked the FBI. But now, he said aloud: "Even the referendum idea wasn't ours. It was theirs. Without their connivance through Sam Muhammed, there wouldn't have been an attempt to negotiate a separate nation."

He removed his forearm from over his eyes and folded his arms across his chest, breathing heavily. He remembered something Preston Jr. had written just last week, in one of his periodic letters. "If out of this struggle," his son had written, "sufficient numbers of us emerge with wills strong enough to be men and women, with viewpoints firm enough to keep our individual natures inviolate, then we will survive. It doesn't matter that much whether we coexist with white people in this country or create a new nation, if we have the guts to keep our personhoods intact, we will flourish." Somewhat overblown, but as near the mark as most other statements on the subject. He hadn't discussed his concerns about the shift in black sentiment to the Rielinski position with Preston Jr., but his son was better than most in reading the signs of the time. He wanted to lend his old man a hand in his dilemma.

He rolled over on his stomach. Preston Simmons, he told himself, the time has come to take a look at yourself as a person. Do you still have concern for people as individuals, the people for whom and with whom you have been working the past four weeks? Or have you grown callous, cynical, too detached and dispassionate, placing yourself above the emotional storms which rage within the people who are at the center of everyday action? Preston Simmons, can you still feel the aloneness of the man who has never had a job, the man you met in the Brown Girl Lounge a few weeks ago? Can you identify with the hopes and the fears of the people who marched with you in the demonstrations two weeks ago? Do you feel the agony of Ted Blackwell's mother? The frustration of Sam Muhammed's best friends?

And what about the women in your life, Preston Simmons? Did you mislead Margaret into thinking that her sense of values could ever be yours, simply because you admired her style? Have you all these years, knowing Rubye's yearning for tenderness beneath the veneer of sophistication and toughness, deliberately withheld your capacity for understanding from her searching eyes? Isn't it possible that, because of her race, you can never deal with Hilda Larsen on an individual basis, yet will continue to tell yourself that the imprecise nature of your relationship is precisely what each of you desire? And isn't it true that while you have not misled Janice by an overt act, you have caused her to mislead herself by permitting her to underestimate the severity of your need for her?

He sat up on the bed. Hold on, Preston Simmons, he told himself. Be careful how harshly you judge yourself. Do not force yourself into a mold from which there is no escape. You have never been easy on yourself, and you have always come off fairly well when subjecting yourself to intense analysis. What has been the yardstick by which you have measured yourself, determined the intrinsic value of yourself as a human animal?

You have told yourself, Preston Simmons, that the world is made up of two kinds of people: the spiteful and the non-spiteful. Spiteful people, regardless of their enthusiasm of the moment or preoccupation with favorite persons, cannot be trusted to deal fairly when the chips are down. They might be lavish in their gifts or extremely demonstrative in their loving, yet they cannot be trusted, for they are always comparing themselves with other people and are ready to lash out when they compare unfavorably. The non-spiteful, on the other hand, regardless of sins of omission or failure to tell the whole truth at times, have no malice toward their fellow men. While some of them have the toughness to fight to the death against the ills of the world, their fight is always against the evil within the person and not against the person. They might not always do everything in their power for the welfare of a particular person, but they will never deliberately do anything against the welfare of any person.

Preston Simmons, you have always told yourself that you belong to the non-spiteful of the world; and that of all the tools in your decision-making arsenal, objectivity is the most reliable of all. Trust yourself, Preston Simmons. You have not failed yourself in the past. Why should you fail yourself now?

He got up from the bed, went over to the dresser and looked into the mirror, searching his eyes, examining his nose, mouth and face. Preston Simmons, he said to himself, you like your eyes, your nose, your mouth and face; you like the quickness of the mind behind your face, the objectivity of your reasoning. In short, you like yourself. There is no need to keep turning this thing over and over in your mind. The facts are all in. Trust yourself to make the right decision.

And the facts were these, he told himself, pulling his face back from the mirror. First, the leaders of the various organizations which had spearheaded the separatist movement were deserting it. Maybe desertion by these leaders wouldn't destroy sentiment for the movement, but their actions would destroy its assertive force. For the separatist movement, despite the large numbers of impoverished blacks who had voted for the referendum, like the civil rights movement of the sixties was basically middle-class led. Second, most of the black leaders who were deserting the separatist movement were joining with Rielinski. And third, Rielinski, like a snowball rolling downhill, was picking up momentum not entirely of his own making, drawing to himself the support of millions of Americans in the process. Yes, the facts were in. The only thing needed now was the courage to push pride aside and accept the message these facts were writing on the wall.

He was amazed at how easy it was. Surprised that the decision came as quickly and as firmly as it did. But suddenly he knew clearly that he would go to the prime members of the Black American Council and tell them that he could no longer serve as their chief negotiator for a separate black nation; that, henceforth, all of his talents would be utilized in helping Rielinski advance democracy in the United States of America.

He turned away from the dresser, smiling to himself, feeling the smile grow. Then he was laughing, silently and deeply. He folded his arms, hugged himself ecstatically, and skipped in a circle about the floor.

He felt very proud of himself.

BOOK II

THE COMING TOGETHER

Chapter 35

9:00 A.M., Sunday, October 25, 1987

ONLY THREE of them were there—Griggs, Rubye and Dr. Patten—the prime members of the Black American Council, sitting around the table in the conference room where he had first met with them the day after being selected chief negotiator. Watching them, in the quiet of Sunday morning, Preston Simmons was acutely aware of how empty the room seemed, overpowered with a feeling of desolation bordering on despair. True, there were three prime members fewer than had been present on that eventful morning, seemingly a lifetime but only a month ago; but the group had been diminished by more than numbers. The dream which had filled them with a burning tenacity was in danger of dissolution—without a dream of equal intensity to take its place.

He twisted around his seat at the head of the table, attempting to free himself from the feeling of gloom. They already knew his decision. He had called Griggs early yesterday and informed him, requesting at the same time that the meeting tentatively scheduled for Monday be held today. He studied each of them, carefully and deliberately, hoping to dispel from their minds any notion that the decision he had reached, and the process by which he had reached it, was contrary to the openness he was exhibiting now.

Rubye and Griggs were on one side of the table and Dr. Patten was on the other. Rubye was looking at him in a half-quizzical manner, her black eyes alight, the trace of a smile on her small, neat mouth. Griggs was sitting up straight, his handsome face relaxed. He appeared much more rested than Simmons remembered him from last week. Dr. Patten had his arms folded, his eyes half-closed, his heavy-featured face in repose.

But where was Albert James? Simmons asked himself. He had noticed the big man's absence, but hadn't inquired of his whereabouts. And nobody had volunteered any information. He studied their faces again. He had been correct at first. They all seemed relaxed. Maybe his feeling of gloom-and-doom was coming from within himself and not from the others, created out of his concern for what they *might* be feeling instead of what they were actually feeling. Anyway, he would soon know.

"Lady and gentlemen," he began, then stopped, conscious of the pompousness of his tone. "Okay," he said, beginning again, "We all know why we are here. I have decided to resign my position as chief negotiator for the Council because I no longer believe the acquisition of a separate nation is achievable. Also, in my opinion, such a state might not be desirable, if there is a probability that the programs being pushed by Rielinski and his supporters stand a chance of becoming a reality. I believe they do stand a chance, and I intend to join the ranks of those who are fighting for the programs." He paused. "Now," he continued. "I suppose you want to hear the reasons why I reached the conclusions I have..."

"Just a minute, Preston," Griggs said, placing his hands on the table and leaning forward. "All that might not be necessary. We should have told you as soon as you arrived." He paused. "When you called me yesterday morning, I called the prime members and we had a meeting. The meeting lasted until ten o'clock last night. We arrived at virtually the same conclusion as you."

Rubye was looking at Simmons, laughing, her fingers playing with a large, globe-like earing. "You sure sounded like you had the world on your shoulders, partner," she said to him. "What the hell do you think we've been doing—sitting on our asses doing nothing?" She tickled the ends of her short, straight black hair, the gold braclets on her wrist sparkling in the diffused light of the room.

Simmons checked his rising embarrassment with conscious effort. Rubye being Rubye, it was only natural for her to needle him. "You didn't *have* to come to the same conclusion," he said to her.

"If we are equally logical, we did," she said, smiling sweetly.

"Okay, then," Simmons said, "since we're being so logical, will somebody please tell me where Albert James is?"

Griggs sighed. "Preston, all the news is not good, after all. We couldn't get Albert to go with us."

"He was at the meeting?" Simmons asked.

"Yes," Griggs replied. "But he wouldn't disavow the separate nation idea."

"Did he say why?"

"There are lots of reasons. But the main one was his son. Wouldn't you say so, Dr. Patten, Rubye?"

"No doubt about it," Rubye said. "When they killed his son, they guaranteed that Al James will never trust white people again."

"That's right," Dr. Patten said. "And James was once the strongest defender white progressives had. A Black/White Unity man for nearly a half century."

Simmons could feel a nerve vibrating violently in the pit of his stomach, and for a second he felt dizzy. He had a lot of affection and respect for Albert James. But more than that: James would fight like hell to keep the separate nation idea alive, therefore the kind of unity he had hoped for would not be forthcoming. But should he really have expected otherwise? The minds, hearts and souls of most Americans carried the wounds and scars of centuries of conflicts and misunderstandings, and it was unrealistic to think that any movement toward reconciliation and progress would be spared. But there were persons against whom he did not want to fight. Albert James was one of them.

"Where is Al now?" he asked.

"He returned to Los Angeles last night," Rubye replied.

"Did he reveal any of his plans?"

"No," Rubye said. "Not to me." Griggs and Dr. Patten shook their heads.

"How firm did he appear to be?"

"Very firm," Dr. Patten said.

"Okay," Simmons said with a sigh. "I suppose that's that. Maybe we can still talk to him, but that's for later."

Griggs sat back in his chair and folded his arms. "Preston," he said, "we reached another conclusion yesterday. We want you to continue as chief spokesman in our negotiations with the Rielinski group."

Simmons had to admit that he had thought about this possibility. However, he had realized that in order for it to occur, the Council first had to agree with his positions of relinquishing the separate nation demands and supporting the Rielinski program. Then there was the problem of the mandate the Council had received from black voters, a problem, so far as he knew, they had not addressed.

"It's easy for me to switch positions," he said. "I'm just a hired hand, so to speak. But as prime members of the Council, you represent that body. And the Council has a mandate from black people."

Rubye shook her head. "The Council had a mandate," she said. "If another vote were taken today, we wouldn't win thirty percent."

Dr. Patten's smooth voice picked up the conversation. "Preston, as you know, public support for the separation demands began to decrease substantially last week, as Rielinski's programs became more widely known. I'm of the opinion that, prior to this, the government's get-tough policy had cut into our support in the more conservative areas, although this might have been offset by hardening of support among militants. In any case, it is evident that we are losing support among blacks and Rielinski is gaining support. We have to move out boldly in support of Rielinski immediately, to keep from being left out of the leadership of the new movement. Because we have demanded so much, we have to remain in the forefront to keep blacks from accepting less."

"I have no argument with that," Simmons said. "Aside from the fact that Rielinski has a good program, the point you just made is probably the strongest single reason for joining him. However, I believe the Council must properly disassociate itself from its old position before embracing the new."

Griggs leaned back in his chair, locking his hands behind his head. "That's been done, Preston," he said. "We weren't just meeting among ourselves yesterday. We were on phones, calling the leaders of the major affiliates, the ones who had not already contacted us. The vast majority of them want to go with Rielinski."

"And the people?" Simmons asked.

"Most of the leaders we talked to swear they are taking their cues from the people. It seems that, as of now, not too many blacks want a separate nation."

"At least," Dr. Patten cut in, "not many any longer believe it is possible to get one. And for our purpose it amounts to the same thing."

So that was that, Simmons told himself. The phenomenon of mass belief in the plausibility of a separate black nation had come to an end, vanishing as mysteriously as it had arisen.

"Okay," he said, "I'm your man if you want me. Now tell me: exactly where do we go from here?"

The three prime members exchanged glances. Finally, Rubye said: "Okay, I'll kick it off. From where I sit, there are three major things to consider. Program, priority, and power. Under program, we deal with what we don't like about Rielinski's ideas. Under priority, we come up with what we think should be pushed the hardest. And under power, we deal with who's gonna be running the show. From where I sit, we should deal with the power question first."

331

Griggs clapped his hands, looking at Rubye with admiration. "I don't know why I should be amazed at Rubye's analysis of the situation," he said. "She does it all the time. But this time she's *really* on target. We must hang tough on this power question. And we must let Rielinski know what we want now."

"Okay, what *do* we want?" Simmons asked.

"Co-directorship of the organization, whatever form it takes," Griggs said. "This is a black and white thing. And that's the way it must be approached. One white director, and one black director. Equals."

"They might want to establish the organization along ideological lines," Dr. Patten said. "Break it down by labor, church, education, civic and other such groups."

"Let them," Griggs said, "but at the second level. Sitting up on top must be one black and one white."

Simmons turned to Rubye. "What do you think?" he asked.

Rubye rubbed the large ring in her ear, smiling. "Why do you think I brought it up in the first place?" she asked. "I agree with Bob. Our demands for a separate black nation gave impetus to Rielinski's movement, altered the climate in his favor. We must be co-equals in leadership."

"Don't think I was disagreeing," Dr. Patten said. "I was only pointing out that an attempt will be made to circumvent our demands—either through the method I stated or by attempting to use the women's groups. A man and women type of leadership."

Simmons nodded. "Your point is well taken," he said.

"That leaves you, Preston," Griggs said. "How do you think we ought to go?"

Simmons felt himself smiling. "I'm a true democrat," he said. "Bob Griggs has as much right to sit on top of the collective organization as does Joe Rielinski."

"Hear! Hear!" Rubye said.

"Another thought comes to mind," Simmons added. "It might not be difficult to get Rielinski to buy the black-white idea. Ideologically, he's a part of the left wing of the trade union movement. It was this group which pushed the Negro-

White Unity theme of the thirties, forties and fifties, along with the blacks like Albert James."

"The theme that failed," Dr. Patten said.

"Exactly," Simmons replied. "It failed because whites refused to let blacks occupy roles of equality. Rielinski might consider it his obligation to correct that."

"I hope *his* feeling of obligation is transferable to his colleagues," Rubye said.

"We all do," Griggs replied.

Simmons stood up, stretched, and sat down again. "Okay," he said. "Rubye had two other points. Program and priority. Who wants to comment on program?"

"I'll open that one," Griggs said. "First, I want to say that the methods Rielinski is proposing for full employment are right on target. I never thought I'd live to see the day when mainstream Americans would seriously consider programs which place people above profits. Well, that day is here. But one thing about Rielinski's pluralistic concept, as it relates to racial integration, worries me."

"What's that, Robert?" Dr. Patten said.

"He seems to believe that human behavior is more static, more controllable than it is. I agree that this is not a melting pot. That people should be given ethnic choices. But these choices can never be permitted to deny freedom of choice to others. What I'm saying is this: We can never go so far in implementing pluralistic programs that we re-legalize segregation."

Dr. Patten looked up at the ceiling, his heavy features animated. "I read Rielinski on this question somewhat differently," he said. "True, he believes in ethnic choices, but he believes that the exercise of these choices will so increase the spirit of cooperation between the races that the need for ethnic choices will gradually decrease, until they are eventually eliminated. Sort of like a withering away of the state in Marxist ideology. He had to have a gimmick to get black and white workers to unite to fight for redistribution of the wealth. He chose the ethnicity gimmick."

333

"Ethnicity is more than a gimmick with him," Griggs said. "It's basic. However, I do believe he thinks increased cooperation between the races around programs of mutual interest will result in decreased animosity. And I agreee with that, to a degree. But we might have to wait as long for racial misunderstanding to disappear as the Communists have waited for their state to wither away."

Everybody laughed.

When the laughter had ceased, Rubye said: "There is a toughness about some of Rielinski's utterances which attracts and scares me at the same time. I'm talking about his stand on breaking the poverty cycle in families who have been on welfare for a number of generations."

"I get your point," Dr. Patten said. "Rielinski's answer is that the parents of welfare recipients must not be left to themselves to direct the destiny of their children. That the government must step in and give *positive* assistance to insure that these children are prepared to participate in a full-employment, people-oriented economy. I believe I can quote him, from a speech he made last year in Detroit before an income maintenance group: 'The establishment does not want these children to break out of the cycle of cultural and social deprivation which has been produced by generations of poverty, neglect and denial. In fact, the establishment—regardless of protestations to the contrary—encourages the type of permissiveness which guarantees that these shackles cannot be tossed off. The establishment doesn't have the guts to institute the policies necessary to change a society'."

"What's wrong with that?" Griggs asked. "It shows the man is not a fool. That he doesn't run from reality."

Rubye grasped her forehead between her thumb and index finger, frowning. "I agree that something has to be done," she said. "But not exactly in that tone of voice, so to speak. Somebody will have to control the controllers."

"What you might be talking about," Griggs said, "is putting the controls in the proper hands. Try this on for size. Establish neighborhood centers for these families, where both the chil-

334

dren and the parents would have to participate in attitudinal correction programs. Of course the experts would have to be consulted to make sure we don't create more psychological problems that we cure. But you get the idea."

"Right!" Rubye said. "Something like that."

"Okay," Simmons said, holding up his hand. "That's the point. We must develop a lot of input before these programs are presented to the people as a platform. Here is what I suggest. Each of you, working with the leaders of your major constituencies, should take the resolutions which came out of Rielinski's convention and develop commentary in the form of position papers. Additionally, develop papers on ideas of your own, whether the questions have been addressed by Rielinski's people or not."

"You are asking for a lot of work, Preston," Griggs said. "When are you suggesting these papers be completed?"

"In about two weeks."

"Hold on a minute!" Rubye said. "Are you saying that we should wait two weeks before joining up with Rielinski's group? That's too long. Now that the momentum is going for us and Rielinski, we must keep it going."

"I'm not saying that at all," Simmons replied. "As soon as this meeting is over, we should call a press conference announcing our affiliation with Rielinski. Some of us should meet with him tomorrow and get things rolling."

"All right, that's better," Rubye said.

"Preston," Dr. Patten said, "I have another idea. Soon after we officially join up with Rielinski, something dramatic must be done to let the country know we mean business. Something which will demonstrate our strength."

"Like a march on Washington?" Griggs asked.

"Only bigger," Dr. Patten replied.

Simmons held up his hand. "I agree," he said, "be we can't solve a problem like that here and now. Joint action is required. There are so many things to kick around, I can't wait to sit down with Rielinski."

Rubye was smiling and looking at Simmons in a coquettish

manner. "Bob," she said, "don't you think its about time to give Preston the other good news?"

"What good news?" Simmons asked, feeling his interest quicken.

"I believe you're right, Rubye," Griggs said, smiling smugly. "Preston, when we finished with our meeting last night we contacted Bill Green and Gene Wild, informed them of our decision, and requested that they reassume their duties as prime members of the Black American Council. They agreed."

Simmons could feel elation rising in him. "You mean they will be sitting with us, instead of with Rielinski, in the coming negotiations?"

"Right."

"We'll have a united black front again. That is, almost."

"Right."

Simmons looked from one to the other. Each, in ways uniquely his or her own, was registering satisfaction at his pleasure. He got the sudden feeling that during the past turbulent month, a bond much stronger than one of trust and respect had developed between them; that, quite probably, they had crossed over the boundary of friendship into the indefinable country of love. He could feel tears teasing the back of his nostrils and dimming his eyes. The information about Bill Green and Gene Wild *was* good news. It made the burden of Albert James somewhat lighter.

"I'll be damned!" he said in a choked voice.

Chapter 36

12:30 P.M., Sunday, October 25, 1987

THE WORK that had to be done that day was completed by noon. With the aid of young Vernon White, Simmons and Griggs drafted a statement on the Council's withdrawal of its separate nation demands and its simultaneous affiliation with the Rielinski group. Both declined media invitations for interviews, insisting that the statement spoke for itself. Rielinski was called at his Washington home and arrangements made to begin preliminary talks on Monday. The initial conferees were to consist of three Council representatives—Simmons, Griggs and Dr. Patten—and three persons of Rielinski's choice. Other Council prime members, including Bill Green and Gene Wild, were to begin working immediately on the position papers with the staff and representatives of affiliated organizations.

"Everybody get some lunch," Griggs said, "then do what you want until tomorrow. Washington is not as dead on Sunday as its reputation pretends."

As if by prearrangement, Simmons and Rubye left the meeting together, getting into the limousine outside Council headquarters, smiling and murmuring their way through pushing and thrusting media representatives without uttering a sentence of consequence. She was wearing a tan, knee-length, three-piece suit of light wool, and as she manipulated the skirt for easy entrance into the limousine, Simmons was reminded again of how shapely her slender legs were.

"What happened to the long skirt today?" he asked as the bodyguard closed the limousine door and walked around the car to get in beside the driver. "Tired of hiding your legs?"

She gave him a sidelong glance. "Yes and no," she replied. "I don't wear as many long skirts and dresses during cool and cold months as I do during the summer. Long dresses should be thin and easy to manage. Imagine sloshing around in the snow with a heavy wool skirt dragging the sidewalk."

"I imagine," he said.

The limousine pulled away from the curb. "Where to?" he asked.

"I'm not hungry," she said. "And I'm not ready to go back to my hotel."

"That's surprising—your not being hungry, I mean. Grieving over your lost love?"

She turned her head to look at him, anger rising in her eyes. "Don't needle me, Preston!" she said.

This was to be one of their days, he told himself. "I'm not needling you," he said. Then in a softer tone: "What did happen, Rubye?"

She shrugged her shoulders, as though attempting to shake away her anger. "I don't really know. Just wasn't anything there in the first place, now that I think about it. Of course, he did say something about my not having any time for him."

"Wanting to change your life style in less than two months, huh?"

"That's about the size of it."

The bodyguard slid open the panel in the sound-proof connecting glass. "Where to, Mr. Simmons?" he asked.

Simmons glanced at Rubye. She spread her hands in a gesture of indifference. "To my hotel," he told the bodyguard, then said to Rubye: "We can have some food sent up to the suite when you get hungry." She gave the indifferent gesture again.

"Rubye," he asked, "is your mother still satisfied with living in New York City? You said she was having a ball the last time I asked you about her."

"She's still having a ball," she said indifferently. "I guess there are even more meaningless teas in New York than Chicago."

"Don't be so hard on your mother."

"I'm not. It's just my mood."

Her mood definitely had changed in the past few minutes, he told himself. True, she had been somewhat sarcastic in the meeting, but her sarcasm had had a brightness to it, so unlike the touchy bitterness she was displaying now. "I hope you get over it before long," he said evenly, "otherwise we might as well go our separate ways."

"I'm sorry, Preston."

"That guy must have meant more to you than you admit."

"He doesn't have anything to do with it."

"What is it then? Your children are okay, aren't they?"

She brightened. "Yes, they're all right. Phyllis is married, you know, and still in Chicago. Her husband's a swell guy. Ray Junior is out in Los Angeles, working in a bank. Doing fine." She paused. "Preston, how is Preston Junior?"

"Fine. Finishing up his last year at Indiana U. Got a letter from him last week. A very thoughtful letter. Intended to call him yesterday, while I was at home, but just didn't get around to it."

"I know. They have their lives—and we have ours." There was sadness in her voice.

"Our lives are okay. At least, we're living the lives we cut out for ourselves."

She sighed. "I'm not knocking our involvement in the movement. I wouldn't exchange that part of my life for anything in the world. But I just don't seem to be able to get my personal thing together."

"You can't have everything, Rubye."

She glanced at him sharply. "No, you can't have everything. But I care about these things. Sometime I wish I were like you.

You just don't give a damn!" She was getting angry again.

"Calm down, Rubye. You don't know about me. You always did think I was something that I'm not—had more strength than I have. What I just said to you applies to me also. A person can't have everything."

She sighed again. "Probably you're right, Preston. Maybe one day I'll learn."

But she remained sullen. She was more angry at herself than at him, he told himself, because she had again revealed her vulnerability. The knowledge made him feel sad. He would not pressure her again.

The mood did not leave her until they were at his hotel suite, fortified with their inevitable drinks—a scotch on the rocks for her and a sherry on the rocks for him. Shaking her glass to mix the scotch, Rubye sat down on the couch, took a long sip, set the glass on the cocktail table and expelled her breath in a long sigh. "Boy, that tastes good!" she said. "A nice way to start a relaxing evening before getting back to the grind." She removed her jacket and vest and threw them across the back of the couch.

Simmons sat down beside her and leisurely sipped his drink. "Who are you going to start working with first?" he asked. "And where?"

Rubye patted her lips with her forefinger, her brow knitted in thought. "I believe I'll start in New York with the Black Media Women," she said. "Get two or three good writers from them and start each working with an organization. Then I'll look the material over before passing it along to you."

"Sounds like a good approach," he said, impressed by her decisiveness.

"A very good approach." She raised her arms above her head and leaned back against the couch. "Your girl is on the ball! But you know that, don't you?" She gave him a coquettish look.

Watching her sitting there, completely at ease for the moment, confident of their friendship, flirting with him without really meaning to, Simmons got a sudden feeling that it was

340

so right for her to be there with him, so logical. The feeling grew and grew, overwhelming him with a sense of contentment. Then his contentment turned restless, and it seemed to him that after all the years of knowing her, fate and poetic justice were at work at that moment, driving him relentlessly toward her. If she had been the center of his adolescent fantasies, he asked himself, why couldn't she be the cornerstone of his middle-aged realities? He got up from the couch and stood looking down at her with what he sensed was a strange stare.

"Rubye," he said, "do you remember what we said to each other the day we had lunch in the outdoor cafe down the street?"

She looked up at him, her eyes becoming serious. "We said a lot of things that day. What are you talking about?"

"About why we had never been lovers, when everybody thought we were."

The serious look remained in her eyes. "I said I'd follow you anywhere in the world, except into the bedroom...because fucking to you was like taking a drink of water."

He waved his hand impatiently. "I know you said that," he said, "but you were just being funny. You said something else: You said, or implied, that every time we had thought about getting together, one of us was seriously occupied with somebody else. But you know something? Neither of us has anybody now."

She didn't shift her eyes from his. "What about Janice?" she asked.

"Finished," he said. "Yesterday."

She stood up from the couch, picked up her glass, drained it, and set it back on the cocktail table. "Preston," she said, "I hate to ask you this, but I must. What about Hilda?" She was looking across the room, away from him.

What about Hilda? It was difficult for him to answer her because he had not answered the question for himself. But there was one thing of which he was sure: Neither he nor Hilda wanted a binding attachment. He placed his hands on Rubye's shoulders and turned her to face him. "Believe me," he said,

341

"there is nothing in my relationship with Hilda which would interfere with us at all. Rubye, I'm suggesting that you and I get something serious started. Immediately." He felt relieved that the actual words were out. There was no backtracking now.

A look of alarm came into her eyes. She raised her hands shoulder high, then dropped them to her side. "Preston, please don't kid me," she said. Her voice was trembling.

"I'm not kidding you, baby. Not this time."

She turned to him, picked up her glass and half-filled it with scotch. Her hands were unsteady. She faced him again without taking a drink. "Preston, do you really think we could...after all these years?"

"We're not that old."

"I know.... But Preston, we couldn't just play with each other. We mean too much to each other for that."

He touched her under the chin, then ran his fingers along her jawline. "Look Rubye," he said, "it's better to take a chance on what you want than on what you know you don't want. I can't guarantee you we'll get along. Maybe we'll be at each other's throats in a week. But I don't think so. We both deserve the chance to try."

The alarm in her eyes gave way to acceptance, then doubt clouded them again. "I don't know..." she said.

He moved closer to her, tenderly rubbing the side of her face. Then, very deliberately, he removed one of her earrings, then the other, and laid them on the cocktail table. Then he unbuttoned the two top buttons on her blouse and began to caress her neck.

"What are you doing?" she asked.

"Taking off your clothes."

"I haven't said yes." Her voice was very low.

"But you haven't said no."

He finished unbuttoning her blouse, pulled it out of her skirt, then unfastened her bra. She stepped back from him, searching his face. Her eyes were wary with indecision.

"Come on, baby" he said, pushing his hands beneath her bra.

Suddenly, she seemed to make up her mind. "I know how to

undress myself," she said. "Remember, I'm a big girl." Her tone was teasing.

"And I'm a big boy, too," he said. "The first one undressed gets a chance to help the other."

Standing undressed before her and looking at her naked body, Simmons marveled at the youthfulness of her figure. Here she was, a woman nearing her middle forties, the mother of two grown children, with a body the envy of most non-mothers twenty years her junior. Her breasts, larger then he had supposed, were firm and undrooped and her waist was amazingly slender without evidence of midriff fat. Her hips, curving away from her waist in a delicate outsweep, tapered into thighs as proportionally slender as her legs. Her pubic hairs, descending from her flat stomach, were dense and black, creating an inviting hollow where the front of her thighs didn't quite come together. She was standing very still, eyes averted, a bashful smile on her lips.

He moved close to her, touched her neck, shoulders, then her breasts. Her skin was cool. She trembled, shivers going through her entire body.

"What's wrong, baby?" he asked, feeling the beginning of an erection.

"I just can't believe it's really happening," she said.

"It's happening, baby," he replied, taking her hand and leading her toward the bedroom.

In the bedroom, she stretched out straight on the bed, on her back, staring at the ceiling. He lay beside her, on his stomach, leaning over her but not touching her, supporting his weight with his elbows.

"What are you thinking about, baby?" he asked.

"About us," she replied.

He began kissing her. First her forehead, then her eyes, nose and mouth, then her breasts. She shuddered, then gradually the shudders ceased. She reached out her hand, stroked his chest, then his stomach, her fingers still reaching. He moved forward, and she took his genitals in her hand, gently rubbing his testicles. As his erection grew, she began caressing his penis,

343

breathing heavily as she spread her legs. He crawled between them, but made no attempt to enter her. Instead, he cupped her breasts in his hands and began rubbing her nipples with his thumbs in gentle circular motions, feeling the nipples swell beneath his touch. She started moaning and thrusting her hips toward him. He permitted his penis to move along the lips of her vagina but refused to let it enter. Every time she would strain toward him, he would move away, continuing to caress the nipples of her breasts. She began tossing her head from side to side, her eyes growing as black as midnight, her mouth forming a silent O. He started whispering to her as she thrashed about on the bed, his loins aching with the unbearable agony of desire. Then he could withhold himself no longer. He met her thrust with a gentle one of his own, feeling himself slide into the hot interior of her. She uttered a groan and quivered in ecstasy, digging her sharp nails into the flesh of his back.

Then, as his climax rose to match her own, a strange feeling of protective compassion consumed him, making him want to cuddle her and hold her to his chest like a baby. It was a tenderness more powerful than any he had ever felt before. He began running his finger gently through her hair and kissing her eyelashes, now wet with tears. She wrapped her arms around his neck and pulled him hard against her, rocking back and forth. He felt at peace with himself and as one with her.

They had lost nothing, even though they had waited a lifetime, he told himself.

Chapter 37

10:00 A.M., Monday, October 26, 1987

EACH PARTICIPANT was dressed in a distinctive uniform, uniquely his or her own. True, no gold braids adorned pressed lapels, no shiny emblems embellished stiff collars, and no brass buttons sparkled on correct jackets. Yet, to Preston Simmons, sitting at a long table in a low-ceilinged room in AFL-CIO headquarters, the six persons present, himself included, definitely were in uniform.

Where Hilda Larsen was concerend, it was the hair which triggered the feeling. In fact, it was the severity of her hair style which had made him think about uniforms in the first place and motivated him to extend the analogy to the appearances and apparels of everybody else in the room. And in a way this was strange, because she was wearing her hair exactly as she had worn it every time he had seen her: drawn tightly across her head and fastened by a clip at the base of her neck. Yet, at other times, especially the last time, the rigidity of her hair style had generated an inquisitive feeling within him: the tightness of the hair on her head had made her features appear more pronounced, creating a sensation of elongated eyes, flaring nostrils and petulant lips. But not this time. Her face looked as though it were made out of plastic, unmalleable and unbreakable, a perfect companion for the blue sack suit she was wearing— buttoned all the way up to the neck.

He sighed. He was losing himself. It was time to stop this reflective bullshit and concentrate on the business at hand. Although they were just six persons quartered in an isolated room, to a watching and waiting world they were much more

345

than that. How had Moses Pennmann put it in his column this morning? "Today, in a room somewhere in the massive structure known as AFL-CIO headquarters, Joe Rielinski, Preston Simmons and two each of their closest associates will begin a dialogue which might well determine the direction of race and class relations in this country for generations to come." A heavy responsibility. No wonder his mind kept reaching out for things beyond the edge of reality, attempting to anchor itself in something less concrete yet, at the same time, more dependable than ordinary forms and philosophies.

Simmons looked deliberately around the room. Sitting alongside Rielinski were Hilda on his right and David Eastman, President of the United Public Workers Union, on his left. On his side of the table, Simmons could feel the presence of Bob Griggs on his left and Dr. Patten on his right. White on one side of the table, black on the other. And that was the way it should be, he told himself, especially at this stage. Specific rights had to be delineated, and there was no need to be hypocritical about it. However, one had to admit that among them there were divisions and differences which had nothing to do with race; in fact, on some issues blacks would side with whites against blacks and whites would side with blacks against whites; if not in this room, definitely among their high-echelon supporters in the field. But on the central issue of where power was to reside in the new movement—that issue had to be decided quickly, here and now, out in the open.

Rielinski picked up one of the two water pitchers from the middle of the table, filled his glass and drank, the heavy muscles of his neck rippling with the flow of liquid through his throat. Rielinski's uniform was very much on display. The open shirt collar had become his trademark.

"I have jotted down a few items," Rielinski said, "which could form the basis for today's agenda, if everybody is in agreement." His voice was as whip-like and direct as Simmons remembered.

"We won't know if we agree until we hear the items, Joe," Simmons replied.

Rielinski smiled as polite laughter came from various places around the table. "I walked into that one," he said. "Okay, I'll list my items, and then we'll see. Add *to* them, or subtract *from* them. Good enough?"

"Good enough," Bob Griggs said.

Rielinski placed his hands on the table, staring intently at his fingers. Simmons realized he was attempting to compress his thoughts into the succinct mold associated with his reputation. "First," Rielinski said, "I believe we should review, generally, the things we stand for: politically, economically, and socially. Sort of state the philosophy of our revolution. Then we should try to agree on the vehicle to be establised for launching, or implementing, this revolution. Next we should talk about projects, how and when to get things started. How does that approach sound to everybody?"

Hilda nodded, her face remaining mask-like. Simmons felt Dr. Patten stir at his right elbow, remembering that the minister was immaculate in a black suit and gray clerical collar. His uniform of firm reasonableness.

"I see nothing wrong with your agenda items, Joe," Dr. Patten said. "However, before we begin, I should like to state how I presently view the previous position of the Black American Council. Maybe separation was not a desirable philosophy, nor a viable strategy, but it was a sound tactic. By pushing it, we showed all Americans the level of black discontent and made it possible for progressive white forces to join with blacks to advance democracy. It is important that whites understand that we have no regrets."

Hilda nodded again, her face relaxing somewhat. David Eastman smiled, his small, slender body erect in his chair, his head sideways as though trying to find a shoulder on which to rest. His smile appeared secretive, as though he were in possession of a morsel of news too good to share.

"Your point is well made, Dr. Patten," Rielinski said. "I am sure Dave and Hilda agree with you, to say nothing of Preston and Bob."

"Indeed I do!" Dave Eastman said, his voice surprisingly big

347

for a man so small. "The war we must wage together is possible only because of the battle you have fought."

David Eastman had begun his climb to the top of the labor movement following Carter's 1978 attempt to change the civil service system. Charging that the Carter legislation was not designed to improve performance but to force federal workers under the thumbs of anti-union supervisors, Eastman began a crusade against passage of the legislation. At the time he was a local union president of the American Federation of Government Employees. At the end of the second year of his campaign, he had become president of the national union; by 1984, he had effected a merger between the Government Employees Union and the American Federation of State, County and Municipal Employees, the largest union in the public service field, to create the United Public Workers Union. When the merger took place, it was only fitting and proper that David Eastman should become head of the combined unions. Joe Rielinski often said, Preston Simmons recalled now—and he agreed with Rielinski in this assessment—that David Eastman had done as much as Rielinski to reawaken class consciousness in American workers.

"My position on the subject is clear," Hilda said, her voice becoming animated as she spoke. "Just like in the fifties and sixties, black militance of the eighties has awakened white progressives to their duty. If I have hit hard at the separatist movement, it's because I'm consumed with making America whole. Now that we have a chance to do it, I want to get on with business." The animation in her voice was tinged with impatience.

Bob Griggs cleared his throat. When he spoke his tone was as precise as always. "Let's get back to Joe's agenda," he said, "the philosophy part. Who wants to get it going?"

"I'll do that," Simmons said. "Since Joe raised the question, the best way to determine if there are disagreements is to let somebody else state the general philosophy of the movement."

"Okay, shoot," Rielinski said.

Now it was his turn to marshall his thoughts for a concise

348

analysis, Simmons told himself. He leaned back in his chair and locked his hands behind his head, vaguely aware that the gesture was one he often used—an integral component of *his* uniform, so to speak. "Industrial and technological management is so complex and all-embracing, it seems ridiculous that a country as advanced in these areas as the United States should leave this function to the whims of private parties," he began. "It's a miracle we have survived as well as we have. Therefore, the cornerstone of our economic philosophy must be the creation of a public-controlled system of planning, design and allocation of economic resources. The forces which control the lives of all Americans, and the lives of billions of peoples throughout the world, no longer can be the tools of corporate expansionism, personal ambition and greed. The passage of those resolutions to nationalize certain industries at the recent AFL-CIO convention was a good start. Those of us joining in this coalition from outside the labor movement must make it clear that we are ready to move in that direction."

Rielinski nodded, his chin in his hand. "Thanks," he said.

"In the past few weeks," Simmons continued, "I've thought a lot about the philosophy which should govern our economy. I have reached the conclusion that the time has come to re-write Marx, in a very specific way."

"How's that," Eastman asked.

"I advocate public ownership of the *means* of production and private ownership of the *ends* of production, and this should be as absolute as possible. That way, in our economic system, both basic social needs of humans will be satisfied—the need for security and the need for self-fulfillment."

Eastman leaned his head further to the side. "The only problem with your re-writing of Marx," he said, "is figuring out where the means end and the ends begin. That could start a whole new war, especially if you stick with your absolute dividing line criteria."

"The war is already going on, as Preston very well knows," Rielinski said. "That was the basic reason why Tito split with Stalin."

349

"As you say, I know that," Simmons replied. "But, as you recall, Tito never admitted that private ownership of the ends of production was a goal. He stated only that circumstances didn't permit the immediate institution of public ownership in all areas, but that it would come. I'm talking about splitting Marx down the middle. Now. Up front."

"And that means splitting capitalism down the middle, also," Rielinski said.

"Right."

"The view Preston just stated was basically the position of Dr. Martin Luther King Jr.," Dr. Patten said. "Dr. King believed that capitalism failed to see the truth in collective enterprise, while Communism failed to see the truth in individual enterprise. He was of the opinion that the real truth was represented by a synthesis of the two views."

"Exactly," Simmons said. "Also, when I used the word 'absolute', I wasn't talking about splitting hairs. I meant that to the best of our abilities, we should define industries which fall in the *means* category and those which fall in the *ends* category."

"I didn't intend to give the impression that I disagree with you philosophically," Eastman said. "As you know, I was one of the first leaders in the American Labor movement to call for nationalization of public utilities and other basic industries. Yet, nationalization frightens me. Once we create the system, how do we control it? How do we prevent the suffocating rigidity found in some Communist societies and eliminate those dehumanizing practices which have become part-and-parcel of our own welfare system? We are talking here about extending public bureaucracy on a massive scale."

"There might not be a way of making the system palatable short of industrial elections," Dr. Patten said softly.

Eastman jerked his head straight. "Are you saying that we should elect industry managers, just like we elect city mayors, state legislators, U.S congressmen, and presidents?"

"I am."

Eastman turned from Dr. Patten and looked deliberately at

350

Simmons and Griggs. Then he twisted around in his chair and looked at Rielinski and Hilda Larsen. The expression on his face indicated that he was looking for intervention. It appeared that he was not rejecting the idea, but wanted to know if any of the others were as surprised at Dr. Patten's suggestion as he was.

Simmons was remembering an article he had read back in 1978. The article had been written immediately after the settlement of a coal strike, and the sharp increases in steel prices imposed by the steel industry as soon as the miners went back to work. After calling for the establishment of a system of universal planning, the article went on to say: "But planning cannot be left to the planners.... It's goals must come from outside the process. Only a renewed democracy can supply them (the goals). In a complex society, it is foolish to pretend that democracy is satisfied by a once-a-year election day. People must be able to 'vote' every day by expressing their values on the job, as newly-aware consumers, in many kinds of groups and organizations, and in a variety of public hearings. Democracy must become as multifaceted and pervasive in daily life as government is now. Planning could then respond, not dictate." He had liked the concept when he had read the article, but he had doubted its effectiveness in practice. He had witnessed the failure of the "many kinds of groups and organizations" in their attempt to help direct the manpower-sharing programs of the seventies, inevitably losing out to the entrenched bureaucrats and special interests. But Dr. Patten was talking about hiring and firing industry management through the electoral process. And that was something else again! Hell, it just might work.

"I think Dr. Patten's suggestion should be considered seriously," he said, feeling his nerves tingle with excitement.

Apparently Hilda was excited as he. She was rubbing her throat with the tips of her fingers and moving her tongue rapidly over her lips. She held up her hand like she was in a classroom requesting permission to speak; nevertheless, she started talking before the permission was granted. "Really, I hadn't thought about that," she said. "I was so satisfied with the full employment in *meaningful* jobs I knew nationalization could bring, that I hadn't concerned myself with the need for democratic checks on operations, other than those provided by the present political process. What I had worried about, and still worry about, is how do we guarantee freedom of expression—first amendment freedoms, if you will—under a system in which the communications industry is also nationalized."

"You wrote an article on that once," Bob Griggs said. "You wrote that all media should be directed by a public corporation, answerable neither to the government nor private interests."

"I know I did," Hilda said, her voice lilting, "but I didn't say how the public corporation was to be established, or how we were to keep the public corporation bosses from getting entrenched. Dr. Patten might have given us the answer to that one also. Elect the top leadership."

Rielinski stood up, took off his jacket and hung it over the back of his chair. He thrust his hands upward, flexed his fingers, then brought his arms back to his sides. The red hair on his arms was dense and appeared to be prickly. Hilda glanced at his arms, then looked quickly away, aware that Simmons had observed her actions.

"What I hear you saying," Rielinksi said, sitting down, "is that the leadership in our industrial and communications systems should be filled through the elective process, similar to that currently employed in the governmental systems. That while this might not guarantee *continuing* democracy, it would come closer than any other method tried so far."

"Exactly," Dr. Patten said, rubbing his hands across his head. "Now you might not want elections in the industrial and communications systems to extend as far down to the local levels as elections in the other areas; yet, on the other hand, you'd try to make sure your lower-level entities in these areas were genuine subdivisions of the national groups—not autonomous bodies like our states, for instance. But then, at a later

352

date, we might want to take a look at that—the states, I mean."

"A much later date," Simmons said. "I'll be damned if we should tackle property rights and *states* rights at the same time."

Everybody laughed.

When the laughter had subsided, Rielinski asked: "Okay, what do we do with this suggestion of electing industrial and communications management?"

"It appears that we have a concensus to make it a plank in our platform," Eastman said.

"I agree that we seem to be in agreement with this policy in this room," Simmons said. "But what is this business about planks and platforms? That comes under Joe's second agenda item—the vehicle to be established for launching the revolution."

Eastman glanced at Rielinski. "I agree," he said. He glanced at Rielinski again. "We might as well go into that?" Rielinski nodded. "How do you like the name United Peoples Party?" Eastman asked the three black men.

"Ummmm." Simmons locked his hands behind his head again. "United Peoples Party. I think the name's all right, if you drop the 'United'. Just plain Peoples Party."

"Why don't you like the 'United'?" Hilda asked.

"It begs the proposition," Simmons said. "Let *them* prove we're not united."

She pursed her lips, glancing at him out of the corner of her eye. It was the first evidence of intimacy she had demonstrated all morning. And that was all right with him. Especially since what happened between him and Rubye. Hilda nodded her head in agreement.

"How are you recommending that this party be organized?" Griggs asked.

"Mostly like any other American party," Rielinski said. "A national party with state and local divisions. In some areas, especially in labor and black strongholds, we might be able to take over the Democratic Party apparatus. Where we can, we should, from my point of view."

Griggs laughed. It was a sardonic laugh. "I think we should steer clear of that. Unless we can take over the apparatus without absorbing the leadership. Where we have the people, we don't need the apparatus; and where we don't have the people, we can't get the apparatus."

"I think it's a matter of circumstances," Eastman said. "It should be a matter of policy that the national committee takes a look at these situations."

"I can buy that," Simmons said. "While I'm inclined to agree with Bob on principle, practical politics occasionally might dictate a different course. But that's down the road. What I'm interested in now is how the national committee will be organized."

Rielinski glanced sharply at him. "What do you mean?" he asked.

"I'm going to bring it down front to you, Joe," Simmons replied. "I'm talking about black co-leadership of the national party. That means the National Committee of the Peoples Party should have two chairpersons—a black one and a white one."

Eastman's head jerked up straight. "But that's instituting racial quotas at the very top of the party," he said.

"Right," Simmons said. "That's the way it should be. Black and white together. At the top."

"Preston, you know the number of blacks who'll be in the new party won't justify that," Rielinski said quietly.

"Oh yes it will. As a symbol for the world to see," Simmons said.

Rielinski looked at Griggs and Dr. Patten. "I can tell you fellows feel the same," he said.

"Correct," said Griggs.

"You bet your life," said Dr. Patten.

Rielinski rubbed his hand across his face. "I don't have anything against it," he said, "but we'll catch hell from below. You might not know it, but many whites, and I mean economically progressive whites, objected to the composition of *this*

354

negotiating committee. They thought more whites should have been on it, something like five whites and three blacks."

Nobody said anything for a few seconds. Simmons could feel the pregnancy of the silence, something akin to a sigh of discomfort, as each person prepared for a battle in which nobody wanted to engage.

Hilda was the first to speak. "Sometime I get the feeling that white people are so *preoccupied* with black people," she said, "so *aware* of the presence of black people, that a lot of us actually *feel* there are more blacks in this country than whites. So your argument about the number of blacks not justifying a co-leadership position, Joe, just doesn't wash, psychologically that is. Hell, let's cut out the bullshit. If blacks and whites are going to be together in this thing—and you and I, Joe, have been preaching this stronger than Preston and his people— then let's declare to the world that it's a partnership. And a real partnership means at the top as well as at the bottom!"

"Amen!" Dr. Patten said.

Hilda was looking directly at Simmons. For a second it appeared to him that she was asking him to be proud of her, to admit that she had redeemed herself for whatever transgression he thought she had committed. Then a veil fell over her eyes and she looked away.

"That's the way you see it, Hilda?" Eastman asked.

"That's the way I see it."

She might be a little screwy about personal things, Simmons told himself, but on the big questions she was all right. She might stare at the hair on Joe's arms because she had not fucked him and ignore him, Simmons, because she had, but she kept the big picture in focus. Maybe that was nature's way of leveling things out—taking from the peaks in order to build up the valleys.

"I hope you fellows got the full impact of Hilda's statement," Simmons said. "This question of co-leadership should not be debatable, at least not in this room. It must be presented to our associates, and to the world, in such a way that they will know

355

there is no alternative: that we didn't even *imagine* there could be an alternative."

"Amen!" Dr. Patten said again.

Rielinski looked at Eastman and Eastman looked at Rielinski, communicating in the secret language of white men who feel inherently that their power is one and the same with their existence. Simmons was almost mesmerized by the exchange.

"Okay," Rielinski finally said, "that's our position. And, Preston, you are right. If we present it like it's one of the eternal truths, they'll buy it."

"Amen!" Dr. Patten said in a parody of himself, and everybody laughed softly in relief.

Chapter 38

9:00 A.M., Tuesday, October 27, 1987

PRESIDENT DORSEY Talbott Davidson could feel a hard knot in his stomach, just below his breastbone. His ulcer was acting up. He would have to insist that Colonel Rapshaff, his much-too-analytical doctor, put him back on Tagamet, the drug which for nearly a decade had curtailed the production of ulcer-creating acids in his stomach. He would just have to take his chances with the slight blood disorder the doctor had detected approximately a month ago. In this case, the witch was worse than the devil.

He leaned back in his chair, ran the fingers of both hands through his long, reddish-brown hair, around the back of his neck, then along the sides of his face, bringing them together at the point of his chin. He smiled bitterly, feeling the jaw muscles in his thin face tighten. That was exactly what he had done on another, more vital front—swapped the devil for the witch: the devil of black separation for the witch of socialist unity. The dullness of the autumn day, pushing into the room through the high Georgian windows of the Oval Office, was depressing. Only time would tell whether this new witch would also prove worse than the old devil.

He glanced again at the Washington Post he had placed on the corner of his desk. The Rielinski-Simmons group, which yesterday had been officially designated The Peoples Party, was hogging all the news. They had scheduled a national convention for early September of next year—after the conventions of the two major parties. The sure hands of master

357

politicians could be detected in their other announcements as well, especially the proposal to hold continuous sessions of their National Committee until May of next year to receive input from "peoples groups" for the development of "an agenda for America". The actual drafting of their platform would take place between May and September. The entire process had been designed to keep their actions continuously in the spotlight. And the payoff was beginning early.

"For the first time in the long history of this country," the lead story in the Washington Post read, "American domestic policy is being shaped not by the President and the Congress but by the newly-created Peoples Party. Despite the fact that not a single member of this party holds an elective office, at this moment it probably is more representative of American opinion than the collective positions of all the elected officials from both major parties." This sentiment was being echoed by the New York Times, the Chicago Sun-Times, the Atlanta Constitution, the Los Angeles Times and many other major papers from throughout the country, to say nothing of most of the radio and television commentators. The President sighed. Couldn't these fools see what they were doing to themselves? If the Peoples Party had its way, the news media would cease to exist in its present framework. Rielinski and Simmons had said as much, right out in the open. Mass suicide was in the air.

The President glanced at his watch. It was one minute after nine. He pushed the intercom on his desk.

"Bernice," he asked in a peeved voice, "aren't Dick Lawrence and Tom Ryan here yet? They were due at nine."

"Mr. Lawrence is just coming in, Mr. President," his secretary replied. Mr. Ryan isn't here yet."

"Tell Dick to come in, Bernice. Send Tom in as soon as he gets here."

Attorney General Richard Lawrence breezed into the office, bringing the loud smell of cologne with him. The President felt like holding his nose. Doesn't the damn fool know he isn't supposed to take a bath in the stuff? he asked himself.

"Good morning, Mr. President," Lawrence said briskly, his

flat face broadened by a smile, the nostrils in his thin nose dilated. "Here I am all ready for action. All ready for action."

"Sit down, Dick," the President said impatiently, "I don't see a damn thing good about this morning."

The Attorney General dropped into a chair facing the President's desk, swinging his right leg over the arm of the chair. "It's the point of view which determines the environment, Mr. President," he said. "The point of view which determines the environment."

The President grunted, wondering again as he had wondered many times before why he had appointed Dick Lawrence to the position of Attorney General, especially during these times of unrest and dissention. Not that the man wasn't a shrewd lawyer, an excellent politician and an unquestioned patriot. But his back-slapping manners, loud cologne and strange habit of repeating the last phrase of every sentence he uttered were unnerving. If he were lucky enough to be elected to a second term, Dick Lawrence wouldn't be a part of it.

"Isn't Tom Ryan supposed to be at this meeting, Mr. President?" Lawrence asked.

"You're damn right," the President cut in, catching Lawrence in the middle of his repeat phrase. "But you know Tom. He's the only sonofabitch I know who's never on time, even for the President."

Lawrence laughed. "He's exercising the perogatives of separation of powers, Mr. President. The perogatives of separation of powers."

The President smiled bitterly. "I hope he understands that we won't have any powers to separate if the so-called Peoples Party has its way," he said. "A Chairman of the Judiciary Committee of the House of Representatives doesn't mean shit to them. Especially now that Tom's Senate counterpart, Sam Leavitt, has defected to the enemy."

"Just like a damn Jew," Lawrence said, "trying to get in on the ground floor, so he can control things. So he can control things."

The President threw up his hand. "It's not just the Jews who worry me. This thing cuts across the ethnic and racial spectrum. I wish you'd take it seriously."

Lawrence leaned back in his chair, his flat face fixing itself into a harsh mold. "I am taking it seriously, Mr. President," he said slowly. This time he made no attempt to repeat himself.

"Then I suppose you have some ideas?"

"Oh, yes, I have some ideas. We stopped the other thing. We'll stop this one. Stop this one."

The President hoped the Attorney General was as confident as he sounded. He knew *he* wasn't. "Maybe we pushed too hard on the other thing," he said.

Lawrence removed his leg from the arm of the chair. "Don't ever say that, Mr. President," he said. "We did what we had to. Anything is better than giving in to a bunch of niggers. Giving in to a bunch of niggers."

The President sighed. "I know. But Simmons and his people came out looking good, as they say. Maybe that last thing with Sam Muhammed was unnecessary."

"Dead men tell no tales," Lawrence said.

"This one did," the President replied.

"But it's not as bad as a live Muhammed saying the same thing."

The President sighed again. "Maybe you're right."

"I know I am," Lawrence replied. "I know I am."

Tom Ryan came into the office, walking on the balls of his feet like a boxer. He folded his arms across his chest in a flexing motion, came over and sat down in the companion chair to the one occupied by Lawrence. His round face carried an expression of concentration. "Sorry I'm late, Mr. President," he said, his words tripping over each other in a hoarse rumble. He nodded in Lawrence's direction.

Despite the things he had said about Ryan to Lawrence, the President was genuinely fond of the chairman of the House Judiciary Committee. Where Lawrence's habit of repeating himself aggravated the President, he found Ryan's jumbled way of talking strangely pleasing.

"Dick and I have been speculating on what to do about the

Peoples Party," the President said. "Nothing concrete yet."

Ryan nodded. He leaned forward in his chair, placing his hands on his thighs. "Have you talked about whether we are in a better or worse situation," he asked, "now that the blacks have pulled away from separation and joined up with Rielinski?"

"Not in so many words," the President said, "but Dick seems to feel we are in a better position."

"It's idle speculation," Lawrence said. "We did what we had to do. That's the only way to deal with niggers. Now we're only fighting on one front. And another thing, the niggers and the whites in the Peoples Party aren't going to get along."

Ryan nodded in agreement. "That's the point," he said. "Most of the whites in the Peoples Party don't like the blacks any better than we do. That's our first move. To exploit the racial differences."

And how do we go about that?" the President asked.

"By starting at the place where it hurts most. Griggs and Rielinski have been selected co-chairmen of the National Committee. A lot of white members aren't going to like that."

"I wonder why they gave Griggs the job instead of Simmons?" the President mused. "Think we can get any mileage out of that? Turning the blacks against each other?"

Lawrence shook his head. "If it had gone the other way, we could have. But Simmons was too smart for that. He doesn't have a strong organizational base like Griggs. He's the real brains, but he doesn't have the base. He doesn't have the base."

Ryan nodded his head in assent. "Dick is right. Our best bet is to play the whites against the blacks."

Lawrence held up his hand. "Not so fast, Tom. That's only one side of the coin, where the niggers are concerned. First, we might as well understand that not all of them are going to desert us. Jim Sneed and the middle-class niggers who cater to him will be with us come hell or highwater. Hell, in a lot of ways they are more economically conservative than we are. Economically conservative than we are."

"I'd rather put it another way," the President said harshly.

361

"They trust the free enterprise system. After all, it's been good to them."

"I'll concede your point, Mr. President," Lawrence said in an apologetic tone. "The bottom line is, that group of blacks are with us, and can be exploited to the hilt. Now, lets go to the other end of the spectrum and take a look at what we have."

"Albert James," the President cut in.

"Right," Lawrence said. "You can't turn people's beliefs and emotions off and on like a faucet. Besides, that Albert James is a very effective leader, much more fire than either Griggs or Simmons. Also, regardless of what Sam Muhammed said in that damn letter, many of his followers are mad as hell at Griggs and Simmons for joining up with Rielinski. Joining up with Rielinski."

"But none of these people are going to support us," the President said.

"I know *that*," Lawrence replied. "The idea is to keep them from supporting *Rielinski*. A few thousand dollars here and there to keep the propaganda rolling will go a mighty long way. Mighty long way."

"The irony in a move like that appeals to me," Ryan said. "Last month we were fighting the separatists like hell, this month we'll be supporting them."

"Anything for flag and country," Lawrence said. "Anything for flag and country."

The President was beginning to feel better. There was nothing like consulting with two top strategists like Ryan and Lawrence to get things moving. Maybe he had been too harsh in his assessment of Lawrence. But talking about a thing wasn't getting it done. There were many genuine Black-White Unity adherents among the leadership of the Peoples Party, and these people were not going to be out-maneuvered by outright racist attacks. Ryan and Lawrence were going to have to put their best experts on the race angles.

"We are up against forces which have been building since New Deal days," he said. "And they are being led by some top-notch strategists. Like that Larsen bitch, for instance."

362

"She'd rather fuck a nigger than eat," Lawrence said.

"Can we make any mileage there?" the President asked.

"Of course," Ryan replied. "Not only where she's concerned, but with lots of others. That's in Dick's department."

"Don't fall into the Hoover trap," the President said.

"We're fighting for our lives," Ryan said. "We must use everything at our disposal. There is such a thing as being too careful."

"I agree with you," the President said. "More importantly, we're fighting for the life of our country."

"I couldn't agree more," Lawrence said. "But as the President keeps implying, these bastards are smart. For instance, take their proposal calling for demonstrations of support in thirteen cities on Thanksgiving Day. *Thirteen cities on Thanksgiving Day.*"

For once, the President had to admit that Lawrence's repetition of himself had a point to it. Thirteen cities on Thanksgiving Day. Modeled after the thirteen original states and the Mayflower. You couldn't get any more American than that. He ticked off the thirteen cities in his mind: Washington, D.C., New York City, Philadelphia, Boston, Chicago, Detroit, Cleveland, Atlanta, New Orleans, Los Angeles, San Francisco, St. Louis, Dallas. The whole country aflame with demonstrations. "And they have placed the burden of keeping the peace on us—by getting the left-wing, violent groups to agree in advance to cool it," he said bitterly.

"If trouble breaks out they can swear we are the ones fomenting it, not them," Ryan added with equal bitterness.

"That doesn't mean a damn thing," Lawrence said. "Most of those left-wing groups are in our pockets. In our pockets."

The President laughed. "Including the Black Liberation Army."

"At least our half of it," Lawrence smiled.

Congressman Ryan stood up, folded his arms across his chest in a hugging motion, then sat down again. "I have another idea," he said. "I heard from a good source just before I came here that one of their tactics will involve attempting to take over some of our state and local central committees. We should make it easy for them to take over *certain* committees."

Lawrence glanced sharply at Ryan, his nostrils flaring with appreciation. "Damn good idea," he said. "Only we can't make it *too* easy."

"Right on target," the President said.

The intercom on the President's desk buzzed. He flipped on the speaker. "Yes, Bernice?"

"The Secretary of State is on the line, Mr. President," Bernice's voice said.

"Tell him to call back in five minutes."

"Thank you, Mr. President."

"Shouldn't he be here?" Lawrence asked.

The President frowned. "Not at this stage. He'll have plenty to do later on. Any other ideas?"

Ryan and Lawrence glanced at each other. Finally Lawrence said: "Tom and I have been kicking around a rather far-out idea. Mind you, Mr. President, it's just an idea. Just an idea." His voice was cautious.

"Out with it, man," the President said impatiently. "We need all the ideas we can get."

Lawrence slumped down in his chair, crossed and uncrossed his legs, then sat up straight. "Well, Mr. President," he said, "Tom and I thought that if things started getting too tough, maybe we should consider merging the two parties. The Democratic and Republican parties, I mean. The Democratic and Republican parties."

At first, the President thought he had misunderstood Lawrence. But he could tell by the expressions on the faces of his companions that his ears were not deceiving him. He could feel anger send a surge of blood to the surface of his face. Were they crazy?

"It was only an idea, Mr. President," Ryan said.

"Just an idea," Lawrence echoed.

By the time the two men finished speaking, the President's anger was subsiding, fleeing before the thoughts emanating from his brain. God knew it was in the interest of both parties to stop the radical surge. But whom would it benefit most? Their party was in, and the other party was out; therefore, their party would have the upper hand in any negotiations. However, the Republican Party, simply because it was out of power, would have less to lose. Maybe, the idea wasn't so bad, after all; an idea which might benefit both parties equally. It would take detailed planning, and correct timing, but maybe the subject could be raised. "Ummm, not a bad idea," he heard himself say.

"You like it, Mr. President?" Ryan asked. His tone was relieved.

"I'm glad you're not angry," Lawrence said.

"I didn't mean that merging the Democratic and Republican parties was not a bad idea," the President said. "That's going too far too fast. However, I can visualize situations where both parties could field single slates of candidates, if this new party shows great strength in certain areas coming into next year's elections."

"Would any such situation include a single candidate for the Office of the Presidency?" Ryan asked.

"It might," the President said irritably. "Depending on the circumstances just before the conventions."

"Dick and I got the idea just last night," Ryan said. "After you scheduled this meeting." His tone indicated that he was still concerned about the President's attitude.

The President was attempting to determine with whom the first contact could be made in the Republican Party. He thought he knew. He still resented Ryan and Lawrence having the nerve to discuss such a radical departure behind his back, but you had to give the bastards credit for some first-rate thinking.

"Let's keep this in this room," he said. "But the idea, as modified, has definite possibilities."

"Mum's the word, Mr. President," Ryan said.

"My lips are sealed," Lawrence confirmed. "Lips are sealed."

"Okay," the President said, standing up from the desk, his manner indicating that the conference was ending. Lawrence and Ryan also stood up.

365

"Get moving on everything we've discussed, except the last item, of course," the President said. "We'll need to have weekly meetings. Just the three of us, for the time being."

"As you see fit, Mr. President," Lawrence said. "As you see fit."

The two visitors headed toward the door. "Thank you, Mr. President," Ryan said.

As he watched them go, the President rubbed his hand across his body. The knot had disappeared from his stomach. He felt in the pink, ready for a fight. Maybe he would permit Colonel Rapshaff to hold off on the Tagamet until the slight blood disorder cleared up.

Chapter 39

5:30 P.M., Monday, November 2, 1987

THE FENCE surrounding the field was composed of interlocking rings of slate-gray metal, corroded now because of years of exposure to the Los Angeles sun, smog and rain. About five feet high, the fence was tied by pliable aluminum strings to slender posts, anchored approximately twenty feet apart in concrete mounds. The fence was topped by long rods of the same material and diameter as the posts, the rods running through ornamental hoops which served as caps for the posts.

The field itself was composed of three or four lots, located at the intersection of a major avenue and a minor street in the predominately single-family, black neighborhood where Albert James lived. According to hearsay, the fence and field had been in place more than twenty-five years. However, James's neighbors were fond of telling him, approximately a decade ago the intersection had been slated for the building of a fast-food restaurant, but their spirited intervention had prevented the disaster, even though a required zoning change was well underway before they found out about the conspiracy. Since that time, the owners of the property had made no further attempt to have the area rezoned. Neither had they, for some unexplained reason, moved to erect the types of buildings on the property which conformed with existing codes. The field, therefore, continued to be utilized in the same way it had in the past—as a playground for neighborhood residents, adults and children alike.

Leaning against the fence, his hands resting on the topping

rod, Albert James was watching three teen-aged black boys and a young black man playing basketball. James was dressed in a blue exercise suit, having stopped at the playground on the last lap of a three-mile walk, which he took most afternoons when he was at home. The basketball players were engaged in the popular game known as "horse", where maneuvers and shots become more and more intricate until every contestant but the most skilled is eliminated. The three boys, whom James knew by sight but not by name, were dressed in after-school street clothes. The young man, however, was wearing expensive-looking shoes, trousers and shirt, with knotted necktie pulled down from open shirt collar. A jacket, which matched his trousers, was hanging on a fence pole near the gate that opened into the basketball corner of the field. James didn't believe he had seen the young man before.

James had been at home in Los Angeles more than a week. He had returned directly from Washington, D.C., after his meeting Saturday before last with Griggs, Dr. Patten and Rubye. He didn't like to think about that meeting. It was too painful. In a way, he had looked for Griggs and Dr. Patten to defect, but he had expected Rubye to support him. He had seen her turn close battles to the side of separation too often not to believe that she favored it deep-down herself. And he still believed she would have supported him if it hadn't been for Simmons. When Griggs had told them of Simmons's decision, that had done it for Rubye. Simmons was one guy, probably the only one, who could make Rubye do anything.

One of the boys made a tricky shot from the right corner of the back-board and one of the three other spectators applauded. The young man said, "Not bad. Not bad."

"Not *bad*," the boy said. "What do you call good?"

"Okay, good then," the young man said.

"Things ain't been standin' still 'round here, man, since you moved out of the 'hood."

So the young man once lived in the neighborhood, James mused. And if the boys, who were about eighteen, knew him as well as they seemed to, he hadn't been gone too long. Probably to college. James looked at the other spectators, studying them closely. There were two black women, in their early thirties, conversing together, standing about twenty feet away. He knew both of them to speak to. In fact, they had exchanged greetings when he had arrived at the playground. The other spectator was an elderly white man. He was standing around the corner from James, on the other side of the back-board, more than fifty feet away.

The call he had received from Simmons last Wednesday night had been brief. It was more of a duty call than anything else, James had told himself, because he knew that Simmons had to find out for himself just where he stood. He realized now that both he and Simmons had been somewhat embarrassed by the necessity of talking to each other.

"We got what we wanted out of Rielinski," Simmons had said. "He and Bob are going to be equals at the top of the Peoples Party."

"Do you really believe that, Preston?" he had asked.

There was a pause on the other end of the line."More or less," Simmons had replied. "But nothing is constant, Al. You know that. Everything has to be fought for everyday." Another pause. "We need you with us."

"I can't change that fast, Preston," he had replied. "I'm with the separation movement, for the duration."

"The people are no longer with you, Al."

"What difference does that make? We've pushed unpopular causes before."

"I know, Al. But now we have a popular cause which might be just as good."

He had laughed. "Do you really think so, Preston? I suppose it all boils down to the fact that you trust white people more than I do."

And that was the way the conversation had ended.

James noticed that two of the boys were standing to the side of the court, away from the players. Apparently they had been eliminated. His assumption was confirmed when the young man said, "Two down and one to go."

369

"It only takes one to stop your show!" the boy who had made the tricky shot replied.

"Tell him, Bubba," one of the young women said.

The young man glanced at the women. "No comments from the peanut gallery," he said. His voice was pleasant, and both women laughed.

James had to admit that in the week since their coming together, Rielinski and Simmons had turned the Peoples Party into the darling of the news media, if coverage meant anything. But, then, their opposition had been relatively silent. He supposed the government was doing what he and his allies were doing—getting their strategy together. Rielinski and Simmons would not be given clear sailing from any quarter. But, of course, they didn't expect they would.

James glanced at the white spectator. As he watched him, the man appeared to grow tired of the game and vacated his place at the fence, heading away from the intersection along the avenue.

One thing really worried him above all others, James told himself. And that was his wife, Sarah. She didn't agree with the stand he was taking. When he returned from Washington Sunday before last, she had shown more elation than she had in a long time. But it had been for the wrong reason. "If they have joined Rielinski," she had said, "now is a good chance for you to wash your hands of the whole business. Forget all this running about the country and stay here, Albert, with me."

But he couldn't, and he had told her so. Her reaction had been the same as it had been for years—silent, respectful disagreement. Yet, this morning at the breakfast table, she had tried again.

"When are you leaving?" she had asked.

"Tomorrow," he had replied. "Heading for New York City. Some of Sam Muhammed's people and some of ours are pulling together a mass rally."

She had nodded. "I wish you wouldn't," she said. "But I know nothing I can say or do will stop you. Tell me one thing, Albert. Are you still doing this for Paul?"

He had been surprised by the bluntness of her question. Yet, the mention of Paul's name had moved him and he had felt water coming to his eyes. "Yes, that's why I'm doing it," he had finally replied. "But isn't that reason enough?"

Loud groans of disappointment from the two young women brought James back to the basketball game. Apparently the young man had just made a spectacular play to end the duel because when James's attention focused, he was raising his arms above his head and waving his hands in the universal gesture of victory.

"Send for me when you grow up," the young man said to Bubba, who was standing dejectedly nearby, his hands folded behind he back. The young man patted Bubba on the shoulder, amending his remarks. "Good game, man," he said. Then he turned away from Bubba, stood still for a second, and announced in a clear voice: "It's all in the arc of the ball."

For a few seconds, the words didn't register with James. Watching the game end, realizing he had been standing there for more than a half-hour, he had begun to doubt if the contact would be made. The mysteriously delivered envelope, which had contained the message to be here at the basketball court, had contained an additional sentence, which he had assumed was a contact code. And these were the words the young man had just uttered. *It's all in the arc of the ball.* He had been looking for somebody to come up and stand beside him and watch the game with him. But now that the contact words had been spoken, it made sense that the young man should be the one. Who had a better right to talk about balls and arcs than somebody playing basketball?

The young man was walking toward the two women, who had not moved from the fence. Bubba, with the resiliency of youth, had joined his friends, apparently for a new game.

"Sorry your brother lost," the young man said to one of the women. "Bubba is your brother?"

"Yes," she said. Then, half-teasingly, "I do know you, don't I?"

"Right. You graduated from high-school the year I came in.

I hit on you once."

"You did? What did I say?"

"You laughed."

"Try me again, " she said, and she and her friend laughed together.

"I just might do that," the young man said. "But first I want to say hello to Mr. James."

"Okay," the young woman said. "We have to go now, but we'll see you around. Give Bubba the message. You can catch him here any afternoon."

"Gotcha."

As the young man came along the inside of the fence toward him, James couldn't help but think about Paul. The young man was tall, taller than Paul had been and almost as tall as his six feet-five inches. He was medium-brown with a round, pleasant face and a short, natural haircut. Establishment was written all over him. They faced each other across the fence.

"How are things going, Mr. James?" the young man asked. His voice was the same as it had been on the basketball court and when talking to the women—confident and pleasant. He was not breathing fast like a person who has just completed a strenuous game, but perspiration was running from his hairline down his neck into the open collar of his shirt.

"I'm doing as well as can be expected," James said.

The young man nodded. "Sellouts can be a bitch," he said.

It was James's turn to nod. "They're tough to get over," he said.

The young man placed his hands on the fence. When he spoke his voice had lost its casual tone. "We have reached a favorable assessment of you," he said, "and have decided to ask you to join us."

"Join you in what?"

"Within a week," the young man said, "there will be a meeting of leaders who still believe in a separate black state. Your name is on the list to participate."

The young man's eyes were boring into him, disconcerting him. "What are you talking about?" James asked. "I haven't

372

helped to plan any such meeting. In fact, I'm going to New York tomorrow to help put together a mass rally. That's the only meeting I know anthing about."

The young man waved his hand. "We know about that," he said. "But I'm talking about something really important. I'm talking about a meeting to map out a *realistic* approach to our problems. After the sellout of the other leaders, don't you think one is needed?"

"Of course," James said, feeling somewhat irritated. "That's one of the reasons why I'm going to New York. The mass rally won't be the only thing we'll talk about."

"I know," the young man said. "But most of the so-called leaders meeting with you in New York City will not participate in the meeting I'm talking about. They're not stable enough."

"Just what are you talking about?" James asked.

"Okay. Here it is. The meeting I'm talking about is being called for the express purpose of merging the military and the political in the battle for a separate state."

Bubba and his friends were keeping up a lot of noise on the basketball court. The women were gone. James and the young man were alone at the fence.

"You said you and your friends have reached a favorable assessment of me," James said. "This means you think I believe a separate state can be won through violence?"

The young man shook his head, smiling with his mouth but not his eyes. "I didn't say that. I said our purpose is to consolidate the military and political aspects of the struggle. Violence, as you call it, will be used only selectively. And under the direction of the political leaders. You are at the very top as a political leader."

"I have never believed in violence," James said.

"You can't win without it," the young man said.

"I don't know about that," James replied. "Martin Luther King did pretty well."

The young man laughed, low and mirthlessly. "The only thing King won without violence was the Montgomery bus boycott. The civil rights legislation of 1964 and the voting

373

rights legislation of 1965 weren't passed until black people started burning cities. And, hell, we're talking about winning a nation. That can't be done without having in place the apparatus to put the fear of God in a few people."

"The fear of God was put in a number of people last month," James said, "but it didn't do any good."

"Do you know why?" the young man asked.

"No."

"Because it wasn't all our fear. Part of it was the government's. And that part which was ours wasn't coordinated. Look, every successful political movement has had a military wing at its disposal. We're determined to have one this time. Your friends have deserted you. You didn't go with them, and we respect you for it. Now, you might as well come with us, if you expect any payoff for all the years you have put into the struggle."

Regardless of the young man's impressive words, James couldn't get over his first impression that basically he was establishment by nature. But what if that appearance and demeanor had been deliberately developed and cultivated? It would be the smart thing to do. A very smart thing to do.

"Which wing of the movement do you belong to, the political or the military?" he asked.

It was a question James had been somewhat apprehensive about asking, but it was one which had to be asked. The young man took it in stride. His only reaction was a slight hardening of the eyes. "If I were part of the strictly political process," he said, "you would know me. Therefore, I must be from the military."

That told him only part of what he wanted to know, James told himself. The answer to his next question, if he could get it, would tell him much more. "Will you be at this summit meeting?" he asked.

The young man smiled. This time he did not hesitate. "Of course," he said.

It suddenly struck James that in their "assessment" of him, the leaders of the Black Liberation Army, or whatever group

374

the young man represented, had decided to expose one of their members to him, to go a long way toward leveling with him, because they were at least partially convinced that he was ready to accept their way of doing things. And in that assessment, they were on the right track. For, truthfully, since the others had decided to go with Rielinski, he hadn't been able to put together a plan of action in which he had confidence. True, he had known he would do something, would keep speaking out. This was the reason he had accepted the invitation to join the mass rally planners in New York, hoping that a more concrete and broader plan of action would materialize out of this project. But he hadn't fooled himself. He needed associates in whom he had confidence: smooth, skilled associates, to take the places of the ones who had deserted him.

"How will I know when this meeting will be held?" he asked.

"We'll let you know," the young man said.

"But how?"

"I don't know that yet myself." The young man's face was stern. "Does this mean you have accepted?"

James could feel his heart pounding with new excitement. What did he have to lose? Paul had to be avenged, to the extent that one man could avenge the wrong done to another. Besides, he liked the young man's style. Here was a brother, no older than Paul would have been, who could flirt charmingly with beautiful young women, comfort a growing boy with sensitivity, and cut the heart out of a white racist, all with the same pleasant smile. If this was the new way of things, so be it. In any case, it would take knowledge of how to operate in this new day, and more, to win a measure of respect from the white rulers of the world.

"Yes, I'm, with you," he said in a firm voice.

Chapter 40

12:00 Noon, Thursday, November 26, 1987

IT WAS high noon, Thanksgiving Day.

Standing on a temporary platform at the entrance to the center section of the Lincoln Memorial, in front of Daniel Chester French's gigantic statue of the Great Emancipator, Preston Simmons looked down the long flight of steps into the great park known as Capitol Mall, where hundreds of thousands of people were assembled. The crowd was so massive that it extended beyond his vision on the left and right. But if the depth of the crowd, he told himself, spilling beyond the Reflecting Pool to the base of the Washington Monument, was any indication of its width, then the outer edges on his left probably reached the downtown business district, while portions of the crowd massed on his right could very well be standing on the banks of the Tidal Basin. He was certain this crowd was the largest ever assembled in the nation's capitol, exceeding the 300,000 who heeded Martin Luther King's call in 1963 and outstripping the half million who participated in the labor-led Solidarity Day demonstration in 1981.

The temperature and weather were ordinary for a late November day in Washington, D.C.—cloudy, cool-cold, with hints of rain in the air. Most of the people, at least those close enough to the platform for him to discern them individually, seemed to be dressed properly for the time and place, wearing topcoats, overcoats or sweaters. At the moment, there was not much movement in the crowd. The people were not exactly standing at attention, but they were, for the most part, assuming postures which indicated that they were aware their long wait was nearing an end: the main event was about to take place.

And the people were right, of course. Joe Rielinski, Hilda Larsen, Rubye Ransome and he were ready to begin their speeches. He felt both nervous and detached, both eager and hesitant about speaking to the massed thousands. He wondered if anybody—no matter how arrogant or humble—ever got used to being a main event.

The preliminaries, emceed jointly by the black Mayor of the city and the head of the district union council, had consisted of songs and short speeches of welcome by local dignitaries. The crowd had joined in the singing with good-natured abandon and had even applauded the speeches without displaying undue impatience. Up to now, it had been a relaxed occasion.

Simmons, Rielinski, Hilda and Rubye were standing in the center of the platform, up front near the microphines. Behind and around them, in a crescent-shaped line, stood approximately a dozen security forces, eyes probing the crowd for unusual movements. The four of them were standing very close together: Rielinski on the left, Rubye next to him, followed by Hilda and Simmons. They were holding hands, with Rielinski's left hand and Simmon's right hand free. The program called for Simmons to speak first, serving somewhat as a master of ceremonies for the four of them. Hilda, Rubye and Rielinski were scheduled to follow in that order.

From the corner of his eye, Simmons looked in front of Hilda and Rubye at Rielinski. Rielinski nodded. In unison, like a well-rehearsed chorus line, the four of them took a step forward, then a step backward, Simmons and Rielinski waving to the crowd with their free hands. The crowd waved back, expectant voices rising to fill the air.

This moment was a fitting climax to the past four weeks of

hard work, of organizing to assure mass participation in the thirteen-city demonstration project, Simmons told himself. He hoped the responses in the other twelve cities, where the projects were likewise headed by high-ranking Peoples Party officials, were as heartening as the response here in Washington, D.C.

He was conscious of Hilda's hand in his, totally unmoving. The impersonal nature of her touch was probably her answer to the slurs which had whirled about their heads during the past weeks, whispers aimed at creating an impossible situation among the four of them. One gossip columnist had written: "Persons in the know are wondering how long Joe Rielinski is going to remain shut out of the black-white-sex unity being practiced at the very top of the Peoples Party by Preston Simmons, Hilda Larsen and Rubye Ransome." They had discussed the slurs openly and frankly and had decided to answer them not with words, but by deeds. The four of them had spent as much time as possible together while organizing the thirteen-city project. The decision to combat the slurs in this manner was the primary reason why Simmons, instead of Griggs, was a member of the foursome now standing on the platform before the Lincoln Memorial. Griggs was heading the project in New York City.

Of course, attacks on the Peoples Party hadn't been limited to gossip about the sex life of its leaders. A number of columnists and commentators had persisted in pushing the theme that the Peoples Party appeared to have a disproportionate number of blacks in high places. Federal grand juries had indicted four labor leaders for misuse of pension funds in the past week alone, and a splinter group of Sam Muhammed's organization was calling upon blacks to boycott future national elections. Albert James and other national black leaders were making it clear that they were going to keep the separatist movement going, and just two weeks ago had held a mass rally in New York City to whip up enthusiasm.

However, the BLA and other violent groups, black and white, right and left, had been strangely silent. He knew they

378

were only playing a waiting game, getting their act together, developing strategy for what they considered to be the proper reaction to the new political alignments in the country. No doubt about it, they would hear much more from the government, the separatists, and all the rest. But the longer some of these groups remained silent and others relatively inactive, while the Peoples Party continued to gain momentum, the harder it would be for any group, or a combination of groups, to keep the Peoples Party from becoming the dominant force in the country.

Simmons felt pressure on his hand from Hilda. He responded in time to keep their rhythm unbroken as the four of them went through the routine of stepping forward, then backward and waving to the crowd. The crowd responded with even more fervor than before.

How did he feel, *really* feel, about the situation in which he was enveloped? Simmons asked himself, dropping his arm as the roar of the crowd subsided, no longer conscious of Hilda's hand in his. Not just about this day, but about the days to come? Did he see victory ahead, or just more and more struggle, until this hope, like the hope of the separate nation, dissipated before the harsh reality of the status quo?

Suddenly, as though drawn into a dream, he was back in Chicago, in the Brown Girl Lounge, and looking into the sad-wild eyes of the tall young man with the mop in his hand and hearing him say in that forlorn voice: "I'm almost thirty years old, and I ain't never had a job."

During a recent trip to Chicago, he had heard that the young man had been beaten up at a construction demonstration, had gone to the hospital, but was all right. Now, standing on the platform at the Lincoln Memorial, acknowledging the cries of the multitude, he found himself wishing fervently that he knew where the young man was at that moment.

The wish became so intense that, vision-like, he could see the tall young man marching down State Street in the Loop, participating in the Chicago version of the thirteen-city project, surrounded on all sides by laughing, singing men, women

379

and children of all races and colors. A gleam of hope and joy had driven the sad-wild look from the young man's eyes.

"We'll wave once more, then you can begin your speech," Rielinski's voice came to him beneath the din of the crowd.

The vision of the tall young man and his laughing companions dissolved into a more somber multitude, still marching, a line so long that it had neither a beginning nor an ending. Simmons told himself that this parade would last forever, for it was the march of humanity into eternity.

If the Peoples Party didn't prove to be an effective vehicle for freedom, he mused, blacks would just have to try again. There was always the scheme Sam Leavitt had mentioned when he and Griggs met with Leavitt and Tom Ryan, the one about blacks migrating to two or three southern states and taking over their governments. The back-to-Africa movement could be started up again, now that there were a number of independent African nations prosperous enough to receive blacks. Of course, the Peoples Party had to be given its best shot, but its failure would not be the end of the world.

In his ears, swelling from that indefinable region beneath the surface of his mind, Simmons could hear the sound of music. It was a gospel song from a treasured album he had purchased years ago, a song which often burst into his consciousness during times of stress or moments of inspiration.

"Lord, don't move my mountain, but give me the strength to climb; Lord, don't take away my stumbling block, but lead me all around!" That just about summed it up, he told himself. It was all a person, or a people, could ask.

The time had come to begin his speech. Dropping Hilda's hand, he turned to his companions. "This is it," he said.

Rielinski nodded, his face set, revealing the confidence of a person ready to play the ball any way it bounced.

Rubye gave him a tremulous smile, concern for him, and herself, showing in her eyes. He smiled his encouragement, holding her eyes in the embrace of his until calmness returned to her face.

Hilda appeared totally unaware of the three of them. She

380

was staring out at the crowd, her face enraptured, as she surrendered herself to the embrace of thousands.

Marveling at the unique individuality of drives and desires by which different persons arrived at the same place at the same time, conscious of the gospel song still beating beneath the surface of his mind, Simmons raised his hands above his head and turned toward the microphones to begin his speech, the roar of more than a half million voices hammering against his eardrums.

THE END